PRAISE FOR SHEER GALL

"Kahn makes you turn pages and he makes you laugh.
You've never rooted for a lawyer the way you will root
for Rachel Gold. It's a puzzle that's so much fun to read
that you never want it to be solved. And you'll never
guess how it ends."
                    —Mark London, author of *Amazon*

"A sheer delight! Fast and funny. I couldn't get enough
of it. Fans of Rachel Gold rejoice!"
                    —Tamar Myers, author of
                      Between a Wok and a Hard Place

"The combination of lawyerly wisdom, first-rate writing,
and a compelling plot."
                    —*Legal Times*

"A not-to-be-missed legal thriller."
                    —Harriet Klausner, *I Love a Mystery*

SHEER GALL

MICHAEL A. KAHN

A SIGNET BOOK

SIGNET
Published by the Penguin Group
Penguin Putnam Inc., 375 Hudson Street,
New York, New York 10014, U.S.A.
Penguin Books Ltd, 27 Wrights Lane,
London W8 5TZ, England
Penguin Books Australia Ltd,
Ringwood, Victoria, Australia
Penguin Books Canada Ltd, 10 Alcorn Avenue,
Toronto, Ontario, Canada M4V 3B2
Penguin Books (N.Z.) Ltd, 182–190 Wairau Road,
Auckland 10, New Zealand

Penguin Books Ltd, Registered Offices:
Harmondsworth, Middlesex, England

Published by Signet, an imprint of Dutton NAL,
a member of Penguin Putnam Inc.
Previously appeared in a Dutton edition.

First Signet Printing, June, 1998
10 9 8 7 6 5 4 3 2 1

For my marvelous son Zack

ACKNOWLEDGMENTS

A special thanks to my good friends Rick and Judy Schiff, who had the sheer gall to let me peek into a most peculiar realm of commerce.

CHAPTER 1

I walked over to my office window and peered through the blinds. Outside, a sudden gust of wind swayed the trees along the sidewalk and snatched off dozens of brown and red leaves. I turned toward Sally Wade, who was seated in the chair in front of my desk.

"The wife?" I asked.

"Closer to ex-wife."

I groaned. "I didn't realize it was a divorce case. I'm sorry, Sally, but I took a blood oath after the last one. I'm never handling another divorce."

Sally smiled. "That's not why I'm here. Everyone has divorce lawyers, and the dissolution papers are already on file."

"Whew," I said with relief. I came back to my desk and sat down. "So who is she?"

"Me."

I paused, trying to mask my surprise. "You're . . . her?"

She nodded grimly. "I'm her."

"Oh."

When Sally Wade had called that morning to schedule

an appointment, I assumed it involved a new lawsuit. After all, Sally was a plaintiff's personal injury lawyer with a growing practice in the state courts of St. Louis and southern Illinois. Although we had never before met, it's not unusual for the younger women attorneys in town, especially the solo practitioners among us, to refer cases back and forth—sort of the young girl version of the old boy network.

Sally Wade did indeed have a new plaintiff's lawsuit for me. I just hadn't expected that she was the plaintiff. Nor had I suspected that the defendant was her (almost) ex-husband. After three years of marriage to Neville Mc-Bride, managing partner of the silk-stocking law firm of Tully, Crane & Leonard, Sally had filed for divorce last month—an event sufficiently noteworthy to find its way into the people column of the *St. Louis Post-Dispatch*.

And now she wanted to sue him for assault.

I pointed toward her upper lip, which was bruised and swollen. "Did he do that?"

She nodded. "And this," she said as she lowered her designer sunglasses to reveal a blackened right eye.

I winced. "Oh, God."

She put her oversized sunglasses back in position. "There's more." She stood, slipped off her peacock-blue cashmere blazer, and hung it carefully on the back of her chair. Pulling down the collar of her black turtleneck, she leaned toward me so that I could see the scratches and dark bruises on the left side of her neck and upper chest.

I felt a surge of anger so fierce it made me dizzy. "That's outrageous."

Without a word, she straightened her turtleneck and sat back down facing me. She crossed her arms over her chest.

I waited for my blood pressure to drop a few notches. "This happened last night?" I asked.

"Around midnight."

"Where?"

"In the house." Her cashmere skirt matched the peacock-blue blazer hanging from the back of her chair, and her black stockings matched her turtleneck.

"Did you let him in?"

She snorted. "Are you nuts? I was sound asleep. I didn't realize the son of a bitch still had a key. He barged into the bedroom, flipped on the light, and started hollering." Her southern-Illinois twang became more pronounced as her ire rose.

"Was he drunk?"

"As a skunk." She shuddered in disgust. "He's an animal. A miserable animal. First he called me names and then he started screaming that I was fucking his partners and fucking the judges and fucking the pool man and everyone else. He went berserk. He slapped me and punched me and then—" She paused, lowering her sunglasses to stare at me, the black eye making her squint. "—and then he tried to rape me." She readjusted her sunglasses and leaned back.

I waited.

She took a deep breath and exhaled slowly. "Fortunately, he was too drunk to get it up."

"I'm so sorry, Sally," I said gently.

She gave me a curt nod. "He's the one who'll be sorry."

"What did the police do?"

"I haven't told the police."

I sat back, puzzled. "Why not?"

She studied me from behind her sunglasses. "I don't want to put him in jail, Rachel. I want to put him in the poorhouse."

"I'm not following you."

She leaned forward, her voice low but intense. "I want to sue the bastard. I want to sue him for assault and I want to sue him for battery. I want to sue him for compensatory damages and I want to sue him for punitive damages. I want a jury of my peers to make that cowardly, blue-blooded piece of shit pay through his high-society nose. He's worth millions of dollars, Rachel, and I want every last penny of it." She leaned back with a frosty smile. "Less your one-third, of course."

I studied my newest client. Sally Wade (briefly, Sally Wade-McBride) was born and raised near Centralia, Illinois. She was in her mid-thirties and had shoulder-length auburn hair cut in bangs over her forehead. She was slender and appeared to be attractive, although it was hard to tell with the sunglasses and swollen lip. As Anthony Trollope once wrote of another attorney, Sally had a face you might see and forget, and see again and forget again; and yet when you looked at it feature by feature, you found it was a fairly good face, showing intelligence in the forehead and strength around the mouth.

It was also a face that matched her reputation. Sally was known as a shrewd adversary and a fearless trial lawyer. She was the type of woman that certain male opponents referred to as "a ballbreaking cunt," usually under their breath in the courthouse hallway after a stinging loss.

Sally had earned her reputation the old-fashioned way. After law school, she went to work for Abraham Grozny, one of the more notorious bottom-fishers in the St. Louis legal community, a five-and-dime shyster who bore a striking resemblance to the actor Lou Jacobi. She started off lugging Grozny's massive briefcase up and down the corridors of the traffic courts on both sides of the Mississippi River as her boss trolled for clients. Sally's job back then was to get the new client to sign the attorney-client agreement right there in the courthouse hallway and take his statement. Over the years, however, her willingness to try cases (no matter how bad the facts, sleazy the client, or small the claim) and her exceptional organizational skills (essential for a litigator with a constantly changing inventory of hundreds of small cases) made her so indispensable that Grozny, the archetypal solo practitioner, offered her a full partnership on her twenty-ninth birthday. She declined, however, and shortly thereafter left to open the law offices of Sally Wade & Associates. Her timing was exquisite. Ten months later, a federal grand jury indicted Abraham Grozny on eighteen counts of mail fraud, wire fraud, bribery, and corruption of justice—a collection of charges that suggested an explanation other than brilliant lawyering for the extraordinary results Grozny routinely obtained before certain judges, all of whom were also indicted. Last winter, midway through the third year of his seven-year prison term, Grozny had died of a cerebral hemorrhage while playing horseshoes in the prison yard.

"Here." Sally reached down and opened her briefcase. "I've already drafted the petition." Completely businesslike, she pulled out a file folder and handed it to me.

I placed the folder on my desk, struck by her transformation from avenging victim to cool professional. It was an impressive performance, albeit just a little creepy.

"It's a working draft," she said casually. "I know you're good, Rachel, but you don't do much personal injury work. This draft will give you language to work with. Feel free to change whatever you want." She smiled. "I realize that I'm the client on this one, not the lawyer. I just don't want to waste any time. I'd love to file it by the end of the week."

I opened the folder and glanced through the allegations as I tried to sort out my own reactions. I looked up and asked, "Was this the first time?"

She frowned. "First time?"

"That he ever struck you?"

She paused, stroking her chin. When she answered, she chose her words carefully. "This was the first time that he struck me without consent."

I repeated her answer to myself. "I'm not following you."

She turned toward my office window, her face impassive. "Neville is a man who has a strong need for control." She spoke slowly, deliberately. "Sexually, that is. It's what turns him on. He likes certain, uh, scenarios."

"Scenarios?" I asked, knowing I needed to hear the specifics but not eager to.

She nodded, still gazing out the window. "Variations on a rape scene." She turned to me with an expression that was almost detached. "Simulated, of course. The pirate and the maiden, the prison guard and the prisoner, the Arab sheik and the harem girl, that sort of thing. Sometimes English."

"English?"

"Bondage. He liked to tie me up. Blindfolds, gags, that sort of thing."

"And you?" I asked after a moment.

"Me?"

"You let him do those things?" The thought of Sally Wade playing the passive role in a fantasy rape game seemed so incongruous.

"Occasionally," she answered coolly, not averting her eyes.

Then again, I acknowledged, I had come across behavior in some of my divorce cases far more incongruous than a tough female trial lawyer who got her jollies playing damsel in distress to a man old enough to be her father.

"But," she continued, leaning forward for emphasis, "we never did anything like what he pulled last night."

"Not even close?"

"Not even close. Whatever he and I did in the past never left a bruise. It was pure fantasy. Last night was no fantasy. It was a nightmare."

"Nevertheless," I said, frowning pensively, "you know what he may try to claim in his defense."

"Don't worry about that, Rachel. First of all, it'd be total bullshit. Simple as that. The guy beat me up and tried to rape me. I never consented to any of it. Second, he'd be too embarrassed to even try to claim that there was anything consensual about what he did. Remember, this is not some lowlife scumbag pervert. We're talking about the distinguished Neville McBride, managing partner of Tully, Crane & Leonard. His reputation is his most precious asset. You think Mr. Wonderful wants to sit up there on the witness stand and tell the world that the only way he can get his rocks off these days is to tie up a woman facedown on her bed and jerk off onto her butt?" She shook her head. "No way, José. Which is why he'll try to settle the lawsuit early on."

I let it sink in.

"Still," I said, "you should have gone to the police."

She laughed. "Come on. You think the police are going to do anything to one of the St. Louis McBrides? Especially when the McBride in question happens to be a member of the St. Louis Police Board? Get real."

"Sally, the man committed a crime."

"Exactly," she said with an angry sneer, "and we're going to make him pay for it."

"That's not the point, Sally. If he did it to you, he might do it to some other woman, too."

She laughed. "You're the one missing the point, Rachel. This is the best way to make sure he never does it again."

I gave her a puzzled look. "Why do you say that?"

"Come on, Rachel." She shook her head in disbelief. "You know what'll happen if I report it to the police? Zilch, that's what." Sally stood up and walked over to the window. "Zilch." She turned to face me. "Look at O. J. Simpson. There's a certified wife-beater. How many times did Nicole report him to the police? And what did they do to him? Nothing. Same here. Neville will bring in some heavyweight lawyer and have one of his powerful buddies talk to the prosecutor or the judge, and the next thing you know the case will be dismissed and the file sealed."

She walked over behind her chair and rested her hands on the top of it. "Believe me, my way is far better. For everyone. Society wants punishment and deterrence. I want revenge and money. This way everyone gets what they want."

"Won't you get plenty of money anyway?"

"How so?"

"In the divorce."

She gave me a sardonic smile. "Don't be naive, Rachel. When you marry a man with that kind of net worth, especially when you're not his first wife, you exchange more than wedding vows."

"A prenuptial agreement?"

She nodded darkly. "And it's airtight, according to my divorce lawyer. I'm entitled to a lump-sum payment of fifty thousand dollars."

"Who's your divorce lawyer?"

She moved around to the front of her chair and sat down. "Sammy Soule."

I raised my eyebrows.

"Exactly," she said. "If that shark says the prenuptial agreement is valid, you can be sure it is. Sammy says there's no way I can get any more money out of him." She leaned back and crossed her arms over her chest. "Until last night, that is." Her lips curled with satisfaction. "Last night Neville McBride handed over the key to the family gold mine."

I studied her. "You still need to go to the police."

"Oh, come on, Rachel. Don't be such a Girl Scout."

"I'm not, Sally. Look down the road. Your case won't come to trial for at least a year. What if Neville denies the whole incident on the witness stand? What if he says it's all a ruse by you to get around the prenuptial agreement? Without a police report, it'll be just your word against his."

She thought it over. "Good point."

"You'll need photographs, too. Preferably in color. A police photographer would be best. If there isn't one available, go to a pro with a solid reputation."

"I know one."

"Good."

She stood up. "I'll call you tomorrow." She handed me the signed attorney-client agreement. "Don't try to call me at the office. I don't want my assistant to know about this. I want an airtight lid on this until we file suit. Okay?"

"Sure," I said. "One more thing."

"What's that?"

"Go see your doctor."

"Excellent point. He'd be a good witness."

I gazed at my gritty, vindictive client and sighed. "Sally, forget about the lawsuit for just a moment. The reason you should go see a doctor is that you're bruised and banged up. You should go see a doctor to make sure you're okay. Do it today."

She grinned and saluted. "Yes, ma'am."

I gave her a stern look. "Today."

"Yes, ma'am."

"Right after you see the police."

She saluted. "Yes, ma'am."

I winked. "Good."

CHAPTER 2

    "I swear, Benny," I said in a voice low enough to keep the others from hearing, "one of these days your penis is going to get you into big trouble."

"Hey, you think it listens to me?"

"I'm serious."

Benny chuckled. "Relax, Rachel. It's not like she's in any of my classes." He peered out his window. "So, do you have service of process on Commander Kinky?"

"Not yet. Probably next week."

He pointed. "What the hell is that?"

I leaned over to see where he was looking. "What?"

We were at the top of the Arch, high above downtown St. Louis. Benny was peering out one of the windows on the east side.

"There," he said, pointing to a factory building on the Illinois side of the Mississippi River. "Jesus, what the fuck are those things on the north side of that building? Cows?"

I squinted. "Yep."

"You're shitting me."

"Those are stockyards, Benny."

"In East St. Louis? I thought they were all closed down."

"Not all of them. That's Douglas Beef."

Benny looked over at me. "Why is it taking so long to get him served?"

It took a moment to shift mental gears. "It hasn't been that long. Sally Wade came in last Wednesday. I filed suit on Friday. Today is only Tuesday."

"Why not hire a process server and get the son of a bitch served right away?"

"Her choice. She wants the sheriff's office to serve the papers." I shrugged. "She's a lawyer, Benny, and she knows it could take the sheriff's office a week or more to get him served." I paused, frowning. "I think she likes the idea of a deputy sheriff showing up at McBride's law firm with the court papers. She thinks it'll embarrass him."

"Sounds like a real sweetheart."

"Hey, she's entitled. Any man who does that deserves to be humiliated."

Benny stepped back and shook his head. "This is one of those goddam optical illusions."

"What is?"

"These windows. How high up are we?"

Shifting mental gears again, I flipped through the National Parks Service pamphlet that I had picked up when we bought our tram tickets down below. "The Arch is six hundred and thirty feet tall."

"Amazing," Benny said.

"What?"

"Down below, looking up, you see these little bitty chickenshit windows, and you think, hey, when I get up to the top of the Arch they'll turn out to be as big as picture windows—it'll be panorama city. But look at them. They're still little bitty chickenshit windows. Weird. I'm telling you, Rachel, there's some strange shit in this town."

"Hey," I said with mock indignity, "I take time out of my busy schedule in the middle of the week to take Mr. New Jersey to the top of the world-famous Gateway Arch, soaring emblem of my proud hometown, and what do I get for my trouble? Nothing but grief."

"I'm not giving *you* grief. You're a total babe, woman. But your hometown." He shook his head. "We're talking weird."

"Come on, grumpy," I said, hooking my arm around his to drag him toward the tram loading area. "Someone who grew up near the Jersey Turnpike ought to remember the old saying about people in glass houses."

"And what about this thing?" he said, stopping to look around. "A humongous stainless-steel arch, planted on the banks of the Mississippi, stuffed with trainloads of yokels cruising up and down inside of it all day long. What the hell is this all about? Some weird Midwest shrine to Ray Kroc?"

He was on one of his harangues, and, as usual, I couldn't help but smile. I also couldn't help but notice how the tourists on either side of us were edging away. Benny Goldberg tended to have that effect on strangers. He was fat and vulgar and loud and obnoxious. He was also brilliant and funny and thoughtful and savagely loyal. I loved him like the brother I never had, although he in no way bore even the slightest resemblance to any brother of my dreams.

We had gone to the Arch on impulse. Earlier that day, just before noon, Benny had dropped by my office after the antitrust seminar he taught every Tuesday morning. We went to lunch at O'Connell's Pub on Kingshighway. It was a sunny autumn day, and on the drive back to Highway 40 after lunch the Arch had been clearly visible to the east, gleaming in the sunlight.

"You ever been in that damn thing?" Benny had asked as we waited for the light to change.

"Not since grade school," I answered. "You?"

He shook his head and then paused, turning to me with eyebrows raised. I had looked at my watch, checked my appointment calendar, and shrugged. "Why not?"

So we went.

"You got plans for later today?" Benny asked as the doors closed and the tram lurched forward. "Around five-thirty?"

Benny and I were seated by a tram window, which had a view of the dark and eerie interior of the Arch. There were two trams, and each ran on special tracks inside the hollow, curving legs of the Arch. One traversed the north leg of the Arch, the other the south. Each tram had eight barrel-shaped segments, and each segment held five passengers. A special leveling device kept the passengers in an upright position throughout the four-minute journey between the subterranean loading zone and the observation deck up top.

"Actually I do have plans," I said. "Why?"

"We have a moot court social function at the law school." He looked over at me and raised his eyebrows. "Big Jake'll be there."

Big Jake was Jacob Sherman, an associate professor of environmental law at the UCLA School of Law. He was at Washington University for the semester as a visiting professor. He was also, according to Benny, a nice Jewish boy. Benny, in his entirely unsolicited role as Yenta the matchmaker, had selected Big Jake as the future Mr. Rachel Gold.

"Well," I said sarcastically, "thanks for the advance notice."

"What's your prior commitment?"

I gave him a wink and pantomimed a few karate chops.

"Oh, for God's sake, not that martial-arts class again. Skip it today."

"No way, Benny. It's only our second week."

"What's going on, Rachel? Since when did you become a Jackie Chan fanatic?"

"I'm not. I'm trying to learn a little self-defense. Considering what's happened in my life the last few years, it's about time."

"Self-defense? I call a crowbar self-defense. Or a .357 magnum. Bowing and jumping around barefoot in goofy white pajamas is hardly self-defense."

I shook my head patiently. "The teacher is great and I love the class."

I had enrolled in a self-defense class for women that was sponsored by the bar association. There were eleven of us, and we met twice a week for six weeks. Although I had been somewhat dubious before the first class, I was hooked already. I was spending forty-five minutes every night practicing the moves our instructor taught us.

"Where do you have those classes?" Benny asked.

"At the Vic Tanny health club in Clayton."

"Oh, really?" he said, suddenly interested.

I looked at him curiously. "Yes, really."

"Well, well." He rubbed his chin thoughtfully. "I may have to drop by one time."

"You? For what reason?"

"Best reason of all: they have an awesome collection of Stairmasters. There must be eight of them, lined up side by side."

I frowned at him. "Oh? Since when did you become a Stairmaster enthusiast?"

"From the beginning. I'm no Johnny-come-lately on that piece of equipment."

I studied him dubiously. "I didn't know you used a Stairmaster."

"Me?" Benny gave me an incredulous look. "Are you nuts? I've never been on one in my life. What's the point? If God meant us to walk up fifty flights of stairs four times a week, he wouldn't have given us elevators."

"Then enlighten me."

"It's easy. There may be some great sights in this city, but nothing can match the rear view of eight babes in leotards and thongs doing their thing on the Stairmaster. As far as I'm concerned, the inventor of the damn thing deserves a Nobel Prize."

I shook my head in wonder. "Would you remind me again why I'm willing to be seen with you in public?"

On our way out, we paused at the south leg of the Arch, craning our heads back to look up at where we had been. I could barely make out Benny's little bitty windows at the top. It was truly an enormous structure: a silver parabola towering over the banks of the Mississippi River, more than twice the height of the Statue of Liberty. The other leg was 630 feet north of where we stood—more than two football fields away. The base of each leg measured fifty-four feet per side, a perfect equilateral triangle that tapered to seventeen feet per side at the top, which was shimmering in the bright sunlight.

A towboat blast made me turn toward the Mississippi River, where a long string of coal barges was gliding south under the Poplar Street Bridge. The tow's powerful screws churned the muddy waters into a cappuccino froth.

Gazing out at the riverfront, you could still feel the history of the place, even though modern gambling casinos and a floating McDonald's were anchored along the cobblestone levee where the grand paddle wheelers once docked. We were near the south leg of the Arch, not far from the boardinghouse where Mark Twain lived during his two-year stint as a gossip columnist for the *St. Louis Evening News*. A hundred feet to the north of Twain's boardinghouse had been the offices of Grant & Boggs, a struggling real estate company owned by a man named Ulysses S. Grant. Each morning, Grant would pass by a house a few blocks to the south of his business that had been let to a Virginia officer of the Army Corps of Engineers who was stationed in St. Louis to solve the erosion problems along the riverbanks. That officer's name was Robert E. Lee. And on the spot where Benny and I were standing, back on a brisk, sunny morning in March of 1804, just days before they left on their famous expedition into the uncharted territories of the Louisiana Purchase, Captain Meriwether Lewis and Lieutenant William Clark had stood at attention in front of the government house as a lone soldier lowered the French flag and raised the American flag.

On the drive back to my office, Benny asked, "Do you think Neville McBride will fight or settle?"

"Hard to say. Sally thinks he'll try to settle."

"And you?"

I sighed. "I really don't know."

"You don't sound too pumped over the case."

I glanced over at him and nodded. "I'm not wild about her."

"How come?"

I gave him a weary shrug. "I know I should be more compassionate. What happened to her is awful. A total outrage. But she's so . . . so cold-blooded about it."

"About what?"

"The lawsuit. All she's interested in is the money."

He laughed. "What did you expect?"

I shook my head. "Something more."

"Jesus, Rachel. She's *supposed* to be interested in the money. That's why she's the plaintiff. You're her lawyer. Remember? You gotta get with the program, woman. You sound like a proctologist who doesn't want to treat a patient 'cause he's got something wrong with his butt. You don't love butts, don't be a proctologist."

"Maybe so," I conceded.

He looked over with a sympathetic smile. "Hey, I understand. You want her to be Joan of Arc, and instead you got the Merchant of Venice in drag."

I nodded glumly. "Sort of."

"Just keep your fingers crossed, woman."

I glanced at him. "For what?"

"For a fight."

"Huh?"

"Let's hope that rich old fart decides to fight it. You know: millions for defense, not a penny for tribute. Then you can turn her into Joan of Arc. War is bliss."

"Wrong, Benny. In this case, peace is bliss. Which is another reason I'm not excited about it." I moaned and shook my head. "Can you imagine the media circus at the trial?"

"So? You'll be a star. I can see it now: Rachel the Jewish Goddess versus the Big Bwana of Bondage. We're talking cover of *Newsweek*, woman."

I gave him a cynical frown. "More like the cover of a supermarket tabloid. Right next to 'Elvis Meets JFK in Secret Michigan Hideout.' It'll be a freak show, Benny. I've been in enough of those for one lifetime."

"Speaking of publicity, how'd you get the lawsuit on file without the press finding out?"

"Jacki handled it."

Jacki was my jack-of-all-trades secretary.

Benny chuckled. "What did she do?" he asked. "Threaten to hogtie the courthouse reporter?"

"No," I said, smiling at the image. Jacki stood six feet three and weighed close to 240 pounds. With plenty of ex-steelworker muscles rippling beneath her dress, she was surely the most intimidating legal secretary in town. "She waited to file the lawsuit until the reporter took his lunch break. With any luck, the press won't find out for months."

Benny turned onto my street and almost immediately applied the brakes. "Oh, really?" he said with a big grin. "Looks like your luck ran out."

I stared through the windshield. "Oh, damn," I groaned.

A 2 News Team van and a NewsChannel 5 van were parked at odd angles in front of my office. Waiting on the sidewalk were the camera crews and two spiffy reporters, a young blond woman in a stylish lavender suit and a young Hispanic man in a blue blazer and gray slacks. Next to them was a rumpled reporter named Neil who covered the city desk for the *Post-Dispatch*. As Benny pulled his car over, the blonde spotted me and pointed with her microphone. She ordered her camera crew into position, and the other crew did the same. As the two TV reporters jockeyed for position on the sidewalk near the car, I saw the guy from the *Post-Dispatch* flip open his shorthand pad. Both camera lenses were pointed at me.

"Like flies to shit, eh?" Benny said.

I gave him a surly look. "Which makes me what?"

"Great shit, babe. The greatest. With a pair of legs to die for." He gave me a wink. "Go get 'em, champ. I'll look for you on the five-o'clock news."

I took a deep breath, glanced over at Benny, and exhaled slowly. *It's show time.* I opened the door.

"Miss Gold?" the blonde shouted as I stepped out.

"Rachel?" the Hispanic said. I'd never met him before in my life. Or her, for that matter.

As I looked from one minicam to the other, I heard Benny's car drive off.

"Over here, Miss Gold," the blonde said with a saccharine smile. Turning to her competitor, she hissed, "Wait your turn, Hector."

Having been through this before, I knew how important it was to assert control early on. If you don't step off the media merry-go-round before it starts spinning, you eventually get hurled off in a daze.

So I assumed the role. I glared at the minicam operator closest to me—a big heavyset guy with a brown beard. In as authoritative a voice as I could muster, I said, "Turn it off."

He gave me an uneasy look and glanced back toward

the blonde. A flicker of uncertainty crossed her face, but she said nothing.

"Both of them," I snapped, pointing at the other mini-cam. "We either start off the record, or we don't start at all."

The two TV reporters exchanged puzzled glances. I waited for a moment and then shrugged. "Your choice, folks. You want me on the record, then we start off the record. Otherwise"—I gestured toward the *Post-Dispatch* reporter—"the only one I talk to is Neil."

Neil grinned sheepishly.

This time the two TV reporters exchanged troubled looks. The Hispanic reporter turned to his minicam operator, a tough-looking fortyish woman with scraggly black-and-gray hair wearing faded jeans and a tie-dyed Hard Rock Beirut sweatshirt. "It's okay, Linda," he said. "We'll get the film later."

I waited until both red lights blinked off.

"Let me guess," I said, mimicking bashful delight. "I just won the Nobel Peace Prize."

They all smiled.

I got serious. "Is this about Sally?"

Several nods.

I shook my head in mild disbelief. "It must be a slow news day."

Curious expressions.

That was stupid, I told myself. *Don't belittle a client's situation.*

I turned to the Hispanic reporter. "How did you find out? From Neville McBride?"

He raised his eyebrows. "Actually, the police."

"Good," I said, pleased. "I'm glad they're getting involved." I looked at the blonde. "Does Neville know?"

"Definitely," she said. "The police have already talked to him."

I smiled. "Let's hope they make him squirm. Uh, that's off the record," I added quickly.

My mind was racing. Sally might not yet be Joan of Arc, but I could start planting some helpful seeds in the media. Even though greed was Sally's primary motivation, with a little spin I could use her case to focus attention on the perils of spouse abuse. The notoriety certainly wouldn't hurt her case, and the increased awareness of the problem just might save a few other women from physical abuse.

"I'm willing to talk in general about battered women," I said seriously, "but I'm not going to answer questions about Neville McBride. We stand by the written allegations of the lawsuit. He's the defendant, and he deserves to be the defendant, but I'm not going to comment further on his actions other than to say that we assume justice will be done. Okay?"

Several nods.

I suddenly realized that I needed to confer with Sally. Neither of us had expected this much publicity so early in the case. We had to talk before reporters started sticking microphones in her face. Whatever I said was just a lawyer flapping her jaws, but Sally was the plaintiff. What she said could be used against her at trial.

"One more thing," I said. "I'd prefer, at least initially, that you talk to me about the case. There may be an appropriate time for you to involve Sally, but she's obviously in no condition to talk now, and it wouldn't be fair for you to try to get a quote out of her." I paused and gave them a plucky smile. "Okay, gang, fire away."

No one said a thing.

I waited, perplexed. The Hispanic reporter looked down at the ground. The blonde and her cameraman exchanged puzzled glances.

"Rachel."

It was Neil, the newspaper reporter. He tugged at his Fu Manchu mustache, his eyes sad. As I stared at him, a warning light clicked on in my head. "What?"

"Sally's dead," he said quietly.

My mind went blank, as if all thoughts had swirled away like startled doves. Somewhere off to the side I was vaguely aware of the whirring of one of the minicams.

Finally, I asked, "When?"

"Late last night," Neil answered.

I moved closer. In almost a whisper I asked, "Where?"

"Her bedroom."

"How?"

He frowned. "Probably asphyxiation."

"Asphyxiation?"

He shrugged. "They won't know for sure until the autopsy."

"Oh, my God, Neil."

He shook his head sadly. "The cops are trying to keep a lid on it for now. I wasn't able to get much."

I studied his face. "What else do you know, Neil?"

He tugged on his mustache. "Apparently, she was tied up on the bed."

"What do you mean, 'tied'?"

He shrugged. "With duct tape. Spread-eagled. Naked. Facedown. A gag in her mouth."

I let that information sink in. "She was strangled?"

"Possibly. Or gagged. Or maybe he just put a plastic bag over her head. He might try to claim it was an accident, but the cops don't think so."

"He?" I said in a hoarse voice.

"They're pretty sure it was a man."

I stared at him, waiting.

He tugged at his mustache, lowering his eyes. "They found some, uh, fluid on her lower back."

CHAPTER 3

It was the lead headline in the morning's *Post-Dispatch*:

WOMAN ATTORNEY FOUND
DEAD IN BEDROOM
Police Question Estranged Husband

The lawsuit of *Sally Wade* v. *Neville D. McBride III* made it into paragraphs seven and eight:

Just five days before her death, in what now seems a haunting omen to some, Ms. Wade filed a $10 million personal injury lawsuit in the St. Louis circuit court against Mr. McBride. In her court papers, she accused her estranged husband of invading her home in the middle of the night and physically assaulting her in her bedroom. Mr. McBride repeatedly struck her with his fists and attempted to rape her, according to the lawsuit, which seeks punitive damages for his alleged conduct, which the petition characterizes as "malicious, willful and reprehensible."

Attempts to reach Mr. McBride regarding the lawsuit allegations were unsuccessful. St. Louis attorney Rachel Gold, who filed the lawsuit on behalf of Ms. Wade, declined to comment on either the lawsuit or her client's violent death.

There was a sidebar story on their marriage entitled "Mixed Doubles." At the top of the story were side-by-side photos of Neville and Sally—photos selected to underscore the contrasts between them. In Neville's photo, he was in white tails and top hat as he escorted his debutante niece down the aisle at the Veiled Prophet Ball. In her photo, Sally was weary but victorious as she stood on the front steps of the Granite City courthouse holding aloft the full-scale model of a human leg that had played an important role in the $1.2 million medical malpractice verdict the jury had just awarded her one-legged client.

I studied her picture as I sipped my coffee. Sally's hair had been a little longer back then, but the sunglasses appeared to be the same model. I wondered whether they were concealing a black eye back then as well.

I stared at the photo of Neville McBride. Although medical science has long since banished phrenology to the Elba Isle of quackery, most of us remain amateur phrenologists. We expect violent criminals to look like violent criminals, members of the polo set to look like members of the polo set, and the rest of the "types" out there to match the specs issued by the Central Casting of our minds. Thus, although I had never seen Neville McBride before, I had a clear mental image of what a distinguished but lecherous managing partner of a powerful corporate law firm would look like: tall, suave, well-manicured, and charming, with just a touch of the satyr.

Wrong. Instead of Cary Grant, I was staring at the bulky, sixtyish grocer who served as treasurer of the local Kiwanis Club. Neville McBride was bald, wore thick glasses, and could generously be described as stocky. He looked more like Sally's father than her husband.

I settled back in my office chair to read the text of the sidebar, which highlighted the differences between the two lawyers—one an influential fifty-five-year-old partner in a major law firm whose roster of clients constituted a who's who of the business, professional, and social elite of St. Louis; the other a feisty thirty-six-year-old solo practitioner whose clients included a motley but lucrative collection of victims—victims of traffic accidents, of medical malpractice, of on-the-job injuries, of defective products, of consumer fraud, of Truth-in-Lending Act violations.

They were, to use a cliché, a study in contrasts. Neville Damon McBride III was the scion of the St. Louis McBrides—a wealthy family that had made its millions in the Missouri lead mines during the early decades of the twentieth century. Sally Wade was the only child of an itinerant carpenter (now deceased) and an alcoholic mother (remarried, divorced, remarried, divorced, and now deceased). Neville grew up in a nine-bedroom home on the grounds of the St. Louis Country Club. Sally Wade grew up in a mobile home on the outskirts of Centralia, Illinois. Neville followed the academic path of his father and grandfather: Princeton College and then the University of Virginia School of Law. Sally became the first member of her family to graduate high school, and then worked her way through Southern Illinois University and St. Louis University Law School.

The two met, according to the article, as members of the bar association committee overseeing the renovation plans for the St. Louis Civil Courts Building. Sally served on the committee because, as a plaintiff's lawyer who regularly appeared in that dilapidated building, it was good politics to be seen as dedicated to improving the working conditions of the judges. Neville served on the committee in part because of his firm's sense of noblesse oblige and in part because his grandfather had donated the imposing bronze sculpture of Louis Brandeis that dominated the lobby. (Brandeis had started his legal career in St. Louis.)

I skimmed through the lead story on the murder one more time before tossing the paper into the recycling bin next to my desk. Then I got up for some fresh coffee. As I was up at the coffee machine, Jacki came in with the morning mail.

"Anything special?" I asked.

She shook her head. "Mostly junk mail. There's an order in the Carson case resetting the pretrial conference for early December."

"Am I okay?"

"Yep. I entered the new date in your calendar." She flipped through the rest of the mail. "They served another set of depo notices in the KSLM-AM libel case. Ah," Jacki said with a chuckle, holding up a piece of correspondence. "And another indignant letter from that lard-ass at Bryan Cave."

"What's he whining about now?"

"Well, it's five pages long." She skimmed the letter. "Seems he's unsatisfied with some of your responses to his latest set of interrogatories."

"Poor baby."

"Are you going to respond to the letter?"

"No way." I took a sip of coffee and gave Jacki an appraising look. She was wearing a navy cardigan sweater over a white cotton blouse, a pleated glen-plaid wool skirt, opaque white pantyhose, and navy Pappagallo flats. "Say, is that a new outfit?"

She smiled hesitantly. "Do you like it?"

"I do. It sort of reminds me of, uh—"

"—the uniforms the girls used to wear at Catholic school?"

I nodded. "Exactly, except without the ugly brown brogues."

"Do you think I'm too old for it?"

"Not at all," I said with as much sincerity as I could muster.

Jacki Brand was a former Granite City steelworker who was putting herself through night law school while working days as my secretary, paralegal, law clerk, and all-around aide. I'd call her my Girl Friday, except that anatomically she was still a he—and would so remain until the operation next summer. Jacki (née Jack) was now in her fifth month living as a woman and her fifth month as the greatest assistant I had ever had.

As for her outfit today, imagine a Green Bay Packer middle linebacker dressed in drag as a senior at Sacred Heart and wearing a Dolly Parton wig, lipstick, and rouge. "You look cute," I assured her. And, oddly enough, she did.

"One last item," Jacki said. "Do you want me to call Mr. Contini to remind him about the pretrial conference tomorrow?"

"Oy," I said with a smile, "that crazy case. Sure. When is it?"

"Eleven o'clock."

"Tell him I'll meet him at court at quarter to eleven."

About an hour later, Jacki poked her head in my office. She was frowning. "What happens to our lawsuit for Sally?"

I leaned back in my chair. "Hard to say. If she had a will, it'll appoint a personal representative." The personal representative is the modern trust-and-estate term for what was once called the executor or administrator. "The personal representative," I continued, "will be the one who'll ultimately decide what happens with the lawsuit."

"And if she didn't have a will?"

"Presumably the probate court will decide. But we've got bigger problems than that."

"Such as?"

"Such as admissible evidence. She was alone when he beat her up. That means our only witness is dead. We'll need to find another way to get her story into evidence." I snapped my fingers. "Which reminds me. I've got to talk to Neil."

Neil Boyer was the reporter from the *Post-Dispatch* who wrote the lead story on Sally's death. As Jacki returned to her desk, I flipped through my Rolodex for Neil's number. Someone at the city desk answered. The call bounced around for a while. One guy put me on hold for a long time and then came back on the line to tell me that Neil was out on assignment. Eventually, I left my name and telephone number.

As I hung up, I heard Benny out in the reception area. He lived in the Central West End, only a few blocks from my office, and occasionally dropped by on his way to or from Washington University, where he was an assistant professor of law. I listened long enough to realize that he was reaching the punch line of one of his favorite jokes. I leaned back with a smile to listen.

"Well, the Hell's Angel slowly walks around the poor guy," Benny said, "and stops behind him. Then there's the sound of a zipper. 'Hey, what's going on?' the guy asks. 'Sorry, little buddy,' the Hell's Angel says, 'but I guess this just ain't your goddam day.' "

Jacki burst into laughter.

"Hello, Professor," I called out.

He strolled in and gave me a wink. "Hey, gorgeous."

I smiled with amusement at his outfit. "I'm glad to see you're finally starting to dress like a real law school professor."

"Never too early to impress upon them the solemnity and dignity of our learned profession." He was wearing a black sweatshirt, a Portland Beavers baseball cap, baggy army pants, and green high-top Chuck Taylor All-Stars. The sweatshirt bore the legend *I Am That Man from Nantucket.* He took a seat and gave me a conspiratorial wink. "Well?"

I looked at him curiously. "Well what?"

"I think ole Neville is up shit creek without a paddle."

"Oh?"

"The cops found some photos."

"Where?"

"In his apartment."

"Really? Of the two of them?"

"Them, and . . ." He paused with a Groucho Marx leer and pretended to remove an invisible cigar from his mouth to flick the ashes.

"And?"

"And a few shots of Neville with other women."

I frowned. "All in the same picture?"

"No, no. One babe per picture. I'm just saying that the guy has, shall we say, a broad collection."

I shook my head in amazement. "I take it these are not the type of pictures one sends home to Mom."

"Not unless Mom happens to be Dr. Ruth. Most are your basic beaver shots."

"Most?"

"Most."

"But not all?"

He winked. "Not all."

I nodded. "So, I take it that this collection includes at least one bondage shot?"

"Damn," he said, "you're good. Score one point for the girl with the All-World Tush."

I felt a chill. "A bondage shot of Sally?"

"Correct again," he said, slipping into his game-show host voice. "Don Pardo, tell her what she's won."

I let the information sink in. "Benny, how in the world do you get access to this kind of stuff?"

"Vee haf our sources, Meez Gold."

"A cop?"

"Maybe, maybe not."

"Reliable?"

"Totally."

I sat back. "I am impressed."

"Me, too. Sometimes I have to pinch myself just to confirm I'm for real."

"Still," I said, contemplating his information, "it doesn't prove he killed her."

"True, but it hurts like hell."

"Yes and no. All it proves for sure is that he or she or both of them happened to enjoy bondage. Bondage is more common than you think. There's even a section on it in The *Joy of Sex*."

"The Joy of Sex?" He stood up, feigning shock. "Good grief, Rachel Gold, what are you doing reading up on bondage in *The Joy of Sex*?" He paused, placing his hand on his chest, as if deeply moved. "Oh, my. Are you finally preparing yourself to become my bride?"

"Right," I said, blushing despite myself.

"Excellent, dude." He sat back down with a satisfied grin. "But be sure to study the section on oral sex, although, alas, I'm sure it's missing from your copy."

"What are you talking about?"

He shook his head sadly. "I have this theory that somehow, through the wonders of modern technology and pursuant to a secret pact with the rabbinical council, the publishers of sex manuals have excised all references to blow jobs from every volume sold to Jewish women and replaced them with an inflammatory and wholly inaccurate essay on oral hygiene."

"Very funny, Benny. Look, my point is that lots of normal people are involved in bondage, and they don't die. It's just a harmless sexual game."

"Maybe, but according to my source, one of the photos has her trussed up in pretty much the way she was when they found her."

I let that one sink in. "Wow," I said softly.

"And his alibi bites. He says he was home alone that

night. He says he watched *Monday Night Football*, which ended around eleven-thirty, and then he went to bed. Pretty lame."

I nodded. "That doesn't do much for him."

"And then there's your lawsuit. Talk about a mortal blow. What did the cops think?"

"Two detectives from the Major Case Squad came by last night around eight to take my statement. They wanted to know all about her injuries, about what she told me about him, about anything and everything I could recall about her. They were extremely interested in her comment about how he liked to tie her up and masturbate."

Benny crossed his arms over his chest. "You realize that if it really was him you're going to end up as a witness at the murder trial."

I sighed. "Probably."

"Which means you'll get to experience the thrill of being cross-examined by the Wolf Man."

My eyes widened. "Really?"

Benny nodded. "I've heard that McBride has already retained him."

The Wolf Man was Jonathan Wolf, a rising star in the criminal defense bar.

"One word of advice, Rachel," he said solemnly. "You better not let the Wolf Man find out about your obsession with sex manuals."

"Benny," I said, exasperated, "why is it that it takes the average woman four years to get through puberty and it takes the average man forty?"

He pretended to ponder the question. "I'll tell you why: to preserve the Blessed Trinity."

I gave him a baffled look. "I give up."

"Moe, Larry, and Curly. Someone has to watch them."

"Ah," I said with a jaded smile, "the Three Stooges Theory of Perpetual Male Adolescence?"

He nodded proudly. "I may write a law review article on it."

Jacki buzzed to tell me that Neil Boyer of the *Post-Dispatch* was on the phone.

I looked over at Benny. "I want to find out why his article doesn't mention any police report. Sally was supposed to file one on Neville's attack. I told Neil there should be one on file."

He stood up, checking his watch. "My class starts in fifteen minutes. It's over at one. How 'bout a late lunch?"

I glanced over at my desk calendar. "Can't today. Tomorrow?"

He squinted as he mentally checked his schedule. "Sure. Where?"

"No more hamburgers," I said as I lifted the receiver. "How 'bout the Sunshine Inn?"

"Oooh, yummy," he said mockingly. "Last time you took me there it was in the middle of that goddam eggplant festival. I had the Hershey squirts for two days."

"Then where, Nature Boy?"

"Llewelyn's Pub."

"Okay," I said reluctantly. I lifted the receiver and placed my hand over the mouthpiece. "Around one-fifteen?"

"Perfect."

I uncovered the mouthpiece and waved good-bye to Benny. "Hi, Neil," I said. "You back at the paper?"

"No. I'm calling from the police station."

"Ah, you found her report on the attack?"

"Not yet. But there's been a new development in the case."

"Really? What?"

"They just arrested Neville McBride."

CHAPTER 4

Jacki came into my office with the morning mail. "Who was that guy?" she asked.

"Barry Morrison." I took the mail from her and started sorting through it. "He's with Laclede Trust Company."

"New client?"

"Maybe."

"What do they want you to do?"

I looked up from the mail. "To be their lawyer in the administration of Sally's estate."

Jacki raised her eyebrows in surprise. "No kidding? How did they come to you?"

I explained the roundabout route. Sally's will, which had been drafted two years ago by an attorney at Neville McBride's firm, appointed Neville and Laclede Trust as co–personal representatives. Neville obviously couldn't serve while the murder charge was pending, and neither could anyone else at his firm. When a trust company finds itself as sole personal representative of an estate, it will often retain as its counsel someone who represented the decedent. In Sally's case, there were only two possible choices.

"Who was her divorce lawyer?" Jacki asked.

"Sammy Soule."

Jacki giggled. "Hollywood Soule is probably a little out of their price range."

"It's more than that. Sammy represented Burt Vinson's wife in their divorce."

"Who's Burt Vinson?"

"The CEO of Laclede Trust. By the time Sammy got done with him in court, Burt would rather pose naked for the next issue of the *American Banker* than allow Sammy to receive a penny of fees from his bank."

"That could be a good client for you."

I looked up at her and shrugged. "I told him I'll think about it."

Jacki studied me with concern. "What's wrong, Rachel?"

I gave her a frustrated sigh. "I'm overdosing on Sally. I'm probably going to be a witness at the criminal trial. Then I've got her lawsuit against Neville, which obviously has developed some major evidentiary problems with her death. And now this. I just don't know how much deeper I want to get into this mess."

Jacki nodded. "I understand."

"Speaking of Sally's lawsuit, will you have time for some research tonight after class?" Jacki was attending night law school at St. Louis University.

"Sure." She picked up a pen and legal pad from my desk. "What do you need me to look at?"

"The Dead Man's Statute."

The so-called Dead Man's Statute, enacted in most states back in the 1800s, was the lawmakers' response to one of the knottiest problems in the law of evidence: who, if anyone, can testify when one of the parties to the lawsuit dies? Although dead men may tell no lies, the courts have long worried that the survivors might. Accordingly, the typical Dead Man's Statute establishes a blanket rule that, at least in theory, places the dead and the living on equal footing by excluding all testimony from the living about any interaction they had with the deceased. Over the years, however, the rule has generated so many unanticipated inequities that the courts have been forced to fashion numerous exceptions, and then exceptions to the exceptions, and then exceptions to the exceptions to the exceptions. As a result, in those infrequent situations where the issue arises in one of my cases, I end up spending hours in the law library taking soundings before I can locate my case within the evidentiary labyrinth of the Dead Man's Statute.

"What's the issue?" Jacki asked.

"Sally gave me a detailed description of what Neville did to her on the night of the attack. In fact, after she left I dictated a memo summarizing what she told me. Can we get her statements to me into evidence? If not, is a statement she made to someone else about the assault admissible?"

"Statements to whom?"

"The police. The photographer who took pictures of her injuries. One of her friends."

Jacki finished scribbling her notes and looked up. "Speaking of the police," she said, "the guy from the *Post-Dispatch* called. He told me to tell you that he checked again and there is no police report."

I leaned back in my chair and frowned. "That makes no sense. I specifically told Sally that it was a condition of my taking her lawsuit." I looked up at Jacki and shook my head. "Sally was a smart lawyer. She understood the evidentiary value of filing a police report."

"Maybe she got tied up." Jacki winced. "No joke intended."

"Brother," I mumbled, "I just hope she had someone to take photos of her injuries."

I walked Vincent Contini to the hallway outside the courtroom.

"They have a final settlement proposal," I told him.

My white-haired client straightened his back skeptically. "What now?"

I peered through the windows of the courtroom door. Cissy Thompson and Milton Brenner were huddled in conversation near the empty jury box. I turned to Vincent. "You're not going to like it."

He crossed his arms over his chest, his face stern. "Tell me."

"Cissy is willing to drop the suit if you agree to give her ten free dresses and a written letter of apology."

He stiffened, his eyes blazing. "Never," he said loudly, shaking his head. "That woman is nothing more than a common thief." He raised his right hand, pointing his index finger toward heaven. "Vincent Contini apologize to a boorish nouveau riche swindler?" He shook his head indignantly. "As God is my witness, that I shall never do."

Several heads turned to stare at the diminutive, elegantly attired gentleman. Although I doubted whether any of them recognized him, I'm sure many sensed that they should have, that they were in the presence of a notable figure, perhaps, say, an Italian duke. He wasn't, but among the more stylish wives of the St. Louis ruling class, Vincent Contini occupied a special spot in the pantheon of fashion deities. He was the haughty proprietor of Vincent's on Maryland, an exclusive designer dress shop in the Central West End. For nearly forty years, my imperious client had been one of the key fashion arbiters in town.

"I understand, Vincent," I said calmly, "and I don't blame you one bit. But I want to make sure you understand that a trial could be expensive, and that if you lose you have the added risk of a big verdict. This is a libel case. She's asking for a million dollars in actual damages and a million dollars in punitive damages."

He shook his patrician head gravely. "I have been an

American citizen for fifty-one years, Miss Gold. I understand my constitutional rights. I chose to exercise them here. I demand my day in court."

I smiled and squeezed his arm affectionately. "Okay, boss. Let's go see the judge."

As we entered the courtroom, Cissy Thompson and Milton Brenner looked over. I gestured toward Brenner, who told his client to wait.

"Wait over there," I said to Vincent, pointing him toward the rows of benches in the gallery.

Brenner approached with a big smile. He was a stocky man in his early sixties with a ruddy complexion, a shock of gray hair, crinkly blue eyes, and a crooked smile that revealed tobacco-stained teeth. Ironically, Brenner had made a name for himself defending media defendants in libel cases, although a good portion of that work was now handled by another firm in town. But with Cissy Thompson involved, it wouldn't have mattered if Brenner had been on retainer as special libel counsel to the *New York Times*, the *Washington Post*, and the *Los Angeles Times*. That was because Cissy Thompson happened to be the wife of Richie Thompson, who happened to be the founder and chairman of Pacific Rim Industries, which happened to account for 32 percent of the annual billings of Brenner's law firm, Harding, Cooper & Brandt. Although that firm was an old-line establishment organization that purported to have a lofty commitment to genteel professionalism, when the wife of your biggest client is pissed off, your loftiest duty is to make her happy, and if that meant tarting up Milton Brenner as a plaintiff's libel lawyer, so be it. Business is business.

"Well, Counselor," Brenner asked with hearty good cheer, "do we have a deal?"

I shook my head. "No dresses, no apologies."

He frowned. "Jesus Christ, Rachel." Pulling on the skin on his neck, he asked, "Does your client understand his exposure here?"

I gave him a plucky smile. "Last time I checked, Milt, truth is a complete defense to a libel claim."

He gave me a grudging chuckle. "You drive a hard bargain, Rachel. Okay, what's your counteroffer? I probably can whittle her down to five dresses."

"No counter, Milt. Let's go see the judge."

Fifteen minutes later, Judge LaDonna Williams leaned back in her chair and stared down at her desk with a scowl. Judge Williams had been on the bench for just two years, having previously served for sixteen years in the city prosecutor's office, where she had been a respected, hardworking attorney. During her years as an attorney, she had also been a guiding force of the Mound City Bar Association, the association of black attorneys, of which she had served two terms as president. Now in her mid-forties, Judge Williams was a plump woman with a gentle Aunt Jemima smile that masked an astute legal mind.

She frowned at me. "Now let me see if I have this straight, Rachel. The plaintiff, Mrs. Thompson, bought a dress from your client, and when she attempted to return it your client refused to take it back. Correct?"

"Yes, Your Honor."

"And the reason being?"

"My client examined the dress and concluded that it had been worn," I explained.

"I see." Judge Williams turned to Milton Brenner. "And how does this incident become a libel claim, Mr. Brenner?"

"Very simple, Judge. When Mr. Contini refused to take back the dress, there was an argument." Brenner shook his head, feigning indignation at the very thought of it. "He accused my client of fraud. He accused her of dishonesty. He accused her . . . of theft. These scandalous charges were overheard by three other women in the store, all three of whom knew my client on a social basis." He paused to shake his head sadly. "Judge, my client's reputation, her most precious asset, her most treasured possession, has been maliciously trashed by Mr. Contini's false and defamatory accusations."

Judge Williams snorted. "Please, Mr. Brenner, let's save the violins for the jury." She turned to me. "Settlement prospects?"

I shook my head. "It doesn't look promising. We have a pair of stubborn litigants, both of whom believe their honor is at stake."

"Honor." The judge shook her head impatiently. "That's what makes lawyers rich. Well, let's pick a trial date, folks." She opened her calendar. "Is this on the jury docket?"

I turned to Brenner. "Milt?"

"Judge," he said, "our first priority is to get this case to trial. My client desperately needs to clear her name as soon as possible. If that means waiving a jury, so be it."

Judge Williams turned to me. "Rachel?"

"We're prepared to do that as well, Your Honor."

Given the size of the jury verdicts in several recent libel cases, I was more than willing to try the case solely to Judge Williams and without a jury. Although I had obtained Vincent Contini's consent to waive a jury, I hadn't thought the opportunity would arise, since libel plaintiffs tend to love juries and juries tend to love libel plaintiffs. However, upon reflection I could see why Brenner's client, whose net worth easily exceeded $20 million, might choose speed over greed. Cissy Thompson was an indefatigable social climber. She certainly needed the money far less than she felt she needed to remove this blemish from her reputation.

Although I had never tried a case before Judge Williams, she had a reputation as an impartial and thoughtful jurist. Moreover, she was far more likely than a jury to resist Milton Brenner's closing-argument histrionics.

"Let's see," Judge Williams mused as she studied her calendar, "this case is only two months old. You won't get on a jury docket for at least twelve more months, and I can't promise it'll be reached then." She looked up. "How long will this case take to try?"

Brenner rubbed his chin. "Oh, two days?"

Judge Williams turned to me. "Rachel?"

I nodded. "Two days."

"Two days," the judge repeated. "Well, you're in luck. I have an opening a week from next Thursday. How's that?"

"Well," Brenner stammered, "that's fine with me, Judge, but I'm sure Rachel could use a little more time to get her case ready."

He was right. I could use a little more time, but I also couldn't ignore that momentary hitch in Brenner's voice. That seemed far more important than additional time.

"Not at all, Your Honor," I said with an easygoing wave of my hand. "A week from next Thursday is perfect. We'll be ready."

"Excellent," Judge Williams said, entering the date on her calendar. She looked up with a smile. "We'll start at nine. I'll see you then."

Out in the hall a somewhat uneasy Milton Brenner said, "Are you going to want to take Cissy's deposition before trial?"

I smiled and shook my head. "What for, Milt? We're already loaded for bear."

We weren't, but bluffing is part of the trial game.

"I don't blame her," I said to Benny. "I'd have booted you out of my house, too."

"What?"

"Benny, you violated a basic law of the universe. When you're trying to impress a woman, you never never never make fun of *Sleepless in Seattle*. Never."

"Wait a minute," he said, giving me an incredulous look as he picked up his chili dog. "You're telling me you liked that chick flick?"

I shrugged. "Sure. It made me cry."

He paused in midbite, staring at me with astonishment. Then he gazed up toward the ceiling and shook his head. "Lord have mercy."

We were having lunch in a booth at Llewelyn's Pub. More precisely, I was having lunch: a plate of red beans and rice and an iced tea. Benny was devouring one of his typical gorge-o-ramas: two jumbo chili dogs with extra onions and a side of jalapeño peppers, a huge platter of Welsh chips doused in vinegar, an order of onion rings, a plate of dill pickles, and a pint of Guinness stout (the most appropriately named of Benny's favorite beverages). It was the sort of cramfest that he would conclude with a satisfied belch and that any normal person would conclude with an ambulance ride to the emergency room.

"By the way," he said, leaning forward with raised eyebrows, "it's looking a little dicier for Neville McBride."

"Oh?"

"They've got the initial test results on that puddle of semen."

"His?"

"They can't say for sure, but he's definitely in the running."

"How so?"

Benny paused to take a big gulp of beer. "To begin with, he has the same blood type as the perpetrator."

"That narrows it some."

"There's more. According to my source, the mystery man was firing blanks."

Firing blanks? I repeated to myself. It took a moment. "He was sterile?" I asked.

"Technically speaking, yes. There wasn't a single sperm cell in the semen."

I looked at him with a frown. "Which means?"

"It could mean several things, but the frontrunner is that the killer had had a vasectomy."

"And Neville McBride has had a vasectomy?"

Benny grinned. "He most certainly did."

"Brother," I mumbled. Over the past two days, the lurid details of the murder had faded in my mind. This information jerked them back into appallingly sharp focus.

Benny chuckled. "Sounds to me like old Neville may be headed for an extended stay at the buttfuck motel."

I gave him a long-suffering stare and sighed. "You actually eat with that mouth?"

Our waiter came over to the booth. "Excuse me," he said. "Are you Rachel Gold?"

I nodded.

"Your secretary is on the phone. She says it's important."

I gave Benny a puzzled look as I stood up. The telephone was at the end of the bar. Harry the bartender, a burly man with a full red beard, smiled as I approached.

"Here you go, Rachel," he said, handing me the phone.

"Thanks, Harry." I took the phone from him. "Jacki?"

"I'm sorry, Rachel. I have an obnoxious lawyer named Jonathan Wolf on the phone. He says he's representing Neville McBride. I told him you were at lunch but he demanded that I find you and get you on the line. I didn't know what to do."

"That's okay. Put him through."

There was a clicking noise on the phone, and then Jacki said, "Go ahead."

"Hello?" I said.

"Hold for Mr. Wolf," a woman's voice answered.

After nearly a minute—a long time to wait on hold—he came on the line.

"Rachel?" he snapped.

Classic alpha-dog tactic, I told myself. Leave your adversary on hold long enough to make her uneasy, and then attack with a snarl. As a final rude touch, be sure to use her first name even though you've never met her before. I shook my head with irritation. Welcome to the Wild and Wacky World of Testosterone.

I paused a beat. "Excuse me?"

"Rachel Gold?" He was on a speakerphone, which made his voice boom.

"Yes?" I answered, keeping my tone civil.

"It's time for us to talk."

"Actually, Mr. Wolf, it's time for me to eat lunch."

"That's fine. We'll meet after lunch. I have an opening at three. I'd like you to drop by. It shouldn't take more than an hour."

I couldn't believe his audacity. It was time to level this playing field.

"Am I on a speakerphone?" I asked.

"Yes."

"Who else is in the room with you?"

There was a pause. "Their identities are not germane," he said.

"Wrong answer. Either tell who they are or pick up the phone."

Another pause. "You haven't answered my question. Can we schedule the meeting for three this afternoon?"

"You haven't answered *my* question, mister. Either identify your eavesdroppers or pick up the phone. I'm going to count to five. One. Two. Three. Four. Fi—"

I heard the sound of the receiver being lifted on the other end. "Okay," he said, his voice slightly less strident coming through the receiver.

"Is there anyone listening on another extension?"

"Of course not," he said in an offended tone.

"Good. Now you tell me why you think we need to meet."

"To discuss this preposterous lawsuit you filed against my client."

"Preposterous?"

I looked over at the bartender, who was listening with a grin as he dried a pint glass. I caught his eye and pointed in disbelief at the telephone. He gave me a sympathetic smile.

"Exactly," Jonathan Wolf said harshly. "It's nothing but a tissue of lies."

I shook my head in amazement at the man's sheer gall. "Why in the world would I want to travel to your office to listen to you tell me that my lawsuit is nothing but a tissue of lies?"

"I'll give you three reasons," he snapped. "First, to avoid a countersuit for abuse of process. Second, to maintain your professional reputation. Third, to protect your law license."

"Those aren't reasons," I said, practically shouting. "Those are threats. Don't you try to pull that schoolyard bully routine on me, buster. You should be ashamed. I wouldn't set foot in your office even if you and your disgusting client offered to carry me there in a sedan chair." I slammed down the receiver and looked over at Harry, my ears burning with anger. "That guy is unbelievable."

Harry chuckled. "That ole boy's gonna think twice before he tries messing with you again."

Seething, I went straight from lunch to Laclede Trust, where I told them that I'd be delighted to serve as their counsel on Sally's estate. I had no idea how, or even if, I could prove her assault claim against Neville McBride, but I'd be damned if I was going to let his arrogant mouthpiece intimidate me into dropping the lawsuit prematurely. I didn't want to risk any piece of evidence slipping through the cracks, and the best way to minimize that risk was to have complete access to her estate.

I spent more than an hour with the trust officer going over their standard practices and procedures for discharging their duties as personal representative of an estate. We also developed a framework for dealing with certain issues unique to Sally's estate, including safeguards to minimize the potential conflict of interest in my evaluation of whether the estate should pursue Sally's assault claim against Neville McBride.

During the meeting I also learned that Sally had maintained a large safe deposit box at the bank. We scheduled a time for the next morning for them to drill the box open in my presence so that I could examine its contents and take an inventory.

At quarter after four I walked through the front door of my office. My secretary was working at her computer.

"Hi, Jacki," I said cheerfully, but my cheer faded when I saw the expression on her face. "What is it?"

She shook her head, wide-eyed. "I wasn't sure."

"What?"

"He insisted on waiting," she said in a loud whisper.

"What are you talking about?"

"That lawyer."

"What lawyer?"

"Jonathan Wolf."

"What about him?"

She jerked her thumb toward my office and silently mouthed the words *In there*.

I glanced at the closed door and back at Jacki. "Jonathan Wolf is in there?"

She nodded. "He waited out here for about a half hour," she whispered, "but then he had to make a phone call. I told him he could go in your office to make it." She shrugged helplessly. "I didn't know what to do."

I stared at the closed door.

CHAPTER 5

I took a deep breath, got psyched, and opened my office door. Jonathan Wolf was standing by the window with his back to me, a portable phone cradled against his shoulder. He turned at the sound of the door opening and gave me a curt nod of acknowledgment. I saw he was holding a small scheduling calendar in his left hand and a Mont Blanc fountain pen in his right.

"Don't waste any time on that issue, Harvey," he said as he jotted something in his calendar. "We don't need it for the motion, and it'll just confuse the judge."

He glanced over at me. I was still in the doorway.

"Should I wait outside?" I whispered.

He shook his head, holding up his thumb and index finger about two inches apart, indicating that the call would be over soon. Then he waved me in, a tad too imperiously for my taste. After all, this was my office, not his. Slightly annoyed, I walked past him to my desk and sat down.

"That's a dead end," Wolf said curtly. He turned toward the window. "Harvey, read the Eighth Circuit's opinion in *U.S. versus Tatem*."

Picking up a draft of a motion for summary judgment, I tried to review it, but I couldn't concentrate. I looked up from the motion. Jonathan was standing in side profile by the window. He glanced over for a moment as he listened. Although I had seen his picture in the newspaper several times, I hadn't realized until then that none of the photos were in color. Believe me, I would have remembered those emerald-green eyes had I seen them before.

While this was our first face-to-face meeting, I was familiar with the Jonathan Wolf lore, having read a lengthy profile of him in *St. Louis* magazine and heard Wolf Man stories from two of his former colleagues at the U.S. attorney's office. Jonathan Wolf was born and raised in Brooklyn. Despite his Orthodox Jewish upbringing, he had displayed an early fascination with boxing. From the time he was ten years old, he hung around the neighborhood boxing gym after school and showed enough ability and drive to induce one of the coaches to work with him. From his bar mitzvah on, he fought in every Golden Gloves competition in the area. At the age of seventeen, he won the Brooklyn title and traveled to Madison Square Garden to compete against the title holders from the other four boroughs. He beat them all. The New York press loved him, partly because of the absolute ferocity of his boxing style and partly because of his yarmulke, which he always wore in the ring. Jimmy Breslin tagged him "the Talmudic Tornado."

After graduating with high honors from Yeshiva University, he spent a year training for a spot as a light heavyweight on the U.S. Olympic boxing team, only to be dropped after breaking his arm when he slipped on icy pavement during his predawn roadwork. He returned to New York and enrolled in law school at NYU, where he met his future wife. After law school, they moved to St. Louis, her hometown, and he took a job in the U.S. attorney's office.

As a prosecutor, Jonathan had been a classic intimidator—a man who seemed less a civil servant than a righteous crusader, who drove himself even harder than he drove his staff, whose bond with the victims and their families seemed almost obsessional, and who earned the nickname Lone Wolf for the long solitary hours he spent preparing his cases. Many a worried defense attorney, driving home along Market Street late at night after a grueling day in trial, had glanced toward a particular window on a particular floor of the U.S. Courthouse and Custom House as he drove past. It was an anxious glance, followed by a groan. No matter what the hour, the light was on.

But five years ago, shortly after his wife died of ovarian cancer, Jonathan Wolf had resigned from the U.S. attorney's office to hang out his shingle as a criminal defense attorney. He had two little daughters, and, according to courtroom pundits, the young widower had decided it was time to provide for their future.

It was an astounding career change. For ten years he had been the Lone Wolf, stalking criminal defendants with ruthless intensity. For ten years he had bored in on hostile witnesses, firing questions at them in that Brooklyn accent, his green eyes radiating chilled heat. And then—*poof*—he was no longer seated in court across from the defendant but at his side. At first it seemed totally implausible—as if Batman had teamed with the Joker. But it was a splendid transformation. Before long, the Lone Wolf had become the Wolf Man, fiery defender of the accused, shrewd tormentor of the accusers. His significant cases since the switch included the startling acquittal of Frankie "the Stud" Studzani on first-degree murder charges and two hung juries in the tax-fraud prosecution of former Missouri congressman Jim Bob Pegram.

The transformation included his courtroom attire as well. Gone were the ill-fitting dark suits, white shirts, scuffed shoes, and bad haircut that seem to be standard issue for assistant U.S. attorneys. No, today, as he stood by my office window browbeating some poor assistant named Harvey, Jonathan Wolf could have stepped out of a *GQ* feature on the successful defense attorney. He was wearing a superbly tailored charcoal chalkstripe double-breasted suit with cuffed and pleated trousers, a crisp blue pinstripe cotton shirt with gold double-knot cufflinks, a bold multistripe silk rep tie, a gold Raymond Weil watch, and cordovan kiltie moc loafers. Although he still wore his dark hair cut short, it was now accompanied by a neat close-trimmed beard. Nevertheless, the most distinctive part of his outfit, and the only holdover from his prosecutor days, was the small embroidered yarmulke he wore on his head.

I studied him as he spoke on the phone. He was in his early forties now, and his black beard was flecked with gray. Close to six feet tall, he still resembled a light heavyweight fighter, right down to the nose that had been broken and never properly reset. Although it scratched him from the pretty-boy category, I had to admit that, despite his insufferable arrogance, there was an alluring masculine aura about Jonathan Wolf. I could well imagine how the younger women on his juries might find themselves wondering, during the slower moments of trial, whether that yarmulke stayed on when everything else came off.

His telephone call was ending. I looked down at the motion papers with feigned concentration.

"That's fine," he said. "Have it delivered to my house. Be sure to let Rose know where I can reach you tonight. Tell her I'll be back in the office by"—he paused to check his watch—"five-thirty." He flipped the portable phone shut as he turned toward me. "I'm glad you're here."

I looked up from the motion papers and met his gaze. "Pardon?"

"Here. At your office." He slipped the portable phone into the pocket of his suit jacket. "I was out in the County Courts Building on a two-thirty arraignment. It ended early. I decided to stop by on my way back downtown. After all," he said with a hint of a conciliatory shrug, "if the mountain won't come to Mohammed . . ."

I smiled reluctantly and gestured toward one of the chairs facing my desk. "Have a seat, Mohammed."

He did. "I'll be brief. I'm here to discuss your lawsuit."

I shook my head. "Forget it."

He nodded. "I understand. But when we spoke earlier, I neglected to tell you the most important reason to dismiss your lawsuit."

I leaned back in my chair and crossed my arms. "Save your breath."

"I understand your misgivings, Rachel." He paused, as if he were mentally weighing something. "Perhaps I came on a little strong on the phone."

"A little?" I repeated sarcastically.

His portable phone started ringing. He reached into his pocket, removed the phone, paused for a moment, and then turned it off. He slipped it back into his pocket and looked at me. "My goal wasn't to offend you."

"I agree. Your goal was to intimidate me."

"Which I obviously didn't," he said with a wry smile, a twinkle in his eyes, "and in the process I most certainly did offend you. Forgive me. I'm sure I'm not the first male attorney to underestimate Rachel Gold." He paused, his face growing solemn. "I didn't come here to try to charm you, Rachel. As you can tell, I'm not a very charming fellow. I came here because I made a mistake. I came here to tell you the most important reason to drop your lawsuit."

I stared at him, waiting. "Which is?"

He leaned forward. "Which is to keep an innocent man from being framed for a murder he didn't commit."

I frowned. "I'm not accusing him of murder."

"Come on," he said impatiently, sitting back in his chair. "That's the only thing your lawsuit doesn't accuse him of."

"That's an awfully big only, Jonathan."

"Rachel," he said, his green eyes intense, "Neville McBride didn't assault your client."

I gave him a tolerant smile. "Jonathan, I saw the bruises."

He studied me for a moment. "You told the police she had a black eye."

I nodded.

"The right eye, correct?" he said.

I paused. "I think so."

He shook his head. "Not according to the autopsy. No black eye. Same with the scratches you saw on her neck and chest. Not one scratch on her neck or chest, Rachel."

I shrugged, growing more irritated. "So maybe they healed."

"In less than a week?"

"It's possible." I leaned forward, pointing my finger for emphasis. "Look, Jonathan, I know what I saw with my own eyes. What's your point?"

"It's simple. My client totally denies your allegations. He swears he was nowhere near her house that night. He swears he hadn't seen her for more than a month. He swears that he never, ever assaulted her."

I raised my eyebrows and gave him a sardonic shrug. "And my client swore that he did."

"What if she lied?"

I laughed, astounded. "What if *he* lied?"

Jonathan didn't smile. "I believe he's telling the truth."

"Okay, Jonathan," I said patiently. "Let's assume for the moment that you're right, which would mean that Sally was the one who lied. What's her motivation?"

"Money, of course. Neville had the money, and this was a good way to get it."

"Fine," I said, going along. "Under your scenario, then, who beat her up?"

He shrugged nonchalantly. "Maybe no one."

I shook my head. "No way. I saw the injuries. They looked real to me."

"So does good makeup." He paused, scratching his beard thoughtfully. "Of course, there are other possibilities. Perhaps the injuries were real but the attacker was someone else."

"Such as?"

He stood up and moved toward the window. "A current boyfriend?" He turned to face me, leaning against the wall with his arms crossed. "Maybe after the beating, as she looked at her injuries in the mirror, she suddenly saw a chance to spin straw into gold: she could concoct a fake story around real injuries and use it to extract money out of my client."

I frowned skeptically. "That's pretty farfetched."

"I've had circumstances far stranger. I'm certain you have as well." He paused. "Here's another scenario. What if Sally didn't hire you?"

I gave him a puzzled look. "But she did."

He nodded, his expression serious. "Did you ever wonder why she decided to hire you?"

"No."

"You don't handle much personal injury work, right?"

"I've had one or two cases."

"Did you know her at all before she hired you?"

"No, but I'd heard of her, and apparently she'd heard of me." I smiled. "Maybe she felt more comfortable with a woman attorney."

Jonathan nodded pensively. "Perhaps. If so, though, there were several women in the personal injury field she knew far better than you. Perhaps she wanted someone who *didn't* know her."

He reached into his suit jacket as he approached my desk and removed a 5x7 photograph. "Here," he said as he handed it to me. "Is that the woman who hired you to sue my client?"

It was a color portrait shot of Sally Wade. I placed it on the desk. "Yep."

"Are you positive?"

I gazed up at him curiously. "Why wouldn't I be?"

"You met her only once. You told the police that she wore sunglasses during most of the meeting and that her upper lip was swollen. Those are less than optimal conditions for accurate observations." He sat down and leaned toward the desk to slide the photograph closer to me. "Look at it carefully, Rachel. Take your time."

I did, and as I studied Sally's face I gradually realized that I couldn't be absolutely certain that I was staring at the same person who had retained me. I was still fairly sure, but I couldn't guarantee it. The problem was that Sally didn't have distinctive features. The hairstyle and hair color looked the same, as I recalled. The eyes in the photo were blue, and that's the color I seemed to remember from the meeting. I couldn't recall the shape of her eyes—just that one of them was swollen and bruised. I couldn't be certain about the shape of her nose, or, for that matter, her lips, or her chin, or her neck.

I looked up from the photo with a frown. "I think it's the same person."

"What if it's not? What if you were hired by an impostor?"

"Oh, brother." I shook my head good-naturedly. "Jonathan, you can spin out these alternative realities all day long, but we both know that the most likely story is the one I've alleged in the lawsuit."

"Unless you believe my client."

"Well, I don't."

"How do you know?"

"Because I believe my client."

"Why didn't she file a police report?"

That was, of course, the very question I'd been asking myself. "I don't know," I conceded.

"But you told her to file one."

"True," I acknowledged. "But it certainly wouldn't be the first time a client failed to follow her lawyer's advice."

He leaned forward. "Don't you see, Rachel? It's just like that photograph. Just as you can't be absolutely sure that Sally Wade was the woman who hired you, you can't be absolutely sure that my client's version of the story isn't the real one."

I smiled and shook my head. "You sound like someone trying to create some reasonable doubt."

He nodded. "Absolutely."

I shrugged. "You haven't succeeded."

"I haven't finished."

I groaned. "What now?"

"I want you to talk to him."

"Neville McBride?"

"Yes."

I tilted my head in surprise. "That's a bit unusual."

"So?" he said, dead serious. "This whole case is a bit unusual, which is why I'd like you to meet with him. Ask him whatever you want. Listen to his answers. Watch him closely. Decide for yourself."

I studied Jonathan. "What if I talk to him and decide he's a liar?"

He shrugged. "I'm willing to take that risk."

I frowned. "I don't understand why."

"Because your testimony could be devastating, Rachel." He leaned forward. "If the jury believes that Sally told you the truth, they're that much more likely to return a guilty verdict. If those jurors believe that he regularly tied her up and masturbated onto her backside, they're going to convict him."

I leaned back in my chair and shook my head. "Jonathan, you seem to overlook the fact that I represent

Sally. I believed her when I filed that lawsuit. I have no reason to doubt her now. In addition, I've been retained by the trust company to help administer her estate. With all that against him, why would Neville risk talking to me?"

"Two reasons. First, you have a reputation for fairness." I laughed. "I'm no saint."

He didn't smile. "Neither is Neville, as you will discover. He's a womanizer, a bit of a racist, and probably not wild about Jews. But I don't believe he's a killer. Neville and I hope that if he gives you a reason to believe him, you'll give him a fair hearing. Second, and just as important, you have a reputation for tenacity. That's crucial here. I believe you were used—either by Sally or by someone else who hired an impersonator. I'm assuming that if you reach the same conclusion, namely, that you were used as part of a murder scheme, you're not going to stop digging until you find out who that someone was."

I got up, walked over to the window, and peered through the blinds. I turned to him. "You're asking a lot."

"I know I am."

"When would you want to have this meeting?"

"Tonight."

"Tonight?"

He nodded. "Name the place. I'll get him there."

I went back over to my desk and glanced down at my calendar. "Tonight isn't good."

"Why not?" he said.

"I have a class at five-thirty, and then I'm going to my mother's house for dinner."

"That's fine. I'll bring him by after dinner. Just give me a time."

"Jonathan," I said, leaning back against my credenza, slightly annoyed and slightly amused, "has anyone ever told you that you tend to be a little too pushy?"

He smiled. "They've never said 'a little.' " The smile

faded. "Rachel, my client is charged with first-degree murder. That's a compelling reason to be a little too pushy." He pulled out his pocket calendar and fountain pen. "When's good tonight?"

I sighed. "Well, how's eight o'clock?"

"We'll be there."

CHAPTER 6

"Assume the position," she ordered.

I did.

"Feet at shoulder width, knees flexed."

They were.

"Grip the ground with your toes."

I tried.

"Tonight we start with the palm-heel strike. Bend your elbows, gals. Hands palm-up at the sides of your ribs. Good. Now pull them back as far as you can."

I did.

"Fingers together. Make sure those elbows are aligned directly behind your hands, just like pistons."

They were.

"Hold that position. Concentrate on your power line."

I did, and as I did, Faith Compton moved slowly around and among us, studying our positions, occasionally pausing to adjust a stance.

The front wall was mirrored. I followed her in the reflection. There were eleven of us in the women's self-defense class, all lawyers, varying body types, all between the ages of twenty-five and fifty. Most of us, including me, were wearing sweatshirts, sweatpants, and sneakers. Two of the women, including the oldest in the class, were in leotards and tights.

Faith Compton was our instructor. She was in her late thirties, stood just under five feet, and looked as if she lifted weights. She had short red hair, intense blue eyes, and an acne-scarred face. According to the class brochure, she held a third-degree black belt USA Goju Karate and a second-degree black belt Aiki Jitsu, whatever those were. She was wearing a gray sweatshirt over black tights and a pair of black leather exercise shoes.

"We start with the palm-heel strike," she announced after she returned to the front of the class. "Remember: strike forward along the power line, fingers up, heel of the palm pushed forward. Keep those shoulders back and still. We'll do the right hand first. You know the move. You've practiced it every night since our last class."

She assumed the stance facing us, arms back, hands up, eyes calm and lethal.

"Make sure your energies are flowing in a straight line," she said, "directly forward from your solar plexus. Prepare yourself. Remember the yell of spirit. I want to hear you scream."

I took a cleansing breath, trying to maintain my focus.

"He's in front of you. Visualize him."

I concentrated, trying to conjure up an attacker. The best I could do was a wavery image of Jonathan Wolf in his thousand-dollar suit. There was a smirk on his face.

"Visualize your palm heel driving through the center of his chest."

I did.

"Ready?"

Definitely.

"Now!"

My arm shot forward. Boom! He staggered backward and lost his balance. Yes!

"Excellent, girls."

I was grinning, my heart racing. I was invincible.

"Resume the chambered position. Good. This time, four hits. Right, left, right, left. Make it fast. Let me hear those screams. Ready? Visualize. *Now!*"

Boom, boom, boom, boom!

I was Wonder Woman, I was Bruce Lee, I was kicking major butt!

Twenty minutes later, I was also totally exhausted. A little hoarse, too, as we prepared to end the class in the same way we opened it. I was kneeling in what Faith called the position of reflection: hands on my lap, ends of my thumbs touching gently, eyes closed. Together, we said the pledge of virtues that Faith said she had learned from her kung fu master, also a woman:

"The martial arts are my secret," I recited with the group. "I bear no arms. I shall find my strength as a woman. I shall always be aware. I shall be quick to seize opportunity. Nothing is impossible."

I opened my eyes, smiling proudly.

Faith caught my gaze and nodded. Then she bounced to her feet and clapped her hands once. "Dismissed."

"What's one more piece?"

"Mom," I groaned, holding up my hands. "I've had three already. I'm *plotzing*."

She put down the plate of *kamishbroit* and shook her head. "Then you'll take some home."

"It's a deal. You know I'm crazy for them."

And I was. *Kamishbroit* is a deliciously crunchy Yiddish pastry, a long, narrow cookie, whose Italian cousin, *biscotti*, became fashionable in the early nineties. Well, my mother's *kamishbroit* makes the finest *biscotti* taste like stale Wonder bread. I don't say that just because I love my brilliant, eccentric, and often exasperating mother, which I dearly do. I say it because it's true. Sarah Gold happens to be an extraordinary cook, and her mastery extends from traditional Jewish cuisine (including knishes to die for and a *cholent* that deserves the Irving Thalberg Award at the next Oscars) to the latest in organic vegetarian cookery (including a vegetable stew that's become a winter special at a local health food restaurant, where the menu lists it as Sarah's West African Groundnut Stew).

"You'll have some more compote, sweetie pie?"

I smiled in surrender. "Okay, Mom, but just a little."

"So," she said as she started spooning the fruit compote into my bowl, "when are they going to be here?"

I glanced at the kitchen clock. "About ten minutes. Whoa, Mom, that's plenty."

"I'll make tea for them."

"Don't bother. You're not the hostess. I'm the one doing them a favor."

"It's no big deal," she said as she got up and walked over to the stove for the teakettle. "In my own house I can at least offer a person tea." She paused for a moment, giving me a severe look. "Even if he murdered his wife and deserves to die in the sewer like a rat."

I held my tongue—as always, the incurably liberal daughter of a mother who believes in capital punishment for murderers, castration for rapists, and slow medieval torture for child molesters.

My mother is the least sentimental woman I know. She has ample reason. She came to America from Lithuania at the age of three, having escaped with her mother and baby sister after the Nazis killed her father. Fate remained cruel. My mother, a woman who reveres books and learning, was forced to drop out of high school and go to work when her mother (after whom I am named) was diagnosed with cancer of the liver. Rachel Linowitz died a year later, leaving her two daughters, Sarah and Becky, orphans at the ages of seventeen and fifteen.

Two years later, at the age of nineteen, my mother

married a shy, cuddly bookkeeper ten years her senior named Seymour Gold. My father was totally smitten by his feisty wife and remained so until the day he died. He was the sentimental one, the one whose eyes quickly welled with tears whether he was listening in the den to one of his Italian operas or reading *The Velveteen Rabbit* to me in bed or saying a prayer of thanks at the beginning of our Friday-night Sabbath dinner.

I remember bringing home *The Great Gatsby* during winter break of my sophomore year of college. He read it in one sitting, spellbound and deeply moved. With some hesitation, he offered it to my mother, a voracious reader of nonfiction who viewed novels with disdain. ("With all my real problems," she says, "who's got time to fret over pretend ones?") She read as far as that wonderful scene where Jay Gatsby, taking Daisy on a tour of his Long Island mansion, throws open his large dressing bureaus to display a rainbow of custom-made shirts. As he tosses them onto the bed, the brightly colored pile of fabrics growing ever higher, Daisy is overcome. "It makes me sad," she sobs, "because I've never seen such—such beautiful shirts before." At that point in the novel, my mother slammed it closed with a snort of disgust and stood up. "I've got no use," she grumbled as she headed toward the kitchen, "for rich people who cry over shirts."

Like her mother before her, my mother had two daughters, me and my younger sister Ann. Although Ann was allowed to be the prissy girl of the family, my mother put me to bed every night with fairy tales about college and medical school. "Someday you'll be somebody," she would whisper fiercely as she kissed me good night, "and not a doormat like your poor father. 'Dr. Gold,' they'll say. 'Please help me, Dr. Gold.'" Those plans changed my junior year in a course called organic chemistry. So it goes.

"Meanwhile," my mother was saying as she came

back to the kitchen table, "what are you doing for that trust company?"

"Basically two things," I explained. "First, I'm going to help wrap up her personal affairs. Second, I'll wrap up her law practice."

"How do you wrap up a law practice?"

"Sally was a solo practitioner. Her assistant's name is Amy Chickering. Jacki called over there this afternoon to tell Amy to put together a status report on all of Sally's cases. I'm assuming there are at least two hundred active cases that need to be transferred to new attorneys. I'll meet with Amy tomorrow. The whole process may take two or three weeks. We've assured Amy that she'll get paid her full salary for as long as it takes plus two months' severance pay."

The teakettle started to whistle. As my mother got up to turn down the gas, she asked, "How do you wrap up her personal affairs?"

"The police have her house sealed off. The trust company will take an inventory of the contents of the house. They've already assumed control of her bank accounts. They've also arranged to have all her bills sent directly to them for payment. Tomorrow morning I'm going down to her bank to have her safe deposit box drilled."

The doorbell rang.

"I'll get it," I said as we both stood up. "I'll talk to them in the living room."

Jonathan Wolf had obviously stopped by his house on the way over, perhaps to have dinner with his children. He had changed out of his courtroom costume and into a navy turtleneck made of heavy cotton, a pair of baggy tan corduroys, and brown leather moccasins.

"Hello, Rachel," he said, stepping into the foyer. "This is Neville McBride."

McBride was even dumpier in person than in his newspaper photo. His lower teeth were crooked, he was bald, and he wore thick wire-rim glasses. The nose pads of the glasses cut into the flesh on either side of his nose, which seemed even more bulbous up close. His gray hair and extra weight made him look at least a decade older than his fifty-five years. Although his glen-plaid suit had probably been made by a London tailor, it was rumpled and lumpy and overdue for a pressing.

But as every lawyer learns early in her career, appearances can be deceiving. Indeed, Neville McBride's rise to power within his law firm and the community was all the more impressive when you realized that he had obtained that success despite his nondescript, almost goofy appearance.

There was nothing nondescript or goofy about his firm handshake and deep voice. "I am honored to meet you, Miss Gold," he said in a subdued, self-possessed tone, "and quite grateful that you are willing to meet with me."

"This is my mother, Sarah," I said, turning toward her. "Mom, this is Jonathan Wolf, and this is Neville McBride."

After everyone shook hands, my mother asked if they wanted tea.

"None for me," Neville said.

"I'll have a cup," Jonathan told her.

"Would you like lemon or sugar?" my mother asked.

"I'll come help you fix it," he said.

"No, you go with the others," my mother said. "I'll bring it to you."

Jonathan smiled and shook his head. "I'll come with you, Mrs. Gold, if you don't mind the company. Rachel and Mr. McBride should meet alone." He glanced over at me. "Right?"

I was a little surprised, having assumed that Jonathan was the sort of control freak who would insist on being present during my conversation with his client. I looked at McBride and then back at Jonathan.

"Sure," I said with a smile. "Let's go to the living room, Mr. McBride. We can talk there."

"Not at all?" I asked him.

He vigorously shook his head. "Never, Miss Gold. Not with Sally. Not with my first two wives, and you certainly don't have to rely on my word for it. I'll be happy to give you their names and telephone numbers. Talk to them directly. Confirm it for yourself." He stood up and walked over to the fireplace. Turning to me with a serious expression, he said, "I absolutely, categorically deny the charge. I have never in my life struck a woman in anger."

"You say 'never in anger,' " I responded, pressing on. "But you did engage in bondage fantasies with Sally, correct?"

"Good Lord," he mumbled, his face reddening. "Yes, but surely nothing like that. Moreover, it was only once, early in the marriage. She asked me to, uh, to tie her up. I did, and we, ahem, had relations. But that was it. Only that one time."

"Maybe with her, but she wasn't the only one, correct?"

He leaned back against the mantel and stared at the ceiling. I waited. After a moment, he took a deep breath, sighed, and looked at me. "I've been with other women, Rachel—do you mind if I call you Rachel? Many women. Before my marriage to Sally, after the marriage ended, and, well, during the marriage, too. Unhappily, our marital relationship soured quickly. All sexual relations had terminated by the end of the first six months of marriage."

He paused, studying the carpet at his feet. "As for other female companions," he continued, still looking down, "occasionally one would express a desire to engage in, shall we say, an unconventional procedure. I will admit that I acquiesced in some such requests, but I can assure you that I am not a"—he paused, searching for the correct word—"a devotee of bondage."

It was, I had to admit, a credible performance. But then again, I reminded myself, lawyers are paid to sound credible. That's what we do for a living. We manipulate judges, lawyers, people in general, clients—especially clients. The best lawyers are masters of manipulation, with skills more akin to those of sorcerers. Surely Neville McBride—managing partner of Tully, Crane & Leonard and a man who had parlayed his mastery of the intricacies of the Internal Revenue Code and his extraordinary contacts within the upper echelon of St. Louis into a flourishing limited partnerships practice—had to be included on any list of the best.

All of which made this discussion even more awkward, given the subject matter and the disparity in our ages. It was like interrogating Walter Cronkite on his favorite masturbation technique.

Speaking of which, I had to concede, as I studied Neville McBride standing by the fireplace, that the image of him hunched naked over the exposed backside of a bound and gagged Sally Wade, his eyes straining, breath rasping, sweat dripping from his face as, in Benny's coarse metaphor, he furiously choked his chicken—well, it was an image so implausible that it seemed preposterous. But then again, given some of the scenarios in my nastier divorce cases, what seemed preposterous often proved genuine.

Leaning back on the couch, I decided to try another approach. "When did you last see Sally?"

He squinted, trying to remember. "About two months ago, in a meeting arranged by our respective divorce attorneys."

"How did it go?"

He seemed to contemplate the question. "She was cool but civil. The meeting lasted an hour and then I left."

I nodded. "And it's your position that you didn't see her after that?"

"It's not simply my position," he said, an edge to his voice, "it's the truth."

No sense picking a fight now. There'd be plenty of time for that if the case continued. Jonathan had brought him here tonight solely for me to assess his credibility, and the jury was still out on that topic. I studied him. Time for the main event.

"I assume you are familiar with the allegations of Sally Wade's lawsuit."

"Oh, yes," he said with a bitter snort. "Yes, indeed. I am quite familiar with every single loathsome fabrication contained therein."

"Okay," I said, aiming for a detached tone. "As you recall, the petition alleges that the assault took place late on that Tuesday night."

He crossed his arms over his chest and stared down at me.

"Where were you on that Tuesday night, Mr. McBride?"

"In my residence."

"Were you alone?"

His lips curled into a smirk. "I was with a woman."

"From when to when?"

"We arrived at approximately nine-thirty. She left the following morning at approximately six a.m."

"Who is she?"

"Her name is Tammy."

I nodded. "Okay. Does she live here?"

"No."

"Where does she live?"

"Actually, I'm not certain."

I kept my expression neutral. "Why is that?"

He tried a smile, but it came off closer to a grimace. "She refused to tell me. She said she enjoyed the mystery of it. No last names, no office addresses, no strings attached—just an occasional, anonymous sexual rendezvous. I was doubtful at first, but it's been quite, uh, well, quite exhilarating."

"So," I said evenly, "you don't know her last name and you don't know where she lives."

"Good God, Rachel, you make something fun sound downright sinister. She's a delightful girl. Although I may not know her last name, I do know that she's an airline stewardess."

"Which airline?"

He gave a nervous chortle. "Actually, I am not certain."

I nodded, keeping my expression blank. "Tell me how you met her."

"Quite simple. It was in the restaurant bar in our office building. About six weeks ago. I met her at happy hour. We hit it off quite well. I invited her to dinner, and afterward she spent the night at my place. Since that night, we have been together twice. The last time, fortunately, was the night of the incident alleged in your lawsuit."

"Fortunately?"

He smiled. "For me. Her testimony will totally refute your ridiculous charges."

"Assuming you ever hear from her again."

He chuckled. "Oh, I'm quite certain I will. Her travel routes bring her through St. Louis every two weeks or so. She calls the night before she's scheduled to fly into St. Louis. As a matter of fact, I should be hearing from her fairly soon. I can guarantee that Tammy will be able to confirm every single thing I have just told you."

He came back over and sat down on the loveseat facing the couch.

I was quiet for a moment. "Her first name is Tammy?"

"Yes."

I considered the story. His key alibi witness was a mystery woman—no last name, no hometown, no employer. By any measure, it was lame. Lamer even than the premises in those thrillers that every attorney in America seemed to be writing except me.

But that was a problem. McBride's story was so lame that it just might be true. After all, Neville McBride was a savvy, ingenious lawyer. He was certainly savvy enough to recognize a lame alibi. He was certainly ingenious enough to concoct a better one. All of which meant that if he didn't have a real alibi for the night in question, he surely could have invented something more compelling than this flat retread of *The Lady Vanishes*. Indeed, the most plausible reason for his Tammy alibi was that it was true.

I stared at him. "I have a few more questions," I said.

He gave me a determined smile. "Fire away."

"Let's go back to your relationship with other women."

"Well?" my mother said after they left. We were back in the kitchen cleaning up.

I sighed and shook my head. "I can't decide. He definitely knows how to make a good presentation. He didn't try to oversell himself, and he made sure to show me some of his warts."

"Such as?"

"Such as failing to honor his marital vows. He's not too good at monogamy."

"That man?" my mother asked in disbelief. "What kind of woman would sleep with him?"

"All kinds, from the sound of things. Secretaries, showgirls, wives of other lawyers. What's that old saying? 'Power is the greatest aphrodisiac'? It apparently works for him."

"Tramps." My mother frowned. "Why would he tell you something like that?"

"So that I could talk to them if I wanted. He claims he's never hit a woman in his life."

She wiped the counter with a sponge. "What about the night your client claimed he attacked her?"

"He has an alibi."

My mother turned to me with a dubious expression. "Oh? Let's hear it."

I told her the tale of Tammy.

My mother scoffed. "No one is going to believe that cockamamie story."

I joined her at the table. "So," I said, weary of the subject of Neville McBride, "how did you and Prince Charming get along in the kitchen?"

She looked at me and raised her eyebrows impishly. "He's not so terrible."

"Terrible? No. Just obnoxious and egotistical and rude."

"I like him."

I laughed in disbelief. "Mom, you've got to be kidding."

She gave me a proud smile. "Did you know he loved my *kamishbroit*?"

"Mom, Saddam Hussein would love your *kamishbroit*. Idi Amin would do cartwheels for it. That doesn't prove a thing."

"He makes it himself."

"Kamishbroit?"

She nodded serenely. "We compared recipes."

"Let me get this straight," I said in amazement. "You and Jonathan Wolf were in here talking about recipes for *kamishbroit*?"

"And why not? Did you know he used to help his *bobba* make it when he was a boy? Now he makes it with his daughters. Oh, my goodness, Rachel," she said, placing her hand over her heart, "do you know about his wife?"

"I know. She died of cancer."

My mother shook her head sadly. "Such a tragedy."

I reached over and squeezed her hand. "Thanks for dinner, Mom." I stood up to gather my stuff. "It's late. I have a big day tomorrow."

As I headed for the dining room to get my purse and briefcase, I called over my shoulder, "Who stays with his girls during the day?"

"He has a housekeeper. An older woman." There was a pause as my mother got up to follow me. "Did you know he keeps kosher?"

"Good for him," I said as I bent down to pick up my briefcase.

"He's not a bad-looking man."

I straightened up slowly. Without a word, I turned toward my mother, who was standing in the doorway.

"I'm not so crazy about a beard," she said, trying to sound offhand, "but otherwise you have to admit that this is a handsome man."

"Mother, please tell me you're joking."

"What?" she asked, pretending to be confused. "You don't think he's good-looking?"

I looked toward the ceiling and shook my head. "No comment." I headed toward the front hall to get my jacket out of the closet.

"All I meant," my mother said, following after me, "is that this is a nice Jewish man, and is it such a crime that he also happens to be tall, dark and—"

"—arrogant," I said, looking back at her.

"Proud, Rachel, not arrogant. Pride is a good thing. As a matter of fact," she said with a wink, "I think I know someone else with plenty of pride. And she happens to be a gorgeous knockout to boot."

I shook my head. "Please, Mother."

"Hush." She gave me a kiss. "My tall, dark, and proud daughter."

We hugged. She stood back to look at me, her eyes bright. "And so beautiful," she whispered. "Here, I'll hold your briefcase."

I handed it to her and slipped on my jacket. "That was a scrumptious meal, Mom."

"Thank you, sweetie pie."

I opened the front door. "I love you, Mom. I'll call you tomorrow."

She walked out on the front porch and handed me the

bag of *kamishbroit*. "Let me know what you find in her safe deposit box, okay?"

"Sure."

As I opened the car door my mother called out, "Rachel?"

"Yes?"

"Did you notice he wears a yarmulke?"

"Good night, Mother."

"Good night, darling."

CHAPTER 7

I waved the Walgreens receipt triumphantly. "Yes!"

Jacki looked up from the inventory list. "What?"

"Bingo." I handed it to her. "Check it out."

Jacki and I were in a small conference room at the main offices of Laclede Trust. Earlier that morning I had watched as two workmen drilled open Sally Wade's safe deposit door. Afterward, they carried the large steel box to one of the conference rooms, where Jacki was reviewing the entries on the inventories of items in Sally's office and home.

Jacki squinted at the Walgreens receipt. "Photo developing?"

"Look at the date."

"October sixteenth." She looked up with a frown. "So?"

"Jacki," I said impatiently, "what was the date Sally came to the office?"

"The sixteenth?"

"Close. The fifteenth."

"Ah," she said with a smile, "you think those are them?"

I gave her a wink and a thumbs-up. "We just might be back in business with that lawsuit. Although," I said, pausing to look down at the receipt with a frown, "I wish she'd had these done by a professional photographer. How're we ever going to find out who took these shots?"

"Do we need to know that?"

I nodded. "It would help. I'm going to have to lay an evidentiary foundation to get the photos admitted into evidence. It'd be nice to have the person who took the shots get on the stand and testify when and where he took them. Moreover, Sally may have told the photographer something about the assault. We might be able to get those statements into evidence."

"Maybe Amy Chickering will know who took them," Jacki said.

"Good point."

Amy Chickering was Sally Wade's assistant. I was scheduled to meet with her at Sally's office after I finished at the trust company.

"Let me have it," Jacki said, reaching for the receipt. She checked the address. "I'll pick them up at lunch." She entered the Walgreens receipt on the inventory she was compiling for the safe deposit box. As she wrote she asked, "What else is in there?"

I peered into the steel box. "Let's see . . . one passport." I flipped to the first page, studied her photograph for a moment, and then handed it to Jacki. I looked back in the box. "One large manila envelope." I took it out, undid the clasp, opened the top flap, and pulled out the contents. "U.S. savings bonds."

Jacki looked up from the passport. "How many?"

I shuffled through them. "Nine, each for one hundred dollars." I put them back in the envelope and placed it on the table near Jacki. She was still paging through the passport.

"Any interesting places?" I asked.

"Lots of trips to Hong Kong."

"Anywhere else?"

"France. Here's one to Spain."

I pulled another manila envelope out of the box and opened it. Inside was a single sheet of paper. At the top of the page, handwritten in blue ink, were the letters BCS. Below it were four rows of numbers, also in blue ink:

BCS
011-41-22-862-1823
108-795-2581-3883
111385
11787

"Bank accounts?" I said, handing it to Jacki.

She examined it a moment and then looked up at me with a puzzled expression. "B-C-S?"

I peered into the safe deposit box. Another manila envelope. This one contained a nine-page handwritten document. Each page had several columns of names and data. The first page was typical of the others:

π		%		
Zenger	Dice	8		
Janney	Johnson	10		
Roberts, L	Johnson	10	$700	12/7/94
Smith, H	Dice	8		
Senn	Magliozzi	8	$350	6/3/95
Gianino	Tubbs	8		
Hartmann	Dice	8		
Blakeman	Rice	10	$1,100	11/8/95
Stahl	Magliozzi	8		

"What do you make of this?" I asked, showing it to Jacki.

She scrutinized it. "These," she said, pointing to the first column, "have to be clients."

"Probably so."

The first column had the π symbol at the top. The π symbol, as every first-year law student struggling to take lecture notes quickly learns, is shorthand for "plaintiff." (Δ is shorthand for "defendant.") Presumably, the names in the first column were plaintiffs, and since Sally had been a plaintiffs lawyer, those names were presumably her clients.

Jacki ran a finger down the second column. "These don't look like defendants," she said. "Too many repeaters."

I nodded. "Maybe defense lawyers. Or maybe the treating physicians." Personal injury lawyers tend to have favorite doctors, which they use as expert witnesses over and over again.

"Or judges," Jacki said. "I'll check the directories when we get back to the office." She pointed to the third column, which had the numbers grouped under the % sign. "What's that?"

"It sure isn't her fee."

Although personal injury lawyers usually charge on a contingent fee basis, the range of typical contingent fee percentages (usually from 30 to 40 percent of the recovery) was far higher than those listed on the document (5 to 10 percent).

"These last two," I said, pointing to the fourth and fifth columns, "must be payment amounts and dates."

"But what kind of payments?"

I frowned at the dates and dollar amounts. "Don't know." I shook my head. "There's something fishy about this."

"Why do you say that?"

"If these are client matters, why did Sally keep the list in her safe deposit box? Why wouldn't she keep it at her office?"

"Maybe there's one there, too," Jacki said.

"I doubt it. Let's make sure we get a copy of this."

Next in the safe deposit box were three savings accounts at three different banks, each in Sally's name
alone, each showing activity before, during, and after her
marriage, each showing a balance of between $12,000
and $35,000. There were also stock certificates from
several corporations, all in Sally's name alone. The stocks,
like the bank accounts, listed Sally's address as a St.
Louis post office box. It didn't take a rocket scientist to
deduce that Sally had concealed these assets from Neville McBride. I handed them all to Jacki and turned back
to the box. We had reached the bottom, and the last item
was a thick manila envelope. I lifted it out, opened it up,
and looked inside.

"Whoa."

Jacki looked up. "What?"

I turned the envelope upside down. Onto the table
clattered twenty packets of paper currency, each bound
with a white paper band.

"Good grief," Jacki said.

We sorted and counted. Ten packets contained crisp
hundred-dollar bills and the other ten contained fifty-
dollar bills. Total: $31,200 in cash.

I summoned the trust officer as Jacki recorded the
cash amounts on the inventory list. When he arrived, we
gave him the cash, bonds, and stock certificates for safe-
keeping. I had him make copies of the various documents I'd found in her safe deposit box, including the
nine-page list.

As Jacki and I rode down the elevator to the parking
garage, I reviewed our tasks. "You'll pick up her pictures at that Walgreens," I said. "You also have to stop
by the post office. Check her post office box."

Jacki nodded, jotting notes on her steno pad in the
elevator.

We stepped off the elevator and headed toward our
cars, which were parked side by side. As we walked, I

said, "I'm heading over to the East Side, to meet with her assistant. What's her name again?"

"Amy Chickering."

"By the way, Jonathan Wolf is sending a messenger to our office to pick up a photocopy of the attorney-client agreement Sally signed."

Jacki gave me a curious look. "How come?"

I opened my car door. "He wants his handwriting analyst to take a look at her signature."

Jacki shook her head in disbelief. "He can't seriously believe that an impostor hired you?"

I shrugged. "He's a criminal defense lawyer. They like to deal in alternative scenarios."

"Right," Jacki said angrily. "Like she wasn't really injured that day, right? Like she was wearing makeup? Alternative scenarios? I think it's disgusting."

I snapped my fingers. "One last thing. Shift gears a sec. Different case. That trial date for Cissy Thompson's libel case is getting close. Check on those two subpoenas. Neiman-Marcus must have something for us by now."

"Will do." She winked. "Keep your fingers crossed on that one."

I smiled. "That's what I'm doing." I held up my hands to show her.

CHAPTER 8

Taking care of business took longer than expected. The firm of Sally Wade & Associates had close to four hundred cases, most of which were garden-variety personal injury matters—slip-and-falls, fender benders, and workers' comp injuries. Curiously, most of her workers' comp claims involved the Douglas Beef slaughterhouse in East St. Louis, the same slaughterhouse that Benny had spotted from the top of the Arch. Presumably, Sally had an in with some official at the meatpackers' union.

Although Amy Chickering, Sally's assistant, had done a fine job grouping the cases into logical categories, it still took far more time than I had anticipated to get through all the files, place a tentative value on each claim, and make preliminary decisions as to which cases should be referred to which attorneys. It was a task for which I was uniquely unqualified, having spent most of my career battling over the issues that arise in complex commercial litigation. Whiplash and loss of consortium have never been much concern under the Sherman Act (except perhaps for the lawyers' spouses), and the key documents in a securities fraud claim do not include spinal X-rays and reports of treating chiropractors.

Fortunately, Amy Chickering possessed enough expertise for both of us. She had been Sally's secretary for almost three years, and, as is true of every good secretary for a solo practitioner, her duties included those performed by paralegals and junior associates at most larger law firms. I watched with deference as Amy picked up a file, sorted through the medical records, and gave me a summary and case value in under five minutes: "Okay, this is a number three lumbar. Seven thousand in specials. Full recovery. Value it at twenty grand. Let's put it in Irv's pile. He'll want this one for sure."

It took us nearly three hours to get through all of the cases, and by the time we finished, both of us were bushed. Our exhaustion was due to more than just the volume of cases. The working conditions were cramped and uncomfortable. Basically, we moved slowly through each file drawer, pulling out one case file at a time, sorting through the papers inside, making notes on a legal pad, returning it to the file drawer, and moving on to the next one.

Amy had dressed for the task. I, unfortunately, had not. Although I shucked my shoes to pad around in my stockings, I envied her yellow cotton turtleneck, faded blue jeans, and jogging shoes.

The pizza we ordered during a coffee and bathroom break arrived a few minutes after we finished the last file. I paid the delivery boy and joined Amy in the kitchen, where she had placed two chilled cans of Pepsi on the small table.

"Boy oh boy," she groaned. She was leaning back against the sink with her hands on her hips as she rolled her head from side to side, trying to loosen her neck muscles. "That was sure one ton of fun."

I put the pizza on the table and took a seat facing her. Amy was in her late twenties and had a cheerful, spunky personality that had me liking her from the start. She was a slender, attractive woman with hazel eyes and curly blond hair that hung in ringlets to her shoulders.

"I keep trying to place you," I said.

Amy closed her eyes and tilted her head back. "What do you mean?"

"You look so familiar."

With her head tilted back, she moved her neck from side to side, working out the kinks. Then she brought her head back down and opened her eyes. "Really?"

I nodded. "It's weird."

She smiled mischievously. "You want a hint?"

"Sure."

She pulled a chair over and sat down. "Pretend this is a water bed." She crossed her legs. "And imagine I'm in a sexy white negligee." She assumed a seductive pose and turned her face as if toward a camera. She paused two beats and started. "When you're old enough to know better," she cooed, "you're old enough for an Uncle Sam water bed. Remember, Uncle Sam wants you." She slowly winked. "And so do I." She paused, and then her face reverted to normal. "Well?"

"Wow," I said, impressed. "That was really you?"

She nodded. "The high point in my less than stellar acting career." She scooted the chair up to the table and reached for a slice of pizza.

"I should ask for your autograph."

"Right," she snorted.

"That was a few years back, right?"

"Four, to be exact."

"Have you done other commercials?"

"Not since then, other than a bit part in a Rothman's Furniture ad right before I went to work for Sally. Before the Uncle Sam gig, I was the girl in the hot pants in the back of the pickup in that obnoxious Jack Bruno Ford commercial."

"Do you do other types of acting?"

"Not for a few years." She paused to take a sip of her soda. "It's hard getting work in St. Louis. I might have had better luck if I'd started on one of the coasts, but let's face it: there are girls with more talent and better looks and bigger boobs waiting tables in Greenwich Village and Santa Monica."

As we ate the pizza, Amy told me more about her background. She had been born and raised in the St. Louis suburb of Webster Groves, where she was homecoming queen her senior year at Webster Groves High. After two years at Stephens College in Columbia, Missouri, she dropped out to follow what had then seemed a promising career as a fashion model. She started off doing fashion "shoots" for local newspaper ads and gradually moved into St. Louis television commercials as well. The work, when she could get it, paid well, but Amy soon learned that modeling and acting, unlike, say, banking, are professions without obvious career paths or steady paychecks. To supplement her income, she signed on with an agency that supplied temporary secretaries to lawyers and accountants. She worked for Sally a few times when Sally was still with Abraham Grozny. She must have impressed Sally, because when Sally left Grozny to start her own firm four years ago, she asked Amy to come with her full-time. Amy declined at first, unwilling to give up on her acting career, but accepted a year later. During her first year with Sally, she tried to do some moonlighting in modeling and acting, but the markets remained tight. Eventually, she threw in the towel.

"Maybe you can try again now," I said.

She shrugged. "It'd be even harder now. I'm just about over the hill."

"You're kidding."

"I wish I was. I'm twenty-nine." She sighed. "Believe it or not, that's middle-aged in the fashion world. As for acting—real acting, I mean—well, that's a tough road."

"Not if it's what you love."

"I know." She gave me a self-conscious look. "I might actually give it another try once we get Sally's cases farmed out."

"Really?"

She nodded. "This killing freaked me out. I mean, there was Sally, zooming along in her career, things getting better every month, big plans for the future, and then, boom, curtain time, strike the set, sayonara, baby." She paused, and shook her head, staring down at the empty pizza box. "It really made me rethink my own priorities." She looked up with a sheepish grin. "I signed up for an acting class yesterday. The first class is tonight. I called my old dance teacher this morning to see if she has room for me. She does."

"Good for you, Amy," I said, reaching across the table to pat her hand. "I say go for it."

She smiled. "We'll see what happens." She paused, her eyes watering. "This really shook me up."

"I'm sure it did."

"And then that horrible thing the other day with that floater. My God, that was dreadful."

I shuddered. "I know."

Two days ago, a family of four from Iowa had been having a pleasant lunch on the floating McDonald's restaurant that was moored to the Mississippi River levee downtown when Junior spotted something bobbing against the side of the boat. It turned out to be the dead, gas-bloated body of a twenty-four-year-old waitress who had lived and worked on the outskirts of Belleville, Illinois. According to preliminary autopsy reports, she appeared to have been shot in the head and dumped in the river somewhere north of St. Louis.

"I used to know her," Amy said, shaking her head sadly. "She was another one."

"Another what?" I asked gently.

"Another struggling actress." Amy looked at me and sighed. "First Sally, then Jenny. It's totally freaking me out. Yesterday I bought myself a gun and a big German shepherd. I bought him from a breeder who trains attack dogs." She shook her head ruefully. "I used to be a bleeding-heart liberal."

"Hey," I said with a smile, "I just started taking a self-defense class for women."

Amy smiled. "All those assholes out there better watch out for us, eh?"

After we cleaned up the kitchen we went into Sally's office. It was plain and functional, with framed diplomas, bar admission certificates, and a few commendations hung on the wall above her credenza. Amy sat on the couch and I pulled up a chair to face her. I took out my notes and started asking questions.

I was surprised to learn that Amy hadn't found out about Sally Wade's lawsuit against Neville McBride until she read about it in the newspaper after Sally was dead.

"I had assumed you typed the draft petition," I said.

"No." She gestured toward the personal computer on the credenza. "Sally prepared many of her court documents in here. Let's see if that petition is there."

She went over to the computer and turned it on. As we waited for it boot up, I said, "Sally came to see me on the afternoon of October fifteenth. That was a Wednesday, the day after the attack. Did she tell you what Neville did to her?"

"That wasn't her style," Amy said, looking over her shoulder at me, "but I knew something was wrong."

"How?"

"When I got to work that morning, Sally was in here, and her door was locked. That had never happened before. Ever. She was gone when I came back from lunch, and I didn't see her the rest of the day."

"Did you see her at all that day?"

Amy shook her head. "Not until Friday."

"What about Thursday?"

"She called that morning to say she wasn't feeling well and wasn't coming in."

"And on Friday?"

"She came in late that morning."

"How did she look?"

Amy frowned, trying to remember. "Her face seemed a little puffy. I didn't think much of it at the time, you know. I mean, she'd gone home sick on Wednesday, called in sick on Thursday. I assumed she looked a little puffy because she still wasn't feeling well."

"What about her eyes?"

"She wore sunglasses the whole time."

"Did that seem odd to you?"

Amy moved her head from side to side, as if weighing the question. "It does now. Back then, maybe not. I know it sounds dumb, but I probably thought the glasses were connected to her illness. I get migraines occasionally, and it helps if I wear dark sunglasses. Cuts down on the glare. I guess I thought she had a bad headache."

"She didn't say anything about the attack?"

"Not a word." She paused. "You need to understand something, Rachel. Sally was strictly business in this office. No girl talk, no gossip, nothing about her personal life. That's the way she was. You know that pizza you and I shared in the kitchen? Well, I worked for Sally for three years, and we never had lunch together." She shook her head. "Not even once. Don't get me wrong, I'm not complaining. We had a strictly professional relationship. She was the boss, I was the employee, and that was the extent of it." She sat back with a faraway expression. "It didn't really bother me. Back when I was a temp, I worked for a real mixed bag of lawyers. You wouldn't believe some of the weird personal stuff they expect their secretaries to handle. Sally wasn't warm and fuzzy, but she was fair." She turned toward the computer on Sally's credenza. "Let's see if we can find it."

I joined her by the terminal screen. She zipped through

the directories with speed and skill. There were hundreds and hundreds of documents in the directories and subdirectories. Amy looked back at me. "You say she came to your office on the fifteenth?" she asked.

"Right."

"Hmmm, maybe this is it." She moved the cursor down to the document entitled PLEADING. It showed a create time and date of 9:49 a.m. on October 15. "Let's take a look."

She typed the instruction to open the document. The screen went blank for a moment, and then the first page of a familiar document appeared:

IN THE CIRCUIT COURT OF THE CITY
OF ST. LOUIS
STATE OF MISSOURI

SALLY WADE,	)
	)
Petitioner,	)
	)
v.	)
	)
NEVILLE D. McBRIDE III,	)
	)
Defendant.	)

PETITION

NOW COMES Petitioner Sally Wade, by her attorney, and for her petition against Defendant Neville D. McBride III alleges as follows:

1. Petitioner is a resident of the State of Missouri and . . .

Amy leaned back in her chair and gestured at the screen. "That explains why she had the door closed all morning," she said. "She came to your office that afternoon, right?"

I nodded. It was eerie to be staring at Sally's handi-work, frozen in time on the computer a few hours before she handed it to me. "Is there anything else she created on that day?" I asked.

"Let's look." Amy returned to the file directories.

"Actually," I said, "let's look at everything she did up to her death."

Amy nodded. "Good idea."

It took about ten minutes to check the origination dates on all the files. The petition was the only document Sally created on the day she saw me. She created no docu-ments the next day, which was Thursday. That jived with Amy's recollection that Sally had called in sick that day.

Sally came into the office on Friday, and according to the computer she created three documents that after-noon: a memo to file on a telephone conversation with defense counsel about settlement of the Brancusi case (a fender-bender, according to Amy), a letter to defense counsel about rescheduling a physician's deposition in the Brenner case (a slip-and-fall, according to Amy), and a rough outline of the questions for that deposition.

No new documents on Saturday and Sunday.

Four on Monday: a letter to the court clerk requesting a hearing date in one case, a memo to file on another telephone conversation with defense counsel in the Bran-cusi case, notes of a telephone interview with an eye-witness in the Stahl case (yet another fender-bender), and a letter to the Bar Association of Metropolitan St. Louis requesting CLE credit for a seminar on structured settlements she was planning to attend in West Palm Beach in November.

There was nothing on Tuesday, of course. Sally was dead by then.

The phone rang as the two of us were staring at the terminal screen. It was Jacki. Amy left the room while I took the call.

"What's up, Jacki?"

"A few things. First, I stopped by the post office and closed out her box."

"Anything in there?"

"Nothing exciting. Two bank statements and a credit card offer from American Express."

"Okay."

"I checked out the second column of names on that nine-page client list we found in the safe deposit box. I ran the names against listings for doctors, attorneys, judges. Even private investigators and court reporters. No luck. I can't find a common denominator."

I pulled a copy of the document out of my briefcase and studied the names in the second column: Johnson, Dice, Magliozzi, Tubbs, Rice.

"Claims adjusters?" I mused.

"Possibly, but I don't know an easy way to run that down."

"I'll take a look at some of her files over here. Maybe the answer is in there. What else do you have for me?"

"Jonathan Wolf called. He wants to talk to you."

"About what now?"

"He didn't say. But as long as I had him on the phone, I asked if he'd heard from the handwriting expert."

"Had he?"

"Yeah, but the guy can't give him a definite opinion. All he can say is that it might be her signature and it might not."

I groaned. "Great."

"How much longer are you going to be over there?"

"Maybe another hour or so. Meanwhile, here's another project. You know that sheet of paper in her safe deposit box that had those long series of numbers on it? The one with the letters BCS at the top?"

"I have a copy in front of me."

"Maybe they're bank accounts. See if our guy at the trust company can have someone run them down."

"Will do. I'll type up the results if I leave before you

get back. By the way . . ." She paused. "I picked up Sally's pictures."

"And?"

Jacki chuckled. "Brother."

"What's so funny?"

"You'll see."

"What's that mean?"

"Hard to describe over the phone. I'll leave them on your chair."

"Not what we expected, eh?"

She laughed. "I don't want to spoil the surprise."

"That's not very nice, Jacki."

"You'll see."

I sighed. "Okay. Anything else?"

"Yes. The libel case. I checked on the two subpoenas."

"And?"

"Good news. Neiman-Marcus will produce their documents and the actual returned item tomorrow afternoon."

"Super. Did they tell you what the item is?"

"Nope, but I'm guessing a purse."

I whistled. "That's an expensive purse."

"Hey, Rachel, Cissy Thompson wasn't exactly shopping at Target."

"What about the other one? The fancy shoe store at Plaza Frontenac?"

"La Femme Elégante." She gave it an exaggerated foreign pronunciation. "They'll produce their stuff tomorrow, too. I'll drive out there and pick them both up after lunch."

"Good work, Jacki."

"Thanks. Whoops, that's the other line. See you later, Rachel."

I sorted through the notes and documents in my briefcase, checking off items from my list of topics. I found Amy back in the file room collating bills.

"Do you know what kind of calendar Sally had?" I asked.

Amy looked up from the documents. "One of those little black ones," she said. "She used to keep it in her purse. Why?"

I shrugged. "It's missing. It wasn't listed on any of the inventories."

Amy frowned. "That's strange. Fortunately, I kept track of most things on a calendar on the computer."

"Do you mind if we take a look at it?"

"No problem. Come on."

I followed her back to her desk. Her computer was already running. She hit a few keys and a calendar appeared on the screen. I leaned forward to study it.

"What are you looking for?" she asked.

"Meetings." I scanned the entries for October 15 through her last day alive. "Rats," I said. "No meetings."

"Why meetings?"

"Meetings have people. People are witnesses. I need a witness."

Amy gave me a perplexed look. "A witness to what?"

"To Sally's physical condition. I need to find someone who spent time with her on that Thursday or Friday. Or even over the weekend. I need to find someone who can testify to her injuries."

"Why?"

"Because Neville totally denies hitting her. He claims he hadn't seen her in months."

"Yeah, right," Amy said bitterly.

"He and his lawyer think she may have faked the injuries."

Amy slapped her hand on the desk. "Those jerks! Typical male reaction. That really pisses me off."

"I know," I said with a weary sigh. "It's exactly what I warned Sally about when she came to see me." I leaned back and rapped a pencil on the desk in frustration. "I still need a witness."

"You've got me."

"But you can't testify to much. You didn't actually see

anything, and she didn't tell you about the incident. I need more than you can give."

"Listen, Rachel," Amy said with quiet intensity, "if you need to prove that her ex-husband is a no-good cheating bastard, I'm your witness."

I stared at her. "What do you mean?"

She leaned forward, her eyes burning. "I met him about six months after they got married. He came over with her one day to check things out." She gave a cynical laugh. "He definitely checked things out. Like my boobs and my legs and my butt. A couple of weeks later, when Sally was out of town on business, he called to say he had a client meeting in the vicinity and wanted to know if I'd join him for lunch. I was kind of caught off guard, and I said yes. Well, twenty minutes into lunch, the guy's downed three Bloody Marys and is trying to slide his hand up my thighs."

I shook my head. "Unbelievable."

"Tell me about it. Well, I survived that lunch, but the guy pestered me for at least a month after that. He'd call me at home, call me at work, trying to get me to go out with him. He had to attend some seminar in Boston and had the gall to ask me if I wanted to join him for the weekend." She shook her head, seething over the memory. "This was all just six months after he married Sally! Can you believe it? He's a total snake, Rachel. If you need a character witness, count me in."

She checked her watch. "Damn. Listen, I've got to run to the Granite City Courthouse for a status call on one of Sally's cases. It won't take long. I should be back in forty-five minutes."

"No problem. I'll lock the door if I leave before you're back."

I was still there when she returned, waiting to ask my one question.

I'd spent most of the time searching for client files that matched the plaintiffs' names on the nine-page handwritten document I'd found in Sally's safe deposit box—the document with the mystery names in the second column. I was able to locate five client files: Zenger, Janney, Gianino, Blakeman and Stahl. The others, I assumed, had been closed and sent off to storage.

Then I brought the files into Sally's office to review them closely. I was looking for any reference to the names that appeared in the second column and some clue as to what the percentages and dollar amounts in the other columns were all about. I jotted down a summary chart:

Client	??	%		
Zenger	Dice	8		
Janney	Johnson	10		
Gianino	Tubbs	8		
Blakeman	Rice	10	$1,100	11/8/95
Stahl	Magliozzi	8		

I slowly paged through every document in each of the five files. Nowhere did any of the names in the second column appear. Four of the five cases were still active; the Blakeman case had settled. I found the Blakeman closing statement in the file:

LAW OFFICES OF SALLY WADE & ASSOCIATES
CLOSING STATEMENT

Client: <u>Randy Blakeman</u>

Settlement Payment:	<u>$33,000.00</u>
LESS:	
Attorney Fee (33 $1/3$%)	<u>$11,000.00</u>
Court Costs:	<u>125.00</u>
Medical Bills:	<u>8,500.00</u>
NET TO CLIENT:	<u>$13,375.00</u>
Date:	November 8, 1995
Accepted:	*Randy Blakeman*

I examined the closing statement and then glanced over at the handwritten entry for Blakeman:

> *Blakeman   Rice   10 $1,100   11/8/95*

The settlement date on the closing statement matched the date on the handwritten entry, but the dollar amounts were different. I looked at the percentage number. Ten percent. My eyes fixed on the $11,000 entry on the closing statement. Ten percent of $11,000 was $1,100, which was the number on the list.

I leaned back in the chair, my brows furrowed. What was the connection between the closing statement and the other document? And why had Sally kept that other document in her safe deposit box? I studied the closing statement. I paged through the nine-page list. I leaned back on the couch and stared at the wall.

And then it clicked.

Amy smiled when she came into the room and saw me. "Still here, eh?"

"I needed to ask you something."

She hesitated. "Okay."

"I want to show you a document I found in Sally's safe deposit box." I paused, choosing my words carefully. "Before I show you the document, Amy, I want you to understand that whatever you tell me will be protected by the attorney-client privilege. Is that clear?"

Amy nodded, her eyes wary.

"Take a look." I handed her the document.

Amy slowly flipped through the pages. She kept her expression blank. When she finished the last page, she carefully closed the document and looked at me.

"Have you seen that before?" I asked.

She nodded.

"Here?" I asked.

"Sally used to keep it here. About a year ago it disappeared. She didn't tell me where it went."

"About a year ago?" I repeated.

Amy nodded.

"What else happened about a year ago?"

Amy gazed at me poker-faced.

"Illinois or Missouri?" I finally asked.

Amy looked down. "Illinois," she said softly.

I nodded. "Is it still pending?"

"I don't know. Sally never said."

"You see the first column on that list?"

She nodded.

"Those are Sally's clients, correct?"

"Yes."

"See the names in the second column?"

She nodded.

"Are those chasers?"

She stared down at the list for a while and then looked up at me.

"Yes," she said.

CHAPTER 9

Benny squinted at the photograph. "What the fuck are these goddam things?"

I shook my head. "I haven't got a clue."

He held the photograph at arm's length, then brought it up close. He tilted it sideways. "Petrified rabbit turds?"

"Wrong size."

"Where do you get size?"

"Here." I slid another one of Sally's photos across my desk toward him. It was a close-up shot of three of the objects alongside a ruler.

Benny scrutinized the picture. "About two centimeters, eh?" He looked over at me. "How big is that?"

"A little under an inch, I think."

He grunted in irritation. "Fucking metric numbers. Who's the yahoo who came up with that system?"

We were in my office. I had returned from Sally's office at quarter to five, and Benny had dropped by twenty minutes later toting his idea of a light afternoon snack: a chilled six-pack of Pete's Wicked Ale, a bag of jumbo pretzels, a huge slab of extra-sharp cheddar, and a summer sausage the size of a Louisville Slugger. Jacki couldn't hang around because her property law class started at five-thirty, so Benny hacked off a thick slab of sausage for her to take along.

Sally's photographs were an enigma. There were twelve in all, and all twelve were shots of what appeared to be rust-colored stones. Some were brown, others yellowish-orange. Most were round, a few triangular or cube-shaped. In six of the twelve shots, about two dozen of the stones were displayed on a white tray. In four of the other shots, three of them were placed against a ruler. Their individual sizes ranged from 1.5 to 3.5 centimeters. The last two pictures had a bunch of them in what looked like a vacuum-packed plastic bag.

"Samples for a rock garden?" Benny said, studying the photographs. "Rusty machine parts?"

I studied the Walgreens photo-processing envelope and shook my head. "The timing makes no sense."

"How so?"

"The day after she hires me—the day after I practically order her to have someone take photographs of her injuries—this is the film she drops off to be developed?" I turned over the envelope. She had filled out the name and address information. "I'll have Jonathan Wolf's handwriting expert look at this."

"Speaking of which, what's the story with the Wolf Man, anyway?"

I shrugged. "I'm not sure. He called while I was out. We've been playing phone tag."

Benny shuffled through the photographs again and handed them back to me. "Maybe his client knows what this weird shit is."

"Maybe." I dropped the photographs into the Walgreens envelope.

Benny pried off the cap of another bottle of ale. "More sausage?" he asked, reaching for the knife.

I shook my head.

He hacked off a big chunk. "So what'd you find over at Sally's office?"

I filled him in on my afternoon. When I finished, he asked, "So what's this Amy like?"

"She seems nice enough."

He took a bite of sausage and washed it down with a big sip of beer. "She hasn't put on a lot of weight, has she?"

I looked at him oddly. "Huh?"

Benny raised his eyebrows lecherously. "I definitely remember her water-bed ad. We're talking blue veiner city."

I let out a long-suffering sigh. "You have such a winsome touch with words, Benny. I'm sure she'd be charmed."

"Now don't go Fem-Nazi on me, woman. When we're talking Amy Chickering we're not exactly talking Margaret Thatcher. We're talking about a woman who poses in a negligee on a water bed with her hooters on display. Something tells me that the goal of that commercial is not to make guys fantasize about a night on the water bed discussing Spinoza."

"Touché," I said grudgingly.

He gave me a leer. "Which is not to say I wouldn't mind discussing Spinoza with her on a water bed. Or Plato, for that matter. After all, it would be a shame to let my undergrad degree go to waste. Maybe you can introduce us."

I gave him a cynical look. "Are you planning to impress her with the size of your epistemology?"

"Hey, woman, as Manny Kant once said, it's not the length of your metaphysics, it's the quality of your categorical imperatives."

"I love when you philosophy guys talk dirty."

The phone rang and I answered it.

"Ah, Miss Gold," my caller said in that familiar nasal

staccato. "I believe you attempted to make contact with me earlier this day."

I gave Benny a wink.

"Who is it?" he whispered.

I said into the mouthpiece, "Hello, Melvin."

Benny grinned broadly. "Melvin? Put that lunatic on the speaker box."

"Melvin," I said, "there's someone else here. Hang on." I pressed down the speakerphone button and replaced the receiver. "Are you still there?"

"I am indeed, Miss Gold."

Benny leaned toward the speakerphone. "Mel, baby, how's the main vein?"

"Oh, no." I punched the mute button. "Not now, Benny," I pleaded.

"Ah," Melvin's voice crackled over the speakerphone, sounding more duck than human, "is that Herr Doktor Goldberg?"

Benny reached over and clicked off the mute button. "Hey, colostomy bag," he shouted into the speakerphone, "I said, 'How's the main vein?' "

Melvin giggled. "Uhh, up tight," he recited, "and, uhh, out of sight."

I groaned and leaned back in my chair. "Not again," I said glumly.

It was too late. They were already several lines into their old routine—the one they'd perfected back in the days when we were all young associates at the Chicago office of Abbott & Windsor. Benny and Melvin had shared an office their first year. Benny detested him from the start. "That turbocharged geek is driving me batshit," he used to complain to me over lunch at our favorite Chinese restaurant, nestled in the perpetual shadow of the Board of Trade.

But then, one fateful night during our first year at Abbott & Windsor, something magic happened. Benny returned to the office late after sharing several rounds of beers with some college buddies passing through Chicago. Melvin was still there—Melvin was always still there— but for the first time, they actually had a conversation, the substance of which Benny never disclosed. And then, wonder of wonders, Benny invited Melvin back to his apartment, where Melvin smoked his first and only joint. (Benny captured it on film, and surrendered the negative several weeks later after extracting Melvin's agreement to help him draft interrogatories for one of Benny's cases.) After the joint, they listened to Benny's Firesign Theater albums, which Melvin committed to memory after just one play. Overnight, Melvin was transformed from circus geek to Benny's science fair project. The two of them worked up a bizarre routine—a grab bag of rock lyrics, Firesign Theater riffs, and movie dialogue— and sprang it on the rest of the junior associates in the firm cafeteria the next morning. It was an instant classic, and remained funny the first ten or twenty times you heard it. This, however, was about the five thousandth time I'd heard it.

"My liege," Benny was saying, "what has happened to your nose?"

"I, uhh, just returned from Rome."

"What-what?"

"What-what-what-what?"

"Excellent, Mel, excellent." Benny looked at me and winked. "This guy is totally awesome. He's so far ahead of the curve it's scary." He turned to the speaker box. "Tell me the truth, Mel. Back in college did you do a lot of acid?"

"Hydrochloric or sulfuric?" Melvin answered, punctu- ating his joke with a machine-gun burst of high-pitched cackling.

I put my finger on the mute button and stared at Benny. "May I proceed, Professor?"

Benny bowed with a sweeping gesture of his hands. "The dude is all yours."

I released the mute button. "Melvin?"

"Yes, Miss Gold."

I paused a beat and gave a weary sigh. "You're allowed to call me Rachel."

"Indeed."

I looked over at Benny and shook my head. Benny snickered.

"Melvin," I said, "do you still have any contacts within the Illinois Disciplinary Commission?"

"I happen to have two exceptional sources of information within that estimable organization. You have in mind a particular investigation?"

"I do. I'm counsel to the personal representative for the Estate of Sally Wade. She was a personal injury lawyer down here in Madison County. I think she may have been the subject of an ongoing investigation."

"I see. Do you happen to know which provision of the Code of Professional Responsibility her inquisitors accuse Ms. Wade of transgressing?"

"The very same one involved in that Lester Fleming lawsuit you worked on."

"Ah-ha! Chasers?"

"Chasers," I confirmed.

"I shall contact my sources in the morning. I should be able to obtain copies of all pertinent investigative materials by the end of the day. Will you be available the following morning?"

I glanced at my calendar. "Sure."

"I shall deliver them to you personally."

"You don't have to do that, Melvin. Just put them in the mail."

"Ordinarily I would, Miss Gold, but I will be traveling to your fair city to attend yet another round of *Bottles & Cans* depositions."

I looked over at Benny in amazement. "Can you believe that case is still going on?" I whispered.

"Shall we say nine o'clock at your office, Miss Gold?"

"That'd be great, Melvin. Thanks."

"I'm teaching at nine, Mel," Benny called out. "I'll hook up with you later in the day."

"Excellent, Benjamin. I shall anticipate our rendezvous with great fervor."

After we hung up, Benny said to me, "Chasers?"

I nodded.

"What did Amy tell you?"

"Not much," I said. "She knew about them, though. One is a real hothead named Dice. Junior Dice. Apparently, Dice had a big fight with Sally over one of his fees. Thousands of dollars. He claimed he brought her some lucrative client, but she said the client came to her because of one of her radio ads. That's about the extent of Amy's knowledge. She says she doesn't know much about the Disciplinary Commission investigation."

"Where's the murder connection?" Benny asked.

I shrugged. "I don't know."

Benny finished off the bottle of ale and set it on the ground next to his chair. He leaned back and pursed his lips in thought. "Rachel," he said, "do you really have doubts about whether Neville killed her?"

I frowned. "The loose ends bother me."

"What else have you learned about Sally?"

I told him about her trips to Hong Kong—nine over the past two years, none for longer than two days. Sally told Amy she went there to shop, and the inventory of her home seemed to support the statement. Her house had plenty of the sorts of things people buy in Hong Kong: watches, jewelry, clothes, camera equipment, stereo systems.

"Still," Benny said, "how much money could she save after adding in the travel costs? What's her ex-husband say about the trips?"

"Neville didn't know about any of them, although I got the sense that communication was never strong in that marriage. According to her passport, she only made four trips to Hong Kong while they were actually living together. Most of her trips came after they separated."

The phone rang again. This time it was Jonathan Wolf.

As usual, he dispensed with the usual pleasantries. "What else do you need?" he asked.

"A confession would be nice."

"I'm serious, Rachel. What more do you need?"

"How about Neville's missing girlfriend?"

"We're working on that."

"I have to tell you, Jonathan, that one's pretty lame."

"As I stated," he said brusquely, "we're trying to locate her."

I told him about the Walgreens receipt, which had another sample of Sally's handwriting.

"Good," he said. "I'll pick it up in the morning on my way to the office. We need to talk."

"I won't be here in the morning."

"Why not?"

I looked over at Benny, who was sorting through the materials in Sally's briefcase. Benny looked up. I gestured to the phone and shook my head in exasperation. "Because, Jonathan, I will be somewhere else."

"Then when can we meet?"

I glanced down at my calendar. "After lunch. I'll come by your office at one-thirty."

"Make it two."

I sighed. "Certainly, Jonathan. Two it is."

After I hung up I turned to Benny. "That guy is unbelievable. Talk about *chutzpah*."

Benny was smiling. "He's perfect for you."

"Yeah, right," I said derisively.

"Mark my words."

I snorted. "Not in this lifetime, buster."

"I'm serious, Rachel."

"Jonathan Wolf?" I shook my head. "No way."

"Were you bullshitting him about being busy tomorrow morning?"

"No, I'm really going to be out. I have to take Ozzie to the vet at eight-thirty, and there's a memorial service for Sally tomorrow at ten."

"You're going?"

I nodded. "I want to see who her friends are. Maybe one of them spent time with her after she retained me. I still need a witness for her case. You want to come along?"

"Maybe." He was studying the monthly schedule of events put out by the bar association. The three-page yellow document had been in Sally's briefcase. "Interesting," he said. "Check it out." He handed it to me. "Look at what she marked."

At the bottom of the second page was a reminder for a meeting of the committee overseeing the renovation plans for the St. Louis Civil Courts Building. The meeting was scheduled for 5:00 p.m. on October 16. Sally had circled it in red.

"So?" I said.

"You're looking for a witness, right? Look at the date of the meeting."

I did. "You're right. It was the day after she retained me." I shook my head. "She didn't go."

"How do you know?"

"Amy told me she called in sick that day."

"Still," Benny said, "she might have called someone on the committee to say she wouldn't be there. There are two state court judges on that committee. She wouldn't have wanted an unexplained absence."

I mulled it over. "You might be right."

"What if she called one of the judges on the committee? Better yet, what if she told him the truth? There'd be a helluva good witness for you."

I looked at the meeting notice again. The only person listed was the committee chair, Lloyd MacLachlan. Lloyd was an older partner at one of the insurance defense firms downtown. Fortunately, I knew him. He'd represented one of the parties in a coverage dispute I'd worked on about a year ago. I called his office.

Unlike Jonathan Wolf, he did not dispense with the usual pleasantries, which, in Lloyd MacLachlan's case, were quite pleasant. Lloyd was one of the senior statesmen of the local bar, a gentleman lawyer with courtly manners, Southern charm, and a marvelous white handlebar mustache with twirled ends kept stiff with mustache wax. After inquiring about my health, my practice, my mother, and my dog, Lloyd said, "To what do I owe the pleasure of this call?"

"I'm helping wrap up Sally Wade's estate."

"Oh, what a tragedy. I had the privilege of becoming acquainted with that young lady during the past year. She served on a bar committee I chair."

"Actually, that's what I'm calling you about."

"Well, I can assure you that Sally Wade was a splendid member of our committee. She was bubbling with ideas and enthusiasm, and was always willing to take on extra responsibility. Why, at the last meeting she agreed to serve as our liaison to the architects, which is no small undertaking. My goodness, that still haunts me."

"Why, Lloyd?"

"That poor woman was dead less than a week later."

I looked over at Benny with surprise. "You mean Sally was at your meeting on October sixteenth?"

Benny raised his eyebrows and leaned forward.

"She most certainly was," Lloyd said. "It made the news of her death even more shocking."

"How did she look?"

"How did she look?" he repeated, perplexed.

"Physically."

"Oh," he said with an awkward chuckle, "she looked lovely."

"Really? Did you notice a black eye?"

"A black eye? Good heavens, are you serious?"

"Dead serious, Lloyd. I take it you didn't notice any bruising around her eye?"

"Not at all."

"Or a puffy lip? Did she look like she'd been in an accident?"

"Gracious, no. Sally sat directly across the table from me during the meeting, and nothing about her appearance seemed to be amiss."

"You're sure?"

"Quite sure." He chuckled softly. "Although it may be a mortal sin in these politically correct times, I plead guilty to having an eye for the lovelier ladies of the bar, very much including yourself, Rachel. I can assure you that on the day in question Sally looked as pretty as a peach, poor thing."

CHAPTER 10

It wasn't that I disliked Marvin Vogelsang, because I didn't really. I barely knew him. My negative feelings were triggered more by his obvious discomfort. Marvin Vogelsang was one of those people who are so ill at ease around people that they make the people around them ill at ease as well. To begin with, he only made sporadic eye contact when I spoke to him, and when he spoke his focal point shifted starboard. Worse yet, he had a slight stammer, and when he tripped on a bad consonant his eyes rotated up and his eyelids fluttered.

The fact that he was a principal in the Vogelsang Funeral Home didn't help matters. Embalming is, to be sure, an ancient and venerable profession, but the thought of what morticians do for a living just plain gives me the willies. Although my initial contact with Marvin Vogelsang was at Sally's funeral, he had come not to bury Sally but to praise her. Literally. Marvin had delivered one of four eulogies. Although his had been short and not particularly stirring, I had driven to his funeral home directly from the memorial service and was now seated in his strange office because of one sentence in his eulogy: "I was privileged to be with Sally throughout the last weekend of her life."

Marvin Vogelsang seemed a thoroughly unlikely candidate for the role of Sally's boyfriend. He was tall and skinny and pale, with a long oval face, thick purplish lips, and dark eyes sunk deep beneath heavy eyebrows. His thinning black hair was carefully combed and swirled over the top of his head in an obvious and obviously unsuccessful effort to camouflage his bald spot. Even worse, the hair that had fallen from the top of his head seemed to have resprouted on other parts of his body, including his knuckles, his nostrils, and his ears. He was, in short, a thoroughly unattractive man. As Benny commented during the memorial service, "I've seen better heads on a cabbage."

His office decor added another strange touch. Along the back wall behind his desk were four porcelain Buddhas of various sizes, each on a marble Greek column pedestal. In a lighted display case against one side wall were a half-dozen Chinese vases. The other wall was hung with four Japanese scroll paintings.

"It was a beautiful eulogy," I lied.

His eyes shifted starboard. "You are kind to say so." His eyes shifted back to me.

"How long have you known Sally?"

Eyes away. "Three m-m-months." Eyes back.

"From what you said about her in your eulogy, I got the sense that you spent lots of time with Sally her last weekend."

Pause. "Almost the entire weekend."

"Here?"

"No. I attended an out-of-town sem-m-m-inar. Sally accom-m-m-"—eyes up, eyelids fluttering—"m-m panied me."

"Were did you go?"

It took a while to get out the word "Milwaukee." The letter "M" seemed to be a problem for him.

I asked about his relationship with Sally. Their intimacy did not seem to extend beyond the physical part. Although she had told him about her pending divorce, she hadn't shared any of her feelings about her soon-to-be ex-husband. They talked only once during the week before their trip to M-M-M-M-Milwaukee—a single brief telephone conversation, during which Sally made no mention of Neville's assault and attempted rape.

Although that was disturbing to hear, it wasn't why I had driven all the way over to Belleville, Illinois, to visit him. For my purposes, the best possible boyfriend for Sally would have been a physician, but a mortician was a close second. Both were familiar with signs of trauma on the human body.

I tried to gently steer the conversation toward the questions I had come here to ask, but with his personality quirks and speech mannerisms it was anything but a smooth approach. Finally, however, I caught sight of the runway.

"So the first time you saw Sally after the assault was Friday evening?"

He nodded slowly, staring off to the side.

"Did you notice any bruises and injuries on her face?"

He shook his head.

"No black eye?"

He shook his head again, still staring off to the side. His watch started beeping. He held it up to eye level and squinted at the dial. He turned to me, apparently hesitant about what to do.

"Uh, excuse me," he finally said, pulling open a desk drawer. Giving me a furtive glance, he took out what looked like an eight-ounce white plastic bottle of pills. He unscrewed the cap and shook out a gold tablet into his palm. Turning sideways, he popped the tablet into his mouth and crunched it up. His face puckered from the taste. Holding the bottle out of my line of sight, he started screwing on the top. The telephone rang. The

noise made him start, and the cap fell onto the floor. I
heard it hit the plastic mat under his chair and roll beneath the desk. Flustered, he glanced at the phone, peered
under his desk, and then looked at the pill bottle in his
hand. He put the bottle on the desk and reached for the
phone. "Uh, yes?" he said.

As he listened, he bent down to retrieve the cap. While
he was hunched beneath the desk, I leaned toward the
plastic bottle. It was half filled with gold-colored tablets.
The label was in English and Chinese. The English part
read *Shim Lai Porpoise Virility Pills*. I leaned closer to
read the writing beneath the brand name:

Ingredients: Top-quality testicle and penis of porpoise
ground into powder and pilled in form convenient for the
intake.

I sat back as his head came up from beneath the desk.
"Fine," he said into the phone and hung up. He
grabbed the pill bottle, screwed on the top, opened the
desk drawer, put it inside, and shut the drawer. He raised
his eyes to mine, his face reddening slightly. "You were
s-s-s-saying?"

"We were talking about the weekend in Milwaukee," I
said in a matter-of-fact tone, as if I hadn't just watched
him scarf down a powdered puree of Flipper's family
jewels. "I assume that the two of you stayed in the same
hotel room."

He nodded.

"I don't mean to offend you by this next question, Mr.
Vogelsang, and I hope you understand why I have to ask
it. Did you have the opportunity over that last weekend
to see Sally without her clothes on?"

He shifted his stare toward me, his brows knitted, his
thick lips pressed together. He stayed in that position,
virtually immobile, for what seemed a long time. I
couldn't tell whether he was angry or insulted by the

question or just pondering it. Eventually, he looked down at his desktop. "Yes, I did."

"Did she have any bruises or visible injuries?"

With his eyes still down, he lifted a brass letter opener off the desk blotter and rotated it between his fingers. "There was a m-m-m-mild abrasion on her right knee. She said she skinned her knee working in the basem-m-m-ment."

"Was that all?"

He slowly slid the blade of the letter opener in and out of the brass sheath. "I saw n-n-n-nothing else." He looked up, his eyes narrowing. "I have work to do. I'd p-p-p-prefer that you leave now."

The offices of Wolf & Diamond were on one of the upper floors of One Metropolitan Square in the heart of downtown St. Louis. Compared to the usual glitzy decor of a successful criminal attorney, Jonathan's office seemed modest and downright traditional. No chrome, no leather, no bearskin rugs. Instead, there were several comfortable upholstered chairs, a large rolltop desk, two tall healthy ficus, and an old-fashioned oak worktable in the corner piled with stacks of pleadings and legal pads and photocopies of cases. It took me a moment to realize that there was no computer in his office—a rarity these days.

And finally, and most surprising, there were walls, not shrines. There were none of the usual awards and bronzed newspaper articles and plaques and autographed celebrity shots that crowd the walls of so many attorneys, although Jonathan Wolf possessed plenty of displayable laurels, including one priceless memento from Operation Paddlewheel, his most famous criminal case. Operation Paddlewheel, inevitably rechristened PaddleGate by the press, ended in prison terms for several state court judges, court clerks, and local attorneys, including, ironically enough, Sally Wade's old boss, Abe Grozny. When the last of the cases ended, Jonathan's colleagues presented him with the framed, signed original of the Thomas Englehardt political cartoon that had appeared in the *Post-Dispatch* during the height of the prosecutions—the one with Jonathan Wolf standing tall and splendid at the helm of his combat ship, the S.S. *PaddleGate*, ordering his men to fire on the crew of rapscallions frantically poling their raft toward shore. When he left the government for private practice, he left that souvenir behind as well. I knew because I had seen it there just two weeks ago, still hanging on the so-called Hall of Fame in the offices of the U.S. attorney.

Instead of plaques and awards, Jonathan's walls were decorated with art. On one wall, centered and alone, was a large, striking abstract painting—bold brushstrokes in reds and oranges and yellows. The signature in the lower right corner of the canvas read SHEILA WOLF 1991. It took a few seconds for it to click: Sheila was the name of his deceased wife. A lawyer when she married Jonathan, Sheila Wolf had returned to her avocation—painting—after the birth of her first child.

The back wall was crowded with children's artwork: watercolors and crayon pictures and homemade Valentines and school art projects and plenty of I Love Daddys. From the signatures on the artwork, one of the artists was named Sarah and the other Leah. On the roll-top desk were several framed photographs of the artists, including one of both on their father's lap. They weren't trophy photos—those professional jobs with everyone impeccably attired and so carefully posed that the scene reminds you of a tableau at Madame Tussaud's. No, these were warm, casual shots of a dad with his two little girls.

The decorating statement was clear: here works a papa. It was a statement so utterly unexpected that I was momentarily flustered. In the courtroom and the boardroom, there was an intimidating take-no-prisoners aura about Jonathan Wolf that seemed to leave no room for a gentler side. And thus, when he told my mother that he made *kamishbroit* with his daughters, it had sounded so incongruous that I dismissed it as a ploy to enlist her assistance in softening my attitude toward his client. But now, looking at these genuinely affecting pictures of him with his daughters, I found myself wondering again about what was beneath the surface of this intense, aggressive, but very private man.

Fortunately, Jonathan's secretary brought my cup of tea soon after I stepped into his office. By the time I finished fumbling with the tea bag and the lemon slice, I had regained my composure and was able to focus on his description of the results of Sally Wade's autopsy.

Certain details stood out, the most important of which was the absence of the usual signs of a struggle—no scratches or abrasions or contusions on the body, no damage to the face, no skin under the fingernails. The only sign of violence was a blow to the back of her head, apparently with a blunt instrument; however, from the condition of the skin and blood vessels around the head injury, the blow came near or possibly after the time of death. Although there was chafing around her wrists and ankles from the cords, the coroner had concluded that those probably occurred as Sally was suffocating, not before.

I weighed the information. "So that means the killer tied her up without a fight."

Jonathan nodded. "It's an excellent development."

I looked at him curiously. "Why?"

"Why no struggle?" His eyes were bright with zeal. "That's a difficult question for the prosecution. Unless one posits the highly improbable scenario of a kinky boyfriend killer who used the lure of sexual bondage as a pretext for tying her up, the most likely explanation is that her killer had a gun. That was how he was able to tie her up without a struggle. Neville doesn't own a gun."

"He could have bought one for that night."

Jonathan smiled. "That's even more unlikely." I could detect an air of condescension in his voice that reminded me of some of the more insufferable professors I had had at Harvard Law School. "There would be a record if he bought one legally, and there would certainly be a witness if someone as unfamiliar with the illegal gun trade as Neville McBride tried to buy one on the black market."

I mulled it over. Although when I arrived at Jonathan's office I hadn't been sure whether I wanted to share with him what I had learned from Marvin the mortician—after all, the absence of bruises and scratches on her body just a few days after Neville's alleged assault further undercut my lawsuit—I decided to anyway. The coroner's conclusions about the absence of such injuries were probably even more damaging to my case than Marvin's observations; moreover, one of Jonathan's investigators was no doubt planning to ask Marvin the very same questions I had asked him this morning.

So I told him what I'd learned. When I finished, Jonathan leaned back and nodded thoughtfully. "Excellent."

I shook my head doubtfully. "Even if I dismissed my lawsuit, which I'm not yet prepared to do, you're not that much closer to getting your client exonerated."

"Oh, but I am."

He stood up and stretched his back. He walked over toward the bay window and its commanding view of the Arch and the riverfront and the muddy waters of the Mississippi River. Today he was sporting another *GQ* look: a full-cut navy pinstripe suit with pleated pants, a crisp red Bengal-striped broadcloth shirt with French cuffs, and a British regimental silk tie in red, navy, and gold.

"Why?" I asked.

He turned to face me, his back against the window,

his arms crossed. "Because now Neville has you on his side."

I laughed. "I beg your pardon."

Jonathan didn't smile. "Sally used you, Rachel—or someone posing as Sally did. You were the dupe in a get-rich scheme. Agreed?"

I didn't respond.

He nodded, his green eyes honing in. "That makes you our MVP."

I frowned. "What in the world are you talking about, Jonathan?"

"Motivation. Someone made a fool out of you. You're not going to let them get away with it."

I shook my head. "They already have."

"To quote Yogi Berra, 'It ain't over till it's over.' "

I gave him a dubious smile. "And why, pray tell, am I all of a sudden so motivated?"

"Because we both know that whoever used you also had something to do with your client's murder. That means that when you figure out who made a fool out of you you'll be a lot closer to figuring out who killed Sally."

"Those are a lot of assumptions."

He shook his head. "Hardly. Indeed, Neville has authorized me to retain you to find out who set you up."

"Oh?" I said, mildly annoyed to discover that he and his client had presumed to select my role in their case. "What makes you so sure I won't just walk away from this mess and get on with my life?"

"Call it a gut feeling, but I don't think I'm wrong."

He wasn't. I was far more than just a curious spectator on the subject of who had used me. I was infuriated. We litigators learn early on in our careers to expect our clients to lie to us. Every client, every case. Not big lies, of course. Little ones. But important nevertheless. Clients seem to believe that they'll have a better-motivated advocate if they fudge the story a little around the edges, maybe omit a few unpleasant details, perhaps slightly exaggerate a few appealing ones. It never works, of course. The unpleasant facts have a way of coming out, and often at the worst possible time and in the most public of possible courtroom settings—during one of those cross-examination ambushes that end in a silent exchange of looks between the flabbergasted attorney seated at counsel's table and his sheepish client in the witness box.

But this went far beyond the usual fudgings and omissions. Sally, or some Sally impostor, had tricked me into filing a lawsuit accusing a possibly blameless man of outrageous misconduct. Worse yet, the allegations in the lawsuit and Sally's statements to me about Neville's actions had been important building blocks in the criminal case against Neville McBride. Although there was now other evidence against him, my actions had played a material role in his arrest and indictment and disgrace, and even if I decided to dismiss the lawsuit, the statements in there could still be used against him at his murder trial.

Jonathan sat down across from me. "I don't think you'll walk away from this. If you did, you'd be giving up, and you're not a quitter."

I gazed at him cynically. "Is this supposed to be a locker-room pep talk?"

He chuckled. "I doubt you need one of those."

"I'll tell you what I need," I said. "About twenty minutes with the mysterious Tammy."

"Me, too." He scratched his beard. "She's far more important than you realize."

"Oh?"

Jonathan nodded. "She's also Neville's alibi witness for the night of the murder."

I raised my eyebrows in surprise. "I thought he was alone."

"He was, but he wasn't supposed to be. She called him the day before to tell him she'd be in town the next night. She called again at five that night to tell him the flight was delayed but she'd be there before ten. He waited for her the whole night."

"She never showed?"

Jonathan shook his head.

"Can anyone else confirm that he was there the whole night?"

Jonathan shook his head.

"Has he heard from her since?"

"No."

I mulled it over. "Who is she, Jonathan?" I finally asked.

Jonathan shook his head with determination. "We'll find her. Neville thought she worked for TWA. They have seven flight attendants named Tammy, but none was on a flight scheduled to land in St. Louis at any time that day. Neville's Tammy had red hair. The only one of the seven Tammys with red hair is forty-seven years old and has enough seniority to work only the JFK flights to London, Paris, and Rome. She hasn't been in St. Louis for three years."

"So she's with another airline?"

"Presumably. I have one of my investigators checking logs for flight attendants on all airlines that fly into St. Louis. It will take several days to complete."

"Maybe she isn't a flight attendant," I said. "Maybe she's someone with a boring day job who acts out a glamour fantasy by pretending she's a stewardess."

Jonathan grimaced. "It's crossed my mind, but I don't want to even consider it yet."

"You'd better. If she was pretending to be a stewardess, she was probably pretending to be a Tammy. Even if she learned that you were looking for her, she might be too embarrassed to come forward. After all, she might be a married woman. And even if she did come forward, Jonathan, she's not much of an alibi witness. Remember, she wasn't actually with him that night.

And that means you're still stuck with the semen problem: same blood type as Neville, and no sperm cells in the semen."

He nodded grimly.

"Well," I said, "at least the absence of sperm cells means you don't have to worry about a DNA analysis."

"Wrong. There still may be enough genetic material in the semen to allow that."

"What are you going to do if they match it to Neville?"

He shrugged calmly. "Just another problem to deal with."

"Just another problem? Good grief, it's like finding your client's fingerprints on the murder weapon."

Jonathan smiled and shook his head. "Not quite, Rachel. It's a little easier to plant doubt in a juror's mind with something that technical. I happen to know the lab the prosecutors are using. There are a few skeletons rattling around in that closet."

I said nothing, struck again not merely by the mindset of a criminal defense lawyer but the totality of the transformation from Jonathan Wolf's days as a prosecutor. He could now vigorously attack the validity and integrity of the very scientific processes that just a few years ago he so vigilantly championed.

Nevertheless, a positive DNA match was a grave peril for the defense. The case against Neville McBride might be entirely circumstantial, but Jonathan Wolf would have to create an ocean of reasonable doubt to overcome a puddle of his client's semen on the body of the victim.

I checked my watch and stood up. "I have to go."

Jonathan walked me out to the elevator lobby. "Can I tell Neville you accept?" he asked as we stood waiting for the elevator.

I gave him a puzzled look. "Accept what?"

"His offer. It's extremely generous, Rachel. He'll pay

you a thirty-thousand-dollar retainer to figure out who was trying to use you."

I smiled. "Oh, I think I can figure out exactly who's trying to use me now."

"That's unfair," he snapped.

"Oh no it's not, Jonathan. But that's okay." I give him a patronizing wink. "I'm a big girl, and I know how this game is played. Tell Neville thanks but no thanks. He can save his money for you and your investigators. I couldn't take it anyway. It could be a conflict of interest. Remember, I represent Sally's estate."

"But—"

I held up my hand. "The estate will pay my fees, which is the way it should be. Don't forget, Jonathan," I cautioned, wagging my finger, "I haven't dismissed my lawsuit yet, and I don't intend to until I fully understand what really happened that night." I paused and gave him a plucky smile. "Meanwhile, don't fret about my motivation. I don't need your client's money to get motivated, and I certainly don't need your pep talks."

The elevator door slid open. I stepped into the elevator, punched the button for the lobby, and turned to face him. He was standing there with an uncertain expression. Seeing Jonathan Wolf off balance was almost too much fun.

I pointed my finger at him and gave him another wink as the doors started to close. "I'll keep you posted, Counselor."

CHAPTER 11

I stared at the purse on the edge of my desk and shook my head in disbelief. "Four hundred and twelve dollars for that?"

Jacki shrugged. "It's a Salvatore Ferragamo. All leather."

"Forget the fucking purse," Benny said. "Who in their right mind would pay five hundred and seventy dollars for a pair of high heels?"

"Oh, but you have to admit," Jacki cooed, touching one of them lovingly, "these are exquisite."

"Hey, girl," Benny said, "if I'm going to shell out nearly six hundred bucks for a pair of pumps, they better be on the feet of a gorgeous chick wearing nothing but a G-string."

It was the end of the day, and Jacki, Benny, and I were in my office. Benny had dropped by around four o'clock to fill me in on some details he'd learned about the police investigation of Neville McBride. Apparently, Neville had joined one of those telephone dating services a few years back, right around the time he started leasing a room at the Marriott hotel downtown. Based on the activity in his dating-service account and his hotel room, Neville McBride was leading a secret life as, in Benny's words, "a two-hundred-pound rat in heat." According to Benny's source, none of the women was named Tammy, although one of them said he tied her up before sex; she admitted, however, that the bondage part was her idea, not his.

As Benny filled me in, Jacki had returned from her trip to Plaza Frontenac carrying two bags. She had gone there to pick up the materials turned over in response to the subpoenas we had served on Neiman-Marcus and La Femme Elégante. As part of my pretrial preparation for Cissy Thompson's libel lawsuit against Vincent Contini, I had obtained a copy of her MasterCard statement for the crucial month of August. It showed the $4,358.56 charge for the Adrienne Vittadini dress she had purchased from Vincent's on Maryland on August 11 and unsuccessfully attempted to return the following week. August 11 was a Tuesday. The next day, according to her statement, she made a $412.35 purchase at Neiman-Marcus and a $570.67 purchase at La Femme Elégante. What made those two purchases noteworthy were the two entries on August 18: a $412.35 credit at Neiman-Marcus and a $570.67 credit at La Femme Elégante. The subpoenas I served asked each store to produce the paperwork surrounding the transaction plus the actual items purchased on the 12th and returned the 18th.

I lifted one of the shoes from La Femme Elégante. It was a sleek black pump by Yves Saint Laurent. I turned it over and studied the sole. There were a few faint scratches around the ball of the foot that suggested, at least to my untutored eye, that the shoe had been worn.

"When is this crazy trial?" Benny asked.

"It starts next Thursday," Jacki said. She lifted the Salvatore Ferragamo purse by the straps and stood up, turning to look at her reflection in the window. Although it was a standard-size black leather bag, against Jacki's bulk it seemed to shrink to a child's play purse.

"It looks smart," I told her.

She gave me a doubtful look.

"You think it'll settle?" Benny asked.

I shook my head. "Neither one is in it for the money." Still holding the pump, I leaned over and placed it alongside one of my shoes. They seemed to be the same size, although it was hard to tell for sure because I was wearing flats. "It's principle versus pride," I said to Benny, looking up at him. "Vincent is convinced that she bought that dress with the intent of wearing it somewhere and then returning it. He claims she's done it before. He sees it as a matter of principle, a line drawn in the sand. For Cissy, it's her social standing. Remember, just ten years ago she and Richie were shopping at Kmart, driving Chevys and Fords, and celebrating their daughter's high school graduation with *mostaccioli* and green Jell-O at the American Legion hall. Now the guy's worth more than twenty million dollars. She's come a long way, and it hasn't been cheap. She's not backing down."

"Jesus," Benny said in disgust. "What does that social-climbing bitch want?"

"Simple," I said as I slipped off one of my shoes. "She wants total vindication, either in the form of a public apology from Vincent Contini or his public humiliation at a trial."

"Can your guy prove she wore the dress?" he asked.

I glanced over at Jacki, who raised her eyebrows and sighed. I looked back at Benny. "Not yet."

"That's great," he said sarcastically. "Who gets to tell the Great Contini that he better be ready next week to bend over and kiss his skinny ass good-bye?"

I slipped my foot into the pump. "Hey," I said with a smile, "it fits." I stood up, wobbling on one heel.

"Here you go, Cinderella," Jacki said, handing me the other one.

I kicked off my other shoe and slipped on the second

pump. I did feel like Cinderella. I'd never owned anything by Yves Saint Laurent. "Do you realize," I said, "that this pair of shoes costs more than all of my shoes combined?"

"Very nice," Jacki said to me admiringly. "They're you, Rachel."

I tilted my head back and fluffed my hair in an exaggerated Hollywood pose. "Thank you, my darling."

I took a few sashaying steps and looked back toward Jacki. We both started giggling like schoolgirls. It was such a nice respite from the daily grind.

Benny looked heavenward and shook his head. "What is this," he said, "a costume party?"

"Oh, hush, grumpy," I said as I returned to my chair and slipped off the heels.

"Rachel," he said, "the trial is just a week away, for chrissakes. This is all you have? A couple of other returns? Jesus Christ, she's gonna testify that she bought this shit, brought it home, and decided she didn't like it. Or maybe her husband didn't like it. Then what are you going to do?"

I put the shoes back on my desk. "Here's what we're going to do." I turned to Jacki. "After lunch tomorrow, go by the public library and get the edition of the *Post-Dispatch* for the Sunday of that week. August sixteenth. There's a section in there called Style Plus. There's a column that covers high-society events, especially charity fund-raisers. Check out the following Sunday as well. Sometimes it runs a week behind."

"What am I looking for?" Jacki asked.

"Best-case scenario," I said, "Cissy's name. Otherwise, you're looking for the names of all events mentioned and all people identified as attending. Then do the same for the *Ladue News*." The *Ladue News* is a weekly paper that covers various high-society events.

Jacki was jotting down my instructions. When she finished, she looked up with a puzzled expression. "Why?"

"A hunch," I said. "In a two-day period, Cissy Thompson spent more than five thousand dollars on a dress, a pair of shoes, and a purse. That's a lot of money. The following week, she returns, or tries to return, everything. Now maybe Benny's right. Maybe she just had second thoughts, but Vincent Contini is absolutely convinced she wore the dress. That gives us an alternative scenario, namely, that she bought the outfit specifically for an upcoming social event. If so, that means the event had to take place sometime between August twelfth, when she bought the shoes and purse, and August eighteenth, when she returned them and tried to return the dress."

Jacki was smiling. "I like it," she said, nodding her head.

"Check with Vincent, too," I said. "If there was some big event that weekend, some of his other customers may have mentioned it." I looked at Benny. "Well, you have any better ideas?"

He shook his head. "Good luck."

CHAPTER 12

Jacki opened my office door, her eyes wide.

"He's here?" I asked.

She nodded.

I grinned. "Send him in."

A moment later: "Greetings and salutations, Miss Gold."

There in my doorway stood Melvin Needlebaum, pale eyes swimming behind thick lenses, thinning brown hair slicked back from his domed forehead. He was, as usual, outfitted in what can only be described as a Full Melvin: a wrinkled ill-fitting brown suit that did nothing to disguise a body totally untouched by physical exercise, including those trademark broad hips cantilevered toward his rib cage; a pair of scuffed brown wing tips the size of snowshoes; sagging navy socks; a phosphorescent tie; and an all-season short-sleeve white shirt, the tail of which was no doubt already hanging out at nine in the morning. To this ensemble Melvin had added the final clarifying Needlebaum touch: a pair of humongous briefcases, one in each hand.

"Hiya, Melvin," I said, standing to greet him. "Thanks for coming."

"Before we commence, Miss Gold, I must contact my adversary in this deposition. May I use your telephone?"

"Sure. I'll wait outside with Jacki."

"Excellent, Miss Gold, excellent."

I walked out to Jacki's desk. She looked at me with raised eyebrows. "Wow."

I smiled. "He's a classic."

Not an original, but a classic. Indeed, every significant law firm in America has at least one Melvin Needlebaum. But never more than three. Abbott & Windsor's Melvin Needlebaum is actually named Melvin Needlebaum. You can look it up.

Except among law-firm cognoscenti, Melvin Needlebaums are easy to misjudge. They remind some of the extra-chromosome types who were vice presidents of the audiovisual club and ran the movie projector in driver's ed. They remind others of the geek in a Depression-era circus freak show—that manic wacko whose sole genius was the ability to bite the head off of a live chicken.

But first impressions are misleading, as any attorney who's had the misfortune of opposing a Melvin Needlebaum can testify. It's not just that Melvin Needlebaums are brilliant workaholics, which they are. Nor is it merely their ability to crank out interrogatories, motions to compel, and fifty-page briefs at a speed that seems to defy the laws of human endurance. And it's certainly more than their encyclopedic recall of even the most obscure judicial opinions and federal regulations. No, what truly distinguishes the Melvin Needlebaums of the legal profession is the astounding level of belligerence within their disheveled bodies. It's a veritable witch's brew of malevolence, and they focus all of it on the opposing attorneys in their lawsuits. They never lose that edge, either. For most litigators, a chance encounter with a former adversary is a time for shared laughter and reminiscence. But for a Melvin Needlebaum, there is no such thing as a former adversary. Every case is a blood feud.

Moreover, and perhaps most important, they are extraordinarily profitable to their firms. They work twelve hours a day, seven days a week—and every minute of their time is billable to a client. When you multiply three thousand billable hours a year by a rate of $225 per hour, you tap into hitherto unknown reserves of tolerance among partners.

I heard an outraged squawk noise from my office. Melvin's telephone call with opposing counsel seemed to be taking that all too familiar path. I gestured to Jacki to join me. Melvin was standing in front of my credenza, his back to me. We watched him from just beyond the doorway.

"Patently absurd!" he quacked, his arms jabbing spastically.

There was a pause as he listened to his opponent's response.

"Get real!" Melvin snarled. "Anyone with the brains God gave a goose would know that was patently absurd." A pause, then another squawk of outrage. "You, sir, can assure your client that I shall make it an unforgettable deposition. By eleven hundred hours I shall be storming through the rice paddies and taking no prisoners." Another pause, arms twitching in silence as he listened. And then, "You, sir, have launched the first missile. *Prepare for Armageddon!*"

He slammed down the receiver and leaned forward to squint at my monitor screen. "Do you have WestLaw on this terminal, Miss Gold?"

"Sure do," I said, walking in. I signaled Jacki to join me. We each took a chair facing Melvin, who stood behind my desk.

He turned to squint at Jacki. "Madam, are you conversant in the fundamentals of WestLaw?"

"She is," I said. "Jacki is going to law school at night."

Melvin nodded and flashed one of his goofy grins. "Excellent," he said, rubbing his hands together eagerly. "I have a premonition that this deposition may become somewhat turbulent." He turned to me. "In the event that I should suddenly require research on certain rules of discovery, Miss Gold, my firm's client will be more than happy to compensate your secretary for her time. Speaking of which"—he paused to check his watch—"we should commence."

"Sally Wade & Associates," I said.

"Aha!" he barked, seating himself in the chair behind my desk, his eyes on fire. "The queen of southern Illinois chasers, self-appointed defender of the lumpen proletariat, champion of the congenitally clumsy, and, up until her dramatic departure from the active practice of the law, the target of the do-gooders at the Disciplinary Commission." Melvin leaned back with a lopsided grin.

I had to smile. Melvin was definitely a trip. "What is this," I said, "a briefing or a celebrity roast?"

Melvin winced. "A celebrity *what*?"

"Never mind," I said. "Tell us why the commission was interested in Sally."

Melvin sat back, his eyes wild. Here we go, I thought. On a good day I could speak in complete sentences. Melvin spoke in complete paragraphs.

"We shall begin with the supporting cast of characters. The so-called associates of Sally Wade & Associates. This rogues' gallery consists of a marginal actress turned legal amanuensis by the name of Amelia Suzanne Chickering. The rest of the supporting cast is composed of three and perhaps as many as nine chasers prowling the highways of southern Illinois with police radios in their cars."

"What are chasers?" Jacki asked.

Melvin's eyes seemed to blaze behind the thick,

smudged lenses. "The lifeblood of a personal injury lawyer's practice, Miss Brand," he explained, "especially in the era before the lower echelons of our learned profession succumbed to the siren call of a full-page ad in the Yellow Pages and the lure of a sleazy thirty-second spot on *The Late Late Show*. Chasers, Miss Brand, are the bounty hunters of the personal injury trade, the sleazy mercenaries who find the prospective clients and haul them to the lawyers. For a fee, of course."

"But isn't that illegal?" Jacki said.

Melvin gaped at her. "Of course it's illegal, Miss Brand. More precisely, it violates Section 2-103 (d) of the Illinois Code of Professional Responsibility, which provides, in pertinent part, that a lawyer shall not give another person anything of value to initiate contact with a prospective client on behalf of that lawyer."

"Oh," Jacki said meekly.

Melvin glanced at me with another lopsided grin. "Miss Brand," he said, turning back to her, "when we are dealing with Sally Wade we are not dealing with the Sandra Day O'Connor of Madison County. Compliance with the Code of Professional Responsibility was hardly the decedent's strong suit."

"Now, Melvin," I said gently, "Jacki hasn't been a law student long enough to become cynical."

Melvin squinted at me in confusion. "I beg your pardon, Miss Gold?"

I turned to Jacki. "Under the code, Sally Wade violates the rules if she pays a chaser two hundred dollars for a case worth two grand in fees. Meanwhile, no one raises an eyebrow if a lawyer at Neville McBride's firm spends five hundred dollars wining and dining a CEO in the hopes of landing a case worth fifty grand in fees." I smiled at Melvin. "I, on the other hand, have been a lawyer long enough to be cynical."

"Those two scenarios are not analogous," Melvin protested.

"They most certainly are," I said, "but we're not here to debate ethics. Tell us more about the Sally Wade investigation."

Melvin took off his glasses, tilted the smudged lenses toward the light overhead, and then put them back on. "The clients of Sally Wade & Associates," he continued, "are primarily semiliterate blacks, Hispanics, and southern Illinois rednecks, brought to the firm by the chasers, usually within an hour of the automobile accident that has given rise to their sudden allure as potential clients. Either Miss Wade or her assistant has—or rather, had—the accident victim sign an attorney-client contingent fee agreement on the spot, pursuant to which the client agrees to pay the firm a hefty percentage of any recovery, plus expenses."

"I assume Sally's alleged chasers were the focus of the commission's investigation?" I asked.

Melvin snickered. "Some focus. Those bumblers have been after her for years, but they could never put together the evidence to nail her. It drove them berserk." Melvin shook his head in disgust. "Anyone with the brains God gave a goose knew how she got her clients."

Melvin shuffled through his papers. "I happen to be acquainted with two of the commission's investigators," he said, "and they slipped me some of the files. It's great stuff, Miss Gold, great stuff. Listen to this one. It's a letter to the commission from one of her clients. 'Dear Sirs,' " Melvin read in a weird accent with no connection to any known race, creed, or geographic region, " 'I was hit by a pickup truck on Route 3 on November fifth of last year. After the police left a big black dude named Dice in a Buick Deuce-and-a-Quarter pulls over to the side of the road and tells me to get in 'cause I needs a good lawyer. I was bleeding from my ear and felt like I'd been slapped upside the head 'cause of that pickup, which really wasn't my fault. This Dice drive me to Attorney Wade's office and give me one of her cards and tell me to go see the lady, which I done. When I got to her office some pretty blond lady has me sign papers and now they won't tell me what happened with my case which gets me angry 'cause I think I'm owed a lot of money and now I have to pay Dr. Hernandez who keep calling my home, which ain't right 'cause it upset my mother. Please help.' Signed, E. B. White." Melvin looked up with a demented grin. "Not!" He burst into high-pitched cackles.

"What happened?" I asked, trying to get to the point.

Melvin slapped his hand on the table. "Not a thing! What buffoons. Mr. Dice denied the event, and the complaining witness failed to respond to further inquiries. Here's another," Melvin said, squinting at a document. "Ah, yes. Ramón Valdona. You're going to relish this immensely, Miss Gold. This Hispanic chap contends he was transported to Sally Wade's office directly from the hospital by—guess who?—the police officer at the scene of the accident, one Officer Annie McCarthy. Drove him there in her squad car! El Señor Valdona claims that Officer McCarthy was kind enough to give him one of Sally Wade's business cards and advise him he'd get in big trouble if he didn't go see her." Melvin paused to give us still another lopsided grin. "As you can imagine, the commission was virtually rhapsodic over this claim. Alas, their enthusiasm nearly matched their ineptitude. They subpoenaed Officer McCarthy, who—surprise, surprise—denied it all under oath, as did the decedent, thereby leaving the commission with nothing more than a complaining witness who barely speaks English and doesn't exactly have a Sears Die-Hard upstairs."

"Did they drop the case?" Jacki asked.

"Excellent question, Miss Brand. Actually, this file was still open when the decedent died. As a matter of fact, there was some indication that they had approached Sally about a possible deal with the prosecuting attorney."

"What kind of deal?"

Melvin grinned. "They proposed that Sally turn state's witness against Officer McCarthy."

"Annie McCarthy?" I repeated, glancing over at Jacki. There were several entries for McCarthy on the nine-page handwritten columns of names we'd found in the safe deposit box.

Melvin glanced at his documents. "She is a member of the Alton police force. According to the investigators, she has a boyfriend who works as a nurse in the emergency room of the county hospital. The investigators surmised that he was feeding his lady friend the names of accident victims who might need a lawyer."

Melvin had to leave shortly, so he and Jacki went to the file room to make photocopies of the materials he'd gotten from the Disciplinary Commission. While they were in there, one of my cocounsel in a trademark case called to discuss strategies for an upcoming settlement conference before a federal magistrate judge. As he rambled on, I idly doodled the names Dice and McCarthy on my legal pad. When the call ended, I jotted a note to myself to call Amy Chickering. Jacki poked her head in the office. I looked up and smiled. "Is Melvin off to war?"

She nodded and came in, holding a document. "He may be strange but he is definitely sharp. I showed him this BCS list of numbers," she said, handing it to me.

It was the single sheet of paper that had been in the manila envelope in Sally's safe deposit box—the one with the initials BCS and four rows of numbers handwritten in blue ink:

BCS
011-41-22-862-1823
108-795-2581-3883
111385
11787

"Don't tell me he recognized a bank account number," I said. Jacki had so far drawn a blank in her efforts to turn up an account number that matched any of the numbers on the sheet.

"No," she said, "but he recognized the first number."

"You must be kidding."

"Well, not so much the number as the sequence. He says it's a phone number."

I stared at the first row: 011-41-22-862-1823. I looked up at Jacki. "Overseas?"

"That's what he said. The first three numbers—zero, one, one—are for overseas, and the next two are the country code. Melvin says that forty-one is the country code for Switzerland."

"He's amazing." I pressed the speakerphone button. "Let's check it out." I punched in the number.

We stared at the phone as we waited for the call to go through. It took a while, but we finally heard the short, quick rings of a foreign telephone service, and then the click as it was answered.

"Allo," an accented male voice said. "Banque Crédit Suisse, Customer Inquiries. Your account number, please."

I glanced at Jacki, momentarily flustered, and then looked down at the sheet of paper and read off the second row of numbers.

"A moment, please," the voice said. There was a short pause, and then he said, "Your personal identification code, please."

I looked at Jacki, shrugged, and read off the third row of numbers.

"A moment, please." Another short pause, and then, "Your password number, please."

I read off the last row of numbers. "One, one, seven, eight, seven."

"A moment, please." Another pause.

I looked up at Jacki. She had her fingers crossed.

"Good afternoon, Ms. Wade," the voice said. "How may we be of assistance today?"

I winked at Jacki, who was covering her mouth to stifle her excitement.

"Can I have my account balance, please?" I said.

"Certainly. Account number 011-41-22-862-1823 has a present balance of 114,835 francs."

I looked at Jacki and pressed the mute button. "Swiss francs?" I whispered.

She shrugged.

I took my finger off the mute button. "Sir, how much is that in American dollars?"

"At today's exchange rate, 114,835 francs equals . . . 147,225 dollars."

I wrote the number down. "Thank you very much."

"You are quite welcome, Ms. Wade."

CHAPTER 13

When I called that morning, the desk sergeant told me that Alton police officer Annie McCarthy was not scheduled to come on duty until late that afternoon. Accordingly, I moved Junior Dice to the top of my chaser list and shifted Officer Annie to later in the day.

The fact that I had a chaser list suggested that I also had a coherent plan of attack. I didn't. All I knew was that Officer McCarthy and Junior Dice were two people who dealt with Sally on at least a semiregular basis and, moreover, were two people who, for different reasons, had cause to be unhappy with Sally.

Amy Chickering's description of Junior Dice made him sound dangerous, and the brief bio in the Disciplinary Commission files confirmed her description. Reginald "Junior" Dice, born and raised in the East St. Louis ghetto, was in his late thirties. He listed his profession as boxer, and still fought occasionally in club matches in Moline, Centralia, Decatur, and other Illinois towns. Back in his early twenties, Junior Dice had served eighteen months in Joliet on a manslaughter conviction for killing a man with his bare hands in a barroom brawl. In the space of a year after his release, he was arrested twice on rape charges. The first was dismissed; the second was reduced to simple assault in a plea bargain that resulted in a six-month suspended sentence. Since then, he had remained clear of the law except for a few traffic violations, including an arrest two years ago for going 115 in a 55-mph zone.

Amy knew where he usually had lunch, and insisted on coming with me. "You're not going to want to go in there alone," she explained.

She was right. What made the lunch crowd salivate at Junior Dice's favorite spot was not the food on the plates but the women on the tables. Cherries was its name. It used to be called Derrières, and there were many on display, one per table, each neatly cleaved by a spangled G-string. Fortunately, Junior Dice's preferred seat was in a quiet booth along a darkened back wall of the establishment, and the dominant object on his table was a fully dressed Caesar salad.

He recognized Amy as we approached and broke into a big grin. "Hello, Miss Amy. Allow me to buy you and your foxy girlfriend a drink."

Junior Dice was a large dark-skinned black man. He had shrewd eyes, even white teeth, and a smooth, shaved head. It was the head of a boxer, with scar tissue around both eyes, a nose that had been broken more than once, a small dent in his forehead, and a cauliflower ear. He was wearing an iridescent green sports jacket over a shiny black T-shirt. The jacket was tailored to accentuate his broad shoulders, barrel chest, and narrow waist.

Amy introduced me but did not tell him my connection to Sally. He reached across the table to gently shake my hand. "I am delighted to meet you, Rachel."

A bikini-clad waitress in spike heels arrived at our table to take our orders. She had what looked like maraschino cherries on the points of her bikini top, which was crammed to capacity by a pair of expensive-looking breasts. Dice ordered another glass of chablis, Amy asked for an iced tea, and I passed. As the waitress wiggled back toward the bar, Dice turned to me with a smile. "So, what brings you to this establishment, Rachel?"

"I'm an attorney, Mr. Dice. I'm helping close up Sally Wade's law practice. I understand you believe you have a claim against the estate."

Dice glanced in mild surprise at Amy, who was sitting next to me. Then he looked back at me with a smile. "You must be mistaken."

I shook my head. "I don't think so. I understand you think Sally cheated you out of one of your fees."

He gazed at me with languid eyes. After a moment, he leaned forward and calmly said, "You understand wrong. Sally owes me nothing."

"Hey, Junior, who're the girls?"

The mood shattered, we all looked over at once. The speaker was one of the Cherries dancers, a slender brunette wrapped in a silky blue robe. She was standing at the head of our table, hands on her hips, one foot tapping nervously. She seemed to have pleasant features, although it was hard to tell precisely what was concealed beneath her thick stage makeup. Her scowl, though, would have been visible from the upper balcony.

Junior leaned back in the booth, his smile warming a few degrees. "Be cool, baby. I'm helping clear up some confusion in the minds of these ladies. This is attorney Rachel Gold. I believe you already know Amy Chickering. She worked for the late, great Sally Wade." He turned to us, his smile even warmer. "Ladies, this is my special girl, Jo-Jo. Her last name is Black, but she's just as white as Snow White. And jes' as pretty, ain't you, baby?" He reached out, put his arm around her waist, and pulled her toward him. "Come on down here, Snow White. You on break. Have a seat next to your Junior and let me buy you a drink."

Reluctantly, she sat down next to him. Dice signaled for the waitress, who was heading in our direction with Dice's glass of wine and Amy's iced tea. As he ordered a Bloody Mary for Jo-Jo, I studied her features, trying to imagine how her face would look without the fake eyelashes, heavy eye shadow, and pancake makeup. She didn't look like Sally Wade, or at least the photographs of the real Sally Wade. The problem was that I could no longer clearly recall the features of the fake Sally, if indeed the Sally I met had been a fake. Jo-Jo Black had similar hair color and body type, although hair color proved nothing and the body type I recalled was typical enough to include Amy and plenty of other women, including me.

It was clear that we were done with Dice for the day. For whatever reason, he had decided that his prior business relationship with Sally Wade, including any money owed him, had terminated with her death. But Jo-Jo might be worth one shot before we left.

"You knew Sally Wade?" I asked her.

She glanced uncertainly at Dice, who subtly nodded his head.

"Yeah," she said, "I knew her." She took a pack of cigarettes out of her robe pocket and stuck one in her mouth. "So what?"

"I understood she owed Junior some money."

Dice had her well trained. She looked at him and he slowly shook his head as he flicked his lighter and held it toward her. She leaned forward, lit her cigarette, and looked back at me. She exhaled a stream of smoke and said, "I don't know nothing about that."

On the way out, I told the bartender that I represented two nightclubs in Memphis and asked if Cherries had a publicity shot of Jo-Jo Black. It did, and he gave me one.

"Why did you want her photo?" Amy asked as we pulled out of Cherries' parking lot. Next stop: Alton, Illinois.

"Clutching at straws," I said, glancing down at the photo. I shook my head. "She doesn't look much like Sally."

"Sally?" Amy asked, momentarily confused. "Oh, that," she said, lifting the photo. "No way. Just more wishful thinking by Neville's lawyer."

We drove for a while in silence. I glanced over at Amy. "Did you ever hear Sally mention someone named Tammy?"

"Tammy?" she repeated.

I nodded.

"Who is she?"

I explained Neville McBride's alleged alibi witness. The passage of time hadn't lent it any more credibility.

"Meanwhile," I continued, "I'd like Neville to look at Jo-Jo's picture. It's a long shot, but you never know."

"You think Jo-Jo might be Tammy, too?"

"I don't know what to think, Amy. But the fact that Jo-Jo is Junior Dice's girlfriend sure brings her closer to the center of the action." I turned onto the highway toward Alton. "How much money did Junior claim Sally owed him?"

"About five grand."

"All from one case?"

She nodded. "It was a big fee. He claimed she was racist and was always trying to screw him out of his fee. That's why I ended up handling most of the face-to-face stuff with Junior."

"Was he her only black chaser?"

Amy nodded. "But racism had nothing to do with it. They just plain didn't get along. Believe me, Junior can be a real asshole."

"This may sound crazy," I said, "but did Sally have any case involving rocks?"

"Rocks?" Amy repeated.

I explained the strange pictures that we had picked up

from Walgreens with the receipt I'd found in Sally's safe deposit box. I gestured toward the backseat. "I have one of the shots in my briefcase. Can you reach it?"

Amy handed me the briefcase, and, keeping one eye on the road, I took out the picture. "Do these things look familiar?" I asked.

She stared at the photograph for a long time. "I have no idea," she said.

"That's what I was afraid of."

After a moment, Amy said, "This whole thing has been a real eye-opener."

I looked over at her. "How so?"

She rested her chin in her hand. "You work for someone all that time and you really think you know who she is, right down to her secrets." She flicked the photograph. "I guess I didn't know Sally as well as I thought."

"I wish you could have been there the day she retained me," I said.

Amy frowned. "Why?"

I gave her a rueful smile. "That way at least one of us would have known if she really was Sally Wade."

We were driving north along the Illinois side of the Mississippi River heading toward Alton, an Illinois river town above St. Louis. We were passing the point just north of St. Louis where the Missouri River flows into the Mississippi River after its 2,500-mile journey from its headwaters high in the northern Rockies. Even down near river level along Route 3, the source of the Muddy Mo's nickname was apparent: you could see its brown currents swirling into the Mississippi, staining the clear waters mahogany.

A few minutes later, I pulled into a parking space behind the police department, turned off the engine, and checked my watch. We were early. Turning to Amy, who was reaching down for her purse, I said, "Tell me about Brady Kane."

Amy jolted upright. She gave me a strange look. "What about him?"

"He works at Douglas Beef Processors in East St. Louis, right?"

She nodded. "He's the plant manager."

"You know him?"

She nodded. "Sally handled a lot of workers' comp cases against DBP—that's what people call Douglas Beef. Brady Kane was usually the company rep at the hearings. I've been over there several times—for document productions, to serve subpoenas, to deliver notices, that sort of thing. You have dealings with DBP, you have to deal with Brady Kane."

"What's he like?"

She shrugged. "Sort of a cross between a management hard-ass and a Neanderthal man."

"Has he done anything specifically to you?"

She gave me a puzzled look. "Why do you ask?"

"The way you reacted when I mentioned his name."

She shook her head. "He's just a creep. Last time I was in his office he had two jars of fetal blood on his desk."

"Fetal blood?"

"From a calf fetus they found inside a slaughtered cow." She shuddered. "They sell the stuff. He looks like he'd drink it warm with a ham sandwich and chips."

"That is creepy." I sorted through my notes. "Tell me about Sally's relationship with him."

"Relationship? What do you mean?"

"The police pulled Sally's phone records. She talked to him a fair amount before and after normal business hours. The telephone records show about six telephone calls to him a month—half to his apartment at night, half to his private line at the slaughterhouse early in the morning."

Amy frowned. "Well, we did have a lot of cases against DBP."

"True, but they were represented by attorneys in each of those cases. That was clear from the files. Sally was a lawyer. That meant she couldn't talk directly to Brady Kane, or to any other Douglas Beef employee, about any pending case."

"Why not?"

"It violates the Code of Professional Responsibility. You're not permitted to make direct contact with an adverse party that you know to be represented by an attorney."

Amy gave me a cynical look. "Is that the same code that says you're not permitted to pay a chaser for a case?"

I smiled. "Good point."

"Don't get me wrong, Rachel. I'm not saying there was anything improper about Sally's contacts with Brady Kane. In fact, I have no reason to think there was."

"Then why would she be calling him?"

Amy mulled it over. "Maybe they were friends?"

"Maybe they were lovers?"

Amy made a gagging noise. "God, I hope not."

I thought about the Swiss bank account. "Were there ever any confidential packages delivered directly to Sally from the slaughterhouse?"

Amy frowned. "What are you thinking?"

I shrugged. "Money. Some sort of kickback on cases. It happens."

"I don't think so, and I probably would have known if there had been. After all, I knew all about the chasers."

I sighed. "Damn."

"What's wrong?"

"Instead of crossing names off my list, I keep adding new ones." I checked my watch. "Tomorrow for him. Let's go see Officer McCarthy."

"You go," Amy said. "I'll wait."

"Oh?"

"I never had any contact with Annie. She would only

deal directly with Sally. You'll probably get more out of her if I'm not there."

It would have been hard to get any less.

Officer Annie McCarthy had her story and she was sticking with it, come hell or high water. She met me in a witness interrogation room that included what had to be a one-way mirror on one wall, and she acted as if someone from Internal Affairs were watching from the other side of the mirror.

"That's a total crock of shit, lady," she said, arms akimbo, fists clenched on her hips.

She was in full uniform, with a riot stick dangling from one hip and a handgun strapped to the other. A walkie-talkie in a shoulder holster emitted occasional coughs of static. Even her hairstyle was tough: a ragged macho pageboy. Only her face seemed out of sync with the Rambo demeanor. She was cute, in a Midwestern tomboyish way, with bright blue eyes, a pug nose, and perfect white teeth.

"I understand that's what you told the Disciplinary Commission's investigators," I said.

"And it's what I'm telling you," she said, her chin thrust forward defiantly. "And it's what I'll tell any other asshole who wants to ask. I never drove no accident victim to that lawyer's office, and I sure as shit never collected no fee. Period. End of sentence. Understand?"

"Sit down a moment, Annie," I said, aiming for a soothing tone. I took a chair.

She looked down at me with a sneer. "No need to. We're done. I'm outta here."

I gazed up at her. "I have the payment records," I said calmly.

There was a pause. "What payment records?" Sounding a shade less cocky.

"For the clients you brought Sally. She kept them in

her safe deposit box. Nine hundred dollars for Ramón Valdona. Remember him? Five hundred from someone named Javier. And so on. But I'm not here to build a chaser case against you, Annie. I don't care about that stuff. I want to talk to you about Sally Wade. We can do that in private, just the two of us, or we can do it in public, in some courtroom." I shrugged. "Your choice. If you'd like, I can meet you after your shift ends."

I could almost hear the gears turning inside her head. It took her a long time to respond, and when she did her tone was subdued. "You got a business card?"

"Sure." I pulled one out of my briefcase and held it toward her.

She snapped it out of my hand and swiveled to leave. "Maybe," she said, her hand on the door, her back to me. She opened the door. "Maybe not."

She walked out.

I watched the door swing shut. Slowly, I stood up. I felt exhausted.

I dropped by the office before heading over to my self-defense class. Jacki had left a nice surprise in the center of my desk: a photocopy of the society column from the Style Plus section of the Sunday, August 16, edition of the *Post-Dispatch*. Jacki had highlighted the middle paragraphs, which described the Carousel Auction Gala at the Ritz-Carlton put on by the Friends of the St. Louis Children's Hospital:

> Guests gathered at 6 p.m. on a Friday night under the carousel in the smaller of the two ballrooms at the Ritz, where a bar had been set up in the center of the room with bartenders serving on all four sides. High above the bar was a carousel horse, and at each of its four corners was a smaller gilded carousel horse dressed in burgundy and teal blue. Waiters and

waitresses passed silver trays of delicious hot hors d'oeuvres to guests as they signed up for the silent auction items displayed around the room.

Chairwoman Cynthia Barnstable said the event netted more than $450,000, including $145,000 from the auction itself. The 350 guests paid $150 and up for their tickets to the event. The money will be used for the Neurorehabilitation Unit at Children's Hospital.

I read the excerpt again, nodding pensively. The article included a photograph of two women standing in front of a carousel horse. The caption identified them as Cynthia Barnstable, chairwoman of the event, and Prudence McReynolds, president of the women's auxiliary of Children's Hospital. The photo credit named Charles Morley. I circled his name and drew an arrow to the margin, where I jotted a note to Jacki:

We need to serve this guy with a subpoena.
Let's talk in the morning.

The special tonight was groin-stomping, with a little face action thrown in for variety. I was pumped.

"Assume the position," Faith ordered.

I was there already: feet at shoulder width, toes pointed forward, knees flexed, hands at my sides.

We started with foot-heel strikes, first in slow motion. I pulled my right leg up, inverted my heel, toes pulled back, and then kicked. Ten with the right leg, ten with the left. Then full speed, with our yell of spirit. We sounded awesome—eleven high-kicking women shaking the room with martial-arts screams.

We paired up to practice heel strikes to the knee in slow motion. Because there were an odd number of us, Faith took turns pairing up with each of us. Tonight she picked me.

"Stay low in your stance, Rachel," she said. "That's it. A little lower. Good. Balance is key. If your stance isn't firm, your kick will be weak. Yes. Aim for the top of the knee. Right there."

Another ten minutes of that, and then it was time for some stomping.

"A stomp is a heel strike," Faith explained, "except your target is on the ground. You can kill a man with a face or a throat stomp. You can incapacitate him with a stomach stomp." She paused, her stern features relaxing into a smile. "But tonight we'll start with my personal favorite: the groin stomp. This works especially well when you're wearing heels. Pair up, gals."

"Oh, for chrissakes, Rachel, forget that stomping bullshit," Benny said on the phone. "Let's have a reality check here. Your attacker is on the ground, right? Option number one: try to do a Mexican hat dance on his body while you're screaming like a banshee. Option number two: reach in your purse, pull out a .357 magnum, and blow his fucking head off. I'm telling you, Rachel, you want protection, dump the martial arts and buy yourself a gun."

I was lying on my back on the living-room rug with the phone cradled between my neck and shoulder. My bare feet were propped up on the couch and Sam Cooke was crooning "You Send Me" on the stereo. Whenever the world gets too snarled for me, Sam Cooke helps restore my harmony.

"Actually," I said, "we start on weapons next week."

"Oh, great. No doubt something highly practical, eh? Like nunchakus."

"New subject, please."

"Okay. What's the latest, Sergeant Friday?"

Staring up at the ceiling, I wiggled my toes and sighed. "I feel more like Inspector Clouseau."

Ozzie, my golden retriever, came padding in from the kitchen and plopped down on the rug beside me. I scratched him behind his ear.

"No suspects yet?"

"None?" I said glumly, shifting the phone to the other ear. "How 'bout too many? My head is swimming."

"Tell me," he said.

I described my meeting at Cherries with Junior Dice and Jo-Jo and my subsequent encounter with Officer Annie McCarthy.

"I don't know," Benny said when I was through. "It's not much money to kill for."

"People have killed for a lot less."

"Maybe. The woman cop had plenty at stake, but where'd she get the semen?"

"From her boyfriend."

"Well, I suppose."

"Not his, Benny. He works at the county hospital. It wouldn't be that hard for him to grab a test tube or two from the urology department or the fertility clinic or wherever they store that stuff. Match it to Neville's blood type and you're off and running."

"Where'd he get Neville's blood type?"

"Medical records. All that stuff is on the computer network these days."

Ozzie moved his head onto my stomach with a contented grunt. I hugged his neck.

"So what's Junior's stripper girlfriend like?" Benny asked.

"I'm going to go back and see her alone. Maybe tomorrow afternoon. She knows something. Also, her looks are driving me crazy."

"Huh?"

"Every woman I meet seems like a possible Sally Wade impostor. Whoever hired me had blue eyes, brown hair, and nice average features, and so does Jo-Jo. Actually, Officer McCarthy does, too."

"So what's on the agenda tomorrow?" Benny asked.

"I'm seeing two more guys. Probably both creeps."

"Oh? More morticians?"

"Worse. An environmental lawyer and—"

"Excuse me?"

I had to smile. One of Benny's pet peeves was the Orwellian names of legal specialties: "labor lawyers" represent management; "antitrust lawyers" represent monopolists; "tax lawyers" help clients avoid taxes; "product liability lawyers" fight product liability. As for "environmental lawyers" . . .

"I beg your pardon, Professor," I said. "I meant a pollution lawyer."

"That's better. Who's the other creep?"

"Wait."

"What?"

"My song."

"Huh?"

" 'Cupid.' "

"Oh, God, are you listening to Sam Cooke again?"

I started to sing along, " 'Soooo, Cupid, draw back your bow—' "

"Puh-leeze, Rachel."

"Shush." I hummed along. "Oh, Benny, he's the best."

"Let's get back on track here, girl. Who's the other creep?"

"The head of a slaughterhouse."

"Ah, so you've got a ransacker and a meatpacker."

I smiled. "That's not bad."

"Better yet, a rainmaker and a steak maker."

"That is bad."

"Wait, wait. How about, uh, a lawmaker and a bone breaker?"

"Good night, Benny."

"Wait. Uh, an hourly biller and a cow killer?"

"Good night, Benny."

"Okay. Good night, Rachel."

I replaced the telephone receiver as Sam Cooke began singing "Only Sixteen."

I scratched Ozzie's head as I closed my eyes and tried to remember back to when I was sixteen.

It seemed another lifetime ago.

CHAPTER 14

                    The ransacker was Bruce Napoli. He was a partner at Tully, Crane & Leonard who had been appointed interim managing partner in the wake of Neville McBride's arrest. The meatpacker was Brady Kane, the plant manager of the Douglas Beef packinghouse in East St. Louis.

The ransacker was first on my list. His secretary ushered me into his spacious, tastefully appointed office at nine thirty-five that morning.

"Hello, Rachel," he said in a soothing tone as he came around the antique mahogany desk to shake my hand. He had that polished, low-key, self-assured manner that clients love. Gesturing toward the large, comfortable couch against the side wall, he said, "Please take a seat."

Bruce Napoli had the look and style of a managing partner, and with good reason. Prior to joining Tully, Crane, he had spent six years as chief of staff for Senator Richard Bartlett of Missouri, two years as counsel to the Republican National Committee, and three years as assistant general counsel of the Environmental Protection Agency. Those eleven years inside the Beltway were excellent training for the position of law firm managing partner, a task closely akin to that of herding cats.

Five years ago, Tully, Crane had lured him back to St. Louis with the promise of money and the challenge of creating a national environmental law practice. It was, as those consultant gurus like to say, a win-win situation. Within three years, Bruce had parlayed his legal expertise, his A-list of government contacts, and his personal magnetism into a thriving practice group of eighteen lawyers, seven paralegals, and more than eight million dollars in annual billings.

It earned him a position on the firm's powerful executive committee, simultaneously delighting the younger partners and discomforting their elders. Before long, the Wednesday-afternoon meetings of the executive committee, once as courteous and affable as afternoon tea at the Ritz (where, in fact, they occasionally were held), degenerated into a lawyer's version of *Beyond Thunderdome*. On one side stood Bruce Napoli, leader of the Young Turks, staunch advocate of high tech and high realization (those twin gods of modern law firm management theory), and—in the prayers of many of his admirers—the icy executioner of the Old Guard. Facing him across the great divide was the increasingly implacable Neville McBride, viewed by the restive Young Turks as the very personification of a cautious stewardship that had allowed Tully, Crane's average profits-per-partner to slip below those of the other major firms in town, viewed by the older partners as the last centurion standing guard against the bloodthirsty hordes of bottom-line lawyer barbarians.

Neville McBride's obsession with his law firm nemesis had caused him to compile an extensive dossier on the man, which Jonathan Wolf had passed on to me before my meeting. As a result, by the time I settled into the couch in Bruce Napoli's office, I already knew that he deserved a prominent spot in his law firm's Book of

Firsts. Specifically, he was the first managing partner at Tully, Crane (1) whose name ended in a vowel, (2) whose specialty was something other than corporate or tax, and (3) whose wife, during an otherwise dull dinner party, spent a furtive quarter of an hour bent over an easy chair in an upstairs bedroom with her dress above her waist, her panties at her ankles, and her eyes clenched tight while an unzipped Neville McBride jabbed and thrusted from behind. Unfortunately for Patty Napoli, and for Bruce, she was discovered *flagrante delicto*, the moment of truth occurring while the hostess was conducting an otherwise eye-glazing tour of the upstairs. As the lady of the house droned on about the strain of trying to coordinate valances and light fixtures, she opened the guest-bedroom door on a scene that was, quite literally, reaching a climax.

The only mercy shown by fate that night—and thus the only secret regret of the other dinner guests—was that Bruce Napoli was downstairs at that very moment, innocently refilling his tumbler of Cutty Sark. In the aftermath, some of the firm's wags found a delicious Freudian irony in Neville's clandestine backdoor invasion of Napoli's high-tech domain with the ultimate low-tech gadget, an erect penis.

Nevertheless, the stalemate continued until Neville's arrest forced him to relinquish the title of managing partner. Bruce was the unanimous choice to replace Neville McBride. It was an extraordinary ascent for a poor Italian-American boy, the sixth of nine children of Marcello and Gina Napoli, raised in a cramped apartment over the M. Napoli Bakery on Shaw Avenue and shadowed throughout his legal career by rumors of mafia connections that stemmed from his great-grandfather's role as a lieutenant in the Chicago mob under Al Capone.

Since his arrest, Neville McBride had been consumed with suspicions that Bruce Napoli, embittered and vengeful over his notorious cuckolding, was somehow connected to the murder. While Neville's suspicions, at least standing alone, weren't enough to put Napoli high on my list of possible suspects, they were enough to make me want to talk to him.

As I studied Bruce Napoli, his wife's liaison with McBride seemed even more incongruous. The two men couldn't have been more dissimilar. Whereas Neville resembled the bulky, sixtyish grocer from the Kiwanis Club, Bruce Napoli reminded me of a sexy Al Pacino in one of the later Godfather movies. Dark hair, dark eyes framed by long, black eyelashes, olive skin, strong nose, dark double-breasted suit. He was in his early forties and looked fit and healthy. I noted a Nike gym bag in the corner of the office with a squash racket sticking out. Although he was short—we were at eye level—he more than compensated with an aura of control.

"How can I help, Miss Gold?" he asked once I was seated.

I had my pretext ready. "I'm wrapping up Sally Wade's estate," I explained, "and I was hoping you could fill in some of the gaps."

It turned out he couldn't, but he gave an impressively disarming performance in the process. Leaning against the edge of his desk, his arms casually crossed over his chest, he conceded at the outset that he and Neville had been rivals within the firm.

"I'd describe us as philosophical rivals," he explained. "If I can draw an analogy to my Senate years, Neville McBride represented what I'd label the 'traditional wing' of the party while I tended to side with the 'next generation.' We had vigorous debates." The memory triggered the glimmer of a smile. "But at all times we remained loyal members of the same party. I had, and continue to have, great respect for Neville's legal skills. I rarely agreed with him," he said, pausing to chuckle and shake his head, "but I never came away from one of those encounters without having learned something of value. He is a formidable advocate, and I am proud to call him my partner. We're all pulling for him, Miss Gold."

It was a convincing performance. It almost made me forget that the man Bruce Napoli was speaking of with grudging fondness was the same man who'd been caught doing it doggie-style with his wife.

As for Sally Wade, Napoli said he barely knew her. "I'm certain that we spoke, albeit briefly, at a few of the firm functions during their marriage, but I have no clear memory of that."

"Did you ever have dealings with her on a professional basis?"

He seemed to weigh the question. "Oh, I suppose I couldn't rule out the possibility, although again, I have no clear memory of any dealings." He stood and moved around to the chair behind his desk. "It's not likely that we would have had any professional encounters," he said with a smile. "After all, she was a personal injury lawyer."

As he took a seat, I glanced around the office. It was festooned with plaques, autographed pictures, and other mementos from his years in Washington. There was a gold-framed photograph of his wife on the front of the desk. I frowned at her image, trying to imagine her face with a pair of sunglasses, hoping I'd be able to eliminate her at the outset. I couldn't. I silently groaned. Yet another blue-eyed brunette with pleasant, undistinguished features. The world seemed to be full of them.

On the credenza behind him was a scale model of an armored truck. It was painted Kelly green and had the words NAPOLI SECURITY stenciled across the side in gold letters. That Napoli was a sibling. Although he was the only lawyer among his siblings, they were a diverse group and included a nun, a priest, a baker, a nurse, and, ironically enough, a bank swindler and a bank protector.

Bruce's eldest brother, Anthony, was serving fifteen years for bank fraud arising out of a condo development in the Lake of the Ozarks. Bruce's younger brother John supplied local banks and other institutions with a variety of security services—everything from bodyguards to security guards to armored truck deliveries—through his company, Napoli Security Systems, Inc.

I checked my notes and asked, "Did Neville McBride ever say anything to you to suggest the nature of his marital problems?"

He gave me a patient smile. "Neville was careful to avoid saying anything in my presence that would suggest anything about his personal life."

I spent ten more minutes dancing around the touchiest subject, hoping he'd give me an opening. Finally, I decided the only way in was to take a breath and dive headfirst.

"Mr. McBride is convinced you hate him," I said.

Bruce Napoli gazed at me pensively. After a moment, he said, "Hate is a strong personal emotion."

"Well, he believes you have a strong personal reason to hate him."

Napoli nodded calmly. "He's right about the reason. He's wrong about the emotion. In our professional lives, we're partners. My relationship with my partners is one of trust and respect."

"He wasn't referring to your professional life."

"But I am." Napoli's expression remained unchanged, although there was a hint of displeasure in his voice. "Neville's private life is his own business. Mine is mine. He took advantage of someone at a psychologically vulnerable moment in her life, and that was regrettable. But it was also part of the past. My concerns are the present and the future. I certainly don't wish him ill in his private life, and I certainly don't wish to discuss his private life. Neither his nor mine." He stood up. "I have a busy day, Miss Gold. On behalf of my firm, I can assure you that we are eager to get this unfortunate controversy concluded. Call me if you have any other questions."

Brady Kane was on the phone when his secretary ushered me into his cluttered office. She stood by my side as we waited for the call to end.

"Don't feed me that low-margin horseshit, huh?" he told his caller in a gruff voice. As he listened, he paced back and forth behind his desk, trailing a long, tangled phone cord.

Although the ransacker and the meatpacker were about the same age and had both come from working-class backgrounds, the stark differences in their professional lives were underscored by the portrait each featured in his office. Bruce Napoli's office, with its Persian rug and its commanding view of the Mississippi River, had several framed photos, but the largest by far, taken several years ago, showed him standing in the Oval Office next to a beaming Ronald Reagan. Brady Kane's windowless office, with its fake wood paneling, metal desk, and cheesy desktop nameplate ("Mr. Kane, Plant Manager"), had three bare walls and one photograph—a poster-size shot mounted directly behind his desk. In the picture, a much younger Brady Kane was wearing a bloody apron and standing in front of a blood-splattered tile wall. He had a big grin and was gripping a huge carving knife. Hanging upside down from a meat hook at his side was a decapitated cow.

In the photo, Brady Kane seemed almost as large as the cow. In person, he seemed even larger. He was at least six feet six, with a massive bald head, broad shoulders, powerful arms, and a large gut. With his sunken eyes, crooked nose, and lantern jaw, he reminded me of a professional wrestler—one of those hulking hoarsevoiced giants who glare into the camera during the prematch hype interview and snarl out their threats. But instead of a gold lamé robe over wrestling briefs, he was decked out in a typical plant manager outfit: a white short-sleeved shirt with a pocket protector jammed with pens and pencils, green work slacks, and black leather round-toed shoes with thick rubber soles.

He ended the telephone call by making a counteroffer that expired in twenty-four hours. Slamming down the receiver, he turned to me, his eyes moving from my face on down to my shoes and back up. The meat market metaphor had never seemed more appropriate or more threatening, especially with that gruesome photo on the wall behind him.

Glancing at his secretary, Kane growled, "Who's the girl?"

I introduced myself. He reluctantly shook my hand, which virtually disappeared in his callused paw. I explained my connection with Sally Wade, which didn't make him any friendlier. He sat down heavily behind his desk.

"What do you want?" he asked coldly.

"I'd like to wrap up some loose ends," I said.

He frowned. "What are you talking, loose ends?"

Amy Chickering was right: this was a guy I'd never feel comfortable around. "Sally's phone records show that she called you direct several times a month. I'd like to know why."

He grunted but said nothing. I waited, glancing from the glowering, weathered face in front of me to the younger, grinning face in the photograph behind him. The years and the work had taken their toll on Brady Kane. If ever there was a job with bad karma, this had to be it.

"Well?" I finally said.

He tried to stare me down. When that didn't work, he said, "None of your goddamn business."

"Actually, Mr. Kane, it's most definitely my business. As I explained, I'm here as counsel to Sally Wade's personal representative."

"Yeah?" He crossed his arms over his chest. "Big deal."

"That's exactly what it is." I tried to control my irritation. "At the time of her death, she was handling eight pending claims against your company."

"So?"

"She was a lawyer, Mr. Kane, and your company had a lawyer in each of those cases. Still, she was calling you direct, both here and at your home. I have the phone records." I paused to let that sink in. I saw no evidence that it had.

"In other words," I said, "whatever was going on between you two is *definitely* my business, Mr. Kane, and if you don't want to tell me about it right now in the privacy of your own office, then I'll have the sheriff arrange for you to tell the probate judge about it under oath in open court. Your choice."

Kane turned to the side and stared at the blank wall as he thought it over. "The company lawyers were morons," he finally said.

"What do you mean?" I said.

He turned to me with a scowl. "I've been running this plant for twelve years. They send them pudknockers down from Chicago who don't know diddly about this business or the insurance or the damn claims."

"The workers' compensation claims?" I asked, trying to follow him.

He nodded. "I could move them faster and cheaper than all them fancy lawyers combined." He gave me a defiant look. "So that's what I did."

In response to my questions, he explained that before his promotion to management twelve years ago, he had been president of the local chapter of the meatpackers' union, and thus was used to dealing with lawyers. According to him, Sally often called to get his estimate of what the company might be willing to pay to settle a particular matter. Other times she called for information about certain aspects of plant operations that were relevant to the cause of a specific injury.

"I knew exactly what I could tell her," he said, "and what wasn't any of her goddamn business. I saved this company thousands of dollars in fees and payouts."

"Did the company lawyers know about these contacts?"

He gave me a derisive look. "What are you, nuts? Sally told me to keep it secret. So long as I could keep those Chicago lawyers out of my goddamn operations, it was fine by me."

That was his story. I had my doubts, but he wouldn't budge from it. His answers to my questions became more and more terse, until he was down to yes, no, or maybe. Eventually, he was delivering those one-word answers while glaring at the side wall, his arms crossed over his chest.

"Was Sally the only plaintiff's lawyer you had these conversations with?" I asked.

He answered with a silent nod.

I checked my notes, crossed off the last topic, and stood to leave. As I did, he turned toward me and squinted, as if making an appraisal.

"You ever done a slaughterhouse case?" he asked.

"No."

He gave me a tight smile, revealing a yellowed set of lower teeth. "This ain't Sesame Street, lady. Best bet for you is to get on over to your side of the river and don't look back."

I stared at him for a moment, and he stared right back, his tight smile unwavering. Without a word, I turned and left his office, secretly relieved to be heading back to my side of the river.

CHAPTER 15

"Whoa!" Benny whistled when I described my encounter with Brady Kane. "I'm telling you, Rachel, you got the legs and you got the tush, and if I ever decide to make an exception for smart women with balls, you're first in line for the title of Mrs. Benny Goldberg."

I put down my coffee mug and placed my hand on my chest. "Oh, be still my heart."

It was later that night, and we were having coffee at an espresso bar in the University City Loop, just down the block from the Tivoli Theater, where I had dragged Benny to a showing of one of my very favorite films, *It Happened One Night*. This was my eighth time, and it again confirmed my willingness to marry Clark Gable and have his babies and iron his boxer shorts, even if he refused to convert. Has there ever been an actor as manly and irresistibly sexy as Clark Gable in that movie? He's even sexy giving Claudette Colbert a lesson in the proper way to dunk a doughnut.

"Do you believe Brady Kane's story?" Benny asked.

"I'm not sure."

"It could be a Brandywine scenario," he mused.

Back when Benny and I were junior associates at Abbott & Windsor in Chicago, Johnny Brandywine had been a hotshot young rainmaker at his own litigation boutique. Four years ago, however, a federal jury had convicted him and the assistant general counsel of Marlin Container Company on various charges of mail fraud, wire fraud, and criminal conspiracy, all arising out of a classic kickback scheme: the assistant general counsel sent Johnny lawsuits to handle, and at the end of each month Johnny sent Marlin Container a legal bill, which the same assistant general counsel promptly approved for payment. Unbeknownst to anyone else at Marlin Container, however, Johnny would then transfer 10 percent of his fee into a second account maintained in the name of the infant daughter of that very same assistant general counsel.

I took a sip of my cappuccino and shook my head. "It doesn't fit the pattern."

"Why not?" Benny asked.

"Because Brady Kane wasn't sending Sally the cases. She was getting them on her own."

"Don't be so sure," Benny said. "You said yourself that you need a good union contact to get workers' comp cases. Kane used to be president of the union. Maybe he was steering cases her way for a fee."

"Possibly," I conceded. "That's one of the reasons I'm going to go to the Douglas Beef headquarters in Chicago on Monday morning. I'll see if I can persuade someone in their legal department to run the numbers on the workers' comp cases. See whether those numbers back Kane's story. See whether he really was getting lower settlements in East St. Louis than at their other slaughterhouses."

"And if he wasn't, then maybe we're talking kickbacks."

"Maybe," I said.

"If we're talking kickbacks, maybe she got tired of paying him off and told him so. Maybe that got him pissed enough to kill her."

"That's a lot of maybes." I took a sip of coffee and sat back in my chair. "Oh, Benny," I groaned.

"What?"

"My head is spinning."

He smiled and nodded his head. "Too many suspects?"

"And not enough motives. Even worse, this whole thing could be a wild-goose chase. Maybe Sally really did hire me, and maybe Neville really did kill her. It's still the most logical explanation." I gave a weary sigh. "You know what I really need?"

"A can of whipped cream and a studded dog collar?"

"Benny, I'm serious."

He reached across and squeezed my shoulder. "Sorry, kiddo. What do you really need?"

"A sign."

"A sign?"

"Something to indicate that I'm on the right track."

"Like what?"

"Anything. I'm not picky."

I should have been picky.

I awoke suddenly to the sound of Ozzie scrambling to his feet at the foot of my bed. With a growl, he ran to one of the bedroom windows.

I sat up. "What is it, Oz?"

He stood motionless, ears cocked, body tense. He was making a low, throaty growl.

I glanced over at the clock radio: 2:53 a.m.

Ozzie gave an anxious whine and dashed to the other window, then back to the first one. He tilted his head, his body rigid. Another low growl.

I pulled back the covers. "What do you hear, Oz?"

He started barking. Not a joyous bark or a treed-squirrel

bark or a dog-to-dog bark. This was his ferocious guard-dog bark. It made me just a little jittery. I slid my feet into my slippers and came over to him. He was still barking.

"What, Oz?"

I peered through the blinds. My window looked out over the backyard and the garage, which was on the left. Everything was dark out there. I strained, trying to spot a sign of movement. Ozzie was still barking. I couldn't see a thing.

"Is it an animal?" I asked, as if expecting an answer.

He paused, whining, and ran to the other window, where he growled and started barking again. I joined him at that window and peered through the blinds. It was the same view of the backyard and garage. The same view of nothing.

I went over to my closet and pulled out my robe.

"Come on, Oz," I said as I tied the sash. "Downstairs."

At the sound of the word, he spun toward the bedroom door and charged out. I heard him thundering down the stairs and scrabbling along the kitchen floor.

When I got to the kitchen, he was standing at the back door and barking fiercely. I stood in the doorway watching him, unsure of what to do. It was either an animal—perhaps a raccoon—or a prowler. Whichever it was, all this barking would likely scare it off. I could call the police, but by the time they got here Ozzie would no doubt be sleeping contentedly on the rug at the foot of my bed and I'd have two macho cops swaggering around my house and treating me like the helpless maiden.

I thought of my palm-heel strikes and my groin stomps and my pledge of spirit. But mainly I thought of my powerful, fearless golden retriever. I went into the pantry and came out again with a high-powered flashlight and Ozzie's leash.

"Come here, Oz."

Reluctantly, he came over to let me fasten the leash, and then he dragged me back to the door, where he started whining. I pushed back the curtain covering the door window and clicked on the porch light. There was no one on the porch.

With the flashlight in my right hand and Ozzie's leash wrapped around the other, I unlocked the door and pulled it open. Ozzie immediately leaped against the storm door, whining impatiently.

"Just a sec, Oz."

I unlocked the storm door and pushed it open. Ozzie charged onto the porch, straining against the leash. I clicked on the flashlight as I followed him down the three stairs and into the backyard.

"Wait," I said, trying to hold him back.

I swung the flashlight in an arc around the backyard. There was nothing there, although it was clear that Ozzie had no interest in the backyard. He was lunging and pulling toward the garage, whining and growling. I let him drag me there, where he took up his position facing the door, barking savagely. The hair on his back was standing up.

I stared at the closed garage door, immobilized, unsure. Trying to devise a plan of action, I swung the flashlight around. The beam of light made the bare tree branches leap and whirl in the shadows. I turned back to the garage and stared at the door handle, trying to decide.

"What's going on?"

The voice made me jump. Stumbling backward, I whipped the flashlight around. It was just Mr. Decker, my elderly, somewhat irascible neighbor. He was standing on his side of the waist-high wooden fence. Ozzie had stopped barking.

"What's that dog so riled about?" he asked in his raspy voice. He was wearing a plaid robe over his pajamas.

"I don't know," I said. My voice sounded an octave higher than normal. I took a deep breath, trying to get composed. "I think it's something in the garage."

"Ha!" he said in disgust. "Damn rats is what that is. I had 'em a couple years back. Little bastards ate through the battery wires under the hood of my car. Got 'em with rat poison. Go get yourself some in the morning. Try Central Hardware." He gestured impatiently toward the garage door. "Let the dog chase 'em out of there so the rest of us can get some shut-eye."

He turned back to go inside.

"Thanks, Mr. Decker," I called after him. "Sorry we woke you."

He grumbled something as he trudged up the stairs to his back porch. A moment later I heard his back door open and then close.

I turned back to the garage door and trained the beam on the door handle. Rats? The idea made me shudder. I looked at Ozzie. He was standing vigilant at my side, silent now.

"Did you hear rats?" I whispered.

He glanced up at me and then back at the garage door.

I leaned over to unfasten his leash. "Okay," I said reluctantly. "You heard Mr. Decker. Chase 'em out of there." I leaned down and looked at him. "Ready?" He wagged his tail and whined. I took that for a yes.

I paused, my mind conjuring up a vision of bloated gray rats swarming under the hood of my car. Grasping the garage-door handle, I took a deep breath. Remembering my self-defense class, I closed my eyes and tried to focus my energies. It didn't work. I yanked up hard and leaped backward to avoid the rat stampede, turning my head away.

But there was no stampede. Or any noise at all. When I turned my head back, Ozzie hadn't moved. He was still at attention, facing the garage. The door had slid up halfway, about chest high. Cautiously, I stepped forward, stopping at the entrance. With my left hand I pushed the door up while I used the other to sweep the flashlight beam around inside.

At first I thought they were diamonds. Sparkling little gems, thousands of them, scattered on the garage floor, glittering in the flashlight beam.

And then I realized what they were.

"Oh, no."

I raised the beam. The rear window of my car was gone. So were the side windows. I stepped into the garage. So was the windshield, except for a jagged piece in the lower right corner. Someone had smashed in every window in the car. The garage floor was strewn with broken glass, as was the inside of the car.

As I moved slowly around the car, the flashlight beam illuminated something white dangling from the inside rearview mirror. I approached warily. It appeared to be a small piece of paper taped to the mirror. I reached in through the empty passenger window and pulled it off.

It was a sheet of bond paper that had been neatly folded to the size of a playing card. I started to unfold it and realized with a chill that it was a sheet of my law office stationery. There was writing on it, directly below the letterhead for *The Law Offices of Rachel Gold*. When I had it unfolded halfway, I could read the entire message, which was handprinted in red ink in capital letters:

SEE HOW EASY IT WOULD BE?
THINK ABOUT IT.

The lower half of the stationery was still folded. Pressing my fingers around it, I could tell that there was something folded in there. My hands trembling, I unfolded it, and something dropped to the floor. Bending over, I aimed the flashlight beam at it.

I caught my breath. There, resting face up in the glittering pieces of broken glass, was my Missouri driver's license.

CHAPTER 16

Of all the sundry things I thought might be in progress in the topless showgirls' dressing room at Cherries on a Saturday afternoon, a baby shower was not one of them. But sure enough, I arrived to a chorus of oohs and aahs as an obviously pregnant Natasha Vladimitskov (a/k/a the Russian Minx) removed the gift wrap, opened the box, and held up an adorable one-piece outfit for a newborn.

"Senk you, Mawta," Natasha said with a warm smile.

"Aw, honey, y'all are welcome," Martha answered in a Southern drawl.

Natasha was seated on the floor with her back against the wall. A dozen non-topless women were seated in a semicircle on the floor facing her. There was a small pile of gifts in front of her, a larger pile of used wrapping paper to the side. Jo-Jo Black was next to her with a notepad and a pen. She looked at the newborn outfit and jotted something down.

"Who was that from?" Jo-Jo asked, apparently keeping the list for Natasha's thank-you notes.

Natasha pointed. "Mawta."

Jo-Jo poked her tongue out as she wrote down the name.

I smiled and shook my head. Benny would never believe this. An hour inside the dressing room at Cherries ranked high on his fantasy Top Ten, right up there with his two perennial favorites: a vigorous game of topless water volleyball at the Playboy Mansion and a weekend on a choke chain as the love slave of rock singer Joan Jett.

Well, this particular dressing-room scene had to be as far from Benny's fantasyland as one could imagine. The Cherries showgirls were wearing jeans or sweatpants, baggy shirts or oversized sweatshirts. There wasn't a bare patch of skin below the neck in sight anywhere. There were no high heels. Most had on sneakers. Their hair was pulled back, and I saw little sign of makeup and even less of lipstick. Instead of sultry strippers, these women looked like factory girls on a coffee break or attendees at an Ace Hardware seminar on furniture refinishing. Jo-Jo Black fit right in. With her faded Bud Light sweatshirt, her hair pulled back beneath a green scarf, and a cigarette dangling from her lips, she could have passed for the cashier at a gas-station minimart.

The whole scene was such a contrast to my garage nightmare that it seemed surreal. Of course, part of the altered reality could have been due to my lack of sleep. I'd been up ever since Ozzie first woke me in the middle of the night, and the adrenaline buzz had long since worn off. The University City police were there until close to six in the morning. Then I had to go with St. Louis police to my office to let them inspect it for signs of entry, especially forced entry. They found none at my office, and the University City police found none at my home or my garage.

Although we could narrow the intruder's window of opportunity to sometime between 10:50 p.m. (when I returned in my car from coffee with Benny) and 2:53 a.m.

(when Ozzie woke me up), and probably very close to
the latter, I couldn't help the police narrow the other crucial time, namely, when my driver's license had been
stolen from the wallet in my purse. It could have been
that night, but it could have been a week ago, or even a
month. I simply could not remember the last time I had
looked at it. Nevertheless, the handwritten warning had
been delivered by someone who wanted to impress me
with the ease with which he could invade my personal
space and wreak havoc.

I was impressed.

And rattled.

Enough to place an order for a home security system,
which the company promised to install sometime during
the coming week.

Meanwhile, with a weekend ahead of me and a full
tank of gas in the insurance company's loaner car, I
wanted to wrap up some of the loose ends and then
dump the whole mess into Jonathan Wolf's lap. Which is
why I was standing in the back of the topless showgirls'
dressing room at Cherries at two o'clock on this blustery
Saturday afternoon.

I watched Natasha open the rest of her gifts. As she
did, a few of the women drifted away from the circle to
start applying their stage makeup. I asked one of them, a
zaftig redhead with breasts the size and shape of honey-
dews, about the guest of honor. She told me that Natasha
and her husband, Aleksey, had emigrated to America two
years ago. Natasha had been a schoolteacher in Moscow,
and her husband a chemical engineer. Now he worked
on the minivan line at the Chrysler plant in Fenton. This
would be their first child.

When the baby shower ended, Natasha gathered up
her gifts and gave everyone a tearful hug good-bye.
As she left and the other women headed toward their
makeup tables, I approached Jo-Jo.

"Where can we talk?" I asked.

She shook her head. "I told you before it'd be a waste of time. There isn't like really a whole lot to talk about. I just don't know much."

"Give me five minutes," I said.

She looked around and gave me a weary sigh. "Okay, five minutes." She gestured toward a red door marked EXIT. "Out back, I guess."

We stepped outside into a fenced-off portion of the blacktop. There were several cars and pickup trucks parked inside the fence, and a uniformed security guard was posted at the gate. Attached to the fence were sheets of tarpaulin that screened the enclosed area from view. A brisk wind snapped the canvas.

I put my hands in my coat pockets. "What is this area?"

She looked around distractedly. "It's for the girls. It's where we park. You know, so we don't like get hassled or stuff on the way in. Look, I gotta start getting ready soon. I'm on at like three. What do you want?"

"Tell me what you know about Sally Wade and Junior."

She looked away and crossed her arms over her chest. "Nothing."

"Come on, Jo-Jo."

"He found clients for her, I guess."

"Is that all?"

She glanced over at me and then stared at the fence. "I think he like sometimes served subpoenas, you know, things like that."

"What do you mean, 'things like that'?"

She shook her head, tapping her foot. "Things. Like, stuff. I don't know exactly. Junior, he don't, like, tell me much about his work."

"What *did* he tell you about his work?"

"Just what I said."

"Why did he dislike Sally?"

She scowled. "Jesus, lady, how am I supposed to know?"

"What did he tell you?"

"He thought she was like screwing him out of money."

"How much money?"

She shrugged.

"Hundreds?" I asked. "Thousands?"

She rolled her eyes. "What*ever*."

"Which?"

She shook her head and waved her hands. "Like I'm supposed to know?"

"How well did you know Sally?"

She looked at me warily. "What do you mean?"

"Come on, Jo-Jo. Level with me."

She paused, uncertain, and then shook her head. "I knew what she looked like, and that's all you're getting out of me."

"What else did you know about her?"

She shook her head. "No way. That's all I'm saying. I know about you lawyers and I'm just not gonna talk no more." She crossed her arms over her chest.

Whatever she knew, she was obviously determined not to tell me anything. I wouldn't get any further information from her today except by indirection. There was one subject on which she ought to be a fairly reliable source of information. I decided to give it a shot, even if it meant a little trickery.

"Do you think Sally was having an affair with Junior?" I asked.

She burst into laughter. "Are you crazy?" She shook her head in disbelief. "No way, lady. He couldn't stand that bitch."

"Are you sure?"

She gave me an incredulous stare. "Yes," she said, nodding her head emphatically, "I'm like totally sure."

I frowned. "Well, okay," I said reluctantly, letting my voice trail off.

"Why?"

I shrugged. "Oh, it's probably nothing."

"Just tell me."

I looked at her carefully, as if considering whether to tell her. "Well, they found a red condom at the scene of the murder. I just wondered whether Junior used red condoms."

She laughed. "No way. He won't touch a condom. He hates them."

"He told you that?"

She blushed and then giggled. "He says it's like doing it in a sock. He only rides bareback. That's what he calls it."

I gave her a concerned look. "But aren't you afraid of getting pregnant?"

She shook her head. "He had one of them operations."

"You mean a vasectomy?"

"Yep." Her smile faded, and she crossed her arms. "Look, you gotta go, okay?"

I took one of my cards out of my purse. "Here," I said, holding it out to her.

She kept her arms crossed and made no move to take the card.

"Put it on your dressing table, Jo-Jo, or hide it in your mattress. That way, if you ever should feel like telling me more, you'll have my number. Take it."

She glanced down at the card. "What*ever*," she said, snatching the card and crossing her arms again. "But I'm not calling. No way." She spun toward the door and marched inside.

I followed her in. Now the place was getting closer to Benny's fantasyland. A big blonde in a gold-spangled G-string and four-inch red pumps sashayed past me. She was adjusting a halter top around a pair of nominees for the Academy Award for Best Achievement in Special Effects. Nearby, a statuesque black woman with long muscular legs was standing sideways to the mirror, her hands on her knees, as she ground her hips in time to the music in her earphones and studied her reflection. She was wearing white stockings, a white garter belt, white string bikinis, white pumps, and white breast tassels.

There was a large mirror near the front door. As I moved toward the door, I observed Jo-Jo in the reflection. When she reached her dressing table she opened the drawer and dropped the card in. As she looked in her mirror, our eyes met in the double reflection. She immediately turned toward the woman seated next to her and started an overly animated conversation.

I paused at the door for a moment and then walked out.

"You're sure?"

Neville McBride frowned as he stared at the photograph of Jo-Jo Black. "I suppose there is always room for doubt, but I do not believe that this woman is Tammy."

It was later that Saturday afternoon, and Neville McBride and I were at my kitchen table. I'd arranged this meeting in a phone call to Jonathan Wolf yesterday afternoon, before all the craziness with my garage.

Neville had been waiting for me when I returned from my trip across the Mississippi River to Cherries. He was on my front porch chatting with a uniformed security guard from St. Louis Shield Security. I was fifty minutes late for our appointment, and, as I soon learned, he'd gotten quite a bit accomplished in that time. Apparently, when he had arrived there had been a squad car and an unmarked car in my driveway. From the police he learned what had happened in my garage the night before. Like many powerful attorneys, he felt most comfortable in the role of mover and shaker. Well, he did some moving and shaking in those fifty minutes. First, he tried to reach Jonathan Wolf, but this was Saturday, the Jewish Sabbath, and Jonathan observed it strictly, which meant, among other things, that all the telephones in his house were disconnected. Unable to reach Jonathan, Neville next called the company that had installed his own security system, only to learn that I had already placed an order with them that morning. Annoyed that they had been unable or unwilling to install it that very day, he insisted that they do it on Sunday. He also requested an upgrade (at his expense) of the system I had ordered, and insisted that they post a security guard at the house until it was installed and fully operational.

I was genuinely touched by Neville's concern and efforts on my behalf. Touched enough to give him a hug and make him a fresh pot of coffee before getting down to the tough questions I felt I had a duty to ask him. I told him with a wink that he was certainly the most considerate accused murderer I had ever dealt with. He grunted a thanks.

Like many older corporate attorneys, Neville McBride apparently had only two sets of clothing: a closet of dull business suits, starched white shirts, and boring power ties for the office, and a collection of clown outfits for the golf course. He was wearing the latter today: a long-sleeved polo shirt that was the same Day-Glo orange as a highway hazard cone, a pair of multicolored slacks that bordered on psychedelic, and the mandatory white patent-leather shoes. I continue to marvel at the attire voluntarily worn on the golf course by the St. Louis ruling class, and find it difficult to believe that business deals are actually cut in those preposterous costumes. I mean, would you buy a used subsidiary from a man wearing pants with the same pattern as the Easter gift wrap on clearance last week at Kmart?

Neville shook his head and handed back Jo-Jo's publicity photo. "As I already explained to Jonathan, Tammy had red hair. This gal doesn't."

"You're sure about the hair color? Was she a natural redhead?"

Neville blushed and shifted in his seat. "Jonathan asked me that as well. I don't know. She, uh, preferred the lights out."

"And you never saw her in the shower? Or the bathroom?"

He coughed. "No. She wasn't that way. Some are, of course. But no, not her."

"So she could have been a brunette?"

He shrugged awkwardly. "I suppose. Or a blonde—or bald, for Christ's sake." He caught himself. "Excuse me. Hair color? No, I am afraid I do not know."

I scribbled notes on my pad. "She knew your name?"

"Of course. Why wouldn't she?"

"According to the police report, you didn't always give women your real name."

That made him sit back. "That was not the case with this woman," he said, sounding miffed. He crossed his arms over his chest. "I was separated at the time. Sally had already filed the divorce papers. I saw no need to disguise my identity."

"Did Tammy know what you did for a living?"

He frowned in thought. "She knew I was an attorney with a firm downtown. I did tell her that much."

I glanced at my notes from our prior interview. "You saw her three times?"

He nodded.

"The first night you went to dinner and then back to your place, right?"

"Yes."

"The other two nights she came directly to your place from the airport. Or at least she said she was coming there directly from the airport, right?"

"Correct."

I looked at him for a moment, trying to think of an easy way to do this. I couldn't think of a way. "How many times did the two of you have sex?"

He grunted. "Sweet Jesus."

I waited. It was an old cross-examination trick: wait long enough and most witnesses feel compelled to fill the silence.

"Four times," he finally said.

"Two times in one night?"

He thrust his chin forward. "As a matter of fact, yes."

I fought an urge to applaud. *Beware the fragile male ego.* "That was the first night?"

He nodded.

"And once on each of the other nights?"

He nodded again.

"Did you talk about work with her?"

He paused, trying to remember. "Not much."

"About Sally?"

"I told her I was going through a divorce. I don't recall telling her from whom."

I nodded. "Did she talk about her job?"

"Only vaguely." He made a dismissive gesture. "Neither one of us talked much about our occupations. That was part of the understanding."

"What *did* you talk about?"

He thought it over. "I can't remember."

"Sports?"

He shook his head.

"Politics?"

"No."

"Movies? Art? Literature?"

"Not that I recall."

"Sex?"

He cleared his throat. "What do you mean?"

I shrugged. "It's about all that's left, Neville. You

were with her three times. You didn't talk much about work or Sally. You didn't talk about sports or politics or movies or the rest. The only thing you had in common was sex. Did she ever talk about it?"

He cleared his throat again. "Once."

"When?"

"The second time we were together."

"Tell me about the conversation."

He stood up, touching his collar. "Good God, this is damned uncomfortable."

"So is death row, Neville."

I waited patiently. Eventually, he sat back down and cleared his throat. "She wanted to know about my other experiences. She wanted to know whether I had ever done any of that, uh, kinky stuff. She said it turned her on."

"What did you tell her?"

"I told her about some of my, uh, my experiences."

"Did you tell her about Sally?"

He drew himself up. "Not by name," he said in an offended tone.

I nodded. "Did you show her your pictures?"

He waved his hand distractedly, obviously ill at ease with the entire subject. "I may have. I don't recall. I can assure you that it wasn't an extended conversation."

"Did you do anything kinky with Tammy?"

"Of course not."

"You're positive?"

"Absolutely. Good God, is this line of inquiry really necessary?"

"Yes."

He cleared his throat. "We engaged in standard intercourse. Missionary position only."

"Did she ever spend the night?"

"No. She usually left shortly after we, uh, after we had intercourse."

"Did you use a condom?" I asked.

He coughed again. "Of course."

"Whose?"

He looked at me, perplexed. "Whose?"

"Yours or hers?" I said. "Did you supply them or did she?"

He tilted his head back, trying to remember. "Hers."

"You're sure?"

He reddened. "Yes."

"Tell me about it."

"What?"

"You just blushed. Tell me."

"I cannot believe this." He stood up and walked to the other side of the room, shaking his head. "Have you ever heard of privacy?"

"I'm afraid you've lost yours, Neville. That's what happens in murder cases. Tell me about the condoms."

He paced back and forth, shaking his head and grumbling to himself. Eventually, he stopped by the counter and lifted the saltshaker, as if to examine it. "She had a special type," he said, inspecting the shaker. "Ribbed or some sort of texture or some damn thing. She made a game out of it."

"What do you mean?"

"Sweet Jesus." He exhaled in exasperation and shook his head. "She, uh, she said she liked to put it on. When we were done, she took it off."

"What did she do with it then?"

He looked at me as if I had lost my mind. "Are you serious?"

I nodded.

He shook his head in disbelief. "I have no earthly idea what she did with the damn things."

"It's important, Neville. Try to remember. What did she do with them? Toss them in the trash can? Flush them down the toilet? Drop them on the rug?"

"I'm telling you, I have no idea."

"Bear with me, Neville. Think hard. It wasn't that long ago."

"I'm telling you, I don't recall." He started pacing around the room again, his hands in his pockets, jangling his change. "Now can we please change the subject?"

CHAPTER 17

Vincent Contini crossed his arms over his chest and shook his head firmly. "Never, Rachel. I would view it as a betrayal of my relationship with my ladies."

It was Sunday afternoon, and Vincent and I were in my office going over a few matters in preparation for the libel trial, which was just four days off. Although I don't usually work Sundays, it was a day more convenient for Vincent, and this particular Sunday I didn't mind getting out of my house, which was teeming with employees from St. Louis Shield Security, who appeared to be installing a security system for a CIA safe house.

Ozzie and I had gone for a jog through Forest Park and dropped by Basically Bagels for a snack—an onion bagel with cream cheese and a large coffee for me, a pumpernickel bagel and a small bowl of water for him. Then we drove over to my office, where Ozzie promptly collapsed on the rug with a sigh and fell asleep, his paws over his ears.

"But, Vincent," I assured him, "I can tell these women that I got their names off a guest list for the event. They'll never know my real source."

"But I would know, Rachel. A secret betrayal is no less a sin than a public one."

I leaned back in my chair and silently groaned. Ten thousand retailers in St. Louis, and I end up representing the Sir Thomas More of designer dresses. "It's hardly a sin," I said, trying to hide my frustration. "Three of your customers bought dresses for the Children's Hospital benefit. You said yourself that all three are loyal patrons of yours. If one of them remembers what Cissy Thompson was wearing that night, I'm sure she'd be delighted to help you by testifying at trial."

Another adamant shake of the head. "Out of the question. This unpleasant dispute is entirely my problem, Rachel. I would never ask one of my darlings to sully her hands in a coarse piece of litigation on my behalf. Never."

He reached into the breast pocket of his elegant suit and removed the white handkerchief. He patted it against his forehead and replaced it, making sure to position it perfectly in the pocket. Unlike Neville McBride, Vincent Contini's weekend attire was no different from his outfits for the week. He was in a navy pinstripe double-breasted suit, white shirt, gold-and-gray striped tie, and black Italian shoes buffed to a brilliant shine. We made quite a Sunday contrast, with me in my St. Louis Browns baseball cap (to keep my curly hair out of my face as I jogged), an oversized gray *Jane Austen Rules!* sweatshirt, black jogging tights, and Nikes.

"Vincent," I said patiently, "Cissy Thompson has sued you for millions of dollars. She will swear that she never wore that dress."

"But she's a liar."

I sighed. "Nevertheless, we still have to prove it's a lie. Otherwise, she's entitled to a judgment in her favor."

He gave me a serene smile. "Ah, but that cannot possibly happen."

"Oh? And why not?"

He made a sweeping gesture with his hands. "Because, my dear Rachel, you will not allow it to happen."

I smiled in resignation. "Vincent, my name is Rachel Gold, not Perry Mason. Remember, he had Erle Stanley Gardner to solve his cases for him. I'm limited to admissible evidence, and, frankly, Vincent, we could use some more."

"But, Rachel, I thought that you and your assistant found some. What about that fellow from the newspaper—the chap who took all of the photographs of the event?"

I shook my head. "It doesn't look great. Jacki went through the one roll he developed the day after the event. Cissy isn't in any of the pictures."

He grimaced. "Ah, a pity."

"He thinks there may be a few more pictures from the event on another roll he hasn't developed yet. He promised to do it over the weekend."

Vincent nodded with satisfaction. "There. You see?"

"Don't get your hopes up." I leaned back and sighed. "I'm not optimistic."

"Oh, but you should be." He paused and gave me a warm, paternal smile. "You are such a lovely young lady, Rachel, and so intelligent. God smiles down upon you, my dear. I have great confidence in you. I am certain you will find us our evidence. And if not, well"—he paused and gave me a long-suffering shrug—"such is the way of the world. But," he said solemnly, placing his hand over his heart, "you must not chide me for refusing to allow any of my darling ladies to get dragged into this case."

I rested my chin on my fist and smiled at my courtly white-haired client. "I would never chide you, Vincent."

He leaned over and patted my hand. "I promise to be a good witness. It will be her word against mine. That may be the best we can do. We will pray that justice prevails."

I said nothing. My client was in a sentimental mood, and I saw no reason to shake him out of it. Praying that justice will prevail is a good recipe for losing. Moreover, as any decent lawyer will tell you, justice isn't usually part of the calculus, and praying is beside the point. The goal is to win for your client, and your job as attorney is to make that happen.

This was Sunday. I still had four days to make it happen.

Benny pushed back from my kitchen table and stood up. He walked to the doorway to the living room. From there, the front yard and the street were visible through the window.

"So he's gone?" he asked.

"Who?" Amy Chickering asked. She stood up to see where he was looking.

Benny said, "The security guard. Rachel had one here overnight and then all day today while they installed the security system."

It was Sunday evening, and Benny and Amy seemed to be hitting it off well on their first date. Tonight I was in the role of matchmaker. Benny's on-again-off-again relationship with my best friend from Harvard Law School, Flo Shenker of Washington, D.C., was off again, which meant he was on the prowl for female companionship. With his memories of Amy's television commercials still vivid, he had begged me to fix him up.

I invited them both to drop by Sunday night, ostensibly to discuss issues related to Sally's estate. Benny "spontaneously" suggested that we have dinner, and Amy agreed. He had arrived an hour ago with enough barbecue take-out and Ben & Jerry's ice cream to feed an army.

Benny came back to the kitchen and peered into the take-out carton that had contained the rib tips. "Ah, excellent," he said, lifting it up. "Still some left." He started to dump the contents onto his plate, but paused to look at us. "Anyone care for a tip?"

I shook my head.

"You're still hungry?" Amy asked in astonishment.

"Benny's always still hungry," I said.

"And with excellent reason," he said as he dumped the contents onto his plate. "You ladies have no conception of the sheer volume of protein and complex carbohydrates required to maintain my sexual prowess at world-class performance levels."

I glanced over at Amy with a skeptical expression. She giggled.

"Another beer, you awesome stud muffin?" I asked him.

He nodded, his mouth full. I turned to Amy. She shook her head. I went over to the fridge and took out two bottles of Sam Adams, one for Benny and one for me. Benny was, I had to admit, an acquired taste. The trick was to find a woman willing to stick around long enough to acquire it. Amy had lasted more than an hour so far, and she still seemed in an acquisition mode.

Later, while they were helping me clean up the kitchen, Benny asked, "You still going to Chicago tomorrow?"

I nodded.

"What's in Chicago?" Amy asked.

"The parent company of Douglas Beef," I explained. "I'm going to see whether their numbers back Brady Kane's story."

"What's his story?" Amy asked.

"He told me the purpose of all of those phone calls with Sally Wade was to work out settlements of workers' comp claims. He says he was able to settle cases cheaper by doing an end run around the attorneys. I'm going to do an end run on him and see what they have at the corporate headquarters."

"You don't believe him, eh?" she asked.

I shook my head. "There's something else going on. That's why I had you put together all that information Friday. We'll see how it compares with the information in Chicago."

CHAPTER 18

Betsy Dempsey joined Abbott & Windsor three years after I did, and from the day we met I knew that she had made a profound mistake. She was intelligent, meticulous, and cautious. She could spot potential issues that her superiors missed and propose solutions that worked. She was modest and considerate and a little bashful. She baked a scrumptious carrot cake for my birthday and selected an adorable jumper for her secretary's new baby. She was a little frumpy and didn't play on the firm's coed softball team and didn't curse and preferred to leave the litigation department's happy hours early to get home to her husband, who was in his last year of divinity school at the University of Chicago. She was, in short, completely miscast as a litigation associate at Abbott & Windsor—a macho subculture where even the women strutted and bragged about "kicking butt."

I came of age as a lawyer within that subculture. Like our counterparts at the other powerhouse Chicago firms, we at A&W knew we had more smarts and wile and skills and balls than our opponents. We were the Green Berets, the SWAT teams of the law—gathering each morning in tribal counsels in our conference rooms high above the battlefields, reviewing the day's combat strategies before boarding our paratrooper planes (the elevators) for the forty-floor drop into the war zone. Being a woman meant that you had to be tougher than the guys, or at least pretend to be.

Not surprisingly, the casualty rate in litigation departments is high, especially among women attorneys, many of whom chose to flee private practice entirely for the duller but sheltered life of an in-house counsel. Betsy Dempsey had been one of the casualties. Fortunately for me, her safe harbor was Bennett Industries, Inc., an international conglomerate whose myriad holdings included Douglas Beef Processors and its five slaughterhouses. I had called her last Friday after my meeting with Brady Kane. She sounded thrilled to hear from me, and said she'd be happy to meet on Monday morning.

It was now Monday morning, and I was in the heart of the Chicago Loop, up on the sixty-third floor of the Bennett Industries Tower, standing in the office of assistant trademark attorney Elizabeth R. Dempsey. Although her office was tiny, it was along the south wall and featured a spectacular view of the Chicago Board of Trade below and, farther off, the Field Museum, Soldier Field, and the Shedd Aquarium.

"Oh, my," I said, picking up the framed photograph on her desk. "Are these your boys?"

Betsy beamed. "Roger is four, Peter is two."

"They're absolutely adorable, Betsy." I felt a slight pang of envy. I looked up from the picture and smiled at her. "And you look great."

"Ugh," she said, her broad face reddening. "I'm fatter than ever, and I'm already getting gray hairs. Even worse, I'm going to flunk out of Weight Watchers for the third time. But look at you, Rachel." She put her hands on her broad hips and smiled, shaking her head in admiration. "I always thought that you were the prettiest lawyer in Chicago. All of us used to envy you so. And now you're even more beautiful. You look wonderful, Rachel."

It was my turn to blush.

Her secretary brought us coffee. We talked some about life as an in-house counsel at Bennett Industries (good hours, decent benefits, so-so work, nasty office politics) and reminisced about names and events from our Abbott & Windsor days. It didn't take long to exhaust the conversational topics for two people who shared almost nothing in common beyond their brief time together at the same law firm.

Betsy steepled her fingers under her chin and gazed at me earnestly. "Tell me how I can help."

"I need to look at some numbers on the East St. Louis slaughterhouse, and I probably need to talk to the people up here who ought to know about those numbers."

"What kind of numbers?"

I explained what I had learned about Sally Wade's communications with Brady Kane, the plant manager.

Betsy frowned. "She actually dealt with him direct?"

I nodded. "If Brady Kane is telling the truth, then the comparative settlement numbers ought to show it. Was East St. Louis settling workers' comp cases on the average for less money than your other slaughterhouses? The person up here in charge of the Douglas Beef workers' comp claims ought to know those numbers."

She gave me a guarded look. "Okay," she finally said.

I soon understood the reason for her strange expression.

All Douglas Beef workers' comp claims fell within the exclusive jurisdiction of Lamar Hundra. According to the nameplate on his desk, he was Assistant Risk Manager, North American Operations—all three hundred well-marbled pounds of him. Lamar had a massive bald head, hooded eyes, and a thick, unkempt mustache. There were moist red blotches along the bottom of his mustache which I initially mistook for blood until he tilted a Dominick's bakery bag toward me and asked, "Would you care for one?"

"Uh, no, thanks."

He reached a meaty paw into the bag, pulled out a big jelly doughnut, and held it at arm's length, as if admiring a work of art. "Raspberry," he sighed. "I'm addicted to the damn things."

He closed his eyes and opened his mouth, revealing an uneven set of teeth and several gold crowns. I watched in silence as he proceeded to shove nearly half of the doughnut into his mouth—a maneuver that added an additional smudge of red and smear of glaze to his vile mustache.

Although I had spent countless hours and days around a man with powerful hungers and an ample waistline, Benny Goldberg in no way resembled Lamar Hundra. In Benny, there was a robust, exuberant quality to his prodigious appetites; by contrast, Lamar reminded me of a bloated, lethargic hog at the trough. Benny was my Falstaff—stout, merry, and ribald. Lamar Hundra was just plain gross.

When Lamar and I initially shook hands, I had assumed that he was cursed with a clammy handshake; but now, fifteen minutes later, my hand was still moist, which was making me think that what I had assumed was perspiration was in fact doughnut grease. I watched in disgust as he chewed in bliss.

"I'm getting better," he said with a spark that quickly drowned in those torpid eyes. "Six weeks ago I cut my daily intake from a dozen of these babies to just six."

He took another gurgling chug from his sixteen-ounce bottle of Diet Coke, screwed the top back on, and stifled a rumbling, subterranean belch. There were five empty Diet Coke bottles on his credenza next to his computer, along with several crumpled Butterfingers wrappers. From where I sat, the keyboard looked filthy.

"Okay, let's see," he said, shuffling through what looked like computer printouts. "Damn," he grunted, looking at his index finger.

"What's wrong?"

He put it in his mouth. For one creepy moment I thought he was going to bite it off. "Paper cut," he said, holding it up. A thin line of red was visible. I wouldn't have been surprised to see gravy oozing out.

He was so repulsive that he had to be very good at what he did to be still employed at Bennett Industries. At least that's what I hoped.

Those hopes remained unfulfilled two hours later. Amy Chickering, under my instructions, had prepared a representative sampling of Douglas Beef workers' comp cases over the past three years. We designed it to include what we hoped was a statistically significant number of claims in each of several areas, ranging from carpal tunnel syndromes to amputated fingers to back problems. My purpose in coming to Chicago was to see whether a comparison of those numbers to settlements of similar claims at the other slaughterhouses supported Brady Kane's contention that his back-channel dealings with Sally had enabled him to save the company money. Unfortunately, Lamar Hundra's organizational system, partly computerized and partly manual, made that type of comparative analysis difficult and imprecise, leaving us with no clear pattern one way or the other.

At my request, Amy had also pulled closing statements for about two dozen settled claims. If there was a kickback scheme involving Brady Kane (or anyone else at the plant, for that matter), I thought I might find it by comparing the actual settlement check issued by the company to the amount shown on the closing statement Sally gave to her client. For example, she could have settled a case for ten thousand dollars with Brady Kane but told her client that the case settled for nine thousand. Then when the ten-thousand-dollar check arrived, she could deposit it, send Brady Kane a grand, and prepare a client closing statement showing a nine-thousand-dollar settlement.

To say the least, Lamar Hundra was not intrigued by the kickback theory. After much wheedling by me and grumbling by him, he finally heaved his bulk out of the chair and plodded down to the accounting department to locate the records for the settlement checks. Unfortunately—or fortunately, I couldn't tell which anymore—the closing statements Sally gave to her clients matched the company's check records. In other words, if Sally's closing statement showed that the claim had been settled for ten thousand dollars, so did the company's records. Every time.

I peered out the window. "Rats," I sighed, shaking my head.

"Pardon?"

I turned to the elderly woman in the seat next to me. "I'm sorry." I gave her a tired smile. "Just talking to myself."

"That's quite all right, dear."

I turned toward the window and stared into the darkness. We were, according to our captain, twenty-seven thousand feet in the air heading south from Chicago to St. Louis. I was sipping a glass of apple juice and thinking that I should have ordered a double Jack Daniel's on the rocks.

My head was spinning. For the past week I'd been talking to people and following leads and sorting through evidence, but I couldn't tell whether I was getting any closer or just moving in ever-widening circles. The only tangible thing I could point to was my state-of-the-art home security system, and I wasn't even certain that I could link that to my investigation. After all, the warning note taped to the rearview mirror hadn't referenced anything specific to Sally Wade. Moreover, it was clear from the police detective's questions that when lawyers receive anonymous threats, the first place to look is their divorce cases. Unfortunately, there were plenty of those. During my first year in St. Louis I had, through an odd series of events, represented a succession of wealthy women in bitter contested divorces. When it comes to divorces, hell hath no fury like a man burned, and I'd burned a few.

The plane touched down at 5:40 p.m. On my way out of the airport, I stopped at a pay phone to pick up my voice-mail messages. There were fifteen of them, mostly routine, except for message number eleven:

"Rachel, this is Jonathan Wolf. It's four-fifteen. I'll be here until about six. If you can't reach me by then, call first thing in the morning. Neville received a telephone call from Tammy."

I dialed his number. His secretary told me he was in conference. I asked her to interrupt. He came on a moment later.

"We need to talk, Rachel, but I can't right now. How about in forty-five minutes? I can meet you somewhere for a drink on your way home."

"That's fine."

"You're at the airport. I'm downtown."

"How about the Ritz?" I said. I needed to go by there anyway to talk to someone about the Children's Hospital function, and with the libel trial just three days off, the sooner I did that the better.

"Six-thirty?" he asked.

"I'll see you there, Jonathan."

CHAPTER 19

I thought it over. "I have a better idea."

Jonathan Wolf took a sip of his Bass ale and reached for a handful of roasted almonds. "Let's hear it."

We were seated in a booth in a quiet corner of the bar at the Ritz-Carlton. According to Jonathan, Tammy had called Neville McBride at his office earlier that afternoon to tell him that she'd heard about the murder charge. She wanted to see how he was doing and to let him know that he was in her prayers. It had been a brief call—five minutes tops—and she hung up before Neville was able to find out how to contact her. She had, however, promised to call him again. Jonathan's plan was to have Neville put Tammy in contact with him next time she called.

I took a sip of my sauvignon blanc. "Give her my name," I said. "Have Tammy call me."

He scratched his beard pensively. "I don't know."

"She might be more willing to talk to another woman," I explained.

"Perhaps."

"It's worth a try."

Jonathan's scowl deepened.

"What?" I said.

He shook his head. "After what happened the other night, I'm reluctant to get you more enmeshed in this case."

I shrugged nonchalantly, although I was touched by this unexpected bit of chivalry. "I can't possibly be more enmeshed than I am already, and you've had very little to do with that. After all, I was here first. I was the one who filed Sally's lawsuit."

I could see he was resisting the idea.

"Jonathan, all I'm suggesting is that we give Tammy a choice. If she's willing to contact you, terrific. I'd be delighted to stay out of this loop. But if she won't call you, maybe she'll call me. That way you'll still have a shot at finding out what she knows."

Jonathan stared at the amber ale in his British pint glass. "Assuming she actually calls him again."

"She told him she was worried about him," I said. "That makes me think she'll contact him again. And if she does, as skittish as she sounds, she may not want to deal with you."

He looked at me with a frown.

I gave him a sly wink. "Trust me," I said. "She might find a woman a little less intimidating than an arrogant, pushy, macho defense attorney."

That coaxed a reluctant smile out of him. It was, in fact, a lovely smile, made all the more appealing by those bright green eyes. With that beard and those eyes and the yarmulke, he could have been Joshua preparing for the Battle of Jericho.

"Anyway," I continued, trying to regroup my thoughts, "it would make sense for Neville to refer her to me. I represented his ex-wife, and I'm handling her estate. Thus I'm someone who's naturally interested in talking to her, especially since she's his alibi witness for the night he allegedly assaulted Sally."

We talked it through again, and eventually Jonathan yielded. He said he would call Neville later that night and explain the game plan.

As we sipped our drinks, he brought me up to date on the criminal case. "The prosecution's case is frayed at the edges, but the center is holding. That's why Tammy may be crucial."

"What do you mean by 'frayed at the edges'?"

"Local homicide investigations are a lot sloppier than most people realize. This one is typical." He paused to finish off his ale. "At some point fairly early on, the police decided that Neville was the killer, and that's when their procedures slipped even more. For example, I think every door in the house was opened and closed by at least five different police officers during the first two days, and none of them wore gloves. As a result, there aren't many clear fingerprints, and Neville's are conspicuous by their absence."

I smiled. "Sounds like you're planning to peck them to death at trial."

Jonathan chuckled and nodded. "Welcome to the practice of criminal defense."

We paid the bill—or, rather, I did, over his protest. I promised to let him pay the next one, and actually found myself willing to entertain the prospect of having another drink with this man.

We walked together toward our cars, reaching mine first.

"Well," I said, a little awkwardly, "let me know how your conversation with Neville goes."

He nodded silently. As I started to get into my car, he said, "Are you an observant Jew?"

I paused, eyeing him uncertainly. "It depends on how you define 'observant.'" I had no idea where he was headed. "I light the candles on Friday night. I try to go to services on Saturday, although I don't always make it. I say kaddish for my father, I don't work on Rosh Hashanah, I fast on Yom Kippur."

He nodded silently.

"Why do you want to know?" I asked.

"My daughters and I enjoy having guests share a Sabbath dinner with us. Perhaps you'd care to join us one time."

"That might be nice," I said carefully.

He nodded gravely, checking his watch. "Very good," he said, suddenly formal. "We'll notify you promptly."

I gave him an amused smile. "Notify me?"

"If Tammy calls. Neville is under orders to contact me immediately, no matter what the hour. We'll notify you as well, so that you can be prepared." He paused. "Good night, Rachel."

"Good night, Jonathan."

I watched him stride away as I tried to sort through my feelings. *Okay, let's concede the dark and handsome part at the outset. Big deal. You're not in the market for a cover boy. As a matter of fact, you're not in the market, period. And don't forget, this guy is pushy and arrogant and domineering and hot-tempered and very intense, and who's looking for that in a package deal? Even worse, he's brilliant and knows he's brilliant. Then again, remember your date with stupid who didn't know it?*

I cautioned myself about the probable impact his two little daughters might be having on my feelings. I was just mushy enough to soft-focus his home life into a Jewish version of *Sleepless in Seattle*. Jonathan Wolf was no Tom Hanks, and, for all I knew, his daughters were spoiled little brats.

Still, I told myself, *you know you're curious to observe Mr. Tough Guy around his daughters, to watch the Lone Wolf with his two cubs. And, you've got to admit, on him that yarmulke works.*

Slow down, Rachel, I warned myself as I scooted in

behind the steering wheel and closed the car door. *One step at time, girl.*

Twenty minutes later, I pulled into a space across from my office. I was surprised to see a Shield Security car parked in front of my office building. I was even more surprised at the reason. According to the uniformed guard in the car, Neville McBride had placed an order for installation of a security system in my office as well, and at his expense. Until the actual installation plan was approved by me, Neville had instructed them to post a guard outside from dusk until dawn.

An office security system seemed a bit extreme, but I found myself warming to the concept almost immediately. I sensed that the hand of Jonathan Wolf was somewhere in the background of this transaction, and that was also a pleasant thought.

The guard got out of the car and walked me up the stairs to my office.

"Would you like to come in?" I asked the guard as I unlocked the door. "I can put on some coffee for you."

"No, thanks." He turned on the light switch and poked his head inside. He peered around for a moment and then stepped back into the hallway and gestured for me to go on. "I've got a thermos of coffee. The Blues are on the radio, and, frankly, I'm dying for a smoke. It's a nice night. I'll just sit out there in the car, sip my coffee, smoke a cigar, and listen to the game."

I smiled. "Except for the cigar part, that sounds pretty good."

He chuckled. "Well, I don't drink and I don't gamble and I don't carouse. Way I figure, a man needs at least one vice. I'll be out front."

There was a stack of phone messages on the message spike on my secretary's desk. I lifted them off and moved toward the window as I leafed through them. When I finished, I peered through the blinds. I could see the security guard in his car, the window rolled down, cigar smoke curling into the night sky.

Smiling, I walked around my secretary's desk and opened the door to my office. I flicked on the light and gasped. Seated on the edge of my desk with his arms crossed was Junior Dice.

"Where the fuck you been?" he said angrily. He was dressed in black: black turtleneck, black slacks, black boots, black gloves.

I took a step backward and glanced toward the door.

"Where you goin'?" he snapped.

He uncrossed his arms, revealing a black automatic pistol in his right hand. He aimed it at my forehead and smiled. "Don't even think about it, bitch."

CHAPTER 20

The gun made me flinch.

"Close that door," he ordered.

I did.

Junior Dice put his foot on the chair in front of the desk and slid it toward me. He pointed the gun at the chair. "Sit down."

I did. We were six feet apart.

I was staring at an entirely different Junior Dice from the affable charmer in the strip joint. This was the Junior Dice who had done hard time for manslaughter. He leveled the gun at my chest. "Who's the dude?" he said, tilting his head toward the window.

I looked over toward the window. The shades were closed. "He's a bodyguard." My voice was shaking.

"Bodyguard?" Junior chuckled. "The fuck's he guardin' now? His dick?"

I said nothing.

"Bodyguard? Shee-yit." Junior eyed my legs as he scratched his neck with the muzzle of the gun. "Your body ain't gonna need no guardin' tonight"—he pointed the gun at me—"so long as you don't pull no shit, you hear?"

I nodded.

"This won't take long," he said.

"What are you going to do?" I asked, struggling to control the tone of my voice.

"I'm gonna explain the facts of life to you, Miss Rachel Gold. You got that?"

I didn't, but I nodded anyway.

"Good." He walked around to the other side of the desk, careful to keep the gun trained on me the whole time. He reached down, picked up a pack of Kools, and shook out a cigarette. "Pull your chair closer," he said, the cigarette dangling from the corner of his mouth.

I noticed for the first time the smell of cigarette smoke in the room. As I moved my chair up to the desk, he lit his cigarette with a gold lighter, inhaled deeply, and exhaled two thick plumes of smoke through his nostrils.

"How did you get in?" I asked.

He snorted. "What you think you got here, girl? Fort Knox?"

I waited as he took another drag and flicked the ash into my favorite coffee mug. There was a liquid hiss as the ash dropped.

I flashed back to my self-defense class. Forget it. The gun in Junior Dice's hand won every time.

Junior Dice shook his head angrily. "Goddammit! Who you think she was? Mother Teresa?"

"Who?"

"Who? Sally Wade, that's who. How well you know her?"

"Not well." *Maybe never even met her,* I said to myself.

He gave me an incredulous stare. "Not well? Then what the fuck you doin' snoopin' around stirrin' up all this shit? Not well? Goddamn." He shook his head. "Let me tell you something, Miss Rachel Gold: I've chased cases for some bad motherfuckers in my time, but Sally Wade takes the cake. She was by far the nastiest one I ever dealt with. She fucked me out of my share three times. Three goddam times! The bitch was cold as ice. Talkin' about that poor husband of hers? Murder? Shee-yit. You talkin' justifiable homicide." He paused to take another drag on his cigarette. "You followin' me?"

"I'm not sure."

He exhaled twin streams of smoke through his nose and leaned forward. "Maybe it was her old man, and maybe it wasn't. Who the fuck cares? Point is, she had it comin'. The bitch pissed off plenty of folks. Maybe one of her clients. Maybe one of her chasers. Shee-yit, I felt like doin' her myself that last time. Point is, she's dead. Deal with it, woman. You ain't gonna bring her back, and all you doin' now is gettin' the wrong people riled up."

"Like who?"

"Like me, goddammit," he said, waving his gun menacingly. "This ain't none of your concern anymore. She's dead, her old man's got his own lawyer, and that makes you the odd man out. You out, so stay out." He dropped the cigarette butt into the coffee mug, shaking his head in disgust. "Man like me, I'm diversified. I got all kinds of things goin' down right now. My business associates like things nice and quiet. When things ain't nice and quiet, my associates get spooked, and when they get spooked they don't wanna do no business." He paused to light another cigarette. "I don't want no one spooked."

My anger was building in spite of my fear. *Here you are,* I told myself, *held hostage in your own office by this small-time cretin who's trying to bully you off the case.*

"You hear me?" he said.

I took a deep breath and exhaled slowly. "Yes, Junior. I hear you."

He stood up and came around to my side, the gun still in his hand. He bent down close enough so that I could smell the mixture of tobacco and alcohol on his breath.

"Now I ain't laid a hand on you tonight, girl, and I'm goin' peacefully, so you got no cause to go runnin' to Mr. J. Edgar Hoover out there. But let me tell you something, Miss Rachel Gold: you bother Jo-Jo one more time or you keep askin' people about me, and you gonna need a whole lot more protection than that sorry-ass rent-a-cop motherfucker sittin' out there earnin' minimum wage."

CHAPTER 21

Benny shook his head in disbelief. "Rachel, you must be nuts. Guy warns you not to fuck with him, so what's the first thing you do when he leaves? You fuck with him."

"I did not," I said irritably as I walked past him to get some more coffee. "I had him arrested."

"Oh, I see." He peered through the doorway at Jacki, who was seated at her computer terminal but listening to us. "I'm sure Junior Dice will appreciate that subtle distinction, don't you, Jacki? Rachel didn't fuck with him, she just threw his ass in jail."

It was close to noon. Benny had called around ten to see what was happening, and when I told him about last night he came right over.

I filled my coffee mug and turned to him. "Benny, the man broke into this office, threatened me with a gun, and scared me half to death. I count at least two crimes there. He deserves to be in jail."

"Right," he said in a sardonic tone. "I'm sure he's grateful to be given this opportunity to atone for his sins."

"You're missing the point," I said, shaking my head

with exasperation. I went back to my desk. "You can't let someone terrorize you in your office and then walk away scot-free."

"Rachel, you're the one missing the point. They may lock Junior up, but they're not going to throw away the key. What about when he gets out?"

I took a seat behind my desk and looked up at him. "Benny," I said patiently, "the guy is no fool. He's smart enough to know that he'd be the prime suspect if anything ever happened to me. Putting him in jail is like buying extra life insurance."

He stared at me, slowly shaking his head. "You're putting a lot of faith in that logic."

I sighed. "I'm putting even more faith in my getting out of this case."

Benny came over to the desk and took a seat. "What else do you have left to do?" he asked.

"I'm going to meet with Bruce Napoli's wife this afternoon."

Benny chuckled. "See if she's got any other tips for jazzing up a dull dinner party. What else?"

"I'm going by Sally Wade's place around seven tonight. Wanna come along?"

"What's there?"

"No idea. That's the point. I've never been there."

He thought it over. "That's where she was killed?"

I nodded.

He shrugged. "Sure. Why so late?"

"No other time. I've got Bruce Napoli's wife at two o'clock, a pretrial conference at four, my self-defense class at five-thirty. As a matter of fact," I said, checking my watch, "I'm kicking you out now. I've got to squeeze in some trial preparation. That crazy libel case starts on Thursday."

I met Patty Napoli in the Tea Room at the Junior League. She played bridge there every Tuesday, and, like all such Junior League bridge games, hers followed a rigid schedule: first hand dealt at 11:30 a.m., drink orders placed at 11:45 a.m., lunch orders at 12:10 p.m., lunch served at an adjacent table at 12:30 p.m. When lunch arrives, the ladies stop play, place their hands facedown on the table, and move to the other table. They nibble at their tuna salads and sip their tomato soups until 1:15 p.m., when they return to the card table and resume play until precisely 2:00 p.m.

I timed my Tea Room arrival for 2:00 p.m., and as I walked in I could see various bridge games starting to break up. I tried to imagine what it would be like to have the time to play bridge with your friends for two and a half hours in the middle of the day in the middle of the week. Actually, it sounded delightful.

The Tea Room kitchen was closed, but I spotted a pot of coffee on a hot plate along a side wall. Pouring myself a cup, I scanned the tables. I recognized Patty from her photo and waved. She excused herself and came over.

"I appreciate your meeting with me," I told her.

"You are quite welcome," she said, somewhat primly. She glanced at her watch. "We have a few minutes before my afternoon car pools start."

"Which ones are today?" I asked, hoping to loosen her up with a familiar, nonthreatening topic.

"Well, there's school first, of course. And then after-school activities. Melissa has Brownies today, and that will be at my house. Brucie has soccer practice until five, and then his violin lesson."

I smiled. "You need a chauffeur's license."

Two women came over to our table. One was plump and heavily made up; the other was wafer-thin and deeply tanned, with shoulder-length black permed hair. They apologized for interrupting but said it would only take a moment. They had to pick a date with Patty for the planning session for an upcoming St. Louis Zoo fund-raiser at the Hyatt Regency.

"We can't forget our thank-you notes to the silent-auction people," the plump one declared. "I'll bring my list and we can divide up the names."

I concealed a smile as I recalled one of Benny's many Junior League jokes. Why don't Junior Leaguers like group sex? Answer: It takes too long to write all those thank-you notes.

I studied Patty as she took a pocket calendar out of her purse. She was the very image of composure and control, devoted mother and volunteer, smartly outfitted as if for a photo spread in *Town & Country*. It was hard to reconcile this Patty Napoli with her carnal tryst in the upstairs bedroom with Neville McBride.

Patty apologized for the interruption after the others left. "So," she said, "you represented Sally Wade?"

I nodded. "And now I represent her estate."

She brushed her brown hair off her forehead and glanced quickly around the room. "I see."

"How well did you know her, Patty?"

"Not well. Not well at all." Her hands fluttered nervously as she talked. "We spoke briefly at a few law firm functions. Nothing that I can remember now. We were once at the same table for a Red Cross luncheon."

Might as well cut to the chase. "Patty, who do you think killed her?"

The question made her sit back, as if she'd been slapped. "My goodness," she said, her eyes blinking. "I certainly don't know the answer to that."

"Do you think it was Neville?"

She cut her breath. "Well, I certainly was surprised when they arrested him, but I've heard that the police have a strong case."

"Who told you?"

She giggled nervously, her face reddening. "Oh, different people. Mostly gossip, I'm afraid. As you can imagine, it's become quite the topic here and at the club. It's our own O. J. Simpson scandal."

"Have the police talked to you?"

"Me?" she asked, eyes widening. "Why in the world would they want to talk to me?"

I shrugged. "Perhaps because of your relationship with him."

She stiffened, her expression going cold. After a moment, she said, "We have no relationship, Miss Gold."

"When did it stop?"

"It never began," she said adamantly. She leaned forward, lowering her voice. "I was vulnerable that night. Bruce and I were going through a difficult phase of our marriage. I was under enormous strain. I'd had way too much to drink. Way too much." Her eyes flashed angrily. "Neville sensed that, and he took advantage of me. He violated me. The man is a vulture." She sat back and closed her eyes. She took a deep breath, exhaled, and opened her eyes. "I have never been so humiliated in all of my life. You have no idea."

After a pause, I asked, "Was Neville married at the time?"

She laughed derisively. "As if that would matter." She paused, trying to recall the night. "She wasn't there."

"When did it happen?"

"Three years ago," she said, closing her eyes again. "February twenty-second."

There seemed to be no tactful way to do this. "Patty, was that the only time you and he—"

"Yes," she answered fiercely, her nostrils flaring. "Never before, never again."

I nodded.

"Of course, that didn't stop him," she said in disgust. "Last summer when Bruce was out of town at an ABA conference on environmental law, that man had the nerve to show up unannounced at my home one night. He even had flowers and a bottle of champagne."

"What did you do?"

"I told him I'd call the police if he didn't leave immediately."

"And did he?"

She nodded darkly.

"Did you tell your husband?"

Patty eyed me coolly for a moment. Then she placed her palms on the table and stood up. "I've said enough, Miss Gold. I have car pools to run." She picked up her purse. "Neville is a son of a bitch, pardon my French." She took a deep breath and shook her head. "There. I've said it. Are you satisfied? Now please leave me alone."

She marched out of the Tea Room. I finished my coffee as I replayed the conversation in my head.

Lawyers, like cops and shrinks, learn early on to beware of appearances. While others get a warm, fuzzy feeling at the scenes in those familiar Norman Rockwell paintings, we're taught to look for dark secrets. See the plump, jolly cop seated on the stool at the drugstore soda fountain smiling at the little boy on the next stool? Is that a smile or a leer, or is he simply relishing the protection money the pharmacist just paid him? Look at dear old Dad carving the Thanksgiving turkey with three generations of beaming family members around the table. Is the old guy about to be indicted for securities fraud? Is he perhaps planning to sneak out later for a leather-and-chain rendezvous with Bruno down at the biker bar? And what's the old darling got buried in the crawl space under his kitchen?

Nevertheless, it was nearly impossible to imagine Patty Napoli in the role of criminal accomplice posing as, say, Sally Wade or the elusive Tammy. Although she had been a drama major at Mount Holyoke (according to her Junior League bio), I saw no logical way to connect the motivational dots between the coitus interruptus and the corpus delicti. Revenge? Something even more convoluted? No answer came to mind.

Still, I reminded myself, Sally's death had unquestionably improved Patty's lot. As the wife of the managing partner of a powerful law firm, she became a prominent figure within the law firm's spousal pecking order and thus within her social circle. But was status enough to kill for? In a rational world, obviously not, but who said this was a rational world? Certainly not the daily news. When Mom arranges a contract hit on her daughter's rival for a spot on the cheerleading squad and Junior blows away Daddy with a shotgun because of a strict curfew, no motivation seems too far-fetched.

CHAPTER 22

Benny gave me a dubious look. "This is a weapon?"

I nodded. In my right hand I was holding one end of a twelve-inch choke chain. The other end, which dangled loose at my side, had a set of twenty keys attached to it. I gave the chain a shake. The keys on the end jangled.

Benny eyed the chain. "Where'd you get all those keys?"

I glanced down. "At the hardware store."

He contemplated me and the weapon. "Let's see if I understand," he said, rubbing his chin. "The mugger approaches, you whip that key chain out, he sees those damn keys and thinks, 'Holy shit, she must be the janitor from hell.' "

I gave him a patient smile. "It's a great weapon because it doesn't look like one." I lifted the chain and the keys clinked. "Lots of people have key chains, and lots of people reach for them as they approach their car or their front door."

We were standing beneath a streetlamp outside Sally Wade's town house waiting for the squad car. The property was still under police jurisdiction, and there was yellow crime-scene tape along the perimeters. The police had changed the locks the day Sally's body was discovered, which meant that they had to send someone over with the key to let us in.

"Okay, Bruce Lee," Benny said, "show me something."

"We learned a few moves tonight. Here's one."

I lifted my arm in front of me to chest height, elbow extended. Starting slow, I swung the chain in a figure-eight pattern, the keys jangling loudly. Gradually I picked up speed, and as I did the jangling noise diminished until the dominant sound was the chain cutting through the air.

Whoosh . . . whoosh . . . whoosh.

I kept it going for about thirty seconds and then carefully slowed down until I could grab the chain down near the keys.

Benny gave me a puzzled look. "What was that? Ninja baton twirling?"

"Our instructor calls it the circle of protection. The idea is to keep an attacker away."

Benny raised his eyebrows skeptically. "Maybe. What else can you do with that thing?"

I showed him the two strike moves we'd worked on: striking to the side and striking to the rear. The first was if someone approached you from the side, the second if they approached from behind. In both moves, you start with the chain dangling at your side. Keeping your arm straight, you quickly lift and swing the chain toward the attacker's face—in an arc to the side to repel the side attack, in a diagonal arc over your shoulder for a rear attack. I had Benny pretend to grab me in slow motion, once from the side and once from behind, while I showed him each move. He seemed grudgingly impressed. The squad car arrived just as I was pantomiming the upward swing for a strike to the groin.

Once inside Sally's town house, we started in her den, looking through cabinets and under couches.

"Let me ask you something," Benny said. He was on his belly peering under a sofa. "Let's say this Tammy calls Neville again and he gives her your name. What exactly do you plan to do if she calls you?"

"Talk to her."

"About what?"

I was looking through the videotapes in her entertainment center wall unit. "Oh, about her relationship with Neville." I slid a *Basic Instinct* videotape out of its case and examined it. "She needs to understand her importance to the case. She could be a key witness."

"For chrissakes, Rachel," Benny said, shaking his head in exasperation as he stood up, "enough is enough. This is Neville's problem, not yours."

"Benny, all I'm going to do is try to convince her to meet with Neville's lawyer. Whether she ultimately helps or hurts their case is up to them, not me. That's all I'm doing. Nothing more."

Benny walked over to the bookshelves. "Christ, you've done too much for them already." He turned to me. "When exactly is Tammy the love goddess supposed to call him?"

I shrugged as I slid the *Basic Instinct* videotape back into its case. "She may never call. And even if she does, she may not be willing to talk to anyone but Neville."

"We can only hope. That woman sounds like trouble to me."

"On the topic of women," I said, "how's Amy?"

Benny shrugged. "Pretty good. I'm meeting her for a late dinner at Bar Italia. You want to join us?"

"No, thanks." I got up and walked over to her desk. "I'm bushed. Once we're finished here, I'm going home."

Benny stared at the bookshelves for a moment and then turned to me with a baffled expression. "What exactly are we looking for?"

I groaned. "I have no idea." I pulled open the top

drawer of the desk. "I'm just hoping there's something the police overlooked."

Benny snorted. "Don't hold your breath."

"You might be surprised. The cops went through here right after the crime was discovered. Moreover, they were convinced Neville did it, and that had to influence the focus of their search. Things that didn't seem relevant to their theory of the case might seem very relevant to us."

"Assuming that we had a theory of the case. Dream on, woman."

I sorted through the contents of the top drawer of Sally's desk and discovered absolutely nothing out of the ordinary. The next drawer had packets of canceled checks. I leafed through the first packet. Payments to the gas company, the electric company, Visa, etc. Checks to individuals had short notations: *For Barb's wedding gift; Lunch reimbursement.* Nothing jumped out.

I looked through the other desk drawers and then went into her bedroom, leaving Benny in the den still looking through the bookshelves. Sally's dresser drawers contained nothing but clothing. In her nightstand drawer I found a tube of hand cream, a nail file, a small container of lip balm, a pack of condoms, a battery-operated vibrator, a dog-eared paperback edition of Stephen King's *Insomnia*, and two recent issues of *Vogue* magazine.

"Hey," Benny said as he walked into the bedroom, "look what I found." He had a book in his hand.

"What is it?"

He held it up. It was a slender book bound in red leather with gold lettering. The top half of the cover was in Chinese. The bottom half read:

SHIM LAI GINSENG LIMITED
HEALTH MANUAL

"Shim Lai?" I repeated.

"You know it?" he asked in surprise.

I frowned. "It sounds familiar." I gestured toward the book. "What is it?"

Benny grinned. "Great stuff. All these weird Chinese medicines made out of animal parts." He flipped open the book and read the page. "Like this. Antler slices." He held the open book toward me. "Check it out."

I took the book from him. The pages were printed on stiff glossy stock. The one Benny wanted me to read was captioned "Shim Lai Select Antler." The top half of the page was a high-quality color photograph of a brown antler next to two neat rows of antler slices. The antler slices resembled brown cucumber slices. Beneath the photograph was a series of Chinese characters, and below that, English text:

Ingredients: Specially selected Siberian Antler in slice, available in two varieties (selected and fine); 2 taels for each portion, sufficient for one person to take 10 times.

Indications: Increase of potency, stimulation of vital energy and blood flow, relief of general debility and spermatorrhea.

Benny chuckled. "One thing you can say about the logic of Chinese pharmacology: it sure ain't subtle."

"What do you mean?"

"Like this antler stuff. You want to feel horny, eat some horn."

I closed the nightstand drawer and stood up, shaking my head. "Then I must have eaten some soft-shells, because I'm starting to feel crabby. We're getting nowhere in here." Frustrated, I went over to the bedroom closet.

"Ah," Benny said a few moments later, "here's more literal pharmacology."

"Now what?" I said, starting to lose my patience. I was down on my hands and knees poking around the shoes on the closet floor.

"A cure for 'feeble male genitality.' Porpoise virility pills."

I spun around. "Let me see that."

He came over with the book. "Look at the size of that johnson."

This page was captioned "Shim Lai Porpoise Virility Pills." The top half of the page had a color photograph of what looked vaguely like a twisted riding crop (or an extra-long piece of beef jerky). Next to it was a white bowl filled with gold capsules. As on the page on the antlers, there were a series of Chinese characters beneath the photograph and, below that, English text:

Ingredients: Top quality testicle and penis of porpoise ground into powder and pilled in form convenient for intake.

Indications: Nourishment of the "Yin" body system, kidney, liver, stomach; stimulation of male virility, efficacious for feeble male genitality.

I closed the book and studied the cover. "Where's this book from?"

"China?"

I turned to the first page. "Shim Lai Ginseng Limited," the text read, "was founded in 1925 by Mr. Fook Lai Tsu (1892–1975). The firm is a Hong Kong ginseng firm that is an extension of its head office in China."

I looked up at Benny. "Marvin the mortician had those pills."

"Which pills?"

"The porpoise ones. Remember?"

Benny smiled in recollection. "Oh, yeah. Flipper's family jewels."

"The exact same brand." I held up the book. "Made by these guys. Get it? Made in Hong Kong."

"Okay," he said uncertainly.

"Benny, remember all of Sally Wade's trips to Hong Kong? She must have bought Marvin the pills when she was over there."

"Oh, yeah. Good point. Jeez, that's a hell of a present from your girlfriend. 'Here, honey, I bought you something for your feeble male genitality.' "

I studied the page on the porpoise virility pills, thinking back to my weird encounter with Marvin. I tried to fit the random pieces into the puzzle. I couldn't do it. Not yet.

"Good find." I handed the book to Benny. "Check the kitchen cabinets and drawers, okay?"

He left and I returned to the closet. Clothes. Lots and lots of clothes.

"Hey," he called from the kitchen, "how about some deer dick?"

"What?"

"This stuff is wild. Oh, gross!"

I sighed in exasperation.

"Listen to this," he called. " 'Deer testicles can be sliced, soaked in wine, or prepared as food.' "

"Oh, brother," I mumbled under my breath as I turned back to my work. I finished up in the closet without finding anything worth noting. The same was true in the guest room. I had just searched that closet when Benny came in with the Chinese medicine book.

I turned and groaned. "Now what?"

"This is serious. Remember Sally's mystery photographs—the ones from the film in her safe deposit box?"

I nodded uncertainly. "Okay."

He handed me the book. "Take a look."

I stared at the color photograph. There were two white Chinese bowls, each containing three or four rust-colored stones exactly like those that were in Sally's photographs. There were four additional stones scattered on the white surface between the bowls. As in Sally's photos, some of the stones were reddish-brown, others were yellowish-orange. Most were round; a few were triangular or cube-shaped. The page was captioned "Cattle Bezoar." I read the English text:

Gallstones from the gallbladder, biliary ducts, or ductus hepticus of cattle or ox. A full bezoar is in shape of an egg, a rounded square or triangle. The better variety has a smooth, lustrous, fine, and crisp surface and finely veined cross section without white coating.

Indications: Dispelling pathogenic heat, resolving phlegm, regulating gallbladder and subduing tension. It is also useful for treatment of fever, coma, delirium, insanity, infantile spasm, convulsion, pyorrhea, laryngitis, virulent carbuncle, ulcer and poisoning, chronic hemorrhoids.

Available in pills or powder.

I looked up at Benny, flabbergasted. "Gallstones?"

He shrugged.

I glanced down at the page again. "From cattle," I said quietly.

"Guess whose cattle," Benny said.

I shook my head in amazement, staring at the color photograph. "Oh, brother."

CHAPTER 23

Benny was right. As long as I was going back to Chicago to meet with Betsy Dempsey at Bennett Industries, I might as well drop in on the Shell Answer Man. If anyone outside the Hong Kong pharmacology market was likely to understand the economics of cattle gallstones, it was Melvin Needlebaum. This was not merely because of Melvin's encyclopedic knowledge of various subjects and his perfect photographic recall of even the most minor of details. No, the subject of cattle gallstones would ordinarily be too arcane for even a data demon like Melvin. But, as Benny reminded me, Melvin had a special reason to know gallstones: *Meat-Prod.*

Back when we were all junior associates in the Chicago litigation department of Abbott & Windsor, Melvin had been assigned to Abbott & Windsor's *Meat-Prod* team, a group of eight attorneys and numerous paralegals headed at the time by the late Graham Anderson Marshall III, the firm's senior antitrust partner. The A&W *Meat-Prod* team represented two of the dozens of pharmaceutical companies named as defendants in multidistrict antitrust litigation over, of all things, cattle pancreas glands.

To the uninitiated, it was an alleged price-fixing conspiracy that sounded not merely bizarre but downright ghoulish. *Pancreas glands?* they would ask in disbelief, wondering if perhaps the American businessman's voracious hunger to monopolize, having already gorged on all the tasty morsels in the ordinary channels of commerce, had now taken a grotesque and apocalyptic turn: hoarding the internal organs of corpses.

Far from it. Cattle pancreas glands were an essential raw material in the manufacture of insulin used in the treatment of diabetes. As such, the alleged antitrust conspiracy involved a potential damage exposure far in excess of two hundred million dollars.

Such numbers justified assigning Melvin Needlebaum to the case, for Melvin was an expensive proposition for a client. Not only did he exhaustively research every conceivable legal issue, no matter how inconsequential or abstruse, and generate lengthy, contentious motions over matters others would not contest, he also tended to immerse himself in the facts and the minutia of a case so obsessively that by the time of trial he knew more about the particular subject matter of the lawsuit than any one individual at the company. For someone as thorough and persistent as Melvin, an understanding of the economics of pancreas glands would not have been enough; he would have wanted to understand the economics of every cow by-product, from hooves to eyeballs to gallstones.

Or so I hoped.

My meeting with Betsy Dempsey was scheduled for three that afternoon. According to Melvin's secretary, to whom I spoke after confirming my meeting with Betsy, Melvin was in a deposition that morning but was due back to the office by one o'clock. I could meet with him then.

I spent the early morning at my office putting the final touches on my preparations for tomorrow's libel trial, caught the eleven-o'clock flight to Midway Airport, and was in the Loop by one.

The law firm of Abbott & Windsor occupies the top six floors of the Lake Michigan Bank Building in the heart of the Chicago financial district on LaSalle Street. I took the express elevator to the forty-first floor—my old floor—and stepped off onto the beige carpeting of the main reception area. Although the receptionist was younger and the chairs had been reupholstered, the rest of the reception area—from the austere granite letters of the firm name on the wall to the contorted chunk of stainless-steel "art" squatting on a pedestal near the picture window—looked the same as it had during my days as a junior associate.

The receptionist tried without success to contact Melvin. He was on the phone, she explained, and his secretary was at lunch. She let me go back to his office when I explained that I used to work at the firm, he was expecting me, and I knew exactly where his office was.

I walked down the long carpeted corridor, passing by the secretaries in their little cubicles. Some recognized me, and I recognized some. A few of the nameplates outside the attorneys' offices were familiar, others were not.

I slowed as I reached one of the smaller offices. Inside was an earnest young woman associate frowning at her computer screen and absently tugging at the side of her frizzy red hair with her left hand. There was no wedding ring. Her desk was cluttered with stacks of court pleadings, legal pads, and photocopies of cases. She was working on either a brief or a motion. The message light on her phone was blinking.

I knew this office well. Too well. I glanced at the nameplate on the wall, half expecting to see MS. GOLD. Instead, it read MS. ALTMAN. There was an empty carton of Dannon yogurt on her credenza with an empty banana peel hanging out. It looked like Ms. Altman was headed for another long night. I remembered all those long nights in that same little office. Abbott & Windsor works its associates hard, striving to squeeze every last billable hour out of them. Turnover is high, few make partner, and those who do are scarred along the way, losing their health or their marriage or their ability to recognize the first signs of spring.

I quietly studied Ms. Altman. She was brilliant, had been a high achiever in college, and had compiled a sterling record at a top law school. Those were prerequisites for a job at Abbott & Windsor. She was intense. That was obvious. And she was no doubt feeling overwhelmed at the moment. That came with the territory, as I vividly recalled.

Standing there in the hallway watching her, I had a crazy urge to dash into her office, my old office, grab her by the arm, and, like one of those crazed survivors in a body-snatcher movie, drag her into the hall and plead with her to leave before it was too late. *Just go. Now. Walk down the hall and get on the elevator and don't look back. Go. Please. You can still survive this.*

The urge passed, and I smiled ruefully at my own foolishness. Ms. Altman was her own woman, and for all I knew she'd be the managing partner of Abbott & Windsor someday.

I moved on, past the next corner office and down the west hallway. In the distance I heard that unmistakable nasal staccato: "That is patently absurd!" The mating call of a Melvin Needlebaum.

He was, as always, on his phone and on his computer and on his Lexis terminal, all at the same time. He had a speakerphone, which gave him even greater freedom of movement, and which he was using at the moment to feed a document into his portable fax machine.

His office looked as it always did. The desk was a jumble of yellow legal pads, computer printouts, pleadings binders, and deposition transcripts. There were documents scattered in tall piles on the floor throughout the office. A dead rubber plant sagged against the wall in the corner, one withered yellow leaf drooping from an otherwise bare trunk. I lifted a stack of deposition transcripts off the lone chair and sat down to wait.

"Now, jes' hold your horses, Melvin," a male voice was saying over the speakerphone in a thick Texas drawl. "Ah'm sure we can reach an amicable accommodation on that issue."

Melvin looked up from his fax machine with a demented grin, his eyes swimming behind the thick, smudged lenses of his horn-rimmed glasses. "An accommodation? Hah! If I were you, Mr. Beverly Hillbilly, I'd check my fax machine in precisely three minutes." He paused to feed another page into the fax. "That motion gets filed tomorrow a.m. unless I get relief today. Hah!"

He leaned forward and pressed the disconnect button on the phone. Then he looked up at me, rubbing his hands together manically, his shoulders hunched forward. "Great stuff, Miss Gold, great stuff."

There was a beep from his Lexis terminal, and Melvin spun around to squint at the monitor screen. A lunatic grin gradually spread over his face. "Good golly, Miss Molly!" he said as he spun his chair toward the word processor on his credenza. "A moment if you please, Miss Gold." His fingers flew over the keyboard. He finished typing, spun back toward his desk, typed a new search instruction into the Lexis terminal, and then looked up, his eyes blinking rapidly. "Yessssss?"

I smiled and shook my head in amusement. "Hello, Melvin."

"Greetings and salutations, Miss Gold. What brings you to the windy city?"

"Gallstones."

He winced. "My sympathies, Miss Gold. I hope you have retained the services of a skilled urologist."

"Not mine, Melvin. Cattle gallstones."

"Ah, well, thank heavens, eh? I once had the misfortune of passing a kidney stone. I can assure you that it was an even more execrable experience than arguing a point of law before Judge Carson."

Cook County Circuit Judge Luther T. Carson, a dim-witted political hack with a fierce temper, a pathological mistrust of big-firm lawyers, and an inability to grasp any rule of law more complex than those set forth in the traffic code, had for years played Professor Moriarty to Melvin's Sherlock Holmes.

Melvin paused and gave me a curious look. "Did you say *cattle* gallstones, Miss Gold?"

I nodded. Opening my briefcase, I removed the leather-bound Hong Kong health manual and Sally's gallstone photographs. "Here," I said, handing him one of the photographs.

Melvin studied Sally's gallstone photograph for a moment and looked up. "Cattle, eh?"

"I think so. They look pretty much like the ones shown in that book."

Melvin glanced at the cover of the book and nodded.

"Benny said you might remember something about the economics of cattle gallstones from your days on the *Meat-Prod* team."

Melvin's eyes widened as he flashed a demented grin. "Ah, yes, the *Meat-Prod* case. The stuff of legends, Miss Gold. In the end, you may be interested to learn, the plaintiff's case collapsed as moot. The development of nonorgan sources for artificial insulin has significantly diminished the utilization of cattle pancreas glands." He paused and snapped his finger. "That reminds me of an intriguing issue we had over the use of contention inter-rogatories in that case. Let's see, if I correctly recall—"

"Melvin, cattle gallstones," I reminded him.

"Ah, yes, of course. Cattle gallstones." He craned his head back and squinted at the ceiling, searching his memory. After a moment, he returned his gaze to mine with a look of pride. "Cattle bezoar, as the Chinese say."

"Right," I answered, impressed.

"Just one of many lucrative but little-known edible or medicinal bovine by-products. Did you know that the Koreans are enthusiastic gourmands of beef large intestines? The Japanese prepare feasts of a part of the cow curiously known as the hanging tenders."

"Gross."

"Miss Gold, you may be surprised to learn that the Armour Pharmaceutical Company buys beef warts by the bushel."

I grimaced.

"And should you ever become heavy with child, Miss Gold, and require artificial promotion of uterine contractions during labor, you will find yourself on the receiving end of an injection prepared from the pituitary glands of a cow."

"Fascinating," I said, trying to sound interested. "But can we get back to the gallstones?"

"Ah, yes, cattle bezoar. Slightly more valuable than horse bezoar, but far less valuable than black bear bezoar."

"Bear gallstones?"

"Absolutely, Miss Gold. Find yourself a few choice specimens of same, live long enough to make the sale in Hong Kong, and take the rest of the year off."

"Tell me about cattle gallstones."

"Certainly. The principal source of market-quality gallstones is cows and bulls, not fatted cattle."

"What's the difference?"

"Fatted cattle are the younger animals, primarily steers and heifers. They are the source of steaks and other choice and prime cuts of beef available at your local supermarket and in fine restaurants throughout the nation. The older animals, known in the industry as cows and bulls, are generally between the ages of eighteen months and eight years. The quality of the meat on these animals is inferior. For that reason, they are slaughtered principally for hamburger and for the harvest of that gag-all of items accurately but euphemistically labeled by-products."

"Which includes gallstones?"

"Most definitely, Miss Gold. The older the animal, the larger the gallstone, and, quite often, the better the quality. The better the quality of the gallstone, the higher the price. Just like diamonds." He gestured toward the gallstones in Sally's photograph. "These are from older animals."

"And thus more valuable?"

"Oh, yes. Indeed, several of these might qualify as sheer gall."

"Pardon?"

Melvin cackled, rubbing his hands together. "A term of art, Miss Gold. Sheer, as in unadulterated, or pure. In Hong Kong, the finest-quality gallstones are classified sheer gall. The poorest quality are classified corrupt gall."

I nodded, looking at another one of the photographs. "Do all cows have gallstones?"

"Great Caesar's ghost!" Melvin sat back, stunned. "All? No way, Miss Gold, no way."

I had to smile. Melvin was the only person other than Perry White who used that expression.

"We are speaking of a tiny fraction, Miss Gold. If one could draw an analogy, searching for stones in cattle gallbladders is a bit like searching for pearls in oysters. Except"—he paused with a manic grin—"you don't need a face mask and snorkel." He burst into weird, high-pitched cackles, enormously pleased with his joke.

When he calmed down again, I asked, "You say these stones are from older cows?"

"Yes, indeed. And thus they come from a particular type of slaughterhouse. Slaughterhouses specialize, Miss Gold. Most handle fatted cattle, a smaller number handle cows and bulls. The population figures for fatted cattle are rather extraordinary. There are thirty-five million of them slaughtered a year. Impressive, eh? Big numbers, but it takes more than seven thousand fatted cattle to yield one ounce of gallstones, and those stones are often of inferior quality. With the older animals, however, one thousand carcasses will yield one ounce of high-quality stones, many of them deemed sheer gall. But, alas, there are less than a million cows and bulls slaughtered each year."

"So that means there's an annual U.S. harvest of less than one thousand ounces of high-quality cattle gallstones?"

Melvin nodded. "You are correct, Miss Gold. However, the unit of measurement in Hong Kong is the kilo, which is, as you may recall from your high school chemistry class, thirty-five point two ounces. That translates into an annual harvest of less than thirty kilos."

I was taking notes. "How valuable are they?"

"Excellent question, Miss Gold, the answer to which depends upon your location within the chain of commerce. A kilo of sheer gall can be worth anywhere from twenty-five to seventy thousand dollars."

"And how many kilos could one slaughterhouse produce a year?"

"The numbers vary, Miss Gold. The average slaughterhouse kills five hundred cows and bulls a day. The larger houses, however, can double or even triple those numbers. I'd say a good annual production would be eight to twelve kilos. With good market conditions in Hong Kong, that could yield more than half a million dollars, although a slaughterhouse would never sell them for anywhere close to that."

"Why not?"

Melvin cackled. "Come, come, Miss Gold. Economics 101. Too many middlemen, commencing with the local by-products dealer. That's the outfit that buys the gallstones, pancreas glands, fetal blood, and other by-products. It sells them to one of the national houses, and so on and so on, until the gallstones finally reach the ginseng houses and folk medicine shops in Hong Kong. The only way to get the top prices is to hop on a plane to Hong Kong and peddle them direct to the retailers."

I quietly absorbed this information.

"If the disclosure is not prohibited by the attorney-client privilege," Melvin said, "I am curious to learn the reason for your sudden preoccupation with the subject of cattle gallstones. I trust it is not because you suffer from pyorrhea, laryngitis, virulent carbuncles, or chronic hemorrhoids or seek alleviation from what the Chinese obliquely refer to as, ahem, endogenous wind."

I laughed. "No, thank goodness."

I explained why cattle gallstones seemed to provide a compelling explanation for Sally's multiple trips to Hong Kong, her Swiss bank account, and her numerous odd-hour calls to Brady Kane, plant manager of the Douglas Beef slaughterhouse in East St. Louis. Even if one assumed a low-end slaughterhouse that processed "just" five hundred animals a day, direct sales of gallstones in Hong Kong—especially ones graded sheer gall—could generate more than a quarter of a million dollars a year. Whatever Sally's cut had been, the money was also apparently tax-free—she certainly hadn't declared it on any of the tax returns that I had reviewed.

"Fascinating, Miss Gold," Melvin said, nodding his head rapidly, his shoulders hunched forward. "How do you propose to test your hypothesis?"

"I'm going to start at Bennett Industries. Douglas Beef is a wholly owned subsidiary of Bennett and operates five slaughterhouses. If someone is skimming gallstones, the numbers ought to show up in the books."

Melvin pounded his fist on his desk. "Superb idea, Miss Gold. By comparing gallstone harvests at the various slaughterhouses, you may be able to identify mani-

fest evidence of gallstone embezzlement. Splendid foren-
sic strategy, Miss Gold. Where is Bennett Industries
located?"

"About two blocks north of us on LaSalle. I'm meeting with Betsy Dempsey in thirty minutes. Remember
her?"

"Of course. Indeed, I specifically remember a research
memorandum that she did for me on a somewhat complex issue under the Lanham Act. An admirable piece of
scholarship."

I leaned back in the chair and smiled at him. "Hey,
you want to come along? You can say hi to Betsy and
maybe help me figure out the financial statements."

He glanced at his calendar and looked up at me, his
lips pursed as he weighed my proposal. He started
slowly nodding his head. "I believe I will, Miss Gold."
His head was bobbing more rapidly now. "Yes, indeed.
As you may know, I am somewhat familiar with the
manner in which slaughterhouse records are maintained."
He placed his hands on the top of his desk and stood up.
"Actually, I may be of material assistance to you on this
matter, Miss Gold."

While we waited for the elevator, I said, "Melvin, how
long have we known each other?"

He gave me a curious look and then tilted back his
head and squinted at the ceiling for a moment as he did
the mental calculation. He lowered his gaze and said,
"Next Tuesday it will be eight years and five months."

"Back when I was at Abbott & Windsor, we worked
on several cases together, right?"

"We did, indeed, Miss Gold. I think especially of the
Bottles & Cans case, and the work we did on the multi-
farious Robinson-Patman legal issues therein. I can fairly
characterize the weekend we spent at the office preparing that emergency petition for mandamus as quality
time, Miss Gold."

I nodded, trying to suppress my smile. "We've also had dinner together in St. Louis."

"Ah yes, an excellent Mexican repast, as I recall."

"In fact, I even got you out of jail in St. Louis."

"You performed laudably on that occasion, Miss Gold, in the face of a gestapo police force and a disgraceful criminal justice system."

I looked at him sincerely. "I consider you a friend, Melvin."

"I'm pleased that you do, Miss Gold."

"Do you consider me a friend?"

He smiled awkwardly. "Yes, indeed."

"Finally," I said, turning to him with a wink, "I believe you've even seen me naked."

He blushed scarlet and coughed. "Purely unintentional, Miss Gold. As I hope you recall, the dressing rooms were unmarked. Upon discovery of my egregious mistake, I immediately averted my eyes. Nevertheless, I can assure you that I continue to feel remorse for that entirely inadvertent mishap."

I smiled. "Forget the remorse, Melvin. My point is that we've known each other for a long time, we're friends, we've been through a lot together, and you're older than I am. So why, after all these years, do you continue to call me Miss Gold?"

The doors slid open and we stepped into a half-full elevator. Melvin turned to face the door as it closed. For the entire forty-one-floor ride, he frowned at the elevator door with a look of total bewilderment.

"Reprehensible," Melvin snarled, shaking his head furiously.

We were walking along LaSalle Street on our return from the Bennett Industries headquarters.

I nodded glumly. "It is disappointing."

Melvin spun toward me, his eyes wide with indignity.

"Disappointing? May I remind you, Miss Gold, that that is a publicly held corporation?"

Melvin was quite a spectacle. His shirt had come untucked in back so that the tail hung below the bottom of his suit jacket. He had forgotten his belt that morning; as a result, his pants were sagging so low that the backs of the cuffs curled under the heels of his shoes. He gesticulated wildly as he talked, his arms jabbing spastically in all directions. Although the sidewalk was crowded, people gave us a wide berth as we passed by.

"Just as appalling," Melvin continued, spraying saliva, "is their inexplicable decision to delegate that level of responsibility to"—he paused, overcome with disgust—"to Jabba the Hut. That distended slug is an embarrassment, and his records are a disgrace."

To say the least, it had not been love at first sight for Melvin and Lamar Hundra. It turned out that oversight of the meat by-products records fell within Lamar's jurisdiction. He was in the process of scarfing down his last jelly doughnut of the day when Melvin and I arrived at his door at three-fifteen. Although I've never thought of Melvin as overly fastidious in the area of personal hygiene, he visibly blanched when Lamar extended his hand for a handshake after first licking his fingers clean.

They were a complete mismatch. Lamar's slack, torpid style was the polar opposite of Melvin's rabid, meticulous approach. I could actually hear Melvin grinding his teeth as Lamar took us on a leisurely jaunt through the financial records of the five slaughterhouses. Eventually, Melvin had exploded, "Goddammit, Mr. Doughnut, we don't care about that rubbish! I want gallstones, and I want them now!"

We eventually got gallstones, but we got them mingled with pancreas glands, fetal blood, bull testicles, beef warts, hanging tenders, and the rest of the by-products. Apparently, Douglas Beef had stopped separately accounting for the sales of particular by-products, such as gallstones, a few years after Bennett Industries acquired the company. Instead, all by-products sales figures were lumped together, thus generating for each plant a single, undifferentiated number. There was no way to determine from Lamar's numbers whether the "official" gallstone harvest at the East St. Louis plant was lower than elsewhere. Further muddying the numbers and our efforts to find meaning in them was the fact that the East St. Louis plant was the only one of the five Douglas Beef slaughterhouses that processed cows and bulls; the other four handled fatted cattle. All we could determine from the numbers was that the East St. Louis plant was processing twelve hundred animals per day, which meant that the monetary value of its gallstone harvest was on the high side of Melvin's estimates, perhaps as much as five hundred thousand dollars a year. Add in a barrel of fresh testicles, a duffel bag of freeze-dried bulls' penises, and a few other equally bizarre items and you'd have ample reason to visit Hong Kong several times a year. And thanks to Lamar Hundra's lack of vigilance, no one at headquarters would ever suspect a thing.

Melvin was still fulminating when we reached the entrance to Abbott & Windsor's building. "I am mightily tempted, Miss Gold, to report that tub of lard to one of the sharks in the plaintiff's class action bar. I should think a nasty lawsuit for securities fraud might be just the thing to turn that bloated buffoon into a genuine Douglas Beef by-product."

"Don't get yourself worked up, Melvin," I said in a pacifying voice. "He's not worth it." I held out my hand. "Thanks. You were really helpful." I gave him a warm smile. "It was awfully good to see you."

"Certainly," he said, eyes averted. He stuck out his hand.

We shook. Instead of letting go immediately, I gave his hand a friendly squeeze. "So long, Melvin."

"Yes, uh, good-bye, uh, Rachel."

He turned and pushed through the revolving door. With a feeling that was almost maternal, I watched him march through the lobby toward the elevator banks. I couldn't begin to imagine what it was like to pass through life as Melvin Needlebaum. He was a true eccentric. Nevertheless, on three separate occasions when he had an opportunity to do so in my presence, Melvin had acted nobly and without hesitation. And, after all these years, he had actually called me by my first name.

With a smile, I turned toward the street and flagged a cab. I checked my watch. With any luck, I could make the five-fifteen flight out of Midway.

CHAPTER 24

The skies were clear heading south. I'm one of those travelers who always request a window seat, and normally I would have spent most of this short flight peering out the window and watching the farmlands and plains and meandering rivers and small towns slowly scroll beneath the plane.

But not today. Although I did spend most of the flight staring out the window, the scenery didn't register. Instead, I was thinking about gallstones and mulling over what Betsy Dempsey had told me when I checked back with her on my way out of Bennett Industries.

I had dropped by her office to thank her for her help. When I explained that the financial records in Chicago didn't include meaningful detail on by-products sales, she told me to wait a moment. She went down the hall to check with the in-house attorney who headed up the environmental law division. Five minutes later she returned with a slip of paper. She explained that slaughterhouses run into lots of EPA compliance issues, especially with the disposal of carcasses and by-products. It was a long shot, she conceded, but if anyone might have more specific numbers on gallstones, it would be the St. Louis law firm that handled environmental matters for the slaughterhouse.

As the plane crossed the Mississippi River in its final descent into Lambert International Airport, I removed that slip of paper from my briefcase and stared at it again:

St. Louis environmental law counsel:
Tully, Crane & Leonard—Contact: Bruce Napoli

"Well?" Jacki said.

I stepped back, crossing my arms as I studied the poster. It was a blowup of a color photograph of two cars parked side by side on a wide circular driveway. The car on the left was a silver Corvette. The car on the right was a silver Mercedes-Benz coupe with gold trim. An ornate Spanish-tile mailbox was visible in the left foreground with the address stenciled in gold: 6 Sienna. Looming above the cars in the background was the 21,000-square-foot mission-style home of Richie and Cissy Thompson. The vanity plate on the silver Corvette read I'M RICH. The vanity plate on the Mercedes read ME TOO.

I looked over at Jacki and smiled. "I like it. I like it a lot."

"Mark it?" she asked, reaching for her trial exhibit stickers.

I nodded. "Definitely. Exhibit H, right?"

"Yep."

It was eight-thirty that night and we were at my office doing the usual last-minute trial preparations—marking trial exhibits, making copies of key documents, outlining direct examinations, making notes for cross-examination. Benny had dropped by to help. He was in a chair in the corner reading through a pile of recent libel decisions in an effort to beef up Vincent Contini's affirmative defenses.

I watched as Jackie peeled off the back of the exhibit sticker and carefully affixed it to the upper right corner of the poster.

"Good," I said. "Now we need to wrap it with the brown paper and write 'Defendant's Trial Exhibit H' on the outside with the black marker." I pointed to the other poster. "Let's mark that 'Exhibit I' and then wrap it up."

I turned to the third poster, which was already wrapped in brown paper and sealed with tape. I picked up the black marker, took off the cap, and walked over to it. "Which makes this one Exhibit J." I bent down and wrote DEFENDANT'S TRIAL EXHIBIT J across the brown paper. I straightened up and replaced the cap on the marker. "There," I said, stepping back to admire my handiwork.

Benny looked up from his cases and chuckled. "Oh, brother. Let's hope you never have to unwrap that present, Santa."

I turned toward him and crossed my fingers. "As my father used to say, from your lips to God's ears."

"Have you told your client about Exhibit J?" Benny asked.

I shook my head. "Not yet. He's nervous enough as it is."

"He's nervous?" Benny said. "Shit." He looked over at Jacki. "What's your reaction to Exhibit J?"

She shook her head and shuddered. "I don't want to even think about it."

Thirty minutes later I announced that we were done for the night. "I'm bushed," I told them. "Vincent is meeting me here tomorrow at eight to go over his testimony. I need some sleep."

On the drive home I remembered I was out of dog food. I stopped by my local Schnuck's supermarket to buy some. As I walked through the parking lot toward the store, I recalled Benny's amused disbelief when he first moved here and discovered that the name of the major supermarket chain in St. Louis is pronounced exactly the same as the Yiddish word for idiot. "Just exactly who are these poor schnooks?" he had asked. "The customers? What's that make the owners? Schmucks?"

I arrived at the checkout line with a ten-pound sack of dog food, two pounds of apples, a half gallon of milk, and a bag of fresh carrots. But by the time I reached the counter, my cart also contained a *Vogue* magazine and a Snickers bar. With the day I'd had and the prospect of a full day of trial tomorrow, I'd decided I deserved some bedtime treats.

It was after eleven when I left the supermarket. I was lost in one of those night-before-trial reveries as I pushed the shopping cart across the dark parking lot toward my car. I was vaguely aware of several delivery trucks on the lot, and a few cars and vans scattered here and there.

I pushed the cart around to the trunk of my car and reached into the pocket of my trench coat for my keys. They were on the end of my choke-chain weapon, along with all the extra keys from the hardware store. I found the correct key, opened the trunk, and dropped the chain back in my pocket.

That's when I heard the sudden rasp of footsteps behind me. Before I could turn, something hard jabbed into the center of my back.

"Don't move," said a deep hoarse voice as he pressed me against the rear fender of my car.

I could feel my knees go weak. "You can have my money," I said.

"Be quiet." I felt his warm, garlicky breath on my neck.

"What do you want?"

"Shut up," he growled.

I waited in the dark, my heart racing, almost dizzy from fear.

He leaned closer. "Get in the trunk."

I looked in the trunk. "What?"

"You heard me."

"Why?" I said, my voice trembling. I struggled to remember what Faith Compton had tried to teach me in the self-defense class. I tried to contain my emotions.

"Just get in it."

"What are you going to do to me?"

"I said get in the fucking trunk, lady." He shoved the hard thing into my back again, and then he moved back a step. "Now, goddammit."

My right hand was in my coat pocket, clenched around the key chain. I looked down to the side, still struggling to control my breathing. I tried to fix his position. I could see black jeans and black running shoes. He was standing about two feet behind me. I tensed my muscles as I tightened my grip on the keys.

"Come on," he said gruffly.

Closing my eyes, I tried to visualize what I had to do. I took a deep breath, held it for the count of three, and then let out a yell as I swung upward with the chain.

The keys snagged for a split second on the coat pocket, throwing the entire swing out of whack. With a grunt, he caught me by the wrist and quickly twisted my arm behind my back and shoved up hard. The fierce stab of pain made me cry out as the key chain crashed to the ground.

"Stupid cunt," he grunted in irritation.

Keeping my right arm pinned behind my back, he reached between my legs with the other hand and hoisted me into the trunk, shoving me in facedown.

"Turn your head away and close your eyes."

I obeyed him.

"What are you going to do?" I said, my eyes squeezed shut. I was shivering, close to tears.

"I got a message for you, and it's real simple. You keep

sticking your nose where it don't belong and you're going to get it cut off. Understand?"

I nodded, my eyes still closed. The trunk carpet was rough against my cheek.

"Now," he said, "I want you to count backward from thirty. I want you to do it loud and slow so I can hear you. Understand?"

I nodded.

"Good." He chuckled. " 'Cause when you reach zero, I got a nice surprise for you. Start counting."

I tried, but the words were barely audible. "Thirty, twenty-nine—"

"Louder. Start over."

I took a breath, fighting for self-control. "Thirty," I said in a louder voice. "Twenty-nine . . ." My voice was shaking, but I kept counting.

By the time I reached ten I was on the verge of hysteria, my eyes squeezed shut, my body rigid with dread. What was his surprise? By the number five I had pulled myself into a ball.

"Three, two, one"—I winced—"zero."

I waited. Silence. The only sound at first was the zinging of blood in my ears. In the distance I heard a truck shift gears. Seconds passed. Then a minute. I opened my eyes. I was staring into the black interior of the trunk.

Hesitantly, I turned my head. The trunk lid was open. I moved my eyes up its length. Beyond the curved end was nothing but stars and the night sky. I waited, straining my ears. Nothing.

I sat up. There was my shopping cart, resting against the side of the car, just where I had left it. I looked around. I saw no one.

I climbed out of the trunk, scanning the parking lot in every direction.

I kneeled down and peered under the car.

I stood up, rubbing my sore right shoulder. As I did, I

saw my key chain on the ground right where it had fallen. I leaned over and lifted it up, the keys clinking together softly. I stared at it and shook my head. Turning with a sigh toward my grocery cart, I dropped the key chain into my coat pocket.

CHAPTER 25

But the show must go on.

Accordingly, at 9:05 a.m. the next morning, bruised and stiff, my right shoulder still throbbing, I rose at counsel's table. Vincent Contini was seated next to me, ramrod-straight, his hands steepled beneath his chin. I placed my hand on his shoulder and announced that the defendant in *Cecelia Ann Thompson v. Contini's on Maryland* was ready for trial.

Judge LaDonna Williams nodded gravely. "We'll start in a moment." She leaned over and said something with quiet authority to her docket clerk, who immediately got to her feet and came around behind the bench to confer with the judge.

As they talked in hushed tones, I turned toward the gallery, which was usually empty save for one or two elderly court watchers. But today there was a crowd of about two dozen scattered on the benches. I recognized the society columnist and the people columnist for the *Post-Dispatch*, seated side by side in the third row. Behind them was a reporter from Channel 5 with a steno pad open on her lap. One row over was Charles Morley, a photographer from the *Post-Dispatch*, here today not as a spectator but as a witness. Jacki had served him with a trial subpoena on Monday. I caught his eye and smiled. He acknowledged me with a nod. I spotted two other witnesses we had served with subpoenas. With any luck this morning, they'd never have to take the stand.

Seated in the first row directly behind us were Vincent Contini's stout wife, Maria, and his stouter son, Tony. I winked at Mrs. Contini, who nodded nervously, fingering her rosary beads. Tony gave me a thumbs-up.

On the other side of the courtroom, in the first row behind plaintiff's table, was Cissy Thompson's husband, Richie. He was flanked by two intense members of his Pacific Rim entourage. By contrast to his grim lieutenants, Richie seemed almost languid. With his heavy-lidded eyes, shiny black suit, and dark, slicked-back hair, he reminded me of a drowsy, well-fed panther.

I looked back at the judge. She jotted something in her calendar and then peered down at us over her reading glasses.

"Counsel," she said to both of us, "I've read your trial briefs and I'm familiar with your legal theories. We'll dispense with opening statements." She turned to my opponent. "Mr. Brenner, call your first witness."

"Thank you, Your Honor," Milt Brenner said in his fawning manner. He turned to his client, who was seated next to him. With a benevolent smile and a sweeping gesture, he announced, "Your Honor, we call the plaintiff herself, Mrs. Cecelia Thompson."

Cissy rose with steely poise and strode across the courtroom to the witness box, where the somber clerk was waiting.

"Please raise your right hand."

And thus the trial began.

I glanced over at Richie, who had momentarily perked up when his wife took the stand. He soon lost interest, though, and turned to one of his assistants to whisper something. The assistant nodded earnestly, jumped to his feet, and scurried briskly out of the courtroom. Richie turned with a dull expression to watch him leave.

He hadn't always been surrounded by these butt boys. Twenty years ago, Richie Thompson had been a penny-ante jobber who was able to corner the U.S. market in cheapo made-in-Singapore work boots at a time when no one cared about cheapo work boots. That was okay by Richie. His margins on the $12.99 schlock that he peddled to the inner-city discount houses were enough to cover the mortgage, the Blues season tickets, and the twice-a-year junkets to Vegas. As he told his buddies, "So long as the niggers and spics keep buying 'em, I ain't complaining."

But then a miracle occurred: the fickle finger of fashion pointed to work boots. Richie was so far ahead of the curve that it took years for the rest to catch up. With his Asian factories working triple shifts, Richie went from penny-ante to pennies from heaven. When he took Pacific Rim public on a Tuesday morning in March eight years ago, in the space of six hours his net worth shot from $23,124 to $12.3 million.

Richie went berserk: he chartered a plane and flew his forty-two best buddies, including the entire duck club, to Vegas for a weekend of booze, broads, and blackjack. Cissy, by contrast, went uptown: she took the wife of Richie's securities lawyer to Hilton Head Island over that same weekend and spent most of the time pumping her for information on how to start moving up the social ladder. Richie returned with a cosmic hangover and a genital rash of indeterminate origins. Cissy returned with climbing ropes and pitons.

She was clearly breathing thinner air these days, and her outfit reflected it. She was wearing a subdued but elegant red wool suit and matching neck scarf that brought out the highlights in her shoulder-length auburn hair. At forty-eight, Cissy Thompson was a striking figure with an aura that was almost regal. And with good reason.

Whatever nature omitted had been supplied by the finest collection of plastic surgeons, orthodontists, personal fitness trainers, hairstylists, fashion consultants, makeup artists, tutors, and diction coaches that Richie's money could buy.

Many who knew her claimed that Cissy Thompson had ice in her veins and the scruples of a contract killer. Just last year, for example, she had refused to pay her ten-thousand-dollar pledge to the St. Louis Special Olympics when, instead of being seated for the luncheon at the "A" table (with guest of honor Barbara Walters and the snooty wives of several CEOs), she found herself at a table that included two of the gold medal winners at the competition. As she indignantly informed the chairwoman of the event immediately afterward, "I didn't shell out ten grand to buy lunch with a couple of retards."

Perhaps to soften that image, Milt Brenner started his examination slow and gentle—name, address, place of birth, marital status, children, pets, hobbies. It took nearly an hour of warm, cuddly testimony before Brenner finally reached the day that Cissy called, in a halting voice, Black Tuesday.

What followed was a performance that had obviously been well rehearsed. We heard about her initial confusion when Vincent Contini responded with a silent scowl to her request to return the dress. Then there was the embarrassment of having him place the dress under a high-intensity lamp and inspect it with a magnifying glass. Then the dismay of trying to maintain her composure while he fired questions at her, his voice "dripping with hostility." And finally, the total mortification of being publicly disparaged.

"There were other women in there," she said, her lips quivering. "Women I knew, women I admired, women whose views I respected." She paused to dab her eye with a handkerchief. "He raised his voice to me. He was practically shouting at me. He called me a liar and a cheat. Those women heard every one of his vile accusations." She paused and took a deep breath, her face a mask of anguish.

Brenner, in a soft, compassionate tone, asked, "Was it painful, Cissy?"

She sighed, her hands fluttering helplessly onto her lap. "Oh, you have no idea."

"Tell the court, Cissy."

As if on cue, she began sobbing, covering her face with her hands. Brenner allowed it to go on until Judge Williams came to the rescue by quietly announcing that the court would be in short recess. Brenner helped her off the stand and walked her out of the courtroom as Richie, barely acknowledging the proceedings, huddled with his two aides.

I used the break to get my exhibits arranged. Brenner had to know that he couldn't possibly top that last scene, and he would likely end his direct examination when court resumed. His expression confirmed as much when he strolled back into the courtroom alone. He could not have looked more pleased with himself.

"Rachel," he said, trying to sound compassionate, "I'm afraid our last settlement offer is off the table."

Ten minutes later, with his restored and completely composed client back on the witness stand, Milt Brenner stood to announce, "No further questions, Your Honor." Turning to me with almost a pompous smile, he said, "Your witness, counsel."

I checked my watch as I stood up. It was eleven-fifteen. We'd break around noon for lunch, which gave me forty-five minutes to set it up. So far, things were going according to the plan—the one I had worked out in the wee hours last night. I'd been so rattled when I got home from Schnuck's that I hadn't been able to fall asleep until three in the morning. Trying to keep my mind off what had happened in the parking lot, I'd used the time awake in bed to map out my cross-examination of Cissy Thompson. If my plan worked, the case would end over the lunch hour. If it didn't, we'd be stuck in a high-stakes mud-wrestling match for at least another day and a half.

I came around the table. "Good morning, Mrs. Thompson," I said politely. "My name is Rachel Gold, and I represent the defendant."

She nodded sternly, once again the imperious ice maiden.

"I have a few questions for you, Mrs. Thompson, but before I ask them I'd like to make sure I understand your claim." I moved back over to Vincent Contini and put my hand on his shoulder. "You've sued my client for libel. You claim he said some false and defamatory things about you, right?"

She looked from me to Contini and then back to me. "That's right," she snapped, sounding almost annoyed by the question.

"In fact, you allege that Mr. Contini called you a liar and a cheat. You allege that he accused you of lying about whether you wore the dress. You allege that he falsely accused you of attempting to cheat him by asking for a complete refund on something that you had already used."

Her nostrils flared. "That's exactly what he said."

I nodded. "And you allege here that those accusations were false, correct?"

She nodded angrily. "They were lies."

"In fact, Mrs. Thompson, you allege that you didn't wear that dress at all, correct?"

"That isn't just an allegation, Miss Gold. That's the truth."

"Thank you." I nodded courteously. "I think I understand your position."

I walked over to the wall hook where the dress was hanging. "Now, I'd like us to go back to Tuesday, August eleventh." I looked toward the dress. "That was the day you bought this pretty Adrienne Vittadini dress from Mr. Contini, right?"

She nodded. "Yes."

"You bought two more expensive clothing items the next day, right?"

She shrugged nonchalantly. "I'm sure I don't remember something that far back."

I smiled politely. "I understand, Mrs. Thompson. I can't even remember what I had for breakfast today. Let me see if I can jog your memory."

I spent the next ten minutes refreshing her recollection with charge receipts, credit slips, and her credit card bill for August. When I was through, Cissy found herself warily eyeing Defendant's Trial Exhibits E and F, which were sitting directly in front of her on the ledge of the witness box. Exhibit E was the pair of Yves Saint Laurent black pumps that she had purchased for $570.67 on August 12. Exhibit F was the Salvatore Ferragamo handbag that she had purchased for $412.35 on the same day.

"Let's make sure our dates are correct," I said, turning to the blackboard. "On Tuesday you bought that pretty dress. On Wednesday you bought the matching pumps and purse. Then, on the following Tuesday, after the weekend, you returned the purse to Neiman-Marcus and the shoes to La Femme Elégante." I turned back to face her and gave her my perky elementary-school-teacher smile. "Right?"

She frowned at the blackboard and then looked down at the receipts already admitted into evidence as trial exhibits. "I suppose," she said quietly.

"Is that a yes?" I said.

She looked at me, her eyes narrowing. "Yes," she hissed.

Another perky smile. "I thought so."

I walked back toward counsel's table. I sat against the

table edge, facing the witness. "Tell us about the night of August fourteenth. That was the Friday of the week you bought the dress and the shoes and the purse."

She laughed. "Come on, lady. That was several months ago. I have no idea what I did that night."

I nodded pensively. *Perfect answer*.

Time to turn up the flame. I leaned across the table and lifted the next exhibit off the pile. Looking back to her, I said, "Let's see if we can refresh that memory of yours."

I walked over to the witness box and held out the document. "I'm handing you what I've marked Defendant's Trial Exhibit G."

I gave a photocopy to the judge and another photocopy to Brenner. Turning back to the witness, I said, "Identify it, Mrs. Thompson." There wasn't a drop of warmth in my voice.

She stared at the document for a moment and then looked over at Milt Brenner with a frown.

"Identify the document," I repeated a little more forcefully as I turned toward Brenner. He dropped his eyes.

"It's a program," Cissy said carefully.

"A program for what?"

"For, uh, a fund-raiser."

"Specifically, the Carousel Auction Gala sponsored by the Friends of the Children's Hospital, correct?" Fortunately, the Ritz-Carlton had kept several copies of the program and had given me one the night I met Jonathan Wolf for drinks.

She shrugged, trying to sound offhand. "That's what it says."

"What's the date of the event?"

She looked at the program. "According to this thing, August fourteenth."

"According to that thing?" I repeated, incredulous. "You can surely do better than that, can't you? You were there, weren't you?"

She sat back with a frown, as if trying to remember. "I might have been. I can't recall for sure."

"Let me help you, then. Let's see if we can jog that foggy memory of yours."

Brenner leaped to his feet. "I object, Your Honor."

Judge Williams peered down at me over her reading glasses. "Sustained."

"Your Honor," Brenner said with an obsequious smile, "perhaps this would be a good time for a break."

I glanced at the clock. Ten minutes to twelve. "Judge," I said, "could I at least conclude this line of questioning? It shouldn't take long."

Judge Williams nodded. "Proceed, counsel."

I turned to Cissy Thompson, who was watching me carefully. "Open that program to page five, Mrs. Thompson." As she flipped to the page, I noted with satisfaction that Judge Williams had also turned to the same page of her copy. "Do you see that list of committee members for the event? Look in the second column, sixth name down. That's your name, right?"

"Yes," she said with a trace of condescension, "but that doesn't prove anything. I serve on committees for many worthwhile causes. That doesn't mean I have time to attend every single one of their events."

"Turn to page three."

She did, the judge did, and Milt Brenner did.

"You see that list of featured auction items? Do you see the fourth item? What is it?"

She looked up slowly, sensing for the first time that maybe, just maybe, she had taken a detour into dangerous territory. "A silver Corvette."

I turned to Vincent Contini. "Mr. Contini, could you set Exhibit H up on the easel."

All eyes in the courtroom followed my client as he walked over to the side wall, where three poster-sized objects wrapped in brown paper were leaning against the wall. The first one was marked in bold black marker EXHIBIT H. He brought it over and set it up on the easel facing the witness box and Judge Williams. Brenner got up and came around to watch.

"Mrs. Thompson," I said, turning to her, "take a look at what I've marked Defendant's Trial Exhibit H."

I glanced over at Vincent Contini and nodded. He reached up and tore the brown wrapping off the poster board, revealing the enlarged side-by-side shot of the two cars in the Thompson driveway. I leaned back against the edge of the table, crossed my arms over my chest, and waited.

Cissy stared intently at the photo, her brows knitted in concentration. You could almost hear those neurons firing. Eventually, she shifted her gaze to me.

"I remember now," she said with a cold smile. "My husband and I attended that function."

"As a matter of fact, you bought the Corvette there, didn't you?"

She gave me a haughty look. "We didn't simply *buy* the car, Miss Gold. We acquired it in exchange for a very generous donation to a worthy cause."

I couldn't help but smile. Might as well take a freebie. "A worthy cause," I repeated as I came over to the witness box and took away the program. As I returned to counsel's table I said, "And what exactly was that worthy cause?"

There was silence. I kept my back to her.

"Objection," Brenner said, scrambling to his feet. "Irrelevant."

I turned around. I'd already scored the point, as was clear from Judge Williams's smile. "I'll withdraw the question, Your Honor."

She nodded.

I turned to my client. "Mr. Contini, could you bring over Exhibit I?"

He walked back to the side wall and fetched the second wrapped poster. This one had EXHIBIT I printed in bold black letters on the brown paper.

I turned to the witness. "Do you recall the article on the event in that Sunday's *Post-Dispatch*?"

Cissy glanced uncertainly at her attorney and then back at me.

I sighed patiently. "Okay, let's see if we can refresh that memory again."

I nodded at Vincent Contini. He tore off the wrapping paper, revealing the blowup of the society column from the Style Plus section of the Sunday, August 16, edition of the *Post-Dispatch*. This one Jacki had found for me. The blowup included the photograph of the two women standing in front of a carousel horse.

I pointed to the caption beneath the photograph. "Do you see this photo credit down here?"

Cissy leaned forward. "Yes," she said cautiously.

"Charles Morley," I read. Turning to her, I said, "Do you remember Mr. Morley?"

Uneasy, she shook her head. "I don't think so."

I turned toward the gallery. "He's out there. Charles," I called, "hold up your hand."

Self-consciously, Charles Morley raised his hand.

I turned back to Cissy. "Remember him? He was there that night. For over an hour. Walking around among the guests, taking photographs." I paused. "*Lots* of photographs."

Her eyes flickered anxiously between the photographer and me. "I . . . I don't remember."

I gave her a look of mild disbelief. "Really? You don't remember him taking *lots* of photographs?"

She looked at Brenner. I turned to look at him, too. He had a forced smile on his face that looked more like gas pains.

"Well?" I repeated.

"I . . . I don't . . . I'm not sure."

I turned to Vincent Contini. "Well, I guess it's time for Exhibit J."

Vincent walked over to the wall and brought back the final wrapped poster. This one had EXHIBIT J printed on the brown paper. As he set it on the easel, I said to him, "Just a moment."

Rubbing my chin thoughtfully, I turned toward the dress hanging from the hook. Then I looked over at the shoes and the purse resting on the ledge in front of Cissy Thompson. Her eyes were wide as her gaze kept shifting from me to the wrapped poster on the easel to her lawyer and back to me again.

"Let me move these to a better position," I said as I walked over to the dress and removed it from the hook. I carried it back to the easel and handed it to my client. "Vincent, could you stand with the dress on this side of the easel?" I steered him next to counsel's table. "There. And hold the dress up."

"Certainly," he said with a dignified smile.

Then I walked over to Cissy, who leaned back as I approached, and I picked up the shoes and the handbag. I carried them over to counsel's table and lined them up on the edge of the table near where Vincent was standing. Then I stepped back, like a set designer, to study the arrangement. As I did, I saw the clock on the back wall. Eleven minutes after twelve. Perfect.

I turned back to the judge with an apologetic smile. "Your Honor, I wonder if we could take a break. Before I move to the next line of inquiry, I would like to ask Mrs. Thompson to put on the dress and the shoes."

Milt Brenner was up like a jack-in-the-box. "Actually, Your Honor, if we're taking a break perhaps we could make it for lunch as well."

Judge Williams looked up at the clock and then back down at me. There was the hint of a smile on her face. "Very well, Mr. Brenner. The court will be in recess until two o'clock. That should give the plaintiff ample time to eat her lunch and put on the dress and the shoes before she returns to the witness stand."

With a bang of her gavel, Judge Williams left the bench. As soon as the door closed behind her, Vincent Contini came over and hugged me.

"Oh, Rachel, you were truly magnificent."

"Wait," I cautioned. "It's not over yet." I glanced nervously at the easel. "Excuse me a moment," I told him and walked over to take down the wrapped poster board marked EXHIBIT J. I carried it over to the bailiff. "I need this locked up," I told him.

He was an elderly black man with a big paunch and a pleasant moon face. "Oh, that's okay, Miss Gold. We lock the courtroom doors here during the lunch recess."

I leaned in close. "I can't leave it in here," I said quietly. "I have to get it somewhere safe."

He shrugged good-naturedly. "Okay, Miss Gold. We can put it in the vault. Follow me."

The vault was three floors down, inside the office of the circuit clerk. Once I got Exhibit J safely stowed, I stopped at a pay phone outside the clerk's office to call Jacki, who was no doubt dying of curiosity.

"Oh, my God," she said, "tell me what's happening."

I filled her in on the morning's events.

"Oh, my God," she said, "what if it doesn't work?"

"I'll improvise."

"Improvise?" She sounded apoplectic.

"I'll have her stand there in that outfit. I'll make sure my witnesses get a good look at her. Maybe it'll jog their memories about what she wore that night. Listen, Jacki, I gotta run. I'll check in later."

"Rachel, Jonathan Wolf has called five times this morning. He says he has to talk to you."

I groaned. "Oh, God, I can't deal with that now."

"Rachel, I promised him you'd call back at the lunch break."

"Tell him you haven't heard from me."

"Rachel, just call him."

I closed my eyes and leaned back against the wall. The whole Sally Wade mess came bubbling back to the surface like a sewage backup. "Okay," I finally sighed. "Can you conference him onto this call?"

"Hang on." About a minute later, he came on the line. "Rachel, we need to talk."

"Please, Jonathan, I'm in the middle of a trial."

"Then tonight. I'll come by your office after court."

I closed my eyes and rubbed my forehead. Actually, seeing him in person wasn't such a bad idea in light of what I had to tell him. The one thing that last night's adventure in the car trunk had convinced me to do was drop out of the Sally Wade investigation ASAP. I wasn't a criminal lawyer, I wasn't a private eye, and in light of my performance in the parking lot I definitely wasn't a ninja warrior. Life was too short to try to run with that crowd.

"Okay," I said, "but not for long."

"What time?"

Judge Williams was unlikely to keep us in court beyond five o'clock. At five-thirty I had my self-defense class. After last night, I said to myself, maybe Faith Compton could teach me how to disarm a first-grader with a water pistol. "Seven-thirty," I said.

"Fine. At your office?"

The class was only five minutes from my house, and I'd be hot and sweaty afterward. I could take a shower and grab a bite to eat before he got there. "No," I said. "Come by my house."

"I'll be there. I'll see whether Neville can join us."

"Neville?" He was the last person I wanted to deal with tonight. "Why him?"

Jonathan paused. "Because he got a call from Tammy this morning."

I grimaced. "Did he give her my name?"

"He did," Jonathan said. "And mine as well."

"Oh." The case seemed to have a relentless gravitational field that kept yanking me back into its orbit.

"I'll fill you in tonight," he said.

I hung my head down.

"Rachel?"

"Fine," I said indifferently.

"Good luck."

"Pardon?"

"In your trial. Good luck."

"Oh. Yeah. Thanks."

I was still in a funk when I got off the elevator on Judge Williams's floor. I checked my watch. It was almost one o'clock. Although I didn't have an appetite, I could hear my mother's voice telling me I had to keep up my strength for the afternoon. Also, she would no doubt add, you have guests: your client, his wife, and their son.

Yes, Mother.

I headed back to the courtroom to gather the Contini clan and take them to lunch somewhere near the courthouse. As I approached the door I tried to get myself properly focused. The Sally Wade situation was tonight. This was now, and for Vincent Contini this was also one of the most important events in his life.

He jumped to his feet as I came through the door. "Ah, Rachel, hurry. They're waiting for you in the judge's chambers."

I frowned. "Who's waiting?"

"Her lawyer and the judge. Her clerk told me to send you back there immediately. They need to see you right away."

Thirty minutes later I emerged from Judge Williams's chambers and found Vincent pacing in the hallway while his wife and son watched from a bench. When he saw me he came dashing over.

"Well?" he asked anxiously.

I smiled. "I have a new settlement proposal from them."

He straightened, his expression wary. "What is it?"

"Thirty thousand dollars."

His eyes widened in outrage. "I wouldn't pay that woman a dime."

I put my hand on his shoulder. "I know that, Vincent. Their original proposal was to drop the lawsuit in exchange for your agreement to keep the settlement terms confidential. I told them you were willing to keep the terms confidential but you expected to be reimbursed for your time and your legal fees. They offered a thousand. I demanded fifty. The judge persuaded them to raise their offer to thirty thousand. I told them to wait while I sought your approval."

He stared at me in wonder. "*She* will pay *me* thirty thousand dollars?"

I nodded.

"*Mama mia,*" he mumbled. Then he stiffened, suspicious. "What exactly are these confidential settlement terms?"

"Simple," I said with a smile. "We have to destroy all photographs of her, and we can't let anyone know that they paid you money to get rid of the lawsuit."

Vincent made me repeat the settlement proposal. He nodded slowly as I explained it. There were tears in his eyes when I finished. "Rachel," he said, his voice filled with emotion, "I told you last Sunday that God smiles down upon you." He placed his hands on my shoulders and kissed me lightly on each cheek. "And now," he said, his voice almost a whisper, "I see that God has smiled down upon me as well. Thank you, my dear."

We drew up the settlement papers right there in the courtroom, and Vincent signed them before we left for a victory lunch at Kemoll's in One Metropolitan Square. At Vincent's insistence, I called Jacki to have her join us at the restaurant.

Milt Brenner promised to deliver a fully executed copy of the settlement agreement to Kemoll's along with a certified check for thirty thousand dollars. Both arrived during dessert. By then we were on our third bottle of Chianti, and I for one was feeling no pain.

"Ah," Vincent said with a wistful smile, "I have only regret." He looked at me across the table. "I would have liked to see that woman's expression when you unveiled Exhibit J."

I glanced over at Jacki, who was trying to keep a straight face. I looked back at Vincent. "Then you should have no regrets, Vincent. No one would ever have seen that exhibit."

Vincent frowned. "But it was the next one. It was up on the easel. I put it there myself."

"Remember I had the bailiff lock it away. If trial had resumed after lunch, the easel would have been empty."

Now he was baffled. "But, Rachel, wasn't it a photograph of that horrid woman in my dress?"

I leaned forward. "Can you keep a secret?" I whispered.

He nodded. "Certainly."

I looked around the table with a conspiratorial smile. "The photographer checked the other roll of film. He didn't have a single picture of her that night. Not one. Exhibit J was a blank piece of poster board."

Victor looked at his wife and then back at me. "I don't understand."

"Have you ever played poker?" I asked.

He stared at me for a moment, and then leaned back with an admiring smile. "You were bluffing?"

I gave him a wink and pressed my index finger against my lips. "Shhhh."

CHAPTER 26

Faith Compton adjusted my right arm. "Remember, Rachel, it's a two-step move: out slow until the chain is fully extended, then up and around hard."

I nodded, trying to visualize the move. "Okay."

Faith had sensed something was awry during the self-defense class. When it ended, she pulled me over as the others gathered their stuff to leave. I was reluctant at first to tell her about the key-chain failure in the parking lot the night before. In fact, I was mortified at having performed so miserably. But she wouldn't let go. She pulled the story out of me, and by the end, with tears welling in my eyes, I let all my frustration pour out. She let me vent, and when I was through she gave me a pep talk, her arms grasping my shoulders as her eyes bored into mine.

"You are no one's victim, Rachel," she said fiercely. "You are not the prey."

She showed me the maneuver for getting the key chain cleanly out of a coat pocket without cutting down on the force of the swing. For the past fifteen minutes, she'd been drilling me in the move.

"Are you ready?" Faith asked. She was standing directly behind me. To protect her hands she was wearing a pair of heavy-duty work gloves.

I nodded. "I think so."

"Let's try it three-quarters speed. On the count of three. One . . . two . . . *three*."

I pulled the key chain clear of the pocket without a hitch. She caught the keys in mid-arc.

"Good. Again. One . . . two . . . *three*."

We did it twenty times, and then ten more times at full speed.

"Excellent," she said after the last one. "That's enough for tonight."

I turned toward her, my face flushed with exertion.

She nodded, her jaw firmly set. "You'll be fine."

"I feel so much better, Faith. Thank you."

"Practice that move, Rachel. Practice it every night. Over and over until you can do it in your sleep." She paused, studying me. "You have great natural talent, but you mustn't let it master you. You must strive to become the master of your talent."

First I had to strive to get home in time to shower and change before Jonathan Wolf arrived. I wasn't planning on getting fancy for him, but I didn't want to meet with him in my exercise outfit, which tonight consisted of a plain gray sweatshirt, black exercise tights, floppy white socks, and Nikes.

I got home in time. The problem was that Benny got there five minutes later.

"Oh, hi," I said ambivalently when I opened the door. He had a large bag in his right hand and a six-pack of Rolling Rock in the other.

"Hey, sexy," he said with a big grin, "how about some Chinese takeout for the victorious trial stud? I hear you kicked major butt in court. Mazel tov!"

I didn't have the heart to do anything but feign gra-

cious appreciation and invite him in. I followed him into
the kitchen, padding behind in my socks.

"I figured you'd be getting back from that judo class
around now," he said. "You must be starved."

"That's sweet," I said, trying to muster some enthusiasm. Actually, I was still stuffed from the victory lunch
at Kemoll's. As Benny started to unpack the bag, I
glanced up at the clock. Jonathan would be here in less
than twenty minutes.

"Uh-oh," Benny said, pausing with a white takeout
carton in his hand. He'd caught me looking at the clock.
"Do you have a date tonight?"

"Oh, no," I said, trying to make light of it. "It's just a
Sally Wade matter. Jonathan Wolf is dropping by at
seven-thirty. Strictly business."

He chuckled. "Sure. Strictly business. Bet you've heard
that line before."

"Don't start," I warned.

He held up his hands in surrender. "Just kidding."

"Anyway, he's probably bringing Neville McBride
along." After a moment, I said, "It's just that I hate to
meet him dressed like this."

"What are you talking about? Black tights and those
legs. Damn, girl, you look like a Rockette."

"I'm sweaty and disgusting."

"Trust me, Rachel. You look awesome."

I went over to the cabinet and got out two plates and
some silverware.

"Benny," I said in disbelief as I watched him remove
the sixth white carton from the take-out bag, "there's
only two of us."

"And Ozzie makes three." He looked over at Ozzie
and winked. "Right, big fella?"

Ozzie wagged his tail joyously. Benny and Chinese
takeout were two of Ozzie's favorite things in the world.

"I couldn't make up my mind," Benny explained to
me. "Gotta go with the Kung Pao Squid, right? Same

with Moo-Shu Pork. Hell, a Chinese meal without Moo-Shu Pork is like a day without a good shit."

I sighed. "You have such a winsome touch with the English language."

"Then you got your Mongolian Beef, just sitting there on the menu crying, 'Eat me, Benny, eat me.' And Ozzie loves it, don't you, you Mongolian Maniac?"

Ozzie barked twice, his tail whacking the refrigerator door.

Benny opened one of the containers and peered in. "Ah, yes. Tonight's special. Szechuan Crunchy Duck. Christ, the name alone gave me a woody." He held it toward me. "Take a whiff of that, white girl."

"Smells delicious," I conceded.

"I almost stopped there, but Jesus, they have sixty-two entrees on the fucking menu, and I suddenly realized we didn't have a chicken dish. Gotta go with General Tso's Chicken, right? I was in a militaristic mood anyway. Guy must have been a trip. I mean, shit, how many army guys you know have a chicken dish named after them?"

"Do you realize," I said as I took out two beer mugs, "that if General Tso ever invaded Kentucky, he could have fought Colonel Sanders?"

Benny gave me an appreciative grin. "That is one weird concept."

Just then the doorbell rang. We exchanged looks.

"Hey," Benny said with a shrug, "maybe the Wolf Man likes Chinese."

Ozzie came with me to the door. It was Jonathan, looking as if he had just come back from court in his dark suit, white shirt, and striped tie. It was an unseasonably warm November evening, and he had his suit jacket slung over his shoulder.

"I'm early," he said with an apologetic smile. "When we talked earlier I forgot that this is the housekeeper's night off. I have to leave here in thirty minutes." He leaned over to scratch Ozzie behind the ear. "Neville's still at his firm," he explained. "He's stuck in negotiations over some acquisition, but we can reach him by phone if we need to."

I took Jonathan into the kitchen and introduced him to Benny. They seemed cordial enough as they shook hands, though it was obvious to me that Benny was sizing him up, assuming the role of my big brother. As for Jonathan, if he was wondering about my outfit or what Benny was doing in my kitchen with enough Chinese takeout to feed the St. Louis Rams, he gave no indication. He politely declined Benny's offer of food and glanced at his watch.

"Tell me about Tammy's call," I said. "You can talk in front of Benny. He knows all about the case."

Jonathan loosened his tie and filled us in. Tammy had called Neville at his office that morning. The call lasted twelve minutes and twenty-two seconds. (Neville has a timer device on his phone.) They exchanged pleasantries. She said that she hadn't heard or read anything about the case for a few days and hoped that that was a good sign. Neville explained that the lack of news didn't signify anything. He told her that his attorney was preparing for trial, which was still about a month away. She expressed her concern. He asked if they could meet somewhere. That question seemed to agitate her. She rambled on about her privacy and her fear of the media and the police. Neville asked if she would at least consider talking to Jonathan or, in the alternative, to the attorney for Sally's estate. She was unwilling to make any commitment on the issue, but took down our names and phone numbers, office and home.

"You think she has a criminal record?" I asked.

"Or maybe an outstanding arrest warrant," Benny mused.

Jonathan shrugged. "Possibly. Or perhaps there was an embarrassing episode in her past that she's afraid will be exposed if she comes forward."

"You really think she can help Neville?" Benny asked him.

Jonathan scratched his beard pensively. "She's acting as if she knows something critical." He turned to me. "If she calls one of us, it's likely to be you."

"Oh, brother," I said, shaking my head. "I'll talk to her if she calls, but that's it. I've got to get out of this case."

Jonathan nodded. "I understand."

I shook my head. "No, you don't." I paused, looking at both of them. "I got another threat last night."

"What?" Benny said, appalled.

I told them about the incident in the Schnuck's parking lot.

Benny went ballistic. "This is a fucking outrage," he said, slamming his fist onto the table.

Jonathan was visibly upset. "Have you talked to the police yet?" he asked.

I gave him a helpless shrug. "No. I was so upset I went right home. And then I ran out of time. I had the trial today, all kinds of catching up this afternoon, and then my self-defense class. The time got away from me."

"I bet it's that fucking Junior Dice," Benny said angrily.

I shook my head. "He's still in jail."

Jonathan had me describe the incident one more time so that he could give the police and the FBI all the relevant facts. He was going to call his contacts at both places when he got home. "As far as Tammy goes," he said, "if she should call you, just tell her to call me."

"Oh, I can talk to her," I said to him. "I don't mind that part. I just want to tie up the other loose ends, turn it over to you, and get on with my life." I looked over at Benny. "For example, I've got Amy putting some slaughterhouse files together for me tomorrow."

"Slaughterhouse files?" Jonathan asked.

I gave him a rueful smile. "I'm looking for gallstones."

He frowned. "Pardon?"

I explained the gallstone angle, including the trip to Chicago and my discovery of the Bruce Napoli twist.

The Napoli connection surprised him. "Interesting," he mused.

"It could be just a coincidence," I cautioned. "After all, Napoli's probably near the top of most lists of St. Louis environmental lawyers."

"How many matters is he handling for them?" Jonathan asked me.

I shook my head. "I don't know if he's ever handled any matters for them. In fact, you should talk to Neville McBride about that. See whether he can access the firm's files on Douglas Beef without Napoli's knowledge."

Jonathan checked his watch and went over to the phone. "I'll ask him now."

He reached Neville, quickly described the situation, and listened to his response, which he relayed to me. Although Neville could obtain copies of the firm's client/matter listings, a request for anything more specific might get back to Bruce. All of the environmental practice group files were centrally maintained by a filing clerk who reported directly to Bruce.

"Is she loyal to him?" I asked Jonathan.

He nodded grimly. "She's his niece."

I mulled it over. I'd worked for five years at a big corporate firm and was used to those client/matter listings; by contrast, Jonathan had only worked as a government prosecutor or in a two-man criminal defense firm.

I said, "See if Neville can drop off a copy of the lists at my office tomorrow. I'll take a look at them. If Douglas Beef shows up, you can move to phase two."

"Which is?" Jonathan asked.

I grinned sheepishly. "I was hoping you'd tell me."

* * *

"Come on, Rachel," Benny said. "I've got a squid in here with your name on it."

"No way," I groaned. "I'm *plotzing*."

Benny turned to Ozzie, who was sprawled on the floor in the corner. Tilting the container toward him, Benny said, *"Nu?"*

Ozzie gazed at him but didn't move.

Benny shook his head with pity. "A pair of short hitters."

Jonathan had left for home an hour ago, and shortly afterward Benny had announced his unsolicited approval of the match. He had proceeded to consume the entire carton of Kung Pao Squid while lecturing me on the reasons I should drag Jonathan Wolf up to my bedroom and "knock his yarmulke off." Now that he was finished (the squid and the lecture), he took a swig of beer and reached for a fortune cookie and popped it in his mouth whole. I watched in amusement as he devoured the cookie without bothering to crack it open.

"By the way, Miss Manners," I said, "you just ate your fortune."

"Huh? Eh, fuck it. They're a rip-off anyway. You get aphorisms instead of fortunes. You know the world is going to hell in a handbasket when you get your worldview from your dessert." He paused, as it fully dawned on him. "Jeez, I really ate my fortune?"

I cracked mine open, pulled out the little slip of paper, read it, and shook my head.

"Let me guess," he said. " 'Smile and the world smiles with you.' "

"Nope. It says, 'Large male friend just consumed winning number in Missouri Lottery.' "

"You're a regular comedian, Rachel." He got up and went to the fridge. "Another brew?"

I shook my head. "Not for me." I peered into the bag. "There's another fortune cookie in there."

"It's all yours," he said as he pulled out a beer.

I cracked it open and pulled out the slip of paper.

"What's it say?" he asked as he returned to the table.

I looked up with a smile. " 'Smile and the world smiles with you.' "

"Yeah, right."

I held out the fortune. He read it, and looked up with a triumphant smile. "Need I say more? The prosecution rests."

CHAPTER 27

I knocked.

"Rachel?" Amy called.

"It's me."

"Door's open."

I turned the handle and stepped into the reception area of what had once been Sally Wade & Associates. Amy was seated on the carpet, her back propped against the front of the receptionist's desk. She was wearing a Chicago Bears jersey, faded jeans, and tennis shoes, and she was surrounded by storage boxes. Literally. Boxes on the floor, boxes on the reception desk, boxes on the couch. She had an open box on the carpet between her legs.

"Oy," I said.

Amy uttered an exhausted sigh. "Believe me, this is one job I definitely will not miss."

I looked around. "Wow. I had no idea she had so many Douglas Beef files."

"Hah," Amy snorted. "I had no idea she was so disorganized back then. Every one of these boxes is a mishmash of files. From what I can tell, she'd wait until she had a box worth of closed files and then ship them off to storage. Take this one," she said, gesturing at the box in front of her. She pulled out a file folder and opened it. "What do we have here? Ah, yes, a personal injury case. Auto accident. Settled for, let's see, four grand."

She stuffed the file back in the box and pulled out another. "Let's see . . . this looks like a slip-and-fall. In a National supermarket." She put that one back and started paging slowly through the rest of the folders in the box. "Here we've got a medical-mal case . . . followed by, let's see, another fender-bender. Both closed in August six years ago. Same as the others in the box." She flipped through two more files. "Ah, here we go. Finally." She pulled out a folder and held it up triumphantly.

"Douglas Beef?" I asked.

"Yep." She studied the label on the file. "Workers' comp claim." She opened the folder on her lap and started leafing through the pages. "What do we have here? Mmmhmm. Mmm-hmm. Oh, my. Bad times on the loading dock. Looks like someone backed over poor Howie Goodman's left foot with a forklift." She looked up at me and uttered an exaggerated groan. "Explain this again. What am I supposed to be looking for?"

"A needle in a haystack. More precisely, a gallstone in a haystack."

She looked perplexed. "Why just the older Douglas Beef files?"

"According to Sally's passport," I explained, "she made her first trip to Hong Kong four years ago. Assuming she went over there to sell cattle gallstones, she must have made her contact at Douglas Beef before then. There might be a clue in one of the older files."

She nodded. "Makes sense."

I set my purse and briefcase onto the floor and walked over to the couch. "I'll help." I sat down next to a box.

When we called it quits three hours later, I was in a state of total information overload. Between us, we'd found eighteen Douglas Beef files—all workers' comp claims—and we still had half the boxes to go. The files we'd found consisted of dozens and dozens of pages of seemingly irrelevant material. Brady Kane had been a witness in a few of the cases, but there was no indication of any direct contact between him and Sally. Nor was there mention in any of the files of gallstones, organ sales, Hong Kong, or anything remotely connected to the criminal case of *People of the State of Missouri v. Neville McBride.*

When I returned to my office around two o'clock, there was a manila envelope from Tully, Crane & Leonard waiting for me. The envelope contained a handwritten note from Neville McBride paperclipped to two pages photocopied from the firm's Client/Matter Report and two from the firm's Closed File Log.

The Client/Matter Report was arranged alphabetically by client, with separate matters listed beneath each client and the initials of the billing attorney shown at the far right. The first of the two pages of the report were from the B's and had been copied, according to Neville McBride's handwritten note, to show that Bennett Industries (parent company of Douglas Beef) was not currently a client of the firm:

Bender Tool, Inc.	#2342915	(RGB)
Tax Matters	002	
v. Anderson Corp.	005	
Lease Negotiations	006	
Bennett, Earl, M.D.	#4326863	(LRA)
Practice Group Contract	001	
Estate Planning	002	
Bentley Enterprises	#3376215	(TMN)
D&O Insurance Review	009	
Wage-Hour Dispute	011	
Stock Option Plan	014	
Yardley Inc. v.	015	

The second page from the Client/Matter List was from the D's. Neville had highlighted the entries for Douglas Beef:

Douglas Beef Co.	#2375490	(BRN)
General	001	
Environmental	002	
Labor	003	

The document showed three current matters for Douglas Beef, all identified in the most generic possible way. The BRN stood for Bruce R. Napoli, which meant he was the partner in charge of the client.

The second two pages in the packet had been copied from the Closed File Log. The first page showed two matters for Bennett Industries—"Opinion Letter re Drabble" and "Missouri Franchise Tax re Drabble." Both had been closed for more than five years. The initials of the billing attorney were HLD (Harrison L. Dawber, according to my Tully, Crane telephone directory). Neville McBride had scribbled in the margin: "Spoke to Harry re Bennett—says our firm retained for limited purposes re sale of Drabble Plastiform Co. to Condesco Inc.— Harry and 1 associate did all work on both matters." The second photocopied page was from the D's and showed that there were no closed matters for Douglas Beef.

I called McBride. "Can you get a billing and collections report on Douglas Beef?" I asked.

"I have it in front of me."

"What's it show?"

"Year to date, we've billed Douglas Beef $56,750. Last year, we billed them $83,500. The year before, $64,355."

"What are Bruce's origination numbers?"

"Just a moment." I heard him rustling through papers. Law firms track various numbers for each partner: hours billed, realization rate on those hours, and the like. But for a rainmaker like Bruce Napoli, the most important numbers are the origination numbers, which represent the dollars his clients pay the firm for services rendered. The bigger the origination numbers, the larger the compensation and the greater the power.

"Here we go. Year to date, Bruce has three point eight million dollars. Last year, four point five million dollars. The year before three point nine."

I jotted the numbers down. Douglas Beef was not a significant client of his, at least from a dollars angle.

I rapped the eraser end of my pencil on the legal pad as I studied the photocopied materials. "Tell me about your computer system."

He chortled. "You are asking the wrong person, Rachel. My level of expertise in modern office technology extends no further than my portable dictation machine, which I started using for the first time this summer when my secretary was on vacation and the temp didn't know shorthand."

"Are your computers networked?"

"Yes, although I'm not quite sure what it means other than that people can send e-mail messages to each other. I get the damn things all day long."

"The firm has a D.C. office, right?"

"Indeed we do. We also have offices in Orlando and West Palm Beach."

"I assume all of your offices are on the network?"

"Oh, yes. That was a big selling point for the system."

I smiled. "Excellent."

"Really?"

"Trust me."

I said good-bye and placed a call to Henderson Consulting in Chicago.

"Mr. Henderson, please," I told the breathy receptionist.

Next to answer was his secretary, sounding even more sensual than the receptionist.

I had to smile. "Can I talk to him?" I asked.

"For whom shall I tell Mr. Henderson is calling?"

I paused long enough to decide her sentence didn't parse. "Tell him it's Rachel Gold."

"Just a moment, Ms. Gold."

Another delay, and then a familiar voice. "Yo, Rachel. What's up, girl?"

"Who you calling 'girl,' Ty? That's 'woman' to you."

"I'll call you woman, girl, when you finally acknowledge reality and become *my* woman."

"You know the rules, Ty. Mom says it has to be a nice Jewish boy. Until you join *my* religion, I can't become *your* woman."

"Hey, baby, you ain't talking to no Sammy Davis, Jr."

"And you ain't talking to no honky bimbo. Speaking of which, Mr. Henderson, who is that phone sex brigade answering your phones?"

"Ain't they something? Those girls give good phone, and don't my clients love it, heh, heh."

Tyrone Henderson was one of my favorite people, and his success over the years had been marvelous to observe. We had joined Abbott & Windsor the same year: he fresh out of high school as a minimum-wage messenger, I fresh out of Harvard Law School as a litigation associate at the going rate back then of forty-eight thousand a year plus bonus. Tyrone spent his days delivering draft contracts and court papers to other firms in the Loop and his nights taking courses in computer programming. When he earned his certificate from night school, he applied for an opening on the firm's *In re Bottles & Cans* computer team. By the time I left the firm, Tyrone was the head programmer for the national *Bottles & Cans* defense steering committee. Over the years he helped design many of Abbott & Windsor's computer systems, including the network linkup with all of its branch offices. Two years before, he'd left Abbott &

Windsor to start his own consulting firm specializing in the design of computer systems for law firms.

"By the way," I said, "I finally got your picture framed."

"About time, girl."

Last winter, Tyrone had been featured in a *Chicago* magazine piece on the city's most eligible bachelors. I'd picked up a copy of the issue, cut out the page with his photograph, and sent it to him for an autograph. He sent it back, signed: *To Rachel, We'll always have Paris. Ty.*

"But I'm having a problem with the glare, Ty."

"What glare?"

"Off your shaved head. That thing is shinier than an eight ball. What did you do, Ty, have them buff it before the shot?"

He chuckled. "Drives the ladies wild. So what's up, girl?"

"I need a computer consultant."

"You dialed the right number."

I described the situation to him.

"I see," he said, his voice instantly becoming utterly professional. Tyrone Henderson could downshift from Cabrini-Green rap to corporate consultant diction and back up again in a nanosecond. "I take it that access to the files themselves is not a viable option."

"Definitely," I said. "I'd have to go through his niece, and that would get right back to him."

"So we talkin' 'bout a little breakin' and enterin'?"

"Well, yes. If there was a way to get into the firm's computer network without being physically present at a terminal in their offices, I could look through the Douglas Beef documents in the system without anyone knowing about it. Can that be done?"

"Easier than you'd imagine. I spend half my time preaching computer security to managing partners. Most law firms have almost no protection. If that firm is typical, I'll be able to get you in."

"My hero."

"Ain't that the truth. Now here's what you need to do. You call over there pretending that you're some lawyer's secretary from, say, Detroit, and ask to talk to someone in their systems department. Tell them that you're supposed to modem a document over there next week and you need some information about their system."

Tyrone proceeded to run through a list of questions for me to ask. He also gave me reasonable answers to questions that the Tully, Crane systems person might ask me. I wrote them down word for word, since I understood less than half of what he told me.

His strategy worked. I got the information he needed, and the systems person at Tully, Crane actually asked me two of the questions Tyrone had prepared me to answer. I called him back and passed on the information. He called me back an hour later with my instructions.

"You call me, Rachel, if you have problems."

"Okay."

"You'll need a password to get in those files or to read old e-mail messages. Here's the one I assigned to you." He read off seven numbers. "Got that?"

"Yep," I said as I wrote it down.

"One more thing. So long as you're going in there, let me tell you how to retrieve documents someone may have deleted from the system."

"How can I retrieve what's been deleted?"

"The computer doesn't physically erase anything. It just sort of forgets where it is. Here's a command that'll make it remember where to find the discards. Write this down."

I did.

"You all set, girl."

"You're totally wonderful, Ty. Next time I'm in Chicago, dinner's on me."

"You got that right."

I hung up and turned toward my credenza. It was nearly five-thirty. I was due at my sister's house at six for Friday-night dinner, but I was itching to see whether Tyrone's instructions would actually get me into the system. If so, I could browse through the Tully, Crane network tomorrow afternoon.

I activated the modem, punched in the telephone number Tyrone had given me, and pressed TRANSMIT. When the computer on the other end answered, I followed Tyrone's step-by-step instructions until the screen displayed the message:

PASSWORD?

I typed in the password Tyrone had given me and hit the Enter key. The screen went blank for a few seconds and then displayed a new message:

GOOD AFTERNOON, FOXY LADY.
WELCOME TO THE TULLY, CRANE & LEONARD NETWORK.
PRESS ANY KEY TO CONTINUE.

Foxy lady? I repeated with an amused smile. Classic Tyrone. Then again, it was certainly better than having the Tully, Crane computer greet me as Rachel Gold. My name was the last thing I needed floating around in their computer network.

I pressed a key and the screen immediately displayed a new message:

YOU HAVE 1 NEW E-MAIL MESSAGE.
DO YOU WISH TO REVIEW IT NOW (YES/NO)

E-mail message? Intrigued and a tad edgy, I typed in *Yes* and hit the ENTER key. A new message unfurled on the screen:

To: Foxy Lady
From: The Man of Your Dreams
Re: Breakin' and Enterin'

    Congrats, girl. You in. Happy hunting. Meanwhile, I'm making reservations for two at L'Escargot, and you're buying.

    Oh, yeah. Almost forgot. Good Shabbos.

I smiled at the message on the screen. "Good Shabbos, Ty," I said.

CHAPTER 28

       The St. Louis weather in November could charitably be described as whimsical. Just two nights before, it had been sixty-eight degrees when Jonathan Wolf arrived at my front door. Last night, we'd had our first killing frost. My patch of basil and bed of impatiens were not the only casualties. My car wouldn't start. All new windows and the same old engine. The timing was terrible: in fifteen minutes I was supposed to pick up my niece and nephew. We'd made our plans after dinner last night at my sister's house. The three of us were going rollerblading through Forest Park in the morning, then to lunch at the Crown Candy Kitchen, followed by a movie of their choice (unless I could talk them into *Old Yeller*, which was playing at the Tivoli).

    The car battery seemed okay—headlights worked, engine cranked—but what did I know? After several more tries, I went inside to call for help. The man at the service station promised he'd have someone there in ten minutes. I checked my watch. Time for Plan B. I called my sister and told her the problem. I promised to call as soon as the mechanic arrived.

    I went outside to wait. On a hunch, I tried to start the

car again. No luck. The engine cranked but wouldn't catch. As I got out of the car, I realized that it wasn't in the most convenient place for the mechanic. I had parked it last night at the top of the driveway in front of the garage. The space looked too narrow for maneuvering the tow truck into position. Fortunately, my car was light, the driveway was level, and I had plenty of nervous energy. I released the brake and, with one hand on the steering wheel and the other on the doorframe, I pushed the car down the driveway toward the front of the house. As I hopped into the car and put on the brakes, the big red tow truck from Roy's Amoco turned into the driveway behind me.

The driver's door opened and a guy in a tan mechanic's jumpsuit stepped down. According to the name patch stitched above his chest pocket, his name was Danny. He looked fresh out of high school, with tousled blond hair, big blue eyes, a smudge of grease on his cheek, and an adorable pair of dimples. He was so darn courteous and respectful that I felt like a marooned old maid.

Danny lifted up the hood and had me try to start the car while he leaned inside and fiddled with something that was apparently connected to the gas pedal. When that didn't work, he poked around for a few minutes and then came around to my window.

"I think I spotted the problem, ma'am."

"Bad?"

"Not really. It looks like the wire to the coil got disconnected. I bet I can get it up and running in five or ten minutes." He gave me a sweet smile. "You can wait inside, ma'am. I'll come get you when it's all fixed."

As I walked toward my front door, I wondered whether three years at Harvard Law School had started me down the wrong romantic path—a path strewn with discarded Ph.D.s, J.D.s, and M.D.s. Maybe life's pleasures were better shared in the company of an adorable, aboveboard auto mechanic with cute buns. If nothing else, he'd be able to fix the leaky faucet in my downstairs bathroom—an achievement not to be belittled and far beyond the talents of my last boyfriend. As I opened the door, I paused to glance back at him. He was, as my niece Jennifer would say, buttery.

I took the portable phone from the kitchen, pressed the speed-dial code for my sister, and headed back to the living room. Ann answered on the second ring.

"It's me," I said.

"Can you hold a sec, Rachel? I have Joanie on the other line."

I peered through the living-room window. Danny was straightened up from under the hood. He pulled a red bandanna out of the back pocket of his jumper and used it to wipe off his hands.

"Rachel?"

"The mechanic is out there now. He says it's a loose wire or something. He thinks he can fix it right here."

"Oh, good."

I watched through the window as Danny got into the driver's side of the car.

"That was a great dinner last night," I told her.

As I stood by the window, I saw Danny close the car door. The hood of the car was still up.

"Here he goes," I said to her. "Let's see if he's got it fixed."

I watched as he inserted the ignition key.

Looking back, the moment seems fixed in amber, as if someone hit Time's pause button: Danny motionless, key in the ignition. Then Time lurched forward in freeze frames.

Danny frowning in concentration, his head tilted forward.

A crow cawing from somewhere nearby.

Danny turning the ignition key, his elbow cocked.

The engine cranking.

A falling acorn tocking against the window near my head.

The car hood, still propped open, shivering as the engine turned over.

And then—a fast-forward nightmare.

A ball of fire erupted from under the hood, followed by an explosion that blew apart the front end of the car and rattled the living-room window.

Red flames shot out of what had been the engine block. Danny's figure was visible through the smoke, slumped backward in the driver's seat, mouth open.

A tire wobbled across the front lawn.

I stared in horror at what was left of the car.

Danny's head bobbed slightly. He was alive.

"Oh, no," I gasped, starting for the front door, the phone gripped in my hand.

That's when the second fireball ignited, shattering the living-room window with a deafening roar and slamming me onto the floor in a shower of broken glass.

There was an awful moment of silence as I lay facedown on the wood floor—and then the hollow clatter of metal rain.

The emergency-room doctor at the hospital told me I was lucky. Just a concussion and some lacerations.

"Oh, yes, missy," concurred the Pakistani plastic surgeon as he stitched the cuts on my arms and back. "It could have been much worse." The scars would be almost invisible, he promised. Had I still been in front of the window at the moment of the second detonation, the window panes would have exploded like shrapnel into my face. He *tsk*, *tsk*, *tsk*ed, as he tied off the sutures, one by one. "You are one lucky lady," he said.

"Please please please please stop talking," I pleaded, my eyes squeezed shut.

Later, as I lay alone in my curtained-off area of the emergency room, I heard them on the other side. "He was blown to smithereens," a female nurse said in a hushed tone. Some male—sounded like an ambulance driver—described a severed arm dangling high in a tree across the street from my house, "just like a fucking Christmas ornament, man."

Eventually, they moved me to an upper floor "for observation." Because I had lost consciousness after the explosion, the doctors wanted to keep me overnight to make sure there were no neurological problems. I was placed in a room designated private, although it soon felt like Groucho Marx's stateroom in *A Night at the Opera.* First to arrive were two police detectives, who entered immediately after the orderly wheeled me into the room. They asked questions for about twenty minutes before my mother arrived, her eyes red, a handkerchief twisted in her hand. Brushing aside the detectives, she sat on the bed and gave me a fierce hug. There were anxiety and protection in that hug, but there was vengeance, too. She's still my mother, and no one but no one messes with Sarah Gold's little girl.

Next to arrive was my sister, Ann, flustered and scared, followed five minutes later by a stout, officious nurse who announced that it was time for everyone to leave so that "patient" could get some rest—an announcement that my mother immediately and decisively overruled. "I'm her mother," she said, standing up and stepping toward the nurse, "and I'm not ready to leave."

The nurse retreated, her eyes blinking, and almost backed into the next arrival, Jonathan Wolf, who came dashing around the corner and into the room, his cashmere topcoat unbuttoned and trailing behind like a cape. He sidestepped the nurse and approached the bed.

"Good Lord, Rachel," he said with a stricken look on his face, "how are you?"

"A little dizzy, a little sore."

He leaned over and gently took my hand. There was tender concern in his green eyes. "I'm so sorry, Rachel."

I gave him a plucky smile. "Aren't you supposed to be at services this morning?"

He reached up and gently brushed back my curls to reveal a bandage high on my forehead. "Stitches?" he said.

"Not there," I said. "That's where I conked my head."

Benny was next into the room, followed a few minutes later by my secretary, Jacki. Her eye shadow was smudged and her eyes were red. The sight of Jacki buoyed my spirits—in part because of the special place she occupied in my heart and in part because of her, well, her singularity, which seemed amplified in my crowded hospital room. Dressed in a conservative print dress, white panty hose, a powder-blue pillbox hat, and dark flats, Jacki Baird was at least four inches taller, thirty pounds heavier, and capable of bench-pressing one hundred pounds more than any man in the room.

"Oh my God, Rachel," Jacki said, her lips quavering. "Oh my God, oh my God, you poor thing." She fumbled in her purse, pulled out a facial tissue, and blew her nose at an impressive decibel level.

Amid all the commotion, an earnest young male nurse pushed through the crowd. He leaned over to peer into my eyes with his flashlight as he asked me a few questions about my aches and pains. As he took my pulse, I could hear Jonathan Wolf on the phone over in the corner. He was talking to, or, more precisely, commanding someone high up in the police bureaucracy to assign more resources to the case.

Amy called, having heard the news of the explosion on the radio while she was in Sally Wade's offices reassembling all of the Douglas Beef files we had sorted through yesterday. I assured her I was okay. Just as I finished the call, another doctor arrived. He gave a disapproving glance around the noisy room and then looked down at me. I shrugged weakly. The crowd was beginning to get to me, too. My mother must have spotted the shrug, because she started moving around the room suggesting that it was time to leave so that her daughter could get some rest.

One by one, they stopped by my bed on their way out. Jonathan told me he'd drop by tonight after services. Jacki tried to tell me that she would take care of things at the office but started blubbering halfway through. Benny handed me a small paper bag. Inside were two Payday candy bars and a hardbound copy of Elmore Leonard's latest. Ann was next, with an air kiss and promise to make sure that Richie walked Ozzie before bedtime.

That left my mother and me. "Come on, doll baby," she said. "Let's go downstairs. I'll buy you an ice cream cone."

I yawned. "I don't know, Mom, I'm kind of drowsy."

"That's why you should get out of bed. When you bang your *kep*," she said, using the Yiddish term for head, "you don't go to sleep."

I sat up with a groan. "Yes, Dr. Gold."

One delicious hot fudge sundae later, I said good-bye to my mother at the elevator after assuring her that I was fine on my feet and could easily get back to my room. "Mom, I ran five miles this morning. Assuming the doctors let me go home in the morning, I'll run another five tomorrow."

She gave me another fierce hug. "I'll be back by dinner."

As I rode up the elevator, I tried to imagine who was behind the explosion. I had given the police detectives my list of suspects. There was Junior Dice, of course, even if he was still in jail. Marvin the mortician was a possibility, mainly because he was such an enigma. Then there was Alton police officer Annie McCarthy, who would no doubt have access to the sort of people who rigged car bombs. Brady Kane qualified for any list of suspects. Then there was the other possible connection, the one I hadn't had enough time to explore on Friday afternoon. To my surprise, he was in my hospital room when I returned.

Bruce Napoli was standing by the window with the phone in his hand. He smiled and nodded as I walked in. Even though it was Saturday afternoon, he was wearing one of his commander-in-chief uniforms: black pinstripe suit, crisp white shirt, and a silk gray-and-red-patterned Ralph Lauren tie. His thick, coal-black hair was neatly brushed back.

"Tell him I'll be at the club by five," he said, closing his eyes to concentrate. "We can meet in the St. Andrews Room. Then call Patty. Tell her to meet me at the St. Louis Club at seven. Be sure she knows which room the reception is in. That's all for now, Holly."

He hung up and turned to me. "Ah, back on your feet already." He gave an admiring smile. "That's excellent."

I nodded uncertainly, pulling my robe tighter.

As if reading my mind, he said, "I happened to be in the neighborhood. Up on the fifth floor, actually, visiting Burt Washington. He's the chair of our trusts and estates department. Poor fellow is recovering from heart surgery. Quadruple bypass last week. They just moved him out of intensive care. Seems to be doing well."

Keeping my voice neutral, I asked, "How did you know I was here?"

He chuckled and gestured toward the small television set above the bed. "Turn on your TV. Turn on the radio. You're the lead story, Rachel." He peered out the window. "Look down below."

I joined him at the window. In the parking area below were four television news vans, each with a satellite dish tilted skyward. I stepped back from the window. "Good grief," I murmured as I sat down on the bed.

"Actually, it's good news for you, Rachel."

I looked up at him, puzzled. "How?"

"The publicity will put pressure on the police. Capable, motivated police detectives are a scarce resource.

This will force the department to allocate some of that resource to your case. Second, and more important, it ought to deter any second attempts. You're in the spotlight, which makes it far too risky."

"Great," I said glumly.

There was an electronic chirping sound from inside Napoli's suit jacket. "Excuse me," he said, reaching inside the jacket to remove a portable flip phone. "Yes?" he said into the phone. "Fine, Holly. Tell them I'm leaving now. I should be there in fifteen minutes." He flipped the phone closed. "I'm afraid I have to go, Rachel."

I looked up at him, torn between my urge to probe his Douglas Beef connection and my longing to withdraw completely from this mess, to get back to my life and let Jonathan and the police sort through the debris. After a moment's hesitation, I yielded to the latter.

"Thanks for stopping by, Bruce."

"Certainly." He paused. "I want you to know that we at Tully, Crane appreciate the efforts you've made on behalf of Neville McBride."

I shrugged. "It's more on behalf of Sally Wade."

"Nevertheless, Neville has been a direct beneficiary. Assuming that this morning's criminal act was somehow connected with your investigation—an assumption that seems reasonable—you've been injured in the line of duty, so to speak. Accordingly, I've instructed our accounting department to make the necessary arrangements with the hospital to have all bills for your care and treatment sent directly to Tully, Crane & Leonard."

I was taken aback. "You don't have to do that, Bruce."

He smiled magnanimously. "It's the very least we can do, Rachel. We're still old-fashioned enough at Tully, Crane to view our fellow partners as members of an extended family. This is our way of saying thanks for helping one of ours." He held his hand out. "My best wishes for a speedy and full recovery."

I shook his hand silently, struck by the insincerity of his little homily.

I spent the rest of the afternoon dozing off and on. Jonathan Wolf dropped by after services. Somewhat awkwardly, he offered me the guest room in his house when I was released from the hospital.

"That's sweet," I told him, "but I'll be okay. Your client has given me a state-of-the-art security system at my home, and I'll make sure I park my next car in my state-of-the-art garage."

He nodded gravely. "The offer stands. When you get home, if you should feel at all uneasy about being there alone, just call and I'll come get you. It's no burden."

I leaned forward in bed and touched his arm. "Thank you, Jonathan, but please don't be angry if you don't hear from me." I leaned back in bed and sighed. "Someone wants me minding my own business, and that's what I plan to do. If they're still watching me, I don't want to give them any reason to think that I'm back on the case or that we're working together."

Just then, my dinner tray arrived, followed three minutes later by my mother. Jonathan said his good-byes. My mother had brought a container of her chicken soup with matzoh balls and homemade kreplach. Overruling the nurse's objections, she sent away the hospital tray with the imperiousness of a Cleopatra and had them heat up my soup in their microwave.

"That nurse told me there was chicken soup on your dinner menu," my mother said with irritated disbelief as she returned from the microwave. She set a huge steaming bowl on my bed table. " 'With matzoh balls?' I asked the nurse. 'With what?' she says to me. 'What about kreplach?' I asked her, and she looks at me like maybe I called her a dirty name."

I laughed. "Oh, Mom."

My mother waved her hand dismissively. "Like the

goyim know about chicken soup in the first place? They crumble five saltine crackers in the bowl and think all of a sudden it's a feast fit for a king."

If hell ever decides to add a wake-up call to its list of amenities, the staff at the hospital could provide the in-service training. They woke me every hour, and the drill was the same each time: *What's your name? What's your telephone number? Who's the President of the United States?* Then someone would shine a penlight into each eye, check my pulse, take my blood pressure, and depart, only to return for an encore performance sixty minutes later.

Every hour, on the hour, beginning at ten that night and continuing until I finally cried uncle at eight the following morning. When my mother arrived at nine, I was packed and ready to go.

"Ann's bringing Ozzie back this morning," my mother said as she drove out of the hospital parking garage.

"Oh, good. I miss him."

"I've got your lunch packed in back. You'll come to my house for dinner. I made a brisket."

"That's sweet, Mom, but you shouldn't. I'm feeling fine. Even the doctors agree."

"Let me ask you," my mother said in a different, serious tone after she pulled the car out of the underground garage and turned south onto Kingshighway. "Did you notice that man standing by the black car in front of the hospital when we came out?"

I looked over at her. She was frowning at the rearview mirror. I turned around. There was a black Oldsmobile 88 making the turn onto Kingshighway directly behind us. "That car?" I said.

She nodded silently, still staring at the rearview mirror. I watched the car behind us. My mother pulled onto Highway 40 heading west. So did the black Olds.

"What did he look like?" I asked her.

"Big," she said. "He was wearing a dark suit and one of those fedora hats your father used to wear."

The black Olds had a tinted windshield that made the driver invisible.

"A business suit?" I asked.

She nodded, checking the rearview mirror again.

I looked back again at the Olds, my anxiety level starting to rise. "Get off at Skinker," I told her, "and take the Forest Park Expressway west."

She did. So did the black Olds. It kept a steady distance of three car lengths.

My mind was racing. "Where's the nearest police station?"

"University City."

"That's right," I said. "Get off at Big Bend."

She did. So did the black Olds.

"Hurry, Mom."

I cursed as the light at Delmar turned red. "Don't stop."

She rolled through the stoplight and turned right.

"Faster, Mom."

I watched as the black Olds paused at the edge of the intersection and then turned right.

My mother screeched to a halt near the front of the police station. Before we could open our doors the black Olds pulled in directly behind us.

"Oh, my God," my mother said, her eyes widening as she watched in the rearview mirror. "He's getting out of the car."

"Lock the doors!" I shouted as I spun around in my seat.

The driver's door of the black Olds swung open and out stepped a grim, thickset, square-jawed man. He was wearing a black suit, white shirt, narrow black tie, and weathered gray fedora.

"Honk the horn!" I said.

My mother leaned on the horn as the man came around

to my side of the car. "My God," she yelled, following his progress with her eyes. "My God!"

I leaned away from the window toward my mother as the man approached. I watched his hands carefully, waiting for one to dart inside his suit jacket. But instead, he leaned down with a friendly grin.

I looked over at my mother and back at him.

He tapped on the window and motioned for me to roll it down. Then he held out his hands, palms facing me, to show me they were empty.

I opened it a crack. "What do you want?"

He smiled again, revealing well-worn, tobacco-stained teeth. He politely removed his fedora. "I'm sorry to have frightened you and your mother, Miss Gold. It certainly wasn't my intent."

"Who are you?" I demanded.

He pulled a business card out of his shirt pocket. "Here you go, ma'am." He held the card through the slot in the window.

I took it from him. It read:

WALTER BRUNT
Security & Surveillance
Experienced and Professional

I handed it to my mother. She read it and looked at me, perplexed. By now, three uniformed police officers had come out of the station.

The oldest of the three nodded at Walter Brunt. "What's all the racket, Walt?"

Brunt straightened up and nodded toward the speaker. "Hello, George. I was just introducing myself to my new client."

One of the other officers rapped on my mother's window. She rolled it down. "You okay, ma'am?" he asked.

She looked at the officer and then gestured toward Brunt. "Do you know him?"

"Yes, ma'am," he said, touching the bill of his cap. "Mr. Brunt used to be a special agent with the Treasury Department downtown. Secret Service, I believe. He retired about a year ago and opened his own shop." He looked up at Brunt and winked. "He may have lost a few miles off his fastball, but he's still pretty good."

As the police went back inside, I rolled my window the rest of the way down and stared up at Walter Brunt. He could easily pass for a retired G-man. His gray hair was trimmed short in a crew cut. There were crinkly crow's-feet at the corners of his pale blue eyes. He had thin lips and big ears with pendulous lobes. Put him in a ten-gallon hat and cowboy boots and he could pass for the sheriff of Dodge City.

"Let me get this straight, Mr. Brunt," I said to him. "I'm supposed to be your new client?"

"Yes, ma'am."

"Says who?"

"Jonathan Wolf, ma'am. And you can call me Walt."

"Jonathan Wolf?" I repeated.

"Yes, ma'am." He had a flat Missouri drawl—the kind that comes from the farming communities where folks pronounce their home state *Muh-ZUR-uh.*

"I see." I took his card back from my mother and read it again. I looked up at him. "What exactly are you supposed to do for me, Walt?"

He put his fedora back on and leaned down, resting his leathery, powerful hands on the car door. "Well, ma'am, I'm supposed to watch over you for a few days."

"Is that what Mr. Wolf said?"

He nodded. "You've already had one attempt on your life. Mr. Wolf says once is enough. He was pretty durn clear on that point."

I looked up at him with an amused smile. "You mean you're my bodyguard?"

"In a manner of speaking, ma'am. I'm going to go home with you today and make sure your house is secure.

Same with your garage and your office. Then I'm going to coordinate the police patrols by your house and your office. Mr. Wolf has arranged for squad cars to cruise by from dusk until dawn. I'm going to make sure all that happens in accordance with Mr. Wolf's instructions."

I looked over at my mother. She raised her eyebrows and shrugged. I looked back at him with a smile. "Walt," I said, holding my hand out, "I'm pleased to meet you."

We shook. "Same here, ma'am."

CHAPTER 29

       On a drizzly, overcast Wednesday morning, Danny Mathews was laid to rest in a gray metal coffin near his father's grave on a gentle slope overlooking a bend in the Meramec River. The small cemetery was south of the city, out where split-level suburbia fades into cornfields and silos.

According to the obituary, Danny was survived by his maternal grandmother, his mother, and his two older sisters. The three generations of women, all wearing black shawls, were seated in the front row under the tent at the graveside ceremony. Seated in the four rows of folding chairs behind them were the uncles and the aunts and the cousins and the close family friends.

I stood with a group of younger mourners crowded at the edge of the tent on the other side of the coffin. The minister's back was to us. I looked past the minister at Danny's mother. She was staring at the coffin, which was braced above the fresh grave. Seated on either side of Danny's mother was one of Danny's sisters, and each was gripping her mother's hand. As the minister's voice intoned a prayer to Jesus Our Savior, Danny's mother took a deep breath and sighed, her lips quivering. Her eyes lifted slightly, and she seemed to meet my gaze. I gave her a compassionate look. After a moment, she lowered her eyes to the coffin. I watched her for a while, and then looked up and beyond her.

Barely visible, way off in the distance, was the murky outline of the Mississippi River. It was shrouded in patches of fog that seemed to swirl off the water in slow motion. The river continued its journey south from here, tracing the common border of Missouri and Illinois. Just before Illinois gives way on the east side to Kentucky, the river passes the town of Cairo (*KAY-roe*), where the waters of the Ohio empty into the mighty Mississippi after their long journey down from the Allegheny Mountains of western Pennsylvania.

It must have been the wisps of fog hovering over the river that made me think of Huck and Jim on their raft—floating blind past Cairo on that endless foggy night, floating blind past Jim's chance for freedom, the silence of that night occasionally broken by Jim's hopeful shouts of "Dah's Cairo!" and "Dah she is, Huck!"

My father, *alev hashalom,* read me that wonderful novel when I was a child. I had cried at the end of that fog scene, at the cruelty of fate, at the image of Jim, standing at the edge of the raft, peering into the mist, his face lighting up as he sings out, "Dat's de good ole Cairo at las', I jis knows it!" It made me weep back then, and it made me weep today. My vision blurred as I stared at the distant river. A tear trickled down my cheek. I looked at Danny's coffin, suspended over that black hole in the ground. Someone nearby patted me gently on the back. Someone else whispered, "Is that his girlfriend?"

I had come here alone today, filled with grief and anger and guilt. I had come here to watch a family I didn't know bury a boy I didn't know. I had come alone, knowing not a soul and feeling every bit the guilty bystander. But for the tiniest quirk of fate, Danny would be alive today and I would be dead. But for a single loose wire, it would have been me in a coffin near my father's grave.

The minister droned on, invoking Jesus and mercy and paradise and the Lord's divine grace, but they were just words—empty sounds that couldn't soften the harshness of pointless death. A boy had been killed by mistake. Forget about mercy and divine grace and the rest of those rickety formulas for pumping purpose into something so meaningless. This was an unlucky roll of the dice. Danny had come up snake eyes. Period.

But I struggled nonetheless. Standing there at the edge of the tent, I struggled to find a meaning in what had happened. Danny Mathews had died in my place. I refused to believe that chance was the only explanation.

"It's okay, dear."

Dazed, I looked up from the coffin and into the clear hazel eyes of Danny's grandmother. One of Danny's sisters was leading her out of the tent. The funeral was over, people were leaving. The grandmother placed her hand gently on my arm. She smiled, her head trembling slightly. "Danny's in heaven now, dear," she said. "He's singing with the angels. Oh, my, that child had such a lovely voice."

I nodded, unable to speak. She moved past me and down the slope toward the black limousine, leaning on her granddaughter's arm. The rain had picked up slightly. It made a gentle thrumming on the roof of the tent. I waited until the rest of the mourners had shuffled out, until it was just me and the cold gray coffin and the two workmen waiting off to the side.

I nodded to the men and gestured toward the coffin. "Go ahead," I said.

They exchanged glances, and then the older one shrugged and said to the other, "Come on."

I watched as they lowered the coffin into the ground and pulled the straps free and removed the brace. Nearby was the mound of fresh soil, covered with a tarpaulin. As they pulled off the tarpaulin, I stepped toward them.

"May I?" I asked the older man. I placed my hand on one of the shovels. "One scoop?"

He nodded. "Go ahead."

I lifted a shovelful of dirt and held it over the open grave. The gray coffin seemed much farther away than six feet down. As I stood there, staring down into the grave, I thought how nice it would be to believe that Danny was up there singing with the angels. But it didn't work for me. Maybe there were angels, and maybe they were singing, but I didn't hear them. Perhaps life was just too noisy.

I knew that if there was to be a meaning to Danny's death, it would have to be forged by those of us still alive. I could dodge the rest of the case, but I could never dodge this one fact: Danny had died in my place. Whatever else that might mean, I knew what it meant for me.

Tilting the shovel, I watched the clods of dirt slide off the end and clatter onto the coffin below.

"I'll find him, Danny," I said softly. "I promise."

CHAPTER 30

I called Jonathan Wolf the following morning at eight-thirty and told him I needed to meet with him. He had an arraignment and a client meeting that morning but was free for lunch. When I explained that I didn't want others overhearing the conversation, he said he'd arrange for a private room at the Noonday Club.

"Is there something wrong?" he asked with concern in his voice.

"I'll tell you at lunch."

I suspected that he might be disturbed to learn that I was back on the case again, and if he was, I didn't want to conduct that discussion over the phone.

My suspicions were correct, of course. He was quite upset.

"Rachel," he said, shaking his head in exasperation, "that's a terrible idea. This isn't your area of expertise in the first place. You were almost killed five days ago. That's why you got out, remember? You need to stay out."

"I know, Jonathan."

I walked over to the window and looked down at the Mississippi River. A long string of barges was moving downriver, passing beneath the Eads Bridge. The Noonday Club is on the top floor of One Metropolitan Square, the tallest point in downtown St. Louis. We were above the Arch, which looked like a giant silver wicket from this height.

I turned to face him. "I do want out. Believe me, Jonathan. I want out, and I want to stay out." I paused, shaking my head. "But I can't." I came over to the table. "Look," I said earnestly, "I'm not going to do anything crazy and I'm not going to do anything that you or your investigators can handle, but I've got to do whatever I can."

Jonathan was studying me, his face set in a scowl. He crossed his arms.

I took a deep breath and exhaled. "That boy died, Jonathan," I said quietly. "He died in my place. I can't walk away from that. I can't pretend it didn't happen." I took a seat facing him across the table. "So don't start lecturing me, and please don't start issuing orders. I didn't come here for that, and I won't put up with it. You're not my commanding officer on this."

I stared at him, the corners of my mouth curling into a reluctant smile. "But I could sure use a partner."

He looked down at the white tablecloth, his arms still crossed. He seemed to be scrutinizing the weave of the linen. Eventually, he raised his eyes to mine. With a long-suffering sigh, he shook his head in resignation. "Okay," he grumbled, "fill me in."

I grinned. "My pleasure, partner."

Despite himself, he smiled. It was a lovely smile.

The waiter arrived to take our orders and to refill our glasses of iced tea. I waited until he closed the door behind him, and then I described the results of my three hours of wandering around inside the Tully, Crane & Leonard computer network yesterday afternoon.

The computer's search logic had been fairly easy to figure out. I started with a search for all documents concerning Douglas Beef involving environmental matters.

"What did you find?" Jonathan asked.

"Basically, a hodgepodge."

I pulled out my notes. The computer had located nineteen separate documents, including legal research memos, memos to file regarding telephone conversations, and letters to clients and to various governmental agencies. The subject matters ranged from applications for permits under the Clean Water Act to an Illinois EPA proceeding on alleged discharges of animal blood and body parts directly into an open creek.

"Nothing specific to gallstones or Sally Wade," I said.

After that, I explained, I had expanded the search to anything having to do with Douglas Beef. That had turned up a variety of labor matters, including two charges of sexual harassment.

I glanced up from my notes, reddening slightly. "In one, a woman claimed she found a severed bull's penis in her locker."

Jonathan shook his head in disgust.

"The other is more intriguing," I said, "because it involves the plant manager, Brady Kane. The complainant is a woman in the accounting department named April Lindner. She claims he made obscene comments to her at work."

Jonathan looked up, intrigued. "What happened to the case?"

I shrugged. "It settled, but the papers were drafted by the other side, so there was nothing in the computer about the settlement terms."

He nodded silently. "Anything else?"

"Not on Douglas Beef. I found dozens and dozens of letters and memos by Bruce Napoli on other matters, but nothing that seemed relevant. I tried Swiss bank accounts and came up with zip. I even tried gallstones."

"And?" Jonathan asked.

I smiled and shook my head. "I found the wrong kind. The firm is defending a medical malpractice case in Jefferson County over a bungled gallbladder operation."

The waiter arrived with our orders: grilled salmon and fresh broccoli for Jonathan, a fresh fruit plate with a cup of gazpacho for me.

As we ate lunch, I described the rest of what I'd found in the Tully, Crane computer network. The most interesting had been the matches between Bruce Napoli and Marvin the mortician. On a hunch I had requested all documents that mentioned Marvin Vogelsang or Vogelsang Funeral Home. I turned up three fairly routine matters, all supervised by Bruce Napoli: an asbestos-removal problem involving old pipe wrap discovered during a remodeling; an issue as to whether a heating oil underground storage tank dating from the 1940s was exempt under the Resource Conservation and Recovery Act; and a review of the funeral home's procedures for the disposal of hazardous substances used to preserve bodies.

"Any personal correspondence between Napoli and Vogelsang?" Jonathan asked.

I shook my head. "At least not in the computer. But they definitely know each other."

I explained that I had been able to access the time records for all of the attorneys at Tully, Crane & Leonard. According to Napoli's time sheets, he had had three meetings with Vogelsang over the last twelve months. I flipped through my stack of printouts.

"Here," I said, handing him one of the time-sheet entries:

Client	Matter	Time	Narrative
Vogelsang Funeral Home, Inc	General Corporate	2.2 hrs.	Meeting with Mr. Vogelsang to discuss pending matters.

"That particular meeting," I said, "took place on the Thursday before Sally was killed."

He studied it for a moment and looked up at me.

I shrugged. "The entry says 'various pending matters,' " I said, pointing. "As near as I can tell from the billing records, there were no pending matters."

"Can I have this?" Jonathan asked.

"Sure." I lifted up the rest of the stack of printouts. "Take it all. I have a copy at my office."

He took the documents from me and stuffed them into his briefcase. "I'll study these tonight," he said. "I may schedule interviews with both of these men."

I gave him the thumbs-up. "Go get 'em, partner."

He smiled. "What else?"

I told him that the police detectives working on my case had interviewed Junior Dice twice in jail but had so far been unable to connect him to the car bomb. I also told the detectives about Officer Annie McCarthy and her incriminating connection to the chaser investigation, but they hadn't seemed interested in that angle. Jonathan was, however, and said that he would add her to his list.

Finally, I told him of my efforts to run down the gallstone numbers through my Chicago connection at the parent company of Douglas Beef.

"I talked to Betsy again this morning," I said. "I asked her to see if she could get a breakdown on the by-product sales numbers directly from someone inside the accounting department at the Douglas Beef plant. That ought to tell us whether someone's been stealing gallstones."

Jonathan shook his head with amusement.

"What?" I asked.

"Back in my days in the U.S. attorney's office I prosecuted some peculiar embezzlements, including the theft of Civil War bearer bonds, but I must admit I never handled a gallstone swindle."

"Let me assure you," I said with a smile, "there's gold in them thar bladders."

After our lunch meeting, Jonathan rode the elevator with me down to the lobby even though his office was in the building just a few floors below the Noonday Club. It was a nice gesture, and I appreciated it. As he walked with me to the parking garage elevator, he made me promise that I would call Walter Brunt if I wanted to do anything in the investigation that required me to leave the office.

"Protection is what he does for a living, Rachel, and he's the best in St. Louis." He pushed the up button and turned to me. "So no heroics, okay?"

"Okay." The elevator door slid open and I got on. Turning to face him, I said, "Thank you for lunch, Jonathan."

He nodded in acknowledgment. As the doors started to close he stopped them with his hand. "Rachel," he said seriously, "Neville already has him on retainer in the case. Let him earn his fee. Got it?"

It was my turn to salute. "Yes, sir."

He gave me a droll look as the doors slid closed.

Two hours later, I was fumbling through my purse looking for Walter Brunt's business card, which had his telephone number. Betsy Dempsey had just called back with an unanticipated development. It seems that I now had an appointment at the slaughterhouse at seven o'clock that evening to discuss the sales numbers for cattle by-products. The lateness of the hour was due to the fact that Douglas Beef was running overtime all week. The accounting people were staying late to get the quarterly figures compiled and shipped to Chicago by the close of business Friday. The meatcutters were staying late because this week's herd included an unusually high number of pregnant cows, which meant that there would be an unusually heavy demand placed on one of the more lucrative but labor-intensive of the by-products harvesting operations, namely, the collection of fetal calf blood.

All of which put an added, creepy twist on my meeting. For I was scheduled to meet not with one of the pocket protectors in accounting but with Brady Kane himself. Although Betsy had spoken directly to the head of accounting at the plant in an attempt to set up the meeting, Brady Kane had called her back twenty minutes later and asked if Rachel Gold was the person coming to the plant that night. Betsy was so rattled by the call and his point-blank question that she answered yes. Kane told her that was fine with him, since he'd rather meet with me himself. His accounting people had too much to do already without having to waste their time answering questions for some nosy damn lawyer who didn't know shit from Shinola.

"I feel terrible, Rachel," Betsy had told me, her voice trembling with remorse. "That man is so—so coarse. I got so flustered."

I had told her it was okay, that it was probably better for me to ask Brady Kane direct. And maybe it was. In fact, having Betsy involved in setting up the meeting was like buying extra protection. Brady Kane now knew that Betsy knew that I was meeting with him tonight; moreover, in light of what had happened to me less than a week ago, he had to assume I would let others know of the meeting as well.

Nevertheless, that didn't make me any less anxious to get Walter Brunt involved. I found his card and dialed his number. He was out, but his answering service told me they would page him.

As I leaned back in my chair, I thought over one of the more surprising things I had learned about Brady Kane from Betsy. Apparently, he had a special status among the upper echelon of Douglas Beef that made him virtually an untouchable, largely because of the fact that Kane ran the most profitable of the Douglas Beef meatpacking operations. For that reason, the top brass were reluctant to interfere in his internal operations. As long as he was sending all those revenues to Chicago, their attitude was leave him alone. It certainly explained what appeared to be a fairly minimal level of corporate control over the East St. Louis slaughterhouse.

Jacki came in with some draft court papers as I waited for Walter Brunt's call. We talked some about the investigation.

I sat back and rubbed my chin pensively. "I can make connections, but I can't find the motivation."

"What do you mean?" she asked.

"Take Sally and Marvin and Bruce Napoli. Sally and Marvin were lovers, he takes pills made in Hong Kong that she must have bought him on one of her trips, and he's Napoli's client. That's *how* they're connected, but where's the motivation to kill her? Or take Napoli and his wife and Neville McBride. McBride was Napoli's law firm rival; worse, he had sex with Napoli's wife. I could see where that might motivate Bruce Napoli to kill Neville McBride, but where's the motivation to kill McBride's ex-wife?"

"Revenge?" Jacki said slowly, concentrating. "Sally's death leads to McBride's disgrace, which gets him pushed out of Napoli's way at the law firm."

I shook my head dubiously. "That's a roundabout way for Napoli to reach his goal."

We talked through other possible suspects, including Junior Dice, who didn't have a known slaughterhouse connection but had an obvious Sally Wade connection and a girlfriend who could have collected the semen sample direct from the source. So, too, there was Officer Annie McCarthy, with a strategically placed boyfriend and plenty of motivation.

When Walter Brunt called, I told him about my appointment at seven that night. He told me he'd meet me at my office at six sharp to go over security arrangements.

CHAPTER 31

There was a full moon suspended low over the slaughterhouse as I turned into the parking lot. I glanced in the rearview mirror. Right behind me were the wide headlights of Walter Brunt's Oldsmobile 88. The asphalt lot was large enough to accommodate more than one hundred cars. It was about half full tonight, with cars scattered throughout. I pulled into an empty space in the fourth row.

I checked my watch before I turned off the engine. Five minutes to seven. Right on time.

I had a clear view of the front of the building, which housed the administrative offices. The lights were all on. From the outside, it looked like an entirely ordinary two-story brick office building dating from the 1930s. There was nothing about the building facade or the administrative office area, where I had met Brady Kane several days ago, to hint at the methodical carnage that took place in the back end of the building five days a week. Nothing architecturally, that is. Even though my windows were up, the odor made me gag.

As I got out of the car, I strained my ears, but I couldn't hear the animals. There were holding pens behind the building where this week's quota waited. Benny and I had seen those pens from the observation deck in the Arch. To say that they were animals made it no less a death camp and made me no less uneasy about the red meat I occasionally consumed.

Walter Brunt had parked two rows back. I waited for him and then we walked together toward the building. To the left of the entrance in the first row was a shiny black Dodge Ram pickup with a RUSH IS RIGHT bumper sticker. A little sign at the head of that space read RESERVED FOR PLANT MANAGER.

I patted the beeper hooked to the waist of my skirt. There was a spare one in my purse, just in case. Walter had trained me in its use before we drove over. Depending upon the button I pushed, the pager became a walkie-talkie (with Walter on the other end), a homing device, or an emergency alarm.

One of the accounting drones—a slight, middle-aged man with a crew cut and wire-rim glasses—met us in the tiny reception area. He said that Mr. Kane would be detained back in the bleeding facility for at least another thirty minutes. He would be pleased to escort me back there, however, if I didn't want to wait. I glanced at Walter and told the man that would be fine. Walter and I had already agreed that while I talked to Brady Kane he would try to locate April Lindner, the woman in accounting who had filed the sexual harassment charge.

I followed the accountant down the hall to a security checkpoint just outside a large set of double doors. The accountant turned me over to a uniformed guard, who issued me a hard hat with the DBP logo, a white smock, protective goggles, and yellow rubber boots. Once I had on my gear, the guard led me through the double doors, down a short hall, and through another set of double doors that opened into a large area the size of a warehouse.

The stench was overwhelming. For a brief moment,

the scene reminded me of the Chrysler assembly line we had visited on a field trip in elementary school. But only for a brief moment. Here, the swaying hulks suspended from cables and moving slowly down the line were made not of steel but flesh.

I averted my eyes, determined not to get sick, as I followed the guard down a yellow path that was painted on the cement floor of the slaughterhouse. The path curved around the circumference of the work area until we stopped by a glassed-in area. The guard told me to wait there a moment.

I peered through the glass. It looked like an army field hospital. There were about a dozen operating tables, and technicians were moving around in green hospital gowns and matching booties. I looked closer. The "patients" on the tables were dead unborn calves. Each fetus had a pair of rubber IV tubes leading from its body into glass jars that were suspended from metal stands on rollers, just as in a hospital, except that here the bottles were at a lower elevation than the "patients" and they were gradually filling with bright red blood.

I turned away, only to find myself facing something just as bad. Across the way was a long line of headless, legless cattle carcasses hanging from meat hooks. One of the workers turned from his carcass and shouted something. He was wearing a blood-smeared rubber smock and holding a large carving knife. From a distance, another man acknowledged the shout and started approaching, pushing a low metal gurney. As I watched, the first man turned back to his carcass and stabbed the knife high into the flesh. In one downward motion, he sliced from neck to crotch and then backed away. As the carcass swayed from side to side, the long gash slowly bulged and spread open, and then the intestines and organs came sliding out with a wet sucking noise.

The guy with the gurney arrived just as the guts flopped onto the concrete. The two men reached down and lifted up a large bloody sac that I suddenly realized contained a fetus. I turned my head as they heaved it onto the gurney.

The guard approached and pointed to an observation deck above the carnage. "Mr. Kane will see you now."

I looked to where he was pointing. Brady Kane was standing up there—an immense, scowling golem. His bald head resembled the business end of a battering ram. I followed the guard up the stairs and onto the platform. Kane glanced over at me and then back down at the activities on the floor of the slaughterhouse.

I waited for him to say something. He didn't.

"I appreciate your making time to meet with me," I said.

He continued to stare silently at the scene below.

"I understand you have some information for me," I said.

He jerked his thumb toward a small table behind him. On it was a manila folder. I picked it up. Inside was a one-page computer printout entitled BY-PRODUCTS ACTIVITY—MONTH TO DATE. I looked down the page. There were summary inventory counts and sales revenues for a variety of beef by-products, including pancreas glands, fetal blood, beef warts, and a category labeled "miscellaneous (incl. gallstones)."

"Don't you have a separate tally for gallstones?" I asked.

He turned his massive head toward me, his eyes cold. "Used to."

"When did you stop?"

"Can't remember."

"More than a year ago?"

"Maybe," he said, his face impassive.

"Who do you sell gallstones to?"

"Varies." He looked down at the floor operations. "Same with the rest of the by-products."

I held the one-page printout. "This is only November."

He nodded.

"What about the records for the prior months?"

He shook his head. "Gone."

"What do you mean?"

"Kept the hard copy off-site in a warehouse in Sauget. They were destroyed three months ago. Water pipe burst on 'em."

"What about the computer records?"

"Virus." He shook his head. "Zapped them all a couple weeks back. Damn shame."

"All plant records?"

"Just by-products."

"How convenient," I said sarcastically.

"Filed a report on it." He turned toward me, his eyes impassive. "They sent one of their tech boys in from Kansas City. He ran one of them antivirus programs. Filed a report, too. They got a copy up in Chicago." He gave me a chilly smile. "Ought to be safe from here on out."

I looked east in the night sky. Off in the distance I saw the blinking red light atop the Arch. As I gazed at the St. Louis skyline, I heard the sound of male voices. I turned to see two middle-aged men coming through the front door of the Douglas Beef plant. One was skinny and the other stout. They separated at the end of the front path and headed for their cars.

I checked my watch. Eight thirty-five. According to Walter Brunt, the accounting staff got off at eight-thirty tonight.

Next out the door was a youngish, chubby woman with platinum hair worn in an old-fashioned beehive. She was carrying a purse in one hand and a canvas lunch sack in the other. Another man, then another woman, and then April Lindner. Walter Brunt had pointed her out to me as we were leaving the building forty-five minutes ago. She had long brown hair and was wearing a St. Louis Blues jacket over a red miniskirt that spotlighted a pair of ample thighs (*polkas,* as my father used to call them).

I watched her walk rapidly to a white Camaro two rows over. As she got in her car, I started my engine. I pulled out of the parking lot behind her and stayed two cars back in traffic until she turned onto the eastbound entrance ramp to I-64.

Now I had to make my decision. When Brady Kane ended our meeting by announcing that he was going downstairs to drain some fetuses, I had hung around the Douglas Beef parking lot as I tried to decide whether to approach April tonight or set up something for tomorrow.

Tonight or tomorrow?

Tonight.

I followed her up the ramp and kept another car between us until she took one of the Belleville exits. Coming off the ramp, I hung back far enough to blend in with the other headlights in her rearview mirror. She pulled into a filling station. I drove past and turned into a McDonald's parking lot. I turned to watch as she pumped gas, cleaned her windshield, and went inside to pay. She came back out with a pack of cigarettes. Lighting one up, she got back in her car and drove out. I followed her down the road. Just past the next intersection she pulled into a 7-Eleven lot, parked the car, and went inside. I turned into a motel parking lot across the street, backed the car around so that I was facing out again, and waited, the engine idling. After about five minutes, I turned on the radio. It was tuned to an oldies station, which at the moment was playing "Little Red Riding Hood" by Sam the Sham and the Pharaohs. Sam started howling as she came walking out of the store carrying a grocery bag and a six-pack of Budweiser. I had to smile at the timing.

I followed her out of the 7-Eleven lot. Another mile or so down the road she turned off the main road into a residential area. I did, too, first clicking off my head-lights. We were driving through what seemed to be a working-class neighborhood of brick bungalows and small ranch houses. She took a right and then a left and then another right. I hung back, watching from the inter-section as her brake lights came on and she turned into the driveway of the seventh bungalow on the left, stop-ping in front of the garage.

I drove on past, trying to decide what to do. This was definitely the unscripted part. I got to the end of the block and pulled over to the side. The house had been dark when she arrived, which probably meant she was alone. I checked my watch. It was nine-twenty. Not too late. I turned right at the end of the block, and kept turn-ing right until I was back where I started.

I drove slowly toward her house. There was now a big Dodge Ram pickup parked directly behind her car. As I drove slowly past the house, I noted the RUSH IS RIGHT sticker on the rear bumper of the pickup. I kept on going.

I got home at ten-thirty. There was a police car parked in front. Walter Brunt had certainly handled that part of his assignment well: there were squad cars cruising by my house throughout the night. I put my car in the garage and came back out front to see whether the cops wanted something to drink. Behind the wheel was a young white female officer. Her partner was an older, heavyset black man. They thanked me politely but said no thanks. Each of them had a take-out cup of Dunkin' Donuts coffee.

"There'll be a squad car parked out here all night, ma'am," the female officer told me.

I gave her a curious look. "Parked?"

She nodded. "That'll be the routine for the next few nights."

"How come?"

"Just a precaution. Junior Dice made bail about an hour ago. He's back on the streets."

There was a message on my answering machine from Jonathan Wolf with the same information. He ended by asking me to call him when I got in. I did.

"The risk is low," he said. "Junior may be many things, but he's not stupid. Nevertheless, a little extra police attention for the next few nights seems justified."

"Thanks, Jonathan."

"Sure," he said brusquely. "Tell me about your meeting with Brady Kane."

I filled him in, including the part about following April Lindner.

"Rachel, Rachel." He sounded exasperated.

"I drove right past her house and went home."

Ozzie came padding over and sat in front of me.

After a moment, Jonathan asked, "How do you feel?"

I scratched Ozzie behind the ear. "I'm fine."

"You're sure?"

I leaned over and kissed Ozzie on top of his head. "I'm sure."

Jonathan was silent.

I laughed. "Don't worry so much. I'm delighted to have you tough guys in charge. I feel very safe."

"That's good. But if your feelings change, well . . ." He hesitated.

"Well what?"

"Well, if you have any anxiety about being there alone, I've told you we have an extra bedroom here. The bed is made. You'd have your own bathroom."

"Thanks. I'm okay so far." I ruffled Ozzie's coat. "I've got a squad car outside and a big, ferocious dog in here with me. Right, Oz?" He wagged his tail in response.

Nevertheless, when I took my shower that night I had Ozzie stay in the bathroom with me, and before I went to bed I double-checked the electronic security system and

I peered out the front window to make sure there was a squad car parked at the curb. There was.

The only place not secured that night was my unconscious, and it served up a doozy. In the dream I was standing on the foul, slippery concrete floor of the slaughterhouse dressed in a white wedding gown and veil. The gown and the veil were splattered with red. Next to me was Neville McBride, dressed in a business suit that was smeared with blood and offal. Inching toward us on meat hooks was an endless line of headless carcasses—a gruesome, swaying disassembly line. As each carcass stopped in front of McBride, he would slit it open from neck to groin with his carving knife. And all the while, as slimy ropes of intestines coiled at our feet and large gray organs flopped onto the concrete and an occasional spray of warm blood made us shield our eyes, McBride droned on and on about the tax advantages of certain limited partnership investments. As he lectured on the use of passive losses to offset gains, an especially large carcass stopped in front of him.

"Ah ha," he said, eyeing the swaying body, "it's about time, eh?"

He grasped it by the shoulder and sliced it open. But this time, as the red gash bulged out, I saw there was a human body inside, curled in a fetal position with its backside facing out. It slid through the opening and dropped out at my feet, the back of its head thonking against the hard concrete. It was a naked woman, and she was clutching something against her chest. Horrified, I knelt beside the corpse and tried to brush the hair away from the face. My eyes widened in surprise. It was Sally Wade. Her eyelids were open, only the whites of her eyes showing. She was clutching a telephone. As I staggered back, appalled, the phone started ringing. I looked over at Neville, whose eyebrows arched with amusement. "Answer it," he said with a chuckle. "It must be for you."

I awoke with a start and sat up in bed, my heart racing. Ozzie was on his feet, staring at me. My nightgown was wet with perspiration. I realized the phone was ringing. I looked at my clock radio: 2:47 a.m. I sat there rigid. The ringing stopped. I heard my answering machine go on downstairs—the taped message ("Hi, you have reached . . ."), then the beep, then a dial tone, then silence. A minute passed. Then another. My clock radio read 2:49 a.m.

And then the phone started ringing. I stared at it. One ring. Two rings. I picked up the receiver.

"Hello?"

"Miss Gold?" It was a woman's voice.

I paused. "Who is this?"

"My name is Tammy."

CHAPTER 32

It was close to noon on Friday. We were down to our last two boxes. Amy had one of them in front of her, and I had the other in front of me. The two of us were seated on the rug in the reception area of Sally Wade & Associates. As far as I could tell, we knew nothing more about Sally's connection to Douglas Beef than we had when we started.

Stifling a yawn, I moved my head side to side to stretch my neck.

Amy leaned forward with a look of concern. "You look exhausted, Rachel."

I nodded wearily. "I didn't get much sleep last night."

"How come?"

"She called."

"Who?" Her eyes got wide. "Oh, my God, you mean that woman? Tammy?"

I nodded.

"She actually called you? Wow. What did she say?"

"Not much." I frowned. "She said she knew something important about the night of the murder, but she refused to say what it was."

"Why?"

I shrugged in frustration. "She was incredibly skittish. She told me that she was calling from a pay phone and wouldn't talk long because she was afraid that the police would trace the call. I tried to assure her that the police didn't even know about the call, but she told me that I was too naive. She said she might be willing to talk to me in person, but it had to be completely off the record. She said she didn't want her name in the paper or her picture on the news, and if there was any risk of that happening she'd vanish and we'd never hear from her again. Then she gasped and said there was a car coming down the street and hung up."

"This is incredible," Amy said, shaking her head in wonder. "Do you think she'll call again?"

I shook my head. "I have no idea." I paused. "She sounds like she's from Chicago."

"Chicago?" Amy said. "What do you mean?"

"Her accent. Sha-CAW-go. Sout-west. Sounded vintage Chicagoland to me."

"Have you told anyone else about her call?" Amy asked.

"Jonathan Wolf." I gave her a concerned frown. "I told him I've got a bad feeling about that woman."

"What do you mean?"

"Whatever she has to say isn't going to be good for Neville." I sighed. "Just a gut feeling." I shook my head. "And if I'm right, so be it. The most logical explanation for Sally's murder is still the one the police have."

"But what about the explosion? And that creep in the Schnuck's parking lot?"

"Maybe," I said, lifting the next file out of the box, "but not necessarily. Remember, there's nothing that conclusively ties that stuff to this case." I flipped idly through the file. "It could still be an angry ex-husband or a crazy former client. The only direct link to Sally Wade so far is the night Junior Dice broke into my office."

We worked alongside one another in silence for a while, leafing through each of the files in the box.

"How did you leave it with her?" Amy asked.

I looked up and shrugged. "Just the way I described it. Maybe she'll call, maybe she won't."

When we finished the last boxes, Amy left for lunch and a doctor's appointment. I went into Sally's office to check in with Jacki and pick up my messages.

Benny Goldberg had left two for me. I caught him just as he was leaving to teach his antitrust seminar. He wanted to know if he could drop by tonight after dinner.

"I'll rent a movie and we can make some popcorn."

That sounded wonderful—a relaxing night at home with company. "Sure," I told him.

"Should I bring my three-piece latex suit?"

"Should I recharge my rhino stun gun?"

"Never mind."

I returned a few other calls, the last to the lawyer who was representing a witness in an age discrimination case that I was handling for one of my mother's friends. As the lawyer blabbered on about certain attorney-client privilege issues, I flipped on Sally's computer. When I got to the main screen, I poked around until I found the directory that contained the draft lawsuit that she had brought to my office the day she (or someone posing as her) retained me. Eventually, the lawyer talked himself out. Hanging up, I studied the date-created information on the terminal screen. It was the same directory Amy had located for me back when we first looked through Sally's computer. It showed that the draft lawsuit had been created the morning of the day she came to visit me. Fairly compelling evidence. Indeed, the police had made a copy of the computer hard drive for that very reason.

Then again, I reminded myself, the date-created screen wasn't dispositive. Someone could have planted the document. Anyone with a rudimentary knowledge of computers could have taken a document created on another computer, copied it to a floppy disk, transferred it to Sally's hard drive several days later, and voilà—it would look as if Sally had created the document back on the same date the document was originally created.

But, I cautioned myself, *the most obvious explanation is also the most logical, namely, that Sally Wade herself typed the draft lawsuit right here at her own computer terminal just before she came to see me on October fifteenth.*

I sat back and stared at the screen with my arms crossed over my chest.

Then again, if someone could add a document to her computer, someone could delete one as well.

I rummaged through my briefcase and found Tyrone Henderson's instructions for launching the undelete program. I typed in the commands and waited. The screen went blank except for the lower right corner, where the word SEARCHING started flashing. It flashed for almost thirty seconds, and then a new message appeared:

12 DELETED DOCUMENTS HAVE BEEN LOCATED AND RECOVERED. TO VIEW UNDELETED DOCUMENT #1 OF 12, PRESS ANY KEY . . .

CHAPTER 33

Ten minutes after Benny arrived with three bags of microwave popcorn, a jumbo box of Milk Duds, a large bag of M&M's, and two videotapes, the doorbell rang. We exchanged puzzled looks. Benny followed me to the door.

"Who is it?" I called.

"Your mother, doll baby. Let me in."

I gave her a hug and kiss, and so did Benny.

"Here," she said, handing me a covered platter. "I brought something sweet."

"Way to go, Sarah G," Benny said, peering under the cover. "Oh, baby, is that your world-famous banana bread?"

My mother nodded. "I baked it today."

"Let's have some dessert, ladies."

We got out the plates and silverware and I put on water for tea.

As we waited for the water to boil, I filled them in on my day, starting with my review of the Douglas Beef files.

"So what did you expect to find?" Benny said when I

was through. "A bag of gallstones and a signed receipt from Brady Kane?"

"I was hoping to find something in those files."

"Rachel," Benny said, "face it: if there was ever anything incriminating in any of those files, the odds are that Sally deleted it before she sent it to storage."

"Funny you should mention deletions," I said.

"Oh?"

I told them what I had discovered when I ran Tyrone Henderson's undelete program on Sally's computer. For the most part, his program resurrected fragments of materials that were either abandoned or incorporated into larger documents: a partial table of contents for an Illinois appellate brief, a half-written letter to Visa about a disputed charge. But it did locate two complete documents: an outline for the deposition of someone named Browning and an outline of legal points for a hearing in the same case.

"Here," I said, leafing through the stack of undeleted documents that I had printed off her computer. I pulled out the two outlines and handed them to Benny.

Benny studied them. "So?"

"Look at the dates," I said, pointing. "Sally created both documents on October thirteenth. The deposition outline was for a deposition on October fourteenth, and the hearing outline was for a hearing at *one-thirty* on *October fifteenth*." I paused with a smile.

Benny gave me a baffled look. "And the punch line is?"

"Benny," I said impatiently, "Sally was in *my* office at two o'clock on October fifteenth."

"Whoa," he said, raising his eyebrows. "Where was the hearing supposed to be?"

"Springfield, Illinois."

"Which is how far from St. Louis?"

My mother answered, "A ninety-minute drive."

Benny looked at me. "Did the hearing go forward?"

"I don't know," I said. "The court was already closed

by the time I realized what these outlines might mean. I tried to reach the lawyer on the other side. He's out till next Tuesday. I'll call the court tomorrow."

"Tomorrow's Saturday," my mother said.

"Then I'll call Monday," I said. "If Sally was up in Springfield for a one-thirty hearing, that's absolute proof that the person who retained me was an impostor." I paused. "Saturday? Rats. It's Friday night."

Benny gave me a curious look. "You are correct."

I looked at my mother. "I forgot to light the candles."

She patted me on the hand. "It's okay."

"No, it's not," I said.

I fetched the candle holders and two Sabbath candles from the pantry, got my father's wine goblet down from the cabinet, took the Mogen David out of the back of the fridge, and located a yarmulke for Benny in the bottom drawer. I made him put it on. Although the Gold family had never been overly observant while I was growing up, there was one ceremony my father never let us miss: every Friday night he lit the Sabbath candles and said the blessing over the wine, using a silver goblet that had once belonged to his grandfather. When I went away to college, I left those Friday-night rituals behind—until the first Friday after we buried my father. My mother, whose religious beliefs did not survive the Holocaust (in which her grandparents, her father, and all of her uncles and aunts perished), gave me my father's wine goblet after the funeral, and I haven't missed a Friday night since. Tonight, I said the blessing over the candles, and Benny self-consciously mumbled the blessing over the wine.

My mother was yawning by the time we finished. She announced that she was going home to bed.

"Not even one movie, Mom?"

"Not tonight, sweetie."

I walked her to the door and gave her a big hug. "Thanks for coming by."

She waggled a finger at me. "You make sure you lock

up good tonight." She gave me a kiss and a fierce hug. "I love you, doll baby."

"I love you, Mom."

Although Benny had rented two oldies but goodies—Kenneth Branagh's *Henry V* for me and Arnold Schwarzenegger's *The Terminator* for him—we agreed that one movie was enough for tonight, and I went along with his plea for Schwarzenegger over Shakespeare.

When it ended, I stood up and stretched as Benny hit the rewind button.

"Big plans for the weekend?" I asked him.

"Nah."

"What about Amy?"

He made a dismissive gesture. "She's going to Memphis for tomorrow and Sunday to visit a college friend."

"How are you guys doing?"

He shrugged. "Okay, I guess."

I nodded silently, knowing enough to drop the subject. In guyspeak, the phrase "okay, I guess," when referring to the status of a relationship with a woman, means "in the pits."

"How 'bout you?" he asked.

"I'm going rollerblading in Forest Park tomorrow morning with Jennifer and Cory." Jennifer and Cory were my sister's children. "We were supposed to do it last week, but, well, things happened."

Benny slid the videotape out of the VCR. "Anything else going on tomorrow?"

"Well," I said, trying to keep my tone offhand, "I'm having dinner at Jonathan Wolf's house."

Benny turned to me, his eyes sparkling with delight. "No shit?"

I blushed slightly. "He invited me over for a *havdalah* service and dinner. It'll be nice."

"Jesus, Rachel, lighting the Shabbos candles tonight, doing a *havdalah* service tomorrow—to quote Annie

Hall's grandmother, you're getting to be what I'd call a real Jew."

I rolled my eyes. "Yeah, right."

He went into the kitchen and cut himself another slice of banana bread. "Listen," he said, his back to me, "do you mind if I crash here tonight?"

"Pardon?"

"I've got my sleeping bag and a pillow in the car." He turned toward me. "If you don't mind, I'll sack out on the living-room couch."

I gave him a strange look. "What's going on?"

"No big deal." He shrugged and came back to the table. "That asshole Junior Dice is out of jail. You had another delightful encounter with Brady Kane. And, if I correctly recall, you are now on your second loaner car because of a rather dramatic recent problem with your own car." He leaned down and scratched Ozzie. "I know you have the most vigilant guard dog on the block, but the Oz-meister might feel more comfortable with me here, and how can I deny the Oz?"

"That's sweet, Benny," I said, genuinely touched, "but you don't—"

"Whoa, girl, don't get mushy on me. You haven't heard my payment terms."

"Oh?"

He gave me a stern look. "I ain't playing security guard for free, woman. The price of one night of Benny Goldberg's Vigilant Home Protection Service is a home-made Rachel Gold breakfast special consisting of a pot of fresh hot coffee and a tall stack—and I do mean tall—of those incredible homemade buckwheat pancakes. Otherwise, woman, deal's off."

I kissed him on the cheek. "You've got a deal."

"Excellent. Come out to the car, Ozzie. You can carry in my pillow."

* * *

Benny insisted on the living-room couch, even though I had an extra bedroom. He gave me some ridiculous excuse, but I assumed the real reason had to do with his idea of the optimal security position in the house. Whatever the reason, when I tiptoed downstairs in my terry-cloth bathrobe at six-thirty Saturday morning, he was on his back on the couch, snoring away with a crowbar across his stomach. Ozzie was asleep on the floor beside him.

Forty-five minutes later, I woke them both with the smells of breakfast—buttermilk buckwheat pancakes bubbling on the griddle, sausage sizzling in the pan, and fresh-ground Sumatra coffee dripping into the pot.

Benny staggered into the kitchen in his baggy pajamas, scratching himself in the usual early-morning guy places. "Lord have mercy," he whispered hungrily.

I looked over and winked. "Morning, officer. Quiet night?"

I scooped another pancake off the griddle and placed it on top of his tall stack. He came over to the stove and inhaled deeply over the sausage. "My God, what kind is that?"

"*Andouille,* fresh from Louisiana. I got it at Bob's Seafood yesterday. Yummy, huh?"

His jaw dropped in delight as he nodded.

I pointed to the plate. "One tall stack of homemade buckwheat pancakes. There's fresh-squeezed orange juice on the counter. A pitcher of warm Vermont maple syrup in the microwave. The whipped butter is on the table, and the sausage should be ready in five minutes."

Benny got down on his knees and held his arms toward me in supplication. "We're not worthy, we're not worthy."

I laughed and knighted him on each shoulder with a clean edge of the pancake spatula. "Get on your feet, you nut, before you get splattered with sausage grease."

If I say so myself, it was an awfully good breakfast.

Afterward, Benny helped me clean up, and then I went upstairs to take a shower while Benny headed for the den to watch Saturday morning cartoons. After my shower, I peered out the bathroom window to check the weather. It was overcast and windy. I called the weather line as I got dressed. The forecast was grim: showers throughout the day, temperatures in the low forties. Not the kind of day to go blading in the park.

The phone rang as I was pulling on my black leggings and trying to decide on a fun alternative plan. Maybe ice skating. I lifted the receiver, thinking it might be my sister, Ann. "Hello?"

"Rachel?" The voice was tense and familiar.

"Tammy?"

"I think I'm ready."

"For what?"

"To meet with you."

CHAPTER 34

The windshield wipers, set on intermittent, swept across the glass, temporarily clearing our view.

"I don't like this," Benny said.

He had pulled his car over to the curb facing south on Broadway, just beyond the entrance to the downtown Marriott Hotel. Ahead of us on our left was the Stadium East parking garage. Ahead of us on our right was Monument Plaza in front of Busch Stadium. Dominating the plaza was the towering bronze statue of Stan Musial, posed in his signature left-handed batting stance, front leg collapsing toward the back one, bat cocked high, head turned squarely toward the invisible pitcher located somewhere above and behind us.

It was a bleak, miserable day—chilly, overcast, and windy, with a mist of rain blurring our windshield. Nevertheless, a trio of intrepid tourists—mom, dad, and daughter—were smiling in front of Stan the Man as a passerby backed up to frame a snapshot with their camera. The word MUSIAL was engraved in gold letters in the black marble pedestal above their heads. The camera flashed in what seemed a pitiful attempt to brighten the day.

I put my hand on the door handle. "You stay right here," I told Benny.

Benny leaned forward to squint through the windshield. "Where the hell is she?"

I looked around. "Probably watching that statue from somewhere nearby."

He looked at me gravely. "And what if she's not alone?"

"I think she will be, Benny. She was the one who picked the meeting place. I can't imagine a more public spot. It's right out there in the open. Remember, she's the one who's freaked out over this meeting. It took me fifteen minutes on the phone to persuade her to do it."

He shook his head. "I'm not convinced."

"If she wanted to do something bad, why this setup? I think she wants to talk to me."

He looked at me with concern. "What if you're wrong?"

"That's why you're here. If you see anything suspicious, start honking the horn like a maniac." I peered around. "Look over there." I pointed behind us. A mounted police officer trotted by on his horse. "We'll be fine."

"I'm telling you, Rachel, I don't like this."

I sighed. "Benny, try to understand. I need to get this case behind me or I'll go crazy. I have to do it. I'm praying she can help." I put my hand on his arm. "Wish me luck."

"I'll tell you one thing," he said, his hands gripping the steering wheel, "forget that bullshit with the horn. Someone tries anything funny on that plaza," he said, pausing to rev the engine, "and I'll turn them into fucking roadkill."

I gave his arm a squeeze and opened the door. "My hero."

"Be careful out there, goddammit. You're not the Terminator."

I shoved my hands into my coat pockets and headed toward the plaza. Since Tammy and I had never met, we had described our outfits so that we could recognize each other. I'd told her I'd be wearing a black leather bomber jacket, black leggings, thick gray wool socks, and hiking boots. As I walked across the plaza, leaning into the wet, icy wind, I wished that I'd thought to mention a hat, too.

By the time I reached the Stan Musial statue, I was the only person on the plaza. Mom, Dad, and Sis had disappeared into the lobby of the Marriott. I slowly turned all the way around, scanning the area for a woman with red hair wearing a dark scarf, sunglasses, and black trench coat. Two older women came out of the parking garage across the street. One was wearing a dark scarf, but neither had a trench coat or red hair. A father and son crossed the street to the west of me, heading toward the Bowling Hall of Fame.

I looked over at the Marriott, which was directly to my north. That was the most likely place for her. I guessed that she was in there, watching the plaza from one of the windows on the first floor.

The front of the hotel faced east, and I could see Benny's car there, idling at the curb. A cab pulled up to the entrance behind Benny's car, and a uniformed doorman came down the stairs to open the door. He moved back with a friendly smile as an elegantly dressed man and woman stepped out of the cab. Although the woman was wearing a trench coat, she had blond hair and wasn't wearing a scarf. I slowly surveyed the south side of the Marriott, which was the side of the building facing Monument Plaza. Two women and a man were walking along the sidewalk, but neither woman matched Tammy's description.

I moved slowly around to the other side of the statue, scanning the area. I pulled the jacket tighter around me and gazed up at the pedestal. Engraved in the black marble were the words of Baseball Commissioner Ford Frick at the ceremony marking Stan Musial's last baseball game in the fall of 1963:

Here stands baseball's perfect warrior,
Here stands baseball's perfect knight.

I leaned back to look up at the statue. In the mist I could barely make out the number 6 on the back of his uniform.

I checked my watch: 10:42 a.m. I was supposed to meet her at the statue at exactly 10:30 a.m. She was nowhere in sight.

In sight.

The thought made me shiver. Directly behind me was Busch Stadium. Cautiously, I turned to face it. The curved outer rim of the coliseum structure was supported by huge cement columns that reached from the ground all the way up to the roof overhang. The columns were spaced about twenty-five feet apart. From where I stood I could count more than a dozen of them in either direction before they curved out of sight. My eyes moved from column to column, searching for a sign of movement in the shadows. I didn't detect any, but that didn't prove a thing. Each column was wide enough for three or four people to hide behind.

I quickly glanced toward Benny's car and then back again. Nothing. I edged around the base of the Stan Musial statue until there was a solid slab of marble between the stadium columns and me. I turned to face Benny's car, my back against the pedestal.

I checked my watch: 10:52 a.m.

I'd give her five minutes.

A phone rang. The sound came from behind me. I peered around the statue toward the stadium. The gates were locked for the winter. The phone rang again. The sound seemed to be coming from somewhere closer than inside the stadium. I scanned the area. On the five stadium columns closest to me were red-and-gold banners honoring the five Cardinals whose numbers have been retired: Dizzy Dean (17), Ken Boyer (14), Stan Musial (6), Bob Gibson (45), and Lou Brock (20). Concentrating on the sound, I suddenly located the phone. It was against the fence between the Dizzy Dean and Ken Boyer columns. I stared at the phone as I counted the rings. I reached six. I assumed it would stop soon. It didn't.

Eight.

Nine.

Ten.

I looked around. Not a soul on the plaza. No one in sight.

Thirteen.

Fourteen.

Fifteen.

On the eighteenth ring I took a few tentative steps toward the phone, glancing anxiously at the columns on either side. I looked back toward Benny's car and then took another few steps toward the phone. Still it kept ringing.

Twenty-one.

Twenty-two.

I lifted the receiver.

"Hello?" I said, my voice constricted.

"You lied to me."

It was Tammy. "What do you mean?" I said.

"You promised to come alone. You broke your promise."

"But I am alone."

"No you're not!"

I said nothing. I could hear static on the line.

"I saw that man in the car," she said.

"He's my friend, Tammy."

"Sure," she said cynically. "You'd say anything."

"I promise, Tammy. Please believe me."

"You break your promises. I can't trust you. You're like all the rest."

"Please don't hang up, Tammy. He's my friend. He drove me down here. Please believe me."

"He could be anyone. He could be a cop. He could be a TV reporter. How can I believe you? Forget it."

"I'm sorry, Tammy. Please give me another chance."

I had the feeling she was watching me as I spoke. The static on the phone line suggested she was calling from a portable phone. Slowly, I shifted my gaze toward the parking garage. It was a logical place to call from, especially since the upper levels had a panoramic view of the plaza. I scanned along the levels, searching for a woman with a portable phone watching the plaza. I didn't see anyone.

"I knew this was a bad idea," she said, her voice edging toward hysteria.

"No, it wasn't, Tammy," I said, aiming for a calming tone. "We need to talk. It's so important. Name another place. I'll meet you there. Alone. I promise."

North of the parking garage was the Equitable Building, with its opaque reflecting windows. If she was in there, she'd be invisible to me. I turned toward the Marriott. She could be up in one of the rooms facing the plaza. There were a few with the curtains open, but I couldn't see inside.

"Please, Tammy. You pick the place. I'll follow your rules."

There was a long pause.

"I don't know," she said uncertainly.

"Please, Tammy."

There was another long pause. "I probably shouldn't, but okay."

"Great. Where?"

"The Arch."

"Outside?"

"No way. You could have a hundred people hidden outside. Inside. Down in the museum. In exactly ten minutes. Meet me back by the stuffed bison. If you bring anyone with you, forget it. You'll never see me and you'll never hear from me again."

"I won't."

"Don't try any funny stuff, 'cause I'll know it if you do. I used to work there. I know my way around that place."

There was a *click,* and then a dial tone.

"This is good," I said to Benny as I opened the car door.

We were on Sullivan Boulevard, the wide street that runs along the St. Louis levee. Had there been any sun today, we would have been literally in the shadow of the Arch. The Mississippi River was to our east. To our west was a broad flight of stairs leading up to the Arch grounds.

"This is totally fucked up," Benny grumbled. "What the hell am I supposed to do while you're in there with her?"

I got out of the car and turned toward him. "She said she used to work at the Arch. Maybe you can get someone to pull old personnel records." I paused, thinking it over. I opened my purse and found Walter Brunt's card. "First," I said, handing it to Benny, "call Walter. Tell him what's going on. Tell him where I am. He'll know what to do." I gestured toward the hillside leading up to the Arch. "She's probably watching us right now. You've got to go. I'll meet you in the bar at the Adam's Mark in one hour, okay?"

He shook his head. "You must be nuts."

I leaned into the car and smiled. "Order me an Irish coffee."

I straightened up, closed the door, and turned toward the stairs. Tilting my head back, I shaded my eyes from the mist. Towering above me on either side were the massive, curving legs of the Arch. They disappeared into the clouds about halfway up. There was nothing visible directly overhead but dark, swirling clouds.

As I started up the long stairway, I tried to think of ways to calm Tammy. Whatever it was she wanted to tell me, it wasn't evidence. Not yet. It was only evidence if she told it again under oath in front of a jury. If she had witnessed something that would help Neville McBride, I needed to persuade her to be a real witness, i.e., to step forward in open court, raise her right hand, and swear to tell the truth, the whole truth, and nothing but the truth. If, as I suspected was more likely the case, she had witnessed something unfavorable, well, I'd pass that on to Jonathan and let him deal with it. My hope was that whatever she knew would also shed light on the car bombing.

There were more than seventy steps, and when I reached the top I was breathing hard. I took the path toward the north leg of the Arch. Along the way I passed a uniformed park ranger.

"Ma'am," the ranger said in greeting as he touched the stiff brim of his ranger's hat, which was fitted with a plastic cover to protect it from the rain. The Arch is run by the National Park Service.

At the base of the north leg I took the slanted rampway that leads to the underground area directly beneath the Arch. Down there are the Museum of Westward Expansion and the loading zone for the two trams that travel up the hollow curving legs of the Arch. There was a sign at the top of the rampway stating that the north-leg tram was closed for winter maintenance.

As I walked down the wet rampway, I flashed back to that sunny day—last month? a thousand years ago?—

when Benny and I came strolling up this same incline, completely unaware that my newest client was already dead. And now, after tracking the strange parabolic loop of this case, here I was, back at the beginning, heading under the largest parabola in St. Louis.

CHAPTER 35

A bronze statue of Thomas Jefferson stands at the entrance to the Museum of Westward Expansion. When you move past Tom, the underground museum fans out in a semicircle of exhibits and displays that include a Conestoga wagon, sod farmhouses, mannequins in buffalo hunter costumes, a Native American tepee village, a quarter-scale replica of the St. Louis levee from the 1850s, and, not surprisingly, a large section on the Lewis and Clark expedition, including maps, artifacts, memorabilia, and murals.

Off in the distance, near the back wall of the museum, loomed the huge stuffed bison. I didn't move toward it. I wanted to work my way back there gradually and indirectly. Although a cheerful, well-lit museum seemed a perfectly benign setting for our rendezvous, I wanted to scope it out first, get a sense of the layout and, just as important, the people wandering through it. Tammy's repeated insistence that I come alone had started to reverberate within me. I wanted to make sure she didn't have her own accomplice down here.

The museum had a completely different feel today from back when Benny and I had been here. That had been a sunny day in the middle of the week, and the museum area and gift shop had been filled with noisy school groups on tours, moms pushing strollers, older couples, out-of-towners with cameras and guidebooks. There had been lines at the ticket booths. The columns of people waiting to board the trams had snaked all the way up the ramps from the loading zone below.

Today's miserable weather and poor visibility had discouraged the usual weekend crowds. The museum was relatively deserted, and the ramp down to the tram loading zone was empty. The determined few who took the tram ride to the top today would find the observation windows cloaked gray by low clouds.

Slowly, I meandered through the museum, working my way toward the back. As I did, my anxiety level spiked up and down. A young couple were holding hands in front of the steam railroad exhibit. Two homeless men in shabby overcoats were seated on a bench by a stuffed longhorn cow. Two kids darted by me, and a moment later their exasperated mother lumbered past, pushing a toddler in a stroller and muttering under her breath. There were others—maybe a dozen in all. Some young, some old. Some together, some alone. As far as I could tell, there weren't any contract killers or psychopathic conspirators, or at least I didn't see any with a name tag identifying himself as such.

Eventually, I reached the bison. The massive beast was mounted in an alcove that also included a display on beaver ecology. I turned slowly. No one else was near. I moved around the bison display. Along the back wall was a large mural of a scene from the Lewis and Clark expedition. To the left of the mural was an empty, darkened section closed off with a chain. A sign in front of the chain read TEMPORARY EXHIBIT AREA—CLOSED. I leaned over the chain and looked around. The room appeared to be empty. To the right of the mural was a door marked NO ADMITTANCE.

"Miss Gold," someone hissed.

I spun around as a woman in a black trench coat approached. She was wearing mirrored aviator sunglasses and a maroon-and-navy-patterned scarf around her head. She had shoulder-length red hair.

"Tammy?" I asked.

"Hush," she whispered, looking back to see if anyone had heard. She turned and signaled for me to wait.

I watched as she walked over to the door marked NO ADMITTANCE. First pausing to glance around, she pushed the door open and looked inside. She turned and gestured for me to follow her in. I moved to the door.

"Hurry," she hissed.

Warily, I leaned forward and peered inside. The door opened into a well-lit hallway that stretched at least a hundred feet in each direction, with other passageways branching off it. I could see several doors down the hall, each clearly labeled in red block letters: MAINTENANCE SUPPLIES; ELECTRICAL; WOMEN'S LOCKER ROOM.

I stepped inside and let the door swing closed behind me.

"Okay, open your purse," she said. She had a gold front tooth.

"Why?" I asked.

"No secret recordings, that's why. If we're going to do this, we're going to do it by my rules."

I shrugged and handed her my purse.

"Unzip your jacket," she said, poking around inside my purse.

As I unzipped, I studied her. She was wearing heavy pancake makeup, plenty of rouge, and bright red lipstick. There was nothing subtle about her appearance, including the prominent beauty mark on her left cheek.

She handed me back my purse and ran her hands inside my jacket and patted me down. "What's this?" she said, pulling my heavy key chain out of my coat pocket.

"My keys," I said, forcing a smile.

"All of these?"

I shrugged good-naturedly. "It helps me find them when they're with all the other stuff in my purse."

She frowned but handed the key chain back to me. I slid it back into my pocket.

"Okay," she said, gesturing behind her. "There's a room down there."

"Why not here?" I asked.

She shook her head. "People come down this hall all the time. I used to work here, remember?"

I paused. "Okay, then let me see your purse, too."

She frowned. "What for?"

"Your rules, remember?"

Impatiently, she handed over her purse. "Hurry."

Among the contents was a portable phone—presumably the one she had used to call me at the pay phone at Busch Stadium. I handed the purse back to her and said, "Unbutton your coat."

She did. I pulled open her trench coat. She was wearing jeans and a cream-colored fisherman's sweater. I checked the deep pockets of the trench coat and ran my hands down her sides. Nothing.

I stepped back and nodded. "Okay."

"We have to hurry."

"Show me where we're going."

She pointed down the long hallway. "That green door way down on the right."

"What's in there?"

She turned to me, exasperated. "Nothing. That's the point. Come on, before someone comes by."

I followed behind as she walked briskly down the hallway. We walked past what looked and sounded like the boiler room of an ocean liner—a symphony of thumping and ratching and hissing—and past three doors on the left, and finally reached the green door on the right. It was labeled NORTH ELEVATOR. She pulled the door open, poked her head in, and then entered.

"Hurry," she said.

Cautiously, I stepped to the doorway and peered inside. I wanted to make sure we were really alone. The room was small, roughly seven feet square, and dimly lit by one red bulb. There were three fire extinguishers and a canvas fire hose along one side wall and a row of five lockers along the other. Set against the back wall was a service elevator. I stepped into the room and let the door swing shut behind me.

"It's important you understand something," Tammy said, her voice edgy. "I like Neville. I don't want to hurt him. That's not why I'm here. Okay?"

I nodded, and in each lens of her mirrored sunglasses I could see a distorted reddish reflection of myself nodding.

She breathed in deeply and exhaled. "It's just that I have to tell someone what I know. I couldn't live with myself if I didn't." She pointed her finger at me. "So you listen careful, and you tell whoever needs to be told."

She turned toward the elevator, her arms wrapped around her waist. She started tapping her foot. I waited.

"He's lying," she said, her back to me.

"About what?"

A pause. "I was there that night."

I caught my breath. "Where?"

Another pause. "His place. He wasn't there."

I nodded slowly. "You're speaking of the night of the murder?"

She turned to me with a nervous shrug. "I thought I'd surprise him. I had a key to his apartment. I went up at nine. I knocked. No one answered, so I let myself in. No one was there. Do you understand what I'm saying? He was gone." She was wringing her hands. "I waited for him. I waited until midnight. Before I left I wrote him a note and left it on his pillow."

I nodded slowly, studying her. "Are you aware," I

said, "that he claims he spent the night watching *Monday Night Football* and waiting for you?"

"I know, I know." She was wringing her hands again. "That's why I'm here. Don't you see? He's lying."

Tammy's version of the facts was troubling, but it wasn't the only thing troubling about her. Despite the heavy makeup, beauty mark, and gold front tooth, there was something disturbingly familiar about this woman. I tried to place her. The scarf and reflecting sunglasses made it difficult, and the dim light further masked her features.

"When did you first talk to him after that?" I asked, trying to visualize her without the scarf and sunglasses.

"About an hour later," she said. She checked her watch anxiously. "I think we're going to have to leave soon."

"In person?"

"Huh? No. He called me."

"Tell me the conversation," I said, scrutinizing her features, trying to make the match.

"He was hyper, screaming about the note I'd left on his pillow. He said I could never tell anyone I'd been there. He told me he'd take care of me, set me up in a beautiful house, buy me a new car, whatever I wanted, so long as I kept my visit that night a secret forever." She shrugged nervously. "I had no idea what he was talking about then." She shook her head. "Now I do. And now it's in your hands."

I didn't say a thing. I was stunned.

There was no Tammy.

Tammy was an imaginary character, created to set up Neville—to do everything from collecting samples of his semen to performing this charade with me.

I struggled to make the rest of the puzzle pieces fit.

"Miss Gold?"

I snapped out of my reverie. She moved closer to me.

"Pardon?" I took a step backward.

"What's wrong?" she said.

"Nothing," I said, trying to sound nonchalant.

I took another step backward, trying to sense where the door was. "Okay," I said, forcing a smile. "I understand why you don't want to testify."

She frowned and moved in close. "Are you sure you're okay?" Her Chicago accent was gone.

"Sure," I said, reaching behind me for the door handle. "We'll just forget the whole thing."

"Get away from the door," she snapped, her voice suddenly harsh and familiar.

The final puzzle piece dropped into place with such force that I almost lost my balance. "Oh, God."

"Shit," she muttered as she pulled open her jacket. She quickly reached around to the back of her waist. When her hand came out again it was holding an automatic pistol. "Get over to the elevator. Hurry."

She followed behind me, the gun pressed against the back of my neck. "Push the button," she said, jamming the gun against my neck.

I did.

I turned to face her. "Why?"

Amy Chickering pulled her sunglasses down for a moment to stare at me with steely eyes. "Guess I need a few more acting classes before I try Hollywood again, eh?"

I heard the elevator gears and cables engage somewhere above us.

"Did you kill her alone?" I asked.

She nodded smugly. "Never underestimate the skills of a legal secretary." She gave me a self-satisfied chuckle. "They sure don't teach that in law school, do they? Like the way I ran you around out there on that plaza like a puppet on a string." She grinned at the memory. "We were always going to meet here. I threw in the Stan Musial detour just to make sure you didn't bring any company with you."

That made me think of Benny. He was supposed to call Walter Brunt. I prayed that he had, and that Brunt had been around to receive the call. But how would he ever find me back here? There were park rangers in and around the Arch that could help. But they would need time. I needed to get them time.

I looked at Amy. "Brady Kane didn't help?"

That made her laugh. "No way."

"Isn't he your gallstone partner?"

That drew a scornful reaction. "Partner? That goon? He's my supplier. Period. I offered him a bigger piece of the action than that bitch, and he's tickled pink."

The elevator stopped with a clunk. The door slid open. She pressed the gun under my chin. "Get in."

She pushed the top button, marked Level 3. The door slid closed and the elevator started upward with a shudder.

Amy turned and gestured with the handgun. "Sit in that corner. We're going to have a nice, peaceful ride."

I backed into the corner and sat down. "Where are we?"

She had the handgun aimed at my head.

"Inside the north leg of the Arch. Sit on your hands. There, that's good. As you may have noticed on your way in, this leg is closed for winter maintenance. How convenient for us. We'll be all alone. It'll give us a chance to spend some quality time together."

"Where are we going?" I asked.

"Third level, women's lingerie."

We rode in silence as I tried desperately to organize my thoughts. Wherever we were headed, it couldn't be the top of the Arch. Although the high-tech trams could maneuver through the long sweeping curves toward the top, we were inside what clearly was a conventional elevator. Conventional elevators go up and they go down. They don't do curves.

Meanwhile, there was nothing else to do until the elevator reached our destination. Options are limited when you're sitting on your hands on the floor in the corner with a gun aimed at your head.

"Did you kill her just for the money?" I asked.

"Just?" she said with a chuckle. "Just? As if the chance to clear three hundred grand a year isn't the best reason in the world? Three hundred grand tax-free versus the life of one nasty, stingy bitch named Sally Wade." She put her finger against her cheek and pretended to think it over. "Hmmm. No, I suppose I really did it for world peace." She burst into laughter.

A moment later, the elevator thunked to a stop and the door slid open.

"Ah," she said, positioning herself in the open doorway, "we're here." She flipped the elevator switch to off. With the gun trained on me, she backed slowly out of the elevator. "Now get up and put your hands behind your head."

I got to my feet, my hands tingling. I kept my eyes on her the whole time. The gun was pointing at my face.

"That's good," she said. "Now, walk slowly toward me. Slowly. No sudden movements, and none of that karate crap, or they're going to be scraping your brain off these walls for weeks."

I stepped out of the elevator and onto the metal platform. We were inside what looked like a chain-link cage about the size of a walk-in closet. The cage was anchored against the back wall of the north leg of the Arch. In front of me, beyond the front end of the cage, the two side walls of the Arch angled in to meet at the inner point of the triangular leg. Fastened along that inner point was the elaborate system of hoisting cables and transporter track that hauled the trams up and down the Arch.

Amy had her back to the cables and track. She stepped

to the side and gestured with the gun. "Go ahead. Take a look."

I walked to the edge of the cage and looked down. I caught my breath and grasped the chain-link fence.

She laughed. "Nice view, eh? We're a little over halfway up. Three hundred seventy-two feet, to be exact."

I peered down, slightly dizzy. The inside of the north leg of the Arch was dimly illuminated by an occasional bulb, but there was enough light to follow the transporter track and cables all the way down the triangular shaft until they curved out of sight into the tram loading zone beneath the Arch. A stairway zigzagged up the three walls of the shaft. I stepped back and looked up. The stairs continued their zigzag path and disappeared around the upper curve of the Arch hundreds of feet above my head.

"Back when I worked here," Amy said, "I once walked all one thousand seventy-six stairs. That's one hundred and five landings. It's a good workout."

I turned to face her, my back against the cage. "How could you have done it alone?"

"Done what?"

"Killed her."

She shrugged. "Talent, I guess."

"But how did you get her tied up?"

She smiled. "Oh, that was the easy part. I had help."

"Who?"

"Sally."

I looked at her, mystified. "What?"

Amy stepped closer, the gun still aimed at my head. "She loved it."

"I don't understand."

She gave me a sensual wink and did a lascivious bump and grind. "Everybody loves to fuck Amy. Neville McBride did, Bruce Napoli did, even Benny. But no one, and I do mean no one, loved it the way Sally loved it."

She arched her eyebrows and whispered, "Especially when I tied her up. She was a kinky little bitch." She moved closer. "Surprised, Rachel?"

I said nothing.

She stepped up to me and pressed the gun against the side of my forehead. "Actually," she hissed, close enough for me to smell her breath, "even with her fancy diploma and all those awards, Sally Wade was nothing but a grubby piece of white trash." She stared into my eyes as she slid her left hand slowly up my leggings along my right inner thigh. "But you, Rachel—" She paused to lick her lips. "I've always had a thing for high-class pussy." She slid her hand the rest of the way up and grasped me between my legs. Her eyelids fluttered as she pressed her hand hard against me. "What a shame," she said with a carnal sigh.

I tried to mask my revulsion.

She stepped back, her expression suddenly cold, and pointed toward the door in the chain-link fence. It opened onto a stairway landing. "Time for our hike. Let's go."

She followed me to the door. "Open it."

I did. My hands were trembling.

"Up," she said.

I started up the stairs, my eyes scanning the area as I searched for possibilities. The stairs were set against the wall, and the guardrails were chest-high and fenced-in.

"How far?" I asked, my voice a little steadier.

"Five more flights," she said. "We're going up to the scenic overlook."

I turned toward her at the next landing. Fear was churning inside me, but I wasn't going to let myself give up. I needed time, though. I needed time to figure out my options.

"I want to ask you something," I said, surveying the area. I could see boxes of tools and a couple of folded drop cloths on the next landing up. I looked down at Amy. "Who did the car bomb? Junior?"

"Junior?" She laughed. "That incompetent nigger couldn't walk and chew gum at the same time."

"Then who?"

She shook her head ruefully. "You must be referring to my reluctant partner, Brucie Goosie."

I stared at her in amazement. "Bruce Napoli?"

She grinned. "Surprised, eh? Sally gets all the credit there. Maybe Bruce was looking for a revenge fuck at first, but Sally got him hooked on gallstones instead. She cut him in on the action for access to his contacts. And my oh my, they do come in handy."

I frowned. "Contacts?"

Amy nodded. "When your name is Napoli and one of your brothers is in jail and the other runs a security business, you have access to all kinds of talent." She raised the gun toward my head. "Now move it."

I turned and headed up the stairs in silence. We passed the landing with the toolboxes and kept going.

"Were you the one who hired me?" I said as I walked.

"Huh?"

I turned. "Were you the fake Sally Wade who came to my office that day?"

She smiled and shook her head. "Oh, no. I hired a professional actress for that part. She had Sally's bone structure."

"Who is she?"

"That poor floater." She put on a mournful face and made a tsk-tsk sound. "The one they fished out of the river by the McDonald's. She got a little too greedy." She gestured upward with the gun. "Come on."

I turned and started up the stairs. My options were limited and lousy: run or attack. Running seemed the worst of the two. I was at least three hundred stairs from the top and thus three hundred stairs from safety. Amy had the gun and was in good shape, which meant an escape run would most likely end with a bullet in my back. Attacking her wasn't much better, but it was probably my only hope. If I could find a way to get her near me, I could try for the gun.

"Here we are," Amy said as we reached a landing surrounded by chain-link fencing. "We used to call it Lover's Leap."

We were at least two-thirds of the way up the Arch. The curve above us was much more pronounced.

"Over there," she said, gesturing toward the door at the edge of the chain-link cage.

I looked to where she pointed. The door appeared to be a gateway to nowhere, a portal into thin air more than four hundred feet above ground. But as I approached I saw the ladder beneath. It was a steel-runged ladder, attached to the edge of the landing directly under the doorway. It led down to what looked like a huge fusebox anchored to the back wall. I turned back to Amy. She was standing in front of the stairs, cutting off any escape.

"Amy," I said, "this'll only make it worse for you."

She laughed and raised her gun. "It's definitely going to make it worse for you. Open the door."

I turned and grasped the doorknob. I shook the handle, pretending that I was trying to open it. I looked back at her and shrugged. "I think you need a key."

There was a momentary flicker of uncertainty in her expression, and then she pointed toward the corner. "Same drill as the elevator," she said. "Sit down and don't move."

I backed to the corner and lowered myself slowly into a squatting position as Amy stepped to the door. I glanced toward the stairway. Too far. I'd never make it. Frustrated, I jammed my hands in the pockets of my jacket. My right hand bumped against the key-chain weapon. I caught my breath. *Option Three.*

I moved my hand around the chain, searching for the right grip, my mind racing.

Amy held the gun with both hands and aimed at the door lock. Squinting, she pulled the trigger. The gun bucked as I turned my head, squeezing my eyes closed. The roar was deafening. When I opened my eyes there was smoke on the landing and the acrid scent of gunpowder. Through the smoke I could see that the door had swung all the way open.

Amy turned and gestured toward me with the gun. "On your feet."

I watched her carefully as I got to my feet, my right hand still in my coat pocket. I had a good grip on the chain.

"Get back over there," she said, pointing toward the open doorway.

I moved past her slowly. "Amy?"

"What?"

I was facing the doorway. I kept my voice low, hoping it would force her to move closer. "Did you have Sally's death planned out the first time you slept with Neville?"

"Oh, I was considering it back then," she said with a chuckle, "but Neville didn't move to the top of my list until the second night."

"Why then?" I had my legs at shoulder width, knees bent.

"That's when I found that bondage Polaroid of Sally. It was perfect. Sally loved me to tie her up, and I knew it'd be a lot easier to kill her in that position—and it was. Just a plastic bag over her head, three minutes of flopping around, and that's all she wrote."

I glanced down. Amy's feet were right behind me. Keep her talking, keep her distracted. "Did you save his semen the first time, too?"

"Of course." She chuckled. "A girl can't ever be too careful, you know. I have a little jar of Benny's, too. Just in case."

I turned my head, checking her position, tightening my grip on the chain. "Just in case what?"

She raised her eyebrows. "Just in case he gets to be a problem after you're gone."

Get ready, I told myself as I took a deep breath and leaned forward slightly, tensing my arms.

"I don't understand," I said, closing my eyes, trying to visualize Faith Compton's instructions. *It's a two-step move: out slow until the chain is fully extended, then up and around hard.* Carefully, I lifted my right arm, feeling the chain extend. I inhaled deeply.

Amy snorted arrogantly. "Just in case Professor Goldberg decides to pick up where you left off on this case. He's going to find it pretty distracting when I scream rape and the hospital nurses find his sperm inside me."

Her words were just background static. I was ready. The blood was roaring through my veins.

One . . . two . . . *NOW!*

With a yell, I whipped the chain around in an arc and whirled toward her. Her eyes widened in surprise just as the keys smashed into the side of her face. The impact spun her off balance and knocked loose the gun, which clanged along the floor. She staggered back against the cage to the left of the doorway, reaching for her face, her legs wobbling.

I dove across the floor toward the gun. Grabbing it, I spun toward her. She was leaning against the chain-link cage, her hand covering her right cheek and temple. I tried to hold the gun steady with both hands as I gasped for air. She was staring at me in dismay as bright red blood trickled through her fingers.

As we faced each other in silence, we could hear the distant metal clatter of footsteps approaching from above. Amy raised her head toward the sound, and then looked back at me in confusion. I got to my feet, my breath still jagged. As I tried to catch my breath, I looked up. I could see several flashlight beams jumping along the stairways about a hundred feet above us.

"It's over," I said to her.

"No," she said dully, shaking her head.

"Oh, yes." I could feel the wrath building within me. "After Benny dropped me off, he called that security guy. He's up there right now, and it sounds like he's bringing the cavalry along."

She stared at me as if in a daze. The sounds of footsteps were coming closer.

I glared at her with disgust. "You'll need a miracle to avoid death row."

Her eyes seemed to glaze over. She lowered her right hand from her face, revealing a gaping flesh wound above her cheek. Blood was dribbling down her face and neck. There was utter despair in her eyes. She turned toward the open doorway and sank to her knees. Her left hand grasped the chain-link fence, fingers spread wide.

The clattering above grew nearer. A deep male voice shouted, "Rachel Gold? Rachel Gold?"

I looked over at Amy. Her body was leaning through the opening, swaying slightly, her left hand supporting all the weight.

I realized too late. "Amy," I said, starting toward her, "don't."

She released her grip as she turned her head toward me. Our eyes locked for an instant as her body tipped through the opening. Then she disappeared over the edge.

I stood motionless, staring at the opening, trying to ignore the sounds of her plunge.

A moment later a familiar voice said, "Rachel?"

I turned.

It was Walter Brunt. He touched the brim of his fedora as six armed park rangers joined us on the landing, their walkie-talkies crackling. One of them peered down through the open doorway and leaned back, shaking his head.

Walt surveyed the scene on the platform, his seasoned eyes taking in the key chain and the blood and the gun in my hand. He looked at me with solemn eyes and nodded. "Nice work."

CHAPTER 36

Havdalah is Hebrew for separation, and for all the bittersweetness that separation connotes. The *havdalah* service, held at sunset on Saturday, marks the moment of separation from the Jewish Sabbath. It is a wistful pause at the border between the sacred and the secular.

Three symbols anchor the ceremony. One is the goblet of wine, first used to welcome the Sabbath on Friday night and now refilled to remind us of its joys as it departs. Another is the braided candle with two wicks—a symbol of fire that marks the beginning of the work week and a distant echo of the first Sabbath, which Adam ended by building a fire. And last is the box of spices, used to buoy the spirits saddened by the end of the Sabbath and to fix its sweetness in our memories until its return next Friday.

We were seated around the dining-room table—Jonathan at one end, me at the other, Sarah to my right, Leah to my left. They were adorable little girls, dressed in pretty white peasant dresses. Leah was two years older than Sarah. She had long auburn hair and her father's dazzling green eyes. As the big sister, she was

allowed to hold the *havdalah* candle, which was braided
in blue and white wax.

Her younger sister, Sarah, was in charge of the silver
spice box, which she solemnly handed to me. Sarah was
in first grade, a beautiful girl with curly black hair and
dark almond-shaped eyes.

"Thank you, Sarah," I said with a gentle smile.

She blushed and looked down. "You're welcome,
Rachel."

I held the silver box to my nose, closed my eyes, and
inhaled the fragrant mix of cloves, nutmeg, and bay leaf.
The Jewish mystics believe that during the Sabbath each
Jew receives an additional soul, which departs at sunset
on Saturday. We try to comfort the lonely remaining soul
with the spices.

"Mmmm," I said as I handed it back to Sarah. She got
up and walked it around to her older sister. From the
other side of the table, Jonathan watched us with a
peaceful smile.

After the Sabbath day I had just spent, my lonely soul
was sorely in need of comforting. During the first hours
after Amy's death, a busy swarm of homicide detectives
and FBI special agents sketched in the outlines of Amy's
audacious scheme. Indeed, by the end of the day the only
important missing link—and the only one that would
likely remain missing—was the actual event that had
made Amy decide to kill Sally. With both dead, we were
never likely to identify the final, lethal twist in their
complex relationship.

But once Amy made that decision, the plan unfolded
with a fiendish brilliance. Neville McBride was the fall
guy, with "Tammy" doing the semen harvest and making
sure he had the weakest possible alibi on the night of the
murder: home alone. I was the unwitting accomplice: retained by a woman I had never met before to file a lawsuit designed to clinch her ex-husband's status as the
sole suspect. Better yet, there was a good chance that I

might also be hired to serve as counsel to the personal representative of Sally's estate in wrapping up her law practice, thereby providing Amy with a way to monitor the homicide investigation. Her relationship with Benny gave her yet another line of access, along with another source of incriminating evidence that might come in handy someday. (The police found more than a dozen vials of frozen semen in her freezer, each labeled with the name of the unsuspecting donor.)

Had everything proceeded according to Amy's original plan, McBride would have gone on trial for murder. Although the odds favored a conviction, even if he prevailed—perhaps in a second trial after a hung jury in the first—so much time would have elapsed that no homicide detective would have been able to pick up the scent again.

The only flaw in her plan was its complexity. There were too many variables, one of which was the identity of the criminal defense attorney Neville would hire. She hadn't counted on Jonathan Wolf, who sensed from the start that his client had been framed. It was Jonathan who set in motion the chain of events—beginning with his utterly obnoxious phone call to me—that eventually destroyed her.

Although it was still too early to tell for sure, the homicide investigators didn't believe that Brady Kane was involved in any of the murders, although there was most likely a long prison term in his future for embezzlement and fraud.

Bruce Napoli, however, had more serious problems. Amy had described him as a reluctant partner, and from what the investigators had put together so far it seemed to be a particularly apt description. His initial involvement with Sally's scheme might have been slight—a small piece of the gallstone profits in consideration for his access and influence. By the time of Sally's death, however, he was stuck in the embezzlement equivalent of the

La Brea tar pits—not merely unable to extricate himself but sinking deeper with each attempt to get out. By the time I left the police station at five-thirty, Napoli was already in police custody.

After dinner, the girls and I helped clear the table, and then Jonathan told them to go upstairs and get ready for bed. I was going to help clean up, but Sarah came back in the kitchen with her thumb in her mouth. She took it out long enough to ask if I could help her get ready for bed.

I kneeled down in front of her and placed a hand on her shoulder. "I'd love to, Sarah. Maybe I could read you a bedtime story, too."

She smiled around her thumb and nodded.

I followed her up the stairs. Sarah shared a bedroom with her big sister. Leah was lying on top of the comforter on her bed, her head propped up by a pillow. She was reading a Goosebumps book. She grunted a hello when I came in and went back to her book.

Sarah didn't really need help getting ready for bed, but it was nice for both of us to pretend that she did. I helped her hang up her dress and put away her shoes and pick out her outfit for tomorrow, which she carefully arranged on the floor at the foot of her bed. After she brushed her teeth, we sat on the bedroom carpet and she showed me her proudest possessions: her Mighty Morphin Power Rangers figures, her special crystal rocks she'd found at Babler State Park, her first-place trophy from her T-ball team, and, saving the best for last, her Barbie doll and accessories, which, she told me in a solemn tone, "were my mommy's when my mommy was little."

I smiled. "I still have my Barbie doll, too."

Leah joined us on the floor, and we tried on Barbie's different outfits. Our favorite was definitely the Rollerblade Barbie outfit (complete with pads and helmet), although I ranked Junior Prom Barbie a close second. I told the girls what a junior prom was. Leah asked if I had ever gone to one. I told her about mine and described the prom dress I'd worn, which my mother had made for me. In addition to Barbie, they also had a Ken, but we all agreed that he was kind of dull and dorky.

After the day I'd had—indeed, after the month I'd had—it was pure bliss to sit on the carpet with these precious little girls.

When they were ready for bed, I asked them to pick out a bedtime story for me to read. They rummaged through the bookshelf and returned with a tattered old picture book that was missing its cover. Both girls got into Leah's bed as I turned out the overhead light and Leah flipped on the reading light attached to her headboard. I smiled down at the girls. Each of them was holding a threadbare baby blanket against her cheek. I sat down on the edge of the bed and started reading.

The book opens late at night. A young mother is standing over a crib and gazing down at her baby daughter. The mother is beautiful, with long dark hair. Behind her is a window. Outside, a million glittering stars illuminate the heavens. The baby stares up at her mother with big round eyes as her mother tenderly strokes her soft blond hair and sings a special song:

> *I love you more than all the stars,*
> *That sparkle in the sky.*
> *My love will be your cradle,*
> *For as long as I'm alive.*

And as she sings the baby closes her eyes. When the song ends, the mother leans over and gently kisses her along the curve of the bridge of her nose. The baby smiles in her sleep.

I paused after the first page, sensing already that I was in trouble. I looked down at the girls. They were both staring intently at the picture on the page. Sarah was sucking her thumb with the blanket pressed against her hand, her brow furrowed.

The story continued. The little girl grew older. Sometimes she misbehaved, and sometimes her mother punished her, but most nights after the daughter was asleep, even when she had grown to be a headstrong teenager, her mother would sneak into her room late at night and tenderly stroke her hair as she sang their special song, and when she finished the song she would lean over and gently kiss her daughter along the curve of the bridge of her nose. Her daughter would smile in her sleep.

Even when her daughter had grown up and moved to another town, whenever she came home to visit, her mother would come into her bedroom late at night, careful not to wake her, and she would tenderly stroke her daughter's hair as she sang their special song:

> *I love you more than all the stars,*
> *That sparkle in the sky.*
> *My love will be your cradle,*
> *For as long as I'm alive.*

And when she finished the song she would lean over and gently kiss her daughter along the curve of the bridge of her nose. Her daughter would smile in her sleep.

By now my eyes were watering and I was fighting to keep my voice from cracking. I glanced down. My two little listeners were rapt, their eyes focused on the illustration. I could hear the wet noises of Sarah sucking her thumb.

So I took a deep breath and pressed on.

One day, many years later, a doctor called the daughter to tell her that her mother was in the hospital. The daughter traveled home all that day and arrived late at night. When she got to the hospital room, her mother was sound asleep. The daughter stood quietly by the bed. She was a beautiful young woman now, with long dark hair. Behind her was a window. Outside, a million glittering stars illuminated the heavens. The daughter sat down at the edge of the bed and tenderly stroked her mother's soft white hair as she sang a special song:

> *I love you more than all the stars.*
> *That sparkle in the sky.*
> *My love will be your cradle,*
> *For as long as you're alive.*

And when she finished the song she leaned over and gently kissed her mother along the curve of the bridge of her nose. Her mother smiled in her sleep.

I think there were a few more pages after that, but I never reached them. Tears were streaming down my face as thoughts of their mother and my father and Danny and others overwhelmed me. I put the book down and covered my eyes, struggling to regain control.

After a moment I felt a little warm hand on my shoulder. "It's okay, Rachel."

I wiped my eyes with my hands and turned, sniffling. Sarah was kneeling next to me, her face earnest. "It makes my daddy cry, too."

I gave her a blurry smile and a kiss on her nose. "Thank you, sweetie."

Leah reached over and pulled a Kleenex tissue out of the dispenser on her nightstand. "Here, Rachel. There's gook coming out of your nose."

I laughed and took the tissue and blew my nose.

Back under control, I tucked Leah in and kissed her good night. Then I walked Sarah over to her bed and did the same for her.

"Send my daddy up," Sarah told me.

When Jonathan came back downstairs after kissing his daughters good night, I was waiting in the front hall.

"You have two special little girls," I said.

"I know." He smiled. "Sarah told me you're going to bring over your Barbie doll one day."

I nodded. "I promised her." I tried to stifle a yawn. "But first I'm going home and sleeping for twenty-four hours." I reached out and took his hand. "Thank you for a wonderful evening."

"It was my pleasure."

"And thank you"—I paused, trying without success to find the right words—"for everything else."

"Oh, but there wasn't—"

"Enough." I covered his mouth with my hand as I smiled at him. "You can either say you're welcome or you can say nothing." I took my hand away.

He gently pulled me toward him. I closed my eyes and let him hold me against his chest.

"You're welcome," he said softly.

We were swaying ever so slightly, a tranquil rocking motion. I tried to think of something to say but nothing came to me.

I was completely out of words.